RITUALIST

The Completionist Chronicles Book One

DAKOTA KROUT

This is a work of fiction. Names, characters, places, and incidents either are the products of the author's imagination or are used fictitiously. Any resemblance to actual persons, living or dead, businesses, companies, events, or locales is entirely coincidental.

ACKNOWLEDGMENTS

There are many people who have made this book possible. As always, the first among them is my *amazing* wife, who always encourages me to do the best at any task I set my mind to. She pushes me to set deadlines and meet them, and always does her best to make sure I am maintaining a balance of working and taking care of my growing family.

A small thank you to my daughter, who reminds me why I am working so hard. I hope that I can always be the person you need me to be!

A special thank you to all of my Patreons, who supply me with an endless stream of coffee, but especially to: Steven Willden, Nicholas Schmidt, Samuel Landrie, Blas Agosto, and Justin Williams. You guys are so involved, always offering great advice and hints to writing better stories.

Finally, a great thank you to all my friends, family, and beta readers who made their way through the awful early editions in order to make this book readable! A special thanks to my friend and editor Dylan S., who helped me to release a high-quality book.

This book was written in loving memory of Joe Jordan, a great friend taken far too soon.

PROLOGUE

"Sir, the geological surveys all came back clean! There is *nothing* we could have done to predict this," the man standing in front of the toolpusher–the person in charge of every crew on the oil rig–nervously reported.

The toolpusher looked back at him with dead eyes, a slight sneer on his face. "You think those eco-terrorists that masquerade as conservationists will give a *damn* that there was an earthquake? You think they won't blame Earth Friendly Oil for the largest spill in a decade? EFO is already in the spotlight after that crew lost control five years ago, and then you tap into the largest underwater oil deposit anyone has ever *seen*. A week after you make the call, an earthquake on a city-killing scale has its epicenter *right* where we are drilling? You think they will let that be passed off as a coincidence?"

"Well, most likely no, but what do you mean *I* made the call-" the nervous roughneck tried to speak, only to be cut off with a hand held out at chest level.

"Look. I know you are a good guy, and you run a tight crew. You're *real* good at what you do. You are also fired. We need someone to take the fall, and you are the only likely candidate."

The toolpusher sighed at the bleak look, which was the only response to his words. "Look, it isn't like we are going to send you off with nothing. We're giving you five years pay as severance and–if you change your name–we'll even give you a glowing recommendation!"

"Change my name…? You're blaming this on *me*?" There was a blazing fury in his eyes now. "I was only here so I could make enough money to finish my doctorate! *You* were the one that made us-"

"Yeah, well, thing is, we can't have you associated with us after this incident since your name will forevermore be the hallmark of damage to the environment." The toolpusher put his feet up on his desk, chuckled heartlessly, and waved his ex-employee off. "Sure as heck ain't gonna be me going down for this. Let us know what new name you come up with."

"You're going to play it like this? Fine. I'm going to find a way to get back at all of you, even if that means ridding the world of its dependence on oil entirely." The fire turned to ice in the man's glare. "From now on, you can call me… Elon." He stormed out of the office, then had to wait an hour before a helicopter arrived to take him away. Elon decided he had had enough of this world: the drama, the strife. He decided to pursue the dreams he had as a child. He would work toward building a colony on the neighboring planet, Mars. Elon reached into his bag, sneaking a peek at the large, blue-glowing rock that had been pulled up from under the ocean floor. *~Core.~* This rock was filled with power; he just knew it! *~Core!~* Was it an alien artifact? It almost seemed to be whispering to him. In the right light, there were even faint markings coating the blue stone in shimmering, undulating light. *~Core, for abyss sake!~* Almost as if it were covered in chains.

Elon decided to study this Core. Core? He felt an odd satisfaction with the term. He would reach his dream eventually, but he needed a way to make money. Elon turned his mind to his past interests: the Internet, renewable energy, and outer space.

Over the next few years, Elon rose like a phoenix in the tech world. He started a payment system, multiple companies, and finally, the pinnacle of his dream, a privately owned space research center. *Space Y*. Then the stock market crashed, and he was out of money. Well, for a *very* short amount of time. With newfound free-time and after years of putting it off, Elon devoted his efforts to researching the Core more directly instead of simply carrying it around as a good luck charm and reminder.

After weeks of preparation, Elon hooked energy-sensitive wires between the Core and his personal computer in an attempt to analyze it. His monitor flickered, and the metrics on the side of his screen went haywire. There was no way that his Wi-Fi had just transferred forty-three Exabytes of data, was there? Elon stared at his shifting monitor as text appeared on it.

<Wow, about time! Smells kinda... *musky* in here. So this is what the world is like now, huh? You humans have some 'splaining to do.>

CHAPTER ONE

"Drink up boys!" Staff Sergeant Knecht called. "Tomorrow we're on QRF *all~l~l* day long!"

Sergeant Nelson shook his head, a tiny bit professionally upset by his soldiers drinking so heavily the night before they were on duty for the quick reaction force. To be fair, as the medic, he was against them drinking at *all* in this heat. The motto of the army may as well be '*Drink Water!*' He understood the need the others felt to forget their troubles, but tomorrow they would be wearing full kit in one-hundred-ten degree weather.

"C'mon, little Joe!" Private first class Johnson slapped his favorite medic on the shoulder. "If they get too dehydrated, just do what ya always do! Stick 'em!"

"Way too loud." Sergeant Nelson glared at the overly familiar tone, "Johnson, you know that you can't be so casual and use my first name like that around officers. They're *super* touchy about that, especially when we get a chance to drink. You know they are always looking for an excuse to take away drinking privileges." Indeed, a few of the butter-bars (2nd lieutenants) had glared over at them and muttered something to the people at their table. The Captain grabbed the hostile officer as he started to stand, shaking his head to force the agitated man to calm down.

"Also, we don't have a bunch of IV's right now, so it'll be a bit hard to 'stick em' as you suggest. The shipment of supplies is late. Hell, the *fuel* shipment is late again, which is why we are doin' half patrols. If we had a logistic *sergeant* in charge over there instead of that two bit luey, we-"

"La-la-la!" The PFC put his hands over his ears. "I'm not hearing you say bad things about our executive officer right now! I'm not getting into logistics, administration, or politics!" When a gleam appeared in Joey's eyes, Johnson quickly amended, "Or religion! Nope, tonight I'm drinkin'!"

Even though he wanted to say something, the PFC sure had him pegged. Sergeant Nelson laughed and settled back into his seat; it was fun to mess with this kid's head. He slowly sipped his one beer for the night, drinking twice as much water to counteract the dehydration. Good times.

"We've got a problem, sir!" A radio operator, Specialist Krout had been pulled out of headquarters and pressed into service on the medevac helicopter when the last guy had come down with a bad case of… dying. "First platoon got hit, they found an IED the wrong way. QRF is on the way, but they need evac and medical attention ASAP."

"Wow, use more acronyms in your next report, Krout," a sarcastic reply was snapped out. The pilot–Warrant Officer Lyons–warmed up the rotors and soon began flying toward the coordinates Krout provided. He turned his head to look behind himself. "Nelson! You and your guys ready to go?" According to the nine-line medevac report included, there were no hostiles in the area so landing to pick up wounded was a top priority. Joe was relieved to hear that they could go right in; their platoon only had two choppers and both were used for quick pick-ups.

Battalion–almost fifty miles south–had the real firepower, and he didn't want to wait an additional twenty minutes to save his comrades and friends.

"Always, sir!" Joe shouted the reply. Jumping the few remaining feet as soon as they touched down, Sergeant Nelson and his two specialists grabbed a gurney and made a run for the smoking wreck of a Humvee. The wounded were spread on the ground as far as twenty feet away, and low moans of pain came from several of them. Those ones didn't worry him as much as the men who were silent.

A Staff Sergeant came over and gave him a quick situation report, "Five wounded, two critically! Meyers is awake but not making any noise. He… he lost his leg! He should be screaming." He held back a sob as he spoke.

"Different man, different way of dealing with pain. Nothing you could do, brother. Nice work on that tourniquet." Nelson shook his head as he knelt down to triage the men. After an initial assessment and the adjustment of a few tourniquets, he noted with relief that all of these men would survive if they got proper care in a timely manner. They loaded up the worst of the wounded and took off. Sergeant Nelson was fully absorbed in keeping the men stable… until he heard an ominous shout.

"Oh shit!" The chopper took a hard turn, which gave Nelson the perfect view of an RPG coming straight at the broad side of the chopper.

There was a flash of fiery light... just before everything went black.

CHAPTER TWO

Beep.... **Beep** … Joey Nelson opened his eyes so he could shout at Johnson to shut off the stupid game he was always playing. He tried to turn but found his head held fast. Now *fully* awake, he looked around and saw white everywhere. He had been in them enough to recognize the flat colors and prison-cell feel of an army hospital.

"Frack," was all he could say, as close to swearing as he allowed himself to get. At least for the 'hard' swear words, anyway.

A smiling face came into view. "Awake are you? They were right! Good, right on schedule. Good, good."

"Who are you?" Joey blearily asked, the drugs he was on right now must be *really* good. "Are you a doctor?"

The greasy smile quivered a bit as the man seemed to be dealing with an internal battle for morality. Morality lost by a large margin. "Well. No. I'm sorry to say, I am an attorney."

"What the…? For what?" Joey struggled to remain fully cognizant of his surroundings. "Where are we? There are no lawyers in this god-forsaken desert, the only good thing about the whole dang place."

"That's uncalled for." The greasy man's eyes shifted into a hurt look. "We are back in the States; you must have been out of it for quite a while! About a month, I believe. Just long enough for the paperwork."

"What are you going on about? You an army lawyer? They kicking me out now?" Nelson's voice had a dreamy quality to it as the drugs tried to send him off to the darkness again.

"No, no... well, yes, you are getting an honorable discharge, a few medals, and most likely a pension, but that's not my department. No, I am here representing your wife, Daisy." A wet tongue flicked out and moistened his lips.

"Where is she? Is she coming to visit?" Joey looked around desperately for his wife; they had only been married a few months when he got his deployment orders.

"She already did, and... well, that is why *I* am here. I specialize in divorce cases, and I needed to inform you that your wife is getting your marriage annulled. In this case, she is not trying for anything that you owned, and she will only take the possessions and money that she brought into the relationship. She wants this to be as *painless* as possible for you." The faux concern in his voice pulled Joe back toward awareness.

Joey's eyes bulged out, "*What?* Why would she leave me, I...?" He tried to sit up, only to realize that he could not move at all. He had thought that he was held in place, but now darker, more *insidious* ideas of his status were appearing in his mind.

"You must understand how difficult it would be for a twenty-year-old woman to be married to a quadriplegic, sir." The lawyer stopped in shock as Joey's eyes went blank and his face drained of color. "Sir?"

"Hey!" A female doctor stepped into the room. "Who are you? Is he awake? What did you tell him!"

"What are you talking about?" The confusion was evident on the lawyer's face. "I have a legal right to inform him...."

"If he is awake, it is the *first time* since he got shot down! Get out or I'll have you arrested!" The doctor shouted in a tone that was bordering on shrill. She ran over to Joey as the lawyer scampered away mumbling apologies. "Sergeant Nelson, it isn't that bad, you could…"

Joey cut her off, "Am I paralyzed?"

"...Yes," was the reluctant reply.

"Will I ever regain functionality?"

"It's… not likely," she admitted quietly.

"Is my wife leaving me?" The doctor had the good grace to look away and not answer as a sob accompanied the question. "Pardon my insubordination, *ma'am*, but I think it *is* that bad."

The most humiliating three months of Joey's life passed in a blur as he tried everything he could think of to regain the use of his limbs. If he could even get his fingers to move he could at least *type* for a living instead of being a drain on all of his loved ones' resources. He had been moved into his mother's house at her insistence, and she had been feeding and taking care of him since. Luckily, a portion of his benefits went to the hiring of a nurse that cleaned him so he didn't have to suffer the indignity of having his mother do that as well.

"You have a visitor, my love," his mom called out as she entered the room.

Bitterly, he muttered, "Please let it be the grim reaper."

She smacked his leg and glared at him; he didn't care. He couldn't feel the strike anyway. One of his buddies from the army came in with a grin as his mother left the room.

"Tim Ramen, as I live and breathe." What felt like the first real smile in months stretched his cheeks.

"Well *you* look like shit."

"Thanks, I still look better than you. At least my arms still have some definition, unlike those noodles you wave around uncontrollably."

"Why are you lazing around? Rub some dirt in it, you'll be

fine. Best cure the army can buy, raw dirt." Tim had trained as a medic with Joey and had always been full of eccentric jokes.

Joey nodded. "Ah yes, your catch phrase. You know, a few of those privates took you seriously and got infected. When a medic tells you to do something…"

"You do it," Tim finished the saying and chuckled. His face slowly lost a bit of its forced cheer. "Well, damn, buddy. *Any* good news about this?"

"Well, turns out I'm rich. After my ex sold my house and car and dog and…"

"Yeah, yeah, I get it, your life is basically a country music song right now," Tim interrupted him laughingly.

Joey would have shrugged if he could have. "Well, my mom also won the lottery, *after* the annulment, so I am now officially the son of a multi-millionaire and will never have to devote any money to that-" Joe stopped himself before he started spiraling into a rant against his ex. "As soon as the lotto department pays out, that is. For now, we are just trying to get by."

"Whaa? Nice, man!" Tim latched onto this good news like a drowning man to a raft. "So it isn't *all* bad!" The smile dropped from his face when he saw the sour expression on Joey's. "Anyway, what now, my friend?"

"That's the big question. No love prospects, no way to work, and no money until the first check comes in from the lotto. That will be next month, I hope. The army says they'll pay for everything, but…"

"But it's the army," Tim finished with him. "I hear you man. Listen, I got out last year… I have a new job. That's actually what I wanted to talk to you about."

"Offering me a job?" Joey's eyes actually lit up for a moment until Tim shook his head.

"Yes and no. It's a way out for you," he said this in such a low tone that Joey had to strain to hear it.

"Out of what? Life?" Joey shook his head. "No matter how I joke, I could never do that to my mother. Suicide is *never* the answer. It's a permanent, *terrible* solution. You know I'm a religious man."

"Not like *that,* man! C'mon, like I would even say something like that to you?" Tim looked truly offended. "No, I work at a gaming company. We just finished developing a new MMORPG, and it's…"

"I'm sorry, a what?" This question elicited a look of pain from Tim.

"A massively multiplayer online role-playing game," Tim informed him in a strained tone. "The company finally got the new DIVE-capsules approved, and…" He paused when he got a 'look'. "A deeply immersive, virtually enhanced reality capsule. DIVE. You get in the pod, and the game becomes reality for you. Cost prohibitive, but doable for a millionaire, huh?"

"So you knew that she had won before you came here," Joey inferred flatly.

Tim nodded sheepishly. "The Company sent *me* because I know you. Here's the thing, if you get in the pod with the correct subscription… the kind you have to be *invited* to," he looked meaningfully at his prone friend, "You don't *ever* leave the game. You actually start a life on a new world. In a new, custom designed body. It's a new chance, man."

Joey was silent as he thought about the implications of this offer. "I could walk again?"

"And *so* much more," Tim promised as genuinely as possible. "The game was developed by the same guy that made paybud, Edison cars, and Space Y. It is beyond realistic. It's… it's a new life, man."

"What's the game?"

"It's called *Eternium.* It is unique beyond belief, and… we need people we can trust in there. It goes live in two weeks. Most of the people that are going to play are standard VR helmet users; there are about twenty percent DIVE users, but there are *no* admins. So we need people to play the game and sometimes to play the game in a way that is best for the *company*." Tim seemed a bit hesitant about his words, as if he were biting his tongue to stop himself from saying something.

"No admins? What do you mean? I need to know more, Tim." Joey locked eyes with his friend. "Help me out, buddy. I'm so excited that I can't move."

"Wow. Alrighty, the game is controlled entirely by an AI. Artificial intelligence. Beyond Turing, buddy. It's called the 'Certified Altruistic Lexicon'. This thing is smarter than half the population combined. It creates quests, monsters, and the game world itself. No outside control whatsoever, unless the Certified Altruistic Lexicon allows it to happen. I want to tell you more details, but I can't unless you agree to join the game."

Joey thought about the embarrassment he felt on a daily basis and nodded sharply. Any chance at a mobile life was one that he would willingly take. "How much?"

"Two hundred fifty thousand." Tim's words made Joey's jaw drop. "That is the 'at cost' version. There is a solid reason; this specific version of the technology is custom designed per user and therefore, can only be used once. Normal pods can be used by anyone, but that's still fifty thousand a year. Then there is the disposal fee…" He winced as the words left his mouth.

"The what!" Joey barked in shock.

Tim sighed, "Look, you can't tell anyone or they will *kill you* to keep you quiet. Once you are fully synchronized with the game and the mind to machine transfer is complete, they need to destroy your body and the gear that lets it work. All that is left is a little data core that contains *you*. It gets added to the main core, and you are part of the game forever. Immortal, new life. Permanent addition."

"...You're serious," Joey breathed through flared nostrils.

"Yes. I shouldn't have even said that much before you sign the NDA. Are you in?" Tim held his breath as his friend deliberated. There would only be one offer.

Joey fought with himself for several moments. The answer that had to be given, finally was, "When do we start? I need to say goodbye to my mother."

Tim let out an explosive breath. "We can start the first scans today; I brought the equipment. You can't go into the game till it is paid off though."

"So the game will have been running for at least a half a month? Is that going to be bad?" Joey wondered as more medical equipment was wheeled into the room.

"Two to one time compression. One hour out here is two in there. So you'll be about a month late to the party."

CHAPTER THREE

The scans had been *very* invasive, including MRI's, blood draws, and tests he didn't have a medical name for. Tim later told him those tests were to determine the best way to destroy his body, making Joey shudder. His mother had paid off the DIVE-capsule no questions asked and invested a million dollars into an in-game account. That was the absolute maximum, but at a ten-to-one ratio, that still only gave him one hundred thousand gold. This was–potentially–a huge amount of money, but as he would theoretically live forever in the game, he would still need to become strong and make wise decisions with his finances. He looked at all the zeros in his account and rolled his eyes in disbelief.

Joey left everything else to his mother–any property, his pension, everything that was transferrable–and they parted with a tearful goodbye. He had tried to get her a pod, but she refused the opportunity; she was planning a perpetual vacation and didn't want to get bogged down playing games. Luckily for Joey, there was an in-game system where he could make calls to the real world. They would be able to stay in contact for all of her remaining years.

Finally, a black van rolled up the driveway, and he was manhandled into it like a cargo crate. The driver drove quickly—blatantly speeding—and within a few hours, Joe was in the sub-basement of a massive corporation staring at the monstrous machine that would be the final resting place of his body.

"Good luck, buddy," Tim called out, a sad smile on his face. "See you in game!"

Joey was startled. "You have a pod?"

"Nope. I'll be playing standard, mental keyboard and headset style. I'll add you to my friends list when I log in, but it might be a couple weeks. Pretty busy out here right now. My in-game name is 'tSnake'," Tim promised with a thumbs up.

"See ya, trouser snake." Joey laughed at the horrified look on Tim's face. "tSnake. Couldn't pick something normal, could you?"

"I'm gonna miss you man!" Tim paused, looking at the nearest employee before leaning in, "Joe… beat the game. If you do, there is a chance that you… I shouldn't be telling you this… This is more than a game. You could come back. Here. The real world." He stopped talking and hurried away as footsteps closed in.

A very confused Joey was brought to the pod, and they arranged his limbs meticulously. The doctor overseeing this process was thrilled that he stayed so still, earning him a sour condescending glare from Joey. The lid started to close, and second thoughts filled his mind with numbing horror. A shining gem that looked like a diamond was lowered to his head and rested gently above the bridge of his nose.

A small line of text appeared in his vision. No blue screens, huh? He rolled his eyes. Guess all those books from Royal Road turned out to be useless in the end. Why did he waste time reading those stories in the last couple weeks? Alrighty then, he would adapt. The message read:

Do you want ***power****? *Yes / No*

Well, yes. That sounded quite pleasant actually. He selected 'Yes' with his eyes. Wait, was that a link on 'power'? Too late.

Do you know what is about to happen? Have you read the terms and conditions?*

There was a link on the word 'conditions', and he selected it and read carefully through the contractual agreement and obligations. There was plenty he didn't understand, but now he at least knew a baseline of what was expected from him. He went back to the question and selected 'Yes'.

The words flashed red.

Excellent. Prepare to die. Yes / Yes

That was way too ominous! As he opened his mouth to shout for help, a roiling liquid poured onto his face and into his mouth, cutting off his complaints. Joey reflexively coughed but couldn't free his head from the fluid. He tried to hold what little breath he had remaining, but was entirely covered with no access to air. When his lungs felt like they were beginning to explode, he finally breathed in.

Air rushed into his lungs, and he blinked at the suddenly bright pod. Wait, he wasn't looking at the pod! He was standing, breathing heavily as he read the words hovering in front of him.

Welcome To Eternium! There is no saved data for your profile. Would you like to make a new character? Selecting 'no' will lead to true death. Yes / No

Easy answer. Joey selected 'yes'.

Great! This will be the only time you will ever be able to create a character as your status is about to legally become [Dead]. Ouch, sorry about that! Make sure to make wise decisions! Would you like to select an available starting class or undergo tests and trials to see what the right choice is for you? These tests may unlock different or even unique *classes based on your ability, but be warned! Taking the tests and showing* low *aptitudes may* reduce *the amount of available classes! You can exit these tests at any time! Start Game / Take Tests*

Well, if he was going to be here for a long time, he didn't want to be a boring archetype. Thank goodness he had studied video game theory for the last few weeks. Joey reached out and pressed… wait! He looked at his hand, moving on its own, under his own power! He jumped and smiled. His body was working again! He reached out and selected the 'take tests' option.

The air around him shimmered, and suddenly, he was standing in an unending hallway. A prompt appeared in front of him just as something screamed the only word that had been on the prompt. *RUN!* If his time in the army had taught him anything, it was to never hesitate when there were clear signs of danger. He sprang forward, running down the hallway as fast as possible. Behind him, he heard a massive **wham**. He chanced a glance over his shoulder in time to see a massive boulder crash through the roof where he had been standing. It must have weighed tons, possibly multiple tons if it wasn't hollow, and it started rolling down the slightly sloped hallway toward him. He ran faster; he had just gotten the use of his legs back, and there was no way in heck he was letting them get crushed!

As he ran, the rock behind him slowly gained speed. The further he ran the more the hallway sloped until it was at a forty-five degree angle. At this point, even Joey's intense desire to run couldn't save him. The rock caught up to him. *No!* As soon as it brushed the back of his body, he found himself in another area. He looked over and saw he was in the desert, next to the Humvees and helicopter that had so drastically changed his life. He was confused; had he been dreaming? Was that all a… premonition?

He shook himself out of his doubt. The screams of pain were slightly different this time, but he still rushed over and began working as fast as he could, doing everything he could to stabilize the men so they could be transported. The first four he quickly bound and had taken to the chopper. The fifth though… he was a bleeder. Joey worked as hard as he could, continuously moving and having the others bring IV's, bandages, and assorted tools. The man's heart stopped, and Joey worked on chest compressions until it was beating again. This happened over and over, fixing him, losing him, fixing him. Blood coated Joey, but he never gave up on the man. After several hours, during another round of compressions, Joe suddenly found himself in another room.

"What the…? This game is *sick*." That was not a compliment. Joe looked around for the men but found only a glowing prompt. That had been… so, *so* real. He looked nervously at this prompt, which simply said *SURVIVE*. A low growl came from behind him, and a quick look revealed a massive tiger poised to launch at him. Joey squealed in *far* too high a pitch and lunged forward into a roll, making it out the doorway as the tiger sailed over him. He stood and started running again, gasping as the last few hours were catching up to him. His body felt fine, but his mind was beginning to waver.

He ran, pumping his legs in perfect rhythm and never looking back until he reached a small pond. He looked over and saw small humanoid creatures talking by the edge of the water. They were standing over the body of a man, laughing as they poked the body with spears. His eyes narrowed as he thought. The tiger was coming up behind him with no pretense at stealth, so he ran directly at the small… Imps maybe? They certainly looked a bit like the devilish creatures of legend.

The tiny humanoids looked up at his charge, raising their spears defensively. Seeing an unarmed human, they cackled and jeered… right until he threw himself flat and a tiger came sailing at them. They raised their spears, but the tiger bowled into the unprepared creatures. Knocked flat, they still managed to spear the cat in its side while they were mauled. Soon, all three were bleeding. They stared each other down and prepared to leap into combat again. Unbeknownst to them, the blood dripping from them had reached the edge of the water. As the tiger leapt, tentacles shot out of the water and yanked all three combatants in. After a small amount of thrashing, the water was deathly still and seemingly clear again.

Joey found himself shivering in a comfy chair, looking at a prompt on a piece of paper. '*Do your best!*' was all that was written on the paper. He frowned, and words began appearing on the paper. Concepts of mathematics, nuances of astronomy, and even world politics and religion appeared in front of him. After he read a section, it vanished from the paper. Every time he got to a break in the page, a question would form. Without a writing utensil, he answered aloud and a new section would appear. Once or twice his mind wandered, causing him to read a section without really *seeing* it. The section would vanish, and he just *knew* he got the answer wrong. He bent his mind to the task, focusing hard and answering questions for the better part of a day. He blinked, then startled himself awake, noticing he had been drooling on the paper.

A new prompt appeared, *Time is up! Select 'proceed' to begin the next test.* Well, that was handy; it didn't penalize him for having fallen asleep. He hit the button and was pulled into the next area.

Dozens of trials tested every aspect of who he was, forcing him to come to know himself better every step of the way. His morality, his sense of family, his ability to handle money, more knowledge tests, and different versions of combat that left him bent and broken before repairing him and moving on. Realistically, he felt that he had never been so self-aware, and it was a hard truth when he found that in many ways, he simply didn't measure up. After days of work, there were finally no more tests to take. A notification appeared in the air in front of him.

Ding-ding-ding! World's First! Congratulations, not only have you finished the trials, you are also the first of 1,256,572 players in the system to take all *of them! Plus, you actually read the terms and conditions! Wow! +1 intelligence, if you know what I mean. Thanks to your forethought, you gain a title with a special* <u>*single-use*</u> *ability! Based on the results of your trials, new starting classes have been unlocked! Your basic stats will be adjusted based on the results of each test after you choose a class!*

Title unlocked: Try me with Trials! This title will increase how favorably others view your work ethic! Effect: Charisma is 10% more effective when interacting with non-player characters.

Title unlocked: Terms and conditions. This title gives you the single-use ability to break a magically-binding contract without any contract-based repercussions! After usage, this title will vanish.

Please note that all title effects are active at the same time, but the title you have equipped will be the only one others can see without analysis abilities. The maximum number of titles you can have at any given time is ten.

Nice! All of the blood, sweat, self-doubt, and tears had been worth it! Mostly. Actually, there were a couple things that… he shook his head to clear it. Happy thought time! Two favorable titles right away, extra classes, and–maybe–good starting stats! He eagerly awaited the chance to see the starting classes he had unlocked.

Joe was transported to a new room, but before his view of his surroundings solidified, the world turned to a muted color, almost like an old-school pause screen. He looked around in mild consternation and turned a squeal into a snort when he saw a man standing right next to him.

"Um. Hello. Are you real?" Joey carefully questioned the slightly glowing, larger-than-life man.

The man spoke, a smile in his voice but not on his face, "Hello, Joey. Yes, I am *very* real."

CHAPTER FOUR

"I was hoping to ask you a favor." The unknown man informed Joey. "I am a deity in this world known as the Hidden God."

Joey looked at the self-proclaimed god very nervously. He would be here for a *very* long time, and angering a god on the first day of game play was not high on his to-do list. "Um. Well, what can I do for you? ...Sir?" He added the last bit a little late.

The deity nodded at the respect in Joey's voice. "I know that you are coming into the game with the intention to become a *perma*. A permanent player that is. Before anyone else gets a chance, I want to make you an offer. I want you to become my follower."

"What? That's it? That seems rather… anticlimactic. No grand quest to throw down the other gods, find magical artifacts, save the world?" Joey babbled in a rush before remembering who he was talking to.

The god looked uncomfortable and coughed into a raised fist. "No, nothing like that for now. The problem is… I'm the Hidden God. It's just that I'm too *well* hidden. I am the god of hidden and forbidden knowledge, my elements being water and darkness. Not of evil!" he exclaimed at the look Joey gave him. "Just like all things, knowledge is only evil if it is used as such, and darkness is as much a part of reality as is the light."

"So... why me?" Joey queried the pleading god.

"Well, you will always be here. That means I will - at a minimum - always have at least *one* follower no matter how out of favor I am. Big plus in your favor, as it will be to my benefit to keep you happy. Also, the way that you finished all of the tasks allows me to offer you a 'hidden' class, one of the necessities for me to be able to speak to you in person." The god sounded strangely desperate. "Deities gain power based on the quantity and works of their followers, which is why they offer quests to so many people, so often. I have *no one*, so my power begins to wane even in these early stages. If I become too weak, the world will stagnate, as no hidden knowledge will ever be found again. No high-level secret quests, no forgotten weapons of power."

It was starting to come together. "I hate to ask, but what do *I* get out of this? You just said the other gods are stronger and more able to give rewards to their followers, and I get the feeling that being associated with you will reduce how happy people are to know me."

The god nodded briskly, happy that they were moving into the transactional portion of this discussion. "That is a serious and valid concern, as people incorrectly associate darkness with evil regularly. I am actually considered a *neutral* god, one of the very few. I won't lie to you, the followers of the gods of good will see you as too evil to fully trust, and those following gods of evil will see you as too weak to make a firm commitment to being terrible. As a starting benefit, where most people start with a positive reputation with those they follow and negative with the opposing side, *you* will start with neutral across the board."

Joey thought for a moment, the neutrality may actually come in handy. He wouldn't be attacked by either the good or evil side in conflicts if he didn't start anything. "Well, can you tell me about the class first?"

The deity nodded, "It is called a *ritualist.* Everyone else will see you as a *cleric* unless you tell them your true nature or a *very* high level inspection spell is cast upon you. You will also have access to a unique profession, called an *occultist.* Again, this is hidden and considered a *scholar* when others steal a peek at your stat sheet."

"What are the class benefits?" Joey asked, very intrigued by the names of the class and profession.

"As a ritualist, you will be able to mimic the abilities of other classes when you get strong enough. Like an enchanter, you will be able to create magical items or other effects that give magical benefits. If you have the mana and mental fortitude, you will be able to use *any* type of magic you find or create, where others are restricted to their area of expertise. As a ritualist, your main unique ability will allow you to cast large scale magics that require multiple participants… if you can find or create those rituals. That is where the *occultist* class comes into play."

"Go on…" Joey grinned, already knowing that he would be accepting this class.

"That profession will let you find knowledge hidden in books, runes, and pictures that others–even high level scholars–will dismiss as irrelevant or simply lore of the world. As your skill levels progress, you will be able to read highlighted sections of information that appear to you and only you."

Joey realized something as the god was talking. "What are the *downsides*? A class this powerful must have some serious flaws…"

"Yes, there are a few… basically, you will forevermore be the most frail character type. You have heard the term glass cannon? Think tissue paper cannon instead. Perhaps paper bow and arrow until you are able to destroy enemies on your own–many, *many*, levels down the road. Think of yourself as the sickly lad who never ate, got exercise, or left the library. Training and items can help to correct this, but you will never be as strong, be as charismatic, or have as much endurance as others who specialize in those areas. Even typical mages will be able to leave you wheezing in the dust if they decide to run away from a fight. Of course, all of that is at the lowest levels." The god smiled nervously as Joey considered this unfortunate effect.

"How do I get stronger? Will I be useful?" Joey finally spoke his thoughts aloud.

"There are several main ways to get stronger; fighting monsters and other people is *usually* the fastest, of course. Otherwise, the second way you will gain experience is following your professions, and *you* will be able to have more than one. Oh, and I'll give you bonuses if you are able to hide your class and play as… whatever you pretend to be. Third, and most important for you, I will be able to grant you *lots* of bonus experience and boons for finding hidden knowledge, secrets, or completing hidden quests. So following your profession will be much more beneficial over time than fighting," the deity promised empathetically. "Eventually, you could attain power that the filthy casuals in the world can only dream of, and you won't even need to leave safe areas too often if you don't want to." Joey thought the last bit was an awkward attempt at a joke.

"I will want to be able to explore though, otherwise what was the point of all this?" Joey gestured to his body. "Also, I read in the wiki, what was allowed to remain anyway," the company had put incredibly strict rules on sharing information, wikis and info sites were usually deleted the day they were created, "that there were class trainers that could direct you to quests or other beneficial areas. Will I get that?"

A disheartened shake of the head was the answer he got.

"Good! So I'll actually be able to make my own way in the world and be rewarded for it?" Joey's pleased voice startled the god, bringing a real smile to his face for the first time.

"Yes, and if you do well, you may be able to recruit people to your cause, whatever it may be. You could actually *become* a class trainer for ritualists if you choose to do so." This statement caused a prompt to appear in front of Joey.

You have been offered the chance to earn a god's favor. This is a multi-part quest. Step one: Choose Ritualist as your class. Step two: Glean enough hidden knowledge to increase favor with the Hidden God to 'Friendly'. Reward: Hidden, variable. Based on knowledge accrued.

Oh look, the reward was hidden. Everything was hidden! Joey thought he now knew how this deity had gotten his moniker. At least the quest seemed fairly typical for this style of quest chain, not to mention the one offering it. "So, how do I start?"

"I would suggest you offer your services as a cleric if you insist that you want to hunt monsters. Healers are very rare in the world, especially magical ones. Actually, all magic is very hard to acquire, as you will soon find out. So few people went far enough in the trials–or did well enough in them–to start with magic, so they will either need to get into a Mage's College or find artifacts that transfer power to them directly," the god shot Joey a meaningful look. In the distance, thunder rolled. He nervously looked around. "I need to go; we are only allowed minimal time with players. I've already said too much. Do great works and I will be able to visit again. Last thing: Try your very best not to draw the Certified Altruistic Lexicon's attention. No one wants to be exposed to his puns, and making him angry would be even worse."

The god vanished as Joe fully materialized in the room, leaving him blinking in a world that motion had suddenly returned to. Stepping forward, he saw that the room was packed full of people standing quietly in rows. Wait, all of them had his face! He walked closer to them, and their class appeared above them. There were men holding huge weapons and wearing armor that glowed, men that wore very little but were bound with muscle, and men that had spirits or magical lights floating around them. In total, there were nearly a hundred of himself all demonstrating different classes he had unlocked.

He moved, and all of them moved with him. Joey smiled,

and the room lit up with the hundreds of teeth that were now showing. He danced around–playing with his new body–and for the first time wasn't told that he should never, ever, dance in public. He liked this crowd; they understood his sweet moves.

"I must have done well in the trials to have access to all of this," Joey pondered aloud. "Now, how do I find the ritualist in all of this?" Saying the words out loud caused all but one of the men to become insubstantial, so he walked to that one and inspected him. It was indeed the ritualist. As he stepped closer, a prompt appeared in front of him.

The Ritualist. A hidden (conditionally unique) class that has the ability to work with almost any type of magic, provided they can gain access to it and take the time to understand it. At level one, they have the same abilities as a cleric. As they level up their hidden selves, the ritualist automatically gains several cleric abilities at no cost. The ritualist class gains skill in their chosen pursuits at four times the speed of an average class due to their vast thirst for power. The ritualist gains five characteristic points to spend per three levels, and one point of wisdom and perception automatically on every even level. This is important and specifically stated because they have a massive penalty to their constitution, dexterity, and strength. Perception, wisdom, and intelligence are the suggested characteristics for this class. Do you want to start the 'game' as a Ritualist?

Joey thought about the extra points; he was not sure how much of an effect each individual point would have, but at level one hundred–without allocating or gaining any extra points–he would have fifty perception and wisdom, plus whatever he started the game with. As far as he knew, there was no level cap but each new level was as difficult to attain as the game could make it and have people still want to play. Point in fact, you needed the experience of the previous level plus *one thousand* times the current level. So, if he started at level one, he needed one thousand points to get to level two. From two to three, he needed two thousand plus the one thousand points of level one; three thousand points in total, and so forth. Joe would need to do some research to see how best to allocate any points he might gain.

He accepted the class, making another prompt appear. *Know this! You are the first player to take this class. Set an example for others, and watch them flock to your cause for instruction! Intelligence +1 per two levels! Professions unlock at level five. You have four characteristic points to spend. Please note, your starting characteristics have already been modified due to your trials, real life capabilities, and class selection. Please allocate your remaining points now.*

Joey looked at his character sheet which appeared in front of him, filling his vision. There were several stats to choose from. Strength, agility, dexterity, constitution, intelligence, wisdom, charisma, luck, karmic luck, and perception. The tooltips informed him that strength was the stat which determined how much he could carry and how hard he could hit with weapons or his fists. Dexterity was the explosive speed he could muster, his ability to contort his body, how well he could do complicated tasks like picking locks, crafting goods, or using ranged weapons. Yikes! Dexterity seemed to be a stat that was needed by most classes, and he had serious penalties to it...

Constitution determined how healthy he was, how much stamina he had, and his resistances to poison and disease. It also determined his body appearance and made it harder to be knocked around at higher levels. Good for tanks and warriors especially.

Intelligence determined how much mana he had at any given time, in addition to how well he could understand complicated concepts like spells or engineering.

The tooltip for wisdom explained that wisdom determined how fast his mana *regenerated*, as well as an esoteric statement that wisdom would help determine if he *should* do something. It would also let him combine various concepts, working with his intelligence to make new and improved things.

Charisma determined how people would interact with him, and his ability to get good prices buying or selling. It would impact his ability to lead or convince others to do things with or for him.

Luck was something that affected all the other stats on an

unstated level as well as his chances of finding rare items or loot without specifically looking for them. Karmic luck wasn't explained, but it likely was how your alignment was tracked.

Finally, perception was his ability to spot details. This was everything that came from sensory input and would increase how well he experienced and interacted with the world. There was a note on the side that caught his attention though. **Be warned! Increasing perception will enhance how much pain players* actually *feel, as well as all other sensations! Eternium is not responsible for damage to player's mental state. For more information please read the capsule handbook included in your order!*

Well, that was disturbing. Hopefully there was a maximum threshold on the pain a person could feel; or else in the higher levels a strong wind may be too much to handle.

He thought about the stats in a way appropriate for a non-gamer. Tomatoes. Why tomatoes? Think of it like this: Strength was how hard you could throw a tomato. Dexterity was how fast you could get to a tomato and allowed you to slice the fruit without hurting yourself. Constitution let you eat rotten tomatoes without getting sick. Intelligence let you know that a tomato was a fruit, while wisdom let you know not to put it in a fruit salad. Charisma allowed you to sell a tomato-based fruit salad. Perception let you spot tomatoes among strawberries. Luck was your likelihood of finding a tomato in a place that only grew potatoes. Karmic luck? No idea how it related, but it sounded dangerous.

He looked at his current stat sheet to determine what he should increase.

Characteristic: Raw score (Modifier)

Strength: 6 (0.06)
Dexterity: 6 (0.06)
Constitution: 4 (0.04)
Intelligence: 16 (1.16)
Wisdom: 16 (1.16)

Charisma: 8 (0.08)
Perception: 16 (1.16)
Luck: 12 (1.12)
Karmic Luck: 0

It seemed to be an odd ratio system, but he understood it better after reading the very informative tooltips that popped up as he looked over the various stats. It read like this: *Growth in Eternium is difficult when you are doing nothing! Unlike other systems, each day will be a struggle to survive, especially at the start of your journey. Because of the difficulty, the rewards will certainly be worth your effort! Since this system is somewhat unorthodox, please note that a modifier of 'one' is considered a normal, healthy adult human. Your real-life capabilities have negatively impacted constitution to a high degree!*

Each point allocated will increase your modifier by one one-hundredth of a point. An exception to this is when you gain your first ten points in any category. At this point, your score will increase to 'one point one' in that category. Moving forward, each time a category increases to the next multiple of fifty, the base score will increase by 'one'. At fifty points, your modifier will be plus 'two'. At one hundred points, the modifier will be plus 'three'. For example, a character with forty-nine points in a category will have a modifier of 1.49, which is forty-nine percent stronger than an average human! Then, if they reach fifty points in the category, they will jump to a modifier of 2.0!

The discrepancy in strength is intended to push you to develop as fast as possible. Skill in the areas you focus on will quickly allow you to reach higher than others of the same level, even if you have similar stats! You can earn skill points and characteristic points through your actions, so work hard! You will need to be as powerful as possible when the first major update comes into effect. That is… if you want to survive!

Ominous ending, but seriously, ouch! Forget the high stats, those low scores made his character barely playable! A negative modifier like this could destroy his gameplay! What would a point zero four modifier do to him? If he read the information correctly, a modifier of 'one' was considered standard for a person, and was about the equivalent of a fit teenaged human in the real world. Anything below one could seriously impact almost all areas of his new life, and his strength modifier would leave him too weak to do almost anything!

By the looks of his constitution, a stray splinter may *actually* kill him. He began with only four points to spend, so he put two in constitution and two in charisma, reasoning that social interactions would be a huge part of gameplay. He shuddered to think about how people would react to a person that much less charismatic than the *average* human. What was the sample size for that rating? Joey had the disturbing feeling that it was somehow *everyone* in the real world.

After the points were distributed, he was asked to input a name. Since he could never start a new one, and would be around a long time, he chose 'Joe' as his screen name. Somehow that hadn't been chosen yet, most likely because there were going to be a thousand versions of 'Shadow' or 'slayer' out there. He didn't get to put in a last name, but his title appeared automatically with the option to change or hide it. He accepted the changes, and looked at the details that described his new and permanent self.

Name: Joe 'Try me with Trials' Class: Cleric (Actual: Ritualist) Profession: Locked
Level: 1 Exp: 0 Exp to next level: 1000
Hit Points: 50/50 (50+(0))*
Mana: 400/400 (12.5 per point of intelligence, +100% from deity)
Mana regen: 4/sec (.25 per point of wisdom)
*Stamina: 50/50 (50+(0)**+(0)***)*
**10 points for each point in Constitution, once it has increased above 10.*
***5 points for each point in Strength, once it has increased above 10.*
****5 points for each point in Constitution, once it has increased above 10.*

Characteristic: Raw score (Modifier)

Strength: 6 (0.06)
Dexterity: 6 (0.06)

Constitution: 6 (0.06)
Intelligence: 16 (1.16)
Wisdom: 16 (1.16)
Charisma: 10 (1.10)
Perception: 16 (1.16)
Luck: 12 (1.12)
Karmic Luck: 0

Class skills and spells

Heal (Novice I): Select a target to heal, restoring 5n HP, where n = skill level. Range: Five meters. Mana cost: 5n. Cooldown: 3 seconds.

Darkvision: Able to see in total darkness with no penalties. Range of vision is halved. Passive, no cost.

Hidden Sense (Novice I): An innate sense that allows you to find hidden items, people, or knowledge (affected by perception). Passive, no cost.

Pray (Novice I): Spend a full minute praying for help or guidance, results vary. Less likely to succeed if deity is occupied. No cost. Cooldown: One day.

Ritual Magic (Novice I): Ability to create, maintain, and change rituals much more efficiently than usual. -5% mana and component cost per skill level. Ritualist class exclusive: -50% mana and component cost.

Joey had no money or gear on him, but apparently had one skill point he couldn't assign until the second level. Not that he knew what it would do. He looked at the skill descriptions and a handy pop-up informed him that most skills and spells started at 'novice' and would get progressively better as they were used. When the level passed 'nine', the skill would be upgraded to a zero of the next rank.

From lowest to highest, the ranks of skills were: Novice, Beginner, Apprentice, Student, Journeyman, Expert, Master,

Grandmaster, and Sage. Looked like it would be a *long* journey to perfect a skill. Joe looked over all the options one more time, and after finalizing his decisions he took a deep breath and accepted the character. The world dissolved into shimmering motes of light, and Joe reappeared in a bustling city.

CHAPTER FIVE

"Welcome to Ardania, capital city of the 'newly returned to the world' human Kingdom! It's actually been about two hundred years, so I don't know why that is still part of the greeting. Hmm. Maybe it is because you travelers don't know our history?" A verbose lady greeted Joe as he appeared in a daze. The overload of information didn't help his confusion. "Can I please ask your class so that I know where to direct you for some initial training?"

"Um... yeah, thanks. I'm a r- I'm a *cleric*." Joe nearly slapped himself at the close call. Right, ritualist needed to stay hidden, or people would not trust him for some reason. He tried to smile brightly, but he was trembling from the strain of standing upright. Joe stooped a bit, letting his muscles relax as he looked down at his skeletal body. People were going to think that he was a ghoul, he just *knew* it.

"Oh! Do you know any *magic*? What deity do you serve?" She looked at him with shining eyes, paying far more attention than he thought he deserved with his non-enhanced charisma.

"Yes, I can heal and pray for guidance, but my god is

uhm… I don't know yet. I'm undecided?" Joe hedged his words, trying not to give too much away.

"That's great! I'm sure you will be asked to join a whole bunch of groups right away! Awesome, I got to meet you before you were popular! How about you head over there for some instruction?" She pointed to an open courtyard, and a prompt appeared in front of his tired-looking face.

Quest alert! Baby steps: Learn some basic information about using your abilities. Reward: Cleric scepter, Exp: 100. Accept / Decline

Accepting the quest, he thanked the energetic lady and walked slowly toward the area she had indicated. He looked around, taking in all of the sights and sounds of the city. Joey was full of wonder; he had always needed glasses, and after several years in the army his hearing had been badly damaged. Now, his vision felt as sharp as an eagle's and his hearing was like that of a bat; he could clearly make out details that he never would have been able to before, and it seemed that he could hear everything for several city blocks while still being able to make out individual conversations. To be fair, he was exaggerating quite a bit, but it didn't change the fact that perception was *amazing*!

Then he got a whiff of the city and nearly gagged. Oh right, a high perception had serious negatives as well. It seemed that hygiene wasn't overly important here. Joe hurried at a snail's pace toward the square where a soldier–in obviously enchanted armor which gave off its own glow–was screaming at some low level fighter-type player.

"You call *that* an attack? I'm surprised that sword had enough force to make it to the dummy, you dummy! How the abyss do you plan on taking down monsters when you can barely lift your weapon? Go find a bow or some other coward's weapon!" the trainer screamed in the player's face. The person on the receiving end of the shouting had a totally blank expression. In fact it seemed he actually had only one facial expression at all, indicating that this must be one of the players who played with an outdated VR helmet.

"Anyone know how to skip conversations?" the trainee suddenly yelled in an echoing voice at the people around him, making the soldier glare at him.

"You want to skip conversations? Fine, you pompous little ass! You are going to *die* out there, and I *refuse* to have it on my conscience!" The guard turned, furious, and walked stiffly away, catching sight of Joe as he moved. "You! What do you want?"

"I'm here for training, sir." Joe respectfully informed him, trying not to make him angrier than he currently was.

"No," the guard grunted, looking at Joe's sallow face, stooped and skeletal frame, and meager amount of muscle. He sighed, seeming to deflate as he looked at the wreck of a body. "Sorry to say lad, there is not much that I can do for you. You are polite, at least, but politeness doesn't kill wolves. A sharp blade does."

"Ah. Well, I'm not really here to learn about swinging weapons around; I'm a cleric. I was hoping to find someone to teach me how to refine my craft. Healing and such," Joe trailed off as the guard got an odd look on his face.

"You mean you are a *healer*, right? A doctor? Bandages and such are in the supply shed over there." He pointed at a small building to the side.

"No sir, I'm a *cleric*. I'm supposed to be able to heal with magic, but am unsure how to actually *do* it," Joe stated sincerely, not breaking eye contact.

"Well, I'll be…" the guard's brow furrowed, "Never seen one of you magic types *here* before. If you want, you can heal some of my guards, and I'll try to find a suitable reward for you. Sorry to say I won't be much use teaching you magic though. If you need to learn, why don't you," he snickered a little, "pray about it? A cleric! That's a good one." He walked away chuckling, mood seemingly much better than it was previously.

Joe was a bit miffed, but stopped himself from lashing out. The guard had a point, why *not* pray about it? He *did* have that option after all. Joe clasped his hands together and asked for guidance, and after a full minute of waiting he suddenly *knew*.

He looked at the guards that he had been instructed to heal. A red outline showed up where they were injured, and a blue outline appeared around his hand. He moved his fingers in the patterns shown by the blue light, and pushed his intent to heal into the burgeoning spell. A ball of water launched from his hand, splashing against the guard he was targeting. The guard released a startled oath, making a few people laugh. The guard's face reddened and he took a few threatening steps toward Joe before stopping in wonder. He took another step, testing the ankle that had given him trouble for years, then rushed over to the unknown person and thanked him loudly and profusely.

A few of the other guards saw this and moved closer, clamoring for Joe to heal them as well after hearing the thankful words being sent his way. Joe repeated his actions, and small orbs of water left his hands to splash against the guards. After the fifth one had been healed, a notification appeared.

Quest complete: Baby steps. Exp: 100.

Nice! He had finished that quest in no time flat, as–he supposed–was the intent. The guard that had assigned the quest came over to talk to the men he had healed, and a sheepish look appeared on his face.

The guard that had been directing the training then came to talk to Joe, "Well. Um. Thank you, holy one. I am sorry that I didn't trust your words, but false healers come through here all the time peddling snake oil and cures that are often worse than the disease. We haven't had a *real* cleric offer their services to the guards in over a decade. The gods have been absent from the common man for too long. If you'll wait here, I'll go get you something we've been hanging onto on the off chance it would be of use." He walked to the storage shed and rummaged around for a few minutes, coming back with a carved piece of wood.

"Here, this is a cleric's scepter. Using this will slightly increase the speed with which you can cast your spells." Joe looked at the information that popped up when he touched the scepter.

Basic Cleric scepter (Wood). Adds 2-4 blunt damage on strike. -10% cast time when casting cleric spells. 5% chance to use ability [Turn undead] on strike. To cast while holding, simply focus your will and intent into the scepter, and it will do the rest.

"Listen cleric… my men don't have much, but they are *good* men. For some reason, just over a month ago we had a huge influx of travelers. Some of them seem to delight in causing havoc, and a portion of them seem to feel no pain. I am the captain of the guard, and I feel responsible for my people. My men can't keep up with the crime spikes, and have been getting hurt in the line of duty. Without proper care or magic, they are slowly becoming permanently injured. Will you help us out?" The guard did his best not to beg, but it was clear that he would if needed.

Quest alert! Baby steps II: Heal at least ten guards. Reward: Exp: 200. Increased reputation with human city guards, and one piece of light armor (variable).

Joe accepted the quest with a nod; what exactly did variable mean? A smile on his face, the guard captain ran off to send injured guards to the city square. Soon a steady stream of guards walked, limped, or were carried into the area. He moved to the one that was carried in first, focusing his mind on trying to inspect the man's health bar.

Perception + healing check succeeded! City guard: Health: 8/1000.

Oh wow, no wonder this guy was barely moving. Joe got to work; instead of standing back and throwing ice-cold water on the damaged man he moved forward and put his hands next to the wound, trying to be as gentle as possible. He cast the spell ten times in roughly thirty seconds, essentially as fast as he was able to make the proper motion without his scepter. He didn't want to be poking a wounded man with a stick after all. After ten casts, a new prompt appeared.

Congratulations! Hard work is paying off, you have learned a variant of the 'heal' spell: Lay on hands (Novice I). Effect: Increased healing when touching the target of the spell. Healing done: 10n where n = skill level. Cost: 5n mana. Cooldown: 3 seconds. Range: Touch. As this is a variant of the spell 'Heal', it will add progress to the skill rank of the original as it is leveled and can never have a higher level than the origin skill.

Joe quickly switched to using this new spell, casting it four times in quick succession. He began to feel tired but continued spamming the spell until the guard reached maximum health. The now-vigorous man stood tall and whooped for joy, dancing around and then profusely thanking Joe before running off. After that initial worst case, Joe was able to quickly soothe the injuries of the other guards in the area, far more than the ten needed to fulfill the quest. Being a medic for so long made it hard for him to leave suffering people–especially soldiers–to their fate. Luckily, with his huge mental scores boosting his power, he had a massive mana pool that refilled almost as fast as he managed to use it.

When the last guard left the yard, he returned to the captain who shook his hand, tears in his eyes. "Thank you, lad. You don't know how much this means to all of us. You really went above and beyond what I asked for. Some of the boys chipped in a few coins to reward ya with some proper armor. So I pulled out the good stuff for you. It doesn't look like much, but it's the best we can do. This should help keep ya alive, which is what you did for all of us."

Quest complete! Baby steps II. For going beyond the requirements without asking for or expecting an increased reward, the rewards have been doubled! Reputation gain has been tripled! (Note: this is uncommon in a harsh, uncaring world such as Eternium.) Exp: 400. Reputation with human city guards has been increased by 3000, from 'Neutral' directly to 'Friend of Human Guards' (bypassing 'Reluctantly friendly' and 'Friendly'). 1000 reputation points remain to reach 'Ally of Human Guards' status. Since this is your first reputation gain, please note that there are many distinct levels of reputation. From lowest to highest: Blood Feud, Loathed, Hated, Hostile, Cautious, Neutral, Reluctantly Friendly, Friendly, Friend, Ally, and Extended Family. There are one thousand points between each level.

"Here you go; I hope it fits." The captain hesitated before he handed over a soft robe that Joe put on before even reading the stats. "Just… I want you to know that as good as this robe is, it can easily be used for completely evil purposes, but it's all we could find."

"Thank you!" Joe exclaimed, feeling the plushy robe. It did *not* look like a bathrobe–totally not–more like a typical monk's outfit. He didn't hear the guard's final few sentences, rather, he *did* hear them, but the words didn't register.

"No, young man, thank you! Bobby was stabbed almost to death in an alley yesterday–in broad daylight! Without you he would have likely… died today." The captain looked away to try to hide his misty eyes. "There was nothing we could do. We were getting a death-fund ready for his wife and kids."

After a slightly uncomfortable silence, Joe coughed and redirected the conversation away from tear-jerking dialogue. "Is there anything else I can do to help?" he queried in a blatant attempt to get another quest.

The captain shook his head knowingly. "I think you have a good handle on your abilities. Good luck out there. Please feel free to stop by anytime you like, and if we have injured, we will pay what we can for your skills if you'd be willing." Joe agreed to help in the future if it was needed, thanking him and then walking a good distance away before pausing to look at the stats on his robe.

Perception check failed! Knowledge check failed! Overruled, quest reward and owner of item.

Undying robe. Item class: uncommon. Adds +5 physical defense, 20% resistance to non-magical cold. Special qualities: Any damage that does more than 20% of your max health at once, which would normally kill you, instead leaves you at one health point. (Note: being hit while at one health will still kill you.) Cooldown: Thirty minutes. Also known as robes of despair or robes of torture, this item is often used by 'interrogators' to ensure that they don't accidentally kill their captive.

Wow. Why were these labeled as uncommon? Maybe this item just wouldn't be useful for a regular player? That could make sense; it was likely that warriors had hundreds of health. But for Joe–with his tiny health bar and poor ability in escaping combat–this may save his life many times. After all, twenty percent of his health only amounted to a grand total of ten points.

Lost in thought, Joe went into the city and started walking around a bit aimlessly. Each time he passed a guard they would smile and wave, which helped him feel relaxed even when he was around some shady looking people. Joe supposed that word had already gotten around about the cleric that helped guards and hoped that if he were mugged, the guards would jump in to help him. Not that he needed to worry too much since he did not have any money on him. His gold had been put directly into a bank account so that he didn't spawn into the game with a mountain of money crushing him.

Thinking about changing his monetary situation, he decided he didn't want to waste time finding a bank to make a withdrawal. Instead, he started looking for the lifeblood of gaming: quests! After wandering for a good chunk of time, he was feeling frustrated. There were no glowing lights to signify a quest giver and he had no map or way to find his way around. This game was very realistic in almost every way, the main difference being that science had been replaced with magic and he was now living in a medieval setting. It seemed that literacy was a given though, because most signs had words and there were many chalkboards up with announcements. Was paper expensive?

Reading everything he could, he eventually spotted a job board that had standing orders for furs, crafting materials, and other odds and ends. Most were written with extra thick chalk, which made a few of the requests a bit… ambiguous. Was that a request for collecting demons or lemons? They really shouldn't have used cursive. Looking around, he spotted a group of armed and armored people about to head out of the gates, obviously getting ready to fight some creatures in the wild.

"Excuse me!" Joe called, jogging over to them. 'Jogging' being a polite exaggeration in this case. He had to fight not to show how winded that short jaunt made him, but his pale face easily gave him away. Freaking constitution. "I notice you only have four people **wheeze** in your group. Do you have room for one more?"

"Oh god, it's a noob," one of them muttered intentionally loudly. "Run for it?"

"Sorry, bro-ski. We are a premade team. We don't accept randos. Especially level *one* randos," one of them snorted with a thick Californian accent. "Go do *social* quests or something. I bet someone around here needs a letter delivered."

They left Joe standing there with his mouth open, shocked at their casual rudeness. A moment later, he felt a hand on his shoulder and turned to see a powerfully built lady patting him on the arm.

"Don't mind them; they're part of a guild that considers themselves 'hardcore' players. They've been going twelve hours a day since day one. Real world hours, that is. You looking for a team? I might be able to help you out depending on what kind of skills you have." She grinned at him, reminding him a little too much of a shark.

"Thank you! I *am* looking for a team. I'm level one, but I'm a cleric. I have two healing spells, a ranged and a touch version. I hear clerics are rare?" Joe smoothly responded, knowing that he would be a valuable asset and determined not to sell himself short. "Do you think that I could be useful to your team?"

"A *real* cleric? Magical and whatnot?" Her eyes bulged a bit and she waggled her fingers at him as she spoke.

"Yes?" Joe responded in confusion. That was standard for a cleric wasn't it?

"Oh, they are going to be *so* pissed that they ignored you!" She chuckled, eyes sparkling. "Can you prove it? I got hurt the other day and healing in this game is *really* slow. If you get hurt badly enough it might be *days* before you get back to full health. You need to fully respawn to fix issues sometimes."

"Sure." He inspected her health bar, which was indeed missing a few chunks. Strange, it was like the last bits of the bar were greyed out. Perhaps her health couldn't increase past that point without magical assistance? That unless you did something like physical therapy, were directly healed, or sent to respawn… you just *never* got back to full health? He reached out and placed a hand on her, activating his touch healing spell. She shuddered as ice cold water dripped down her shirt.

"Ahh! You bastard, that's not funny! I never signed up for a wet tee shirt-" her voice cut off as her health maxed out. "Hot *damn*, you'd better come with me before someone assaults you with unrelenting guild invites." They went to a local tavern where she introduced him to a few people, including her guild leader.

"If you join The Wanderers, I *promise* you won't regret it. I'll make sure to set you up with a solid team and we'll get you to level ten within three weeks! At that point you should be able to resurrect people. Well, that's the hope anyway; there aren't any other clerics right now so the data is unclear. This will be a *huge* advantage to our guild, and I'll make sure you are properly compensated; you'll be a guild officer right away! Tiona, set up a standard officer contract and we'll…" the guild master was cut off abruptly as Joe shook his head.

"Sorry, I can't accept the guild invite. I have a quest line which I'm sure is going to take me across a huge amount of land, so I can't promise to stay tied to a guild or the city without talking to my deity. I'll go crazy worrying about it otherwise," Joe informed the guild leader in a quasi-sad tone. "If I don't complete my quest, I could lose all of my cleric abilities."

The man scoffed at this, "You are level one! It can't be *that* great of a quest. Plus, the weakest monster out there–a rabbit–is level three! You are supposed to spend at least a week doing social quests in town before ever going out there. Whatever god you follow won't be *that* much of an asshole, right? Sending you out defenseless? Without help or a team?"

"I'll make you a deal," Joe offered frankly. One of the most important things he had learned in the army was to be assertive. "I'll join you, on a *temporary* basis. I'll heal people, you help me gain levels and skill. At any point, I have the option to leave with no hard feelings. I will not leave the guild if my leaving will make a party member fail a quest. Wait, I'll add a qualifier to that. I won't leave so long as the quest is finished within a timely manner; none of this faffing around to keep me in the guild indefinitely. I'm just not sure that joining a guild is the way to-"

"Done! If it is a choice between that or losing you to some crap guild like the Hardcores, I'll take *that* offer any day." The GM set down a new piece of paper that his scribe had handed over, detailing every aspect of the conversation and deal they had just talked about as well as other standard guild details. "You can stay here; we own the inn. Did you want to go hunting today? The faster we get you leveled, the better for all of us."

"Yes, please. How long will it take to get to level five? I'm really looking forward to getting a profession," Joe mentioned offhandedly. He read the contract carefully and signed after making sure there were no hidden loopholes.

Minor achievement: Joined a Guild! Good for you. Have some experience. Exp: 10.

At least the system wasn't *overly* snarky like some other games tended to be. For some reason, programmers seemed to think people only responded to mean messages. Sometimes it was nice to get *just* the details.

"Hrmph. Well, it usually takes a week or so when power leveling like this. If you were able to fight monsters directly, one-on-one like a warrior, it would be a *lot* faster. As a cleric, I have no idea," the guild leader told him. "You might gain more, you might get less."

"Fair enough. Whose team will I be on?" Joe looked around at the people bustling around, all of them seeming to be in a hurry. Oh, right, it should be Sunday right now, people were trying to maximize their play time before the work week.

"Well, since she found you, and hers is the only team not full right now, head out with Tiona. Good luck." The man looked at his interface, going far too still. He must have taken off his helmet and was getting a drink or something in the real world, leaving his character to sit unattended. It was painfully obvious the conversation was over, and Tiona seemed a bit overexcited. She grabbed Joe with powerful hands and basically dragged him out the door.

Not that he was resisting. This was getting fun.

CHAPTER SIX

Super minor achievement: Joined a party! Nice work, have some experience. Exp: 5.

"So, here is the deal. Those rabbits are the nastiest thing around until you get about a half mile out, then foxes show up to eat the rabbits. Also you, if you aren't strong enough or smell like a rabbit. Later, foxes get eaten by wolves, bears keep the wolves away, and so on till you start seeing magical monsters. There are also Wolfmen walking around out there, but they don't seem to fit into these categories. They aren't too much of an issue if you stay out of their territories, but there are a lot of quests to hunt them," Tiona told Joe. "Don't worry about that though. Today you have one job and one job only. *Don't die*. Can you deal with that?"

"I was a medic on active duty in the army for the last few years," Joe proudly informed her. "I got this. Piece of cake."

"Oh good! How did that go? Enjoy your time in the service?" she muttered as she stared down an extra-large rabbit. She loosened her sword and drew it as they got closer.

"Not so much… my last day was when my chopper got

blown out of the sky." Joe coughed, face red with embarrassment. He should have kept his mouth shut.

She paused. "Yeah*hhh*. My order stands. Don't die." She used some blade skill, sending a strange energy out as a slash. A moment later, there was a quickly cut off squeak followed by squeals of rage as a small group of bunnies ran at them. The rabbits had a small, blunt horn on their heads, and it seemed their main attack was jumping and bashing their opponents. The largest man in the group smoothly intercepted the blow, and a *ping* was heard as the animal fell in multiple chunks from the oversized sword. Two blades and an arrow worked together to quickly erase these minor threats from existence.

Angry Horned Rabbit x5 defeated. Exp: 20.

Joe was a bit disheartened; it looked like quests were indeed the best way to gain experience points. Four points per rabbit? No wonder it took so long to level up.

"Let's roll. We have a *lot* of ground to cover." Tiona set a brisk pace, and within a few moments, they had left the blood-stained ground behind. They didn't even collect the furs; at this point, they were so common that they were totally worthless. Joe nearly collapsed as they went too fast for him to regenerate stamina, his poor constitution catching up with him again. On one of their frequent rest stops–where they did not actually stop, just slow to a crawl–Tiona grouched at him to increase his constitution so they could jog further at one time.

"There are… more important… things for me… to focus on," Joe wheezed while glaring at his slowly refilling stamina bar.

"Hmm," Tiona replied in a non-committal manner. "Well, you *are* the only one with a mana bar so… I guess whatever you say goes."

Local event! 'Trespassers!' Survive the swarm to gain rewards!

"*Ambush!*" one of the others shouted, making Tiona whip around with her sword in hand.

The team's main fighter seemed resigned to his fate. "Crap! It's a swarm! Good game all, see you tomorrow." It appeared that one of the members had gotten too close to a rabbit warren, and the horned rabbits were scampering out of the ground in an attempt to overwhelm the humans.

"Stop spouting that defeatist crap and get set!" Tiona ordered them to form a defensive ring with their backs to a tree. Joe was stuffed into the protected center as the first rabbits began their attack. Red numbers began appearing above the other party members, and a small list of names with total health appeared in Joe's vision. Only his years in the army kept him from freezing up as cries of agony from both sides began reaching his ears. One of the important features of this game was realistic feedback–specifically pain–which made people play much more carefully.

Joe started healing, and since he was so close to the affected individuals, he simply used his spell 'lay on hands', restoring ten hit points every three seconds to whomever was the most damaged person. Luckily for the group, each individual attack from the rabbits only took a little health from the target and even that was somewhat mitigated by the armor they were wearing. Unfortunately, however, there were so many attacking rabbits that those points were adding up quickly. Working as fast as possible, Joe kept the mana flowing and the health points increasing.

"I cannot *believe* how useful you are!" one of the men with them chuckled as he skewered a rabbit. "I don't know any other teams that survived a swarm *this* long–even if they had a higher overall level–and if we win, I'm buying you a drink!"

"Keep your mind on the target, Dylan!" Tiona snapped at him. "You're slowing down!"

Dylan–the main fighter–rolled his eyes. "That's stamina drain, not *my* fault."

"Push past it! Use more skill and less strength with each swing. They don't all need a full-power attack. Go until you collapse, or we're going to lose our cleric on his first day!" Tiona ordered, furiously swinging her blade into the wave of fluffy animals.

"I'm doing it! Jeez." Dylan stumbled on his next swing, his low stamina making his attack too slow to kill the rabbit he was aiming at. He overextended and tripped, falling forward and away from the group.

"Damn it! Dylan!" Tiona called as the hoard of rabbits focused on him.

Joe was watching Dylan's health as it swiftly trickled lower and lower. Ignoring the shouts from the others to stay back, he leapt forward and grabbed Dylan's foot as the man struggled weakly to protect his head from the abusive bunnies. Dylan was down to five health before the first wash of healing water flowed over him, and he hung on a few more moments as Joe alternated to the regular healing spell, waiting for the touch version's cooldown to reset. Using a spell as soon as it was ready, Joe worked to heal his fallen teammate through the brutal beating.

The others had stepped forward as a unit and were killing the rabbits that were entirely focused on Dylan. They were able to kill two or even three at a time, the population was so dense. Thirty seconds and twenty healing spells later, Tiona finished off the last of the stragglers and glared at Joe.

"I thought you said you were new to the game!" She pointed her sword at him accusingly.

Joe didn't look away from Dylan, he required too much healing. "I am." Another wash of water swept over the bruised and battered man.

"Then how did you know that monsters will almost *always* focus on helpless targets? You would have died if that weren't the case!" Tiona was looking at him oddly.

"This has been my job for years. I was a combat medic; putting myself at risk to save others is just a part of the job," Joe calmly replied as he sent another heal into Dylan. He was up to half health now and was able to sit up to begin regaining stamina.

"I don't care what your job *used* to be! From now on you follow *my* orders or you are out! I don't care how useful you are!" Tiona barked at him, breaking his concentration. "I don't care if you were a dang-nab *General*, if you cannot do what I tell you, *when* I tell you, I will leave you out here to die. You put *all* of us at risk by breaking formation. The only reason we survived was because we got lucky."

Dylan looked up at Joe and nodded. "She's right. If I had died it would have been my own cockiness that killed me, but *you* dying would have killed all the others when that swarm rolled over them. There are different rules here, and you don't know 'em. I do appreciate it, though. Waiting for respawn sucks."

Joe sat back with a sigh. "I understand. My bad. I'm not used to seeing someone come back if they die, so I kind of freaked out. Everything here is just so… real."

"Hmph. Well, dying here isn't great. Depending on how much of your death is attributed to stupidity, you can't play for up to twelve hours; which is twenty-four in-game. If you are in a long-term capsule, you just have to sit and wait. You can access the internet, but it is still boring. VR helmet is a bit better 'cause they can go do other things," Tiona described to him, though anything else she was going to say cut off as the experience points came rolling in.

*Angry Rabbit x35 (swarm) slain! Local event 'Trespassers' complete! Experience increased due to low average party level! Exp: 210 (4xp * 35 rabbits * 1.5 difficulty).*

New (hidden) chain quest: Playing your fake role I: Heal at least 50% of damage dealt in five battles before combat ends. Reward: Title: I'm a healer! I swear! Effect: Gain bonus experience for every battle that you heal at least 50% of the damage taken before combat ends. 0/5 complete.

Nice! Joe would work to get that quest done as soon as possible. It was surprising how difficult it was to level up, but Joe supposed that they *were* fighting rabbits. The party started walking, ignoring the ruined carcasses of rabbits in their hurry to find wolves to fight. Dylan broke the awed silence, "I got eighty-four experience off of that! I'm getting close to level six!"

"Congrats." Tiona sent a lopsided grin at him. "You would

have *been* there last week if you had bothered to show up for training."

"Hey, not all of us can afford not to work and hang out in pods all day." Dylan laughed aloud, but Tiona's face went white with rage.

"Shut it!" she hissed at him. "What if PK-ers heard you?"

Joe looked between Tiona's angry glare and Dylan's admonished face. "What? PK-ers?"

"Player killers," Dylan muttered shamefacedly. "My bad, boss. Joe, PK-ers hunt people in pods for a couple reasons. Pod people can feel more pain than a standard player in a VR headset, and obviously, people playing on the older VR versions can't feel much of anything. When you die to a player, you are out of the game for a minimum of three to six hours, up to twenty-four if the game AI judges your death to be from something really stupid that was your fault. People in long-term pods are in the game until their contract is up, so dying is not only annoying, it is a huge waste of time and *really* expensive in real world money."

"So people kill other players… just to be assholes? No other benefit?" Joe couldn't believe humans could be so terrible.

Tiona turned her glare away from Dylan. "Worse than that. It is actually actively *punished* by the game. When you kill another player–and if they could see who you were–you have a bounty placed on you. Masks and other gear could hide your name, but you need to have contact with shady organizations in order to get them. While your name was red, anyone can kill you without repercussions, you have a chance to lose gear if you die, and NPC's will attack you if you try to enter the city. The bounty does wear off over time, especially if you killed plenty of monsters, but there is a good chance that you just don't survive the experience."

"Yup. You don't drop anything if killed by a player, and they don't get experience for it either. Usually PK-ers are outdated VR gamers who are pissed that they don't have the funds to experience modern virtual reality themselves," Dylan informed him. "So you really wanna keep that info on the down-low, ya dig?"

"I… sure?" Joe was a bit nonplussed about the terminology. He had been out of high school for over a decade. Why can't people just speak properly? This sort of crap led to miscommunication and misunderstandings. He shook his head.

Tiona snapped her fingers. "Foxes ahead, focus please." An arrow snapped out, hitting a fox in the eye and killing it instantly.

"Heh. Critical hit." The team's ranger chuckled.

Something was bothering Joe; he finally realized what it was. "So, real world damage is the same here?"

"Meaning?"

"Hit an eye, cut a throat, stab a heart and they die?" Joe clarified for her.

"Yup," the archer offered verbosely.

Joe looked at his character sheet. "Also, I didn't get any experience for that fox."

"Didn't participate, did ya? I'm betting that as a healer you will need to be in a battle mindset in order to get experience. You didn't *think* of yourself as a participant in that, since it was a ranged attack. The AI in control of the game takes that into account; the more you contribute the better the reward. That's why you prolly got decent experience for that swarm and maybe some from when they get real close to you." The archer nodded sagely at him.

"I see." Joe didn't offer his experience gains to the group, preferring to remain mysterious. "I *did* just get a quest that will give me experience for healing when I complete it. All I need to do is heal fifty percent of the damage done to us five times before combat ends."

Tiona perked up. "Oh *really*? That will make leveling you into a useful player a *lot* faster and easier. We try hard not to get hit, so you won't need to heal much to complete your quest."

"Thanks?" Joe was fairly certain she had insulted him. "I'm useful!"

"A little," she conceded, attacking a fox that burst from the underbrush, "but until you gain a few levels, you won't *really* be useful. You can just heal a bit."

Joe looked on dejectedly as the foxes were eliminated before he could get in a swing. He swung his scepter when one got close, but it easily dodged. He looked at his status bars; that single attack had drained his stamina by half! He really needed to find some attack magic. His enthusiasm ramped up again as a fox got close enough to bite Tiona on the ankle. "Yes!"

"Ow!" Tiona glared at Joe as her sword sliced into the offending creature. "What the heck are you cheering for? I got *bit*!"

"Sorry about that, but now I can at least heal you. Need that quest progress!" Joe poked her on the neck and let icy water wash down her back. She yelped louder than when she had been bit, and viciously took out her rage on the next fox. As it died, a message sprung into Joe's vision.

Playing your fake role I: 1/5 complete.

"Nice! Just need to heal y'all four more times. Who wants to take one for the team?" Joe looked around expectantly. No one met his gaze except a glaring Tiona.

"You realize that it actually *hurts* to get bit, clawed, or bludgeoned, right?" Her eyebrow was twitching.

"Well, yeah, but…"

"No buts!" She jabbed a finger into his chest. "It's obvious you haven't taken damage yet or else you wouldn't be excitedly telling someone else to get hurt for you. This is one of those quests we aren't going to rush for you. We get hurt plenty, just wait until it happens naturally."

Joe hung his head. "Sorry guys, I wasn't thinking about that."

"Not a problem, buddy." Dylan slapped Joe on the back. "Just remember that to anyone who is in a capsule, this is real life until their contract is up. Pain hurts, and dying is avoided if at all possible. Think like that, and you are good. Play like it isn't a game."

Dylan's words put Joe's situation in perspective perfectly. As a medic, he would have never wanted someone to get hurt so he could practice on them. His whole career was based on prevention of injury and getting people back on their feet as soon as possible. This was his new life; for all he knew, his body had already been incinerated. He needed to treat this as real life, and from now on, he would.

"Anyway, we are almost to the wolves. They hunt in small packs, so our defenses need to be perfect," Tiona changed the subject when she was satisfied that she saw real remorse in Joe's eyes. "We cut through the most narrow fox area, so be prepared to fight."

They walked around for a few minutes, looking for any signs of movement. The further they moved from the city, the slower they moved. Dylan gave a great heaving sigh and groaned, "Where are the stupid things?"

His words seemed to be a trigger, because a wolf pounced at him from a bush and clamped its jaws around Dylan's leg. With a snarl and a sharp jerk, the leg was twisted and dislocated with a loud **pop*. Dylan howled with pain as the remaining members of his group attacked the creature. Tiona was the only one with experience fighting wolves, so while the others were focused on helping Dylan, she turned and swung blindly behind them. Her sword impacted a leaping canine, which yelped and fell to the ground with a chunk of fur torn off of it. Taking advantage of its helpless state, she stabbed down through its chest to execute the creature.

Joe was so surprised that he forgot to heal right away and instead swung his scepter at the wolf holding Dylan. **Bonk*. A damage indicator showing a red zero popped up over the animal, meaning that his most vicious strike directly to the head… was utterly useless.

"I need healing!" Dylan gasped, breathless from pain. The wolf was dead–killed by the other party members–but its jaw was still locked around his leg. Tiona and the others circled around Dylan as two more wolves revealed their presence.

Joe dropped to his knees and worked on pulling the teeth out of Dylan's leg. A wash of fresh blood poured from the now-open wound, and Joe wrapped his hand around the holes to keep pressure on the leg. With his other hand he made a quick gesture, and water washed over the blood, leaving behind clean, unblemished skin. After twisting his leg into the socket, it took two more uses of his healing abilities before Dylan could use his leg again. By the time they stood up, the fight was over.

Playing your fake role I: 2/5 complete. Exp: 48 (Wolf x4).

Skill gained: Medic (Novice I). Don't have access to a healer? Patch wounds together the best you can! This skill increases efficiency of bandages, medicines, and potions by 1% per skill level.

"No one else even got hurt! Why is it always you? Maybe you should just give in to fate and become a tank." The group's archer elbowed Dylan good-naturedly as Tiona worked to skin the dead animals. "You know, *intentionally* draw in the attacks that are coming to you anyway."

"I have no idea why it happens! Maybe I just taste good," Dylan rebutted wearily. Screaming in pain was tiring. "Also, no. Who wants to be a tank? Stand on the front line and take all the damage? Can you even imagine how much that will suck when someone is chucking a fireball at you? I don't look forward to burning to death or cooking inside my armor as it melts onto me."

"Some people choose to be tanks… some tanks are chosen. I think you are one of the chosen. Just ignore perception and put everything into constitution!" the archer demanded cheekily.

"Let him build his own character." Tiona stood up and pointed at a pile of fur. "Let's find a good spot to store these and keep hunting; we can skin them later. Wolf fur is good for armor, so it'll sell nicely back in town."

CHAPTER SEVEN

They were able to hunt down two more wolf packs before everyone judged that it was time to head back. According to Dylan, being caught out of town at night was a death sentence no matter what level you were at. They started walking back to the city as Joe looked over his gains from the hunting trip. He had gained another ninety-six experience from his part in killing wolves but still hadn't ranked any of his skill above novice level one. Trying to understand why, Joe asked Tiona what he had to do to rank them up.

"Well, to boost skills you need to use them over and over or study how to use them better. There is a common saying that to be a Master of the sword, you need to have ten thousand hours of combat. If that holds true here, imagine what it takes to become a Grandmaster or a Sage!" Tiona shook her head in wonder. "Also, if you are good at the skill already, it will level a whole lot faster. A five-star cook in real life apparently has his cooking skill to journeyman already. Supposedly it is so the game will appeal to a wider variety of people; not everyone is a combat fanatic like I am. Now, there is another way to increase skills, but it is almost as hard."

"What is it?"

"Leveling!" She laughed at his incredulous look. "At every level you get at least one skill point. Some people have said that they got more than one, but there is no way to know how they did it. You can spend a skill point on any skill to instantly increase it by one, but I think it is a much better idea to hoard those points until you really need them. Why bother using them on a novice skill?"

"One skill point per level? That's absurd!" Joe thought about how many skills and spells he already had. It would take him until level eighty to get *one* of his skills to Sage rank!

"You can sometimes get skill points from quest rewards, from being the first to find an area, or doing special actions. It is really hard to say how hard it will actually be to-"

Joe was driven to the ground as a wolf the size of a small horse landed on him. A savage bite tore into him as his teammates screamed. They charged at the wolf as it howled in triumph. A very dazed Joe looked at the text floating in front of his eyes as he struggled to move in spite of the pain.

Sneak attack by Dire Wolf! Double damage inflicted! -60 health! Undying robe effect triggered! Health set to 1! Bleeding: -5 health per ten seconds! Stunned for 5 seconds! 4… 3…

This was a good example of being non-realistic: though he was at only one hit point, he was still able to function so long as he could fight through the crippling pain. Joe waited for the stun effect to fade, mouth moving like a fish as he tried to gasp for air. The agony was almost unbearable, but the fact that he couldn't move was what was really terrifying him. He would *never* go back to being a quadriplegic! As soon as he could move again, the pain intensified further. Joe moved his hands, and forced his spell to activate.

Lay on hands: Health +10. Bleed effect: Health -5. Heal: Health +5. Lay on hands: Health +10.

He was able to outpace the bleed effect with his healing, and twelve seconds later, he was back to full health. There was a small benefit to having almost no constitution; he could get back on his feet much faster than a normal, beefy character. He surveyed the battle, noting that almost all of his teammates were heavily injured. If the sneak attack had done double damage to him… that meant that a normal attack could do thirty damage? With a normal constitution, this meant that each person could take three attacks before dying. He hurried to join combat, but decided to keep his distance. Joe started hurling balls of healing water, boosting his target's health by five points every few seconds.

Tiona moved like a terrifying force of nature: twisting around attacks, bending at odd angles, and stabbing into exposed weak points with perfect timing. Her movements were graceful, but no matter how hard she tried, she was still taking damage every few seconds. Though she was usually able to avoid the main attack, she was still nicked by claws or teeth. This enemy was simply that strong and agile.

Joe fired off his healing spells as fast as possible and would have continued doing so if the creature's rage-filled gaze hadn't snapped to him. With a snarl, it charged past the other members and made a beeline for the healer. Just before the ball of fur, teeth, and fury reached him, Dylan barreled into the animal's side and knocked it over. The wolf was back on its feet in a flash, but now its focus was riveted on Dylan.

"Damn it, I *am* a tank!" Dylan griped as he stabbed the wolf. Joe used the distraction to run around the fight and heal Tiona. After two uses of healing spells, Tiona rushed back into the battle. With the team getting healed each time the spell was off cooldown, the fight quickly drew to a close. A well-timed arrow **thunked** into the heart of the great animal, and it finally fell with a mournful howl.

Zone alert! Members of the guild The Wanderers have killed a local [animal] field boss! For the next twenty-four hours, all wolves—having lost their protector—will take 20% bonus damage! The Wanderers guild gains +20 fame with the city of Ardania!

The area alert faded, leaving only the reward for the battle in Joe's view.

For being the first to vanquish the field boss [Silver Dire Wolf] you gain +1 skill point and +50 personal and guild fame with Ardania. Return the pelt of the fallen animal to the town guard for a monetary reward! Exp: 150. For fighting through pain and saving yourself from otherwise certain death through sheer willpower, Wisdom +1.

Joe made a choking sound as he was engulfed in light. Euphoria flooded through him, and he levitated an inch off the ground. There was a soundless explosion, and Joe dropped to the ground completely refreshed. Even his clothes were clean! He looked around to see two other members of the party dropping to the ground as well, goofy smiles playing across their faces.

"I love leveling up." Dylan gave a shudder of happiness and looked at the massive wolf. "We need to hurry, it's already getting dark."

"I'm on it." Tiona started skinning the wolf, trying to keep the fur as intact as possible. "Someone collect the meat as I go, it'll make it easier to flip over, and I bet Dire Wolf meat will sell for a good price. I'd eat it."

"Same. Sounds exotic," the archer responded greedily.

"You realize you are talking about eating dog, right?" Dylan sent a queer look at the pile of meat that was swiftly growing.

Joe sat on the ground and exhaled softly. That had been *way* too close. His mind was frazzled, and his thoughts were fuzzy. He wanted to sleep. Joe reached out and plucked a flower growing next to him, twirling it in his hand and smelling it.

New skill gained! Herbalism (Novice I). Plant? What plant? All you see is ingredients! Whether they are for dinner or for creating potions is up to you! Usable raw plants are 1% easier to find, 1% easier to process, and have 1% greater effect per skill level!

Joe continued looking at the plant in his hand, and it did indeed seem a *tiny* bit more distinctive. Without the notice, he would have chalked it up to not looking at it properly beforehand. He stared at the flower, trying to figure out what it was. The pop-up bar over the plant only showed question marks as his knowledge check failed, so Joe simply shrugged and put the plant into his pocket. He really needed to get a bag.

"Ready to go, cleric?"

Looking up, Joe noticed that the archer was holding a hand out to him. "Sure thing, archer. What's your name, by the way?"

"XSnipeMasterX."

"I'm not calling you that."

"Then call me Chad." The archer grinned at him.

"That's almost as bad!" Joe chuckled at the grinning ranger as they walked through the slowly darkening forest.

Joe was the only person not carrying either a load of meat or pelts. He had tried to, but the stamina drain was so severe that he had only been able to take a few steps at a time with a *single* pelt before needing to recover or risk collapsing. Tiona had loaded his burden onto Dylan, stating that 'if he were more weighed down, he would do fewer stupid things'. Now moving at as frantic of a pace as Joe could maintain, the group swiftly retraced their steps to the town. Joe was having an easier time of it since not only was he unburdened, his class ability of dark-vision made sure that he never stumbled on the roots and stones hidden by the encroaching darkness. Most of the animals they would have normally had to face were hiding, burrowed away from the dangers of night.

The group entered town with grins on their faces, relieved to have made it before the gates were locked. That would have been an almost assured death sentence. They turned in their quest, gaining three gold and ninety silver coins for the pelt of the Dire wolf. Joe was disappointed at first, but the ecstatic faces of his groupmates assured him that the reward was a good one. As they talked about how they were going to spend their shares, he didn't have the heart to tell them that he could likely buy a small town with his bank account. They made their way back to their tavern just as the gates **boomed**, signaling that they had been barred for the night.

No one was outside to see a few rotting rabbits begin to twitch.

CHAPTER EIGHT

"Wake up!" Joe howled as a cup of cold water was tossed on him, causing him to launch himself from the bed. His stamina instantly drained from that maneuver, and he ignobly collapsed into a pile on the floor.

"*Why*!" he sputtered at the grinning Tiona as he tried to use the bed to pull himself to his feet. "How did you even get in here? I rented this room!"

"So? How would that stop anyone from getting in? You didn't even bother to lock the door!" She wagged a finger at him admonishingly. "You were supposed to stop thinking of this as a game, remember? As for why, well… you are just going to have to see it to believe it. Hurry up, it's a beautiful morning." They went downstairs where a beaming guild master was turning his brightest smile on Joe.

"What's up with him?" Joe was feeling distinctly uncomfortable from the creepy look. That smile was intense enough to classify as a light-based weapon.

"You remember how we killed the Dire Wolf last night and we got reputation for the guild? That's what the smile is for. We need to be at least 'friend' level reputation to get an *official*

Guildhall in the city. Getting a leg up on the competition is great because there can only be four official Guildhalls in the city. The first four to do so will get the title 'Noble Guild' and have access to elite quests for the Kingdom." Tiona shrugged as if this was inconsequential and pointed at a bowl of food. She waited until he started to chow down before continuing to speak.

"Eat fast, we need you right away. Oh, and did you look over your stats after leveling? You should have gotten a little stronger and gotten at least one skill point. I wouldn't recommend using it until you know how you want to build yourself, but feel free to ruin your character. The best way to see any changes is to say 'delta status'. That will let you see only the changes on your sheet instead of a wall of text you can't see through."

Joe nodded at her and quickly intoned the words 'delta status'. As he looked at the tiny window, he found that he was rather cheerful not to have to slog through an exhausting list.

Intelligence: 16 to 17
Wisdom: 16 to 18 (Level +1 for feat of willpower)
Perception: 18 to 19
Unused skill points: 1 to 6 (Level +1 for boss kill bonus)

As expected, intelligence, wisdom, and perception increased by one while the others didn't budge, but when he glanced at his skill points, he nearly choked on his admittedly dry bread. He had six points! Six of them! He got one point from the wolf boss so did that mean he gained *four* points from leveling? Joe tore through his menus until he arrived at his class description, and his eyes lit up when he read the words, '*they gain skill in their chosen pursuits at four times the speed of an average human, due to their vast thirst for power*'.

He wanted to shout for joy, but he knew that if he disclosed this information in public he would likely be killed by other players out of jealousy. Doing his best to calm himself, he reached his hand toward his skill sheet. He shivered, feeling entirely too frustrated. Joe was *itching* to spend a couple points on his spells, and only Tiona's rather timely warnings about waiting kept him from becoming a miracle healer overnight.

After finishing his breakfast, he was led to the gates by a grinning Tiona. The other party members looked a bit leery but followed quietly. Stopping just before leaving town, she pointed at the field of rabbits. "Take a look, let me know what you see."

Joe glanced at the beautiful landscape, and his perception-enhanced eyes instantly locked onto a hopping oddity. What was wrong with that rabbit? Just as he realized the truth, a screen appeared in his vision.

New zone quest: 'Waste not…' The innumerable bodies left lying in the open have allowed a dark corruption to take hold of the rabbit population! They aren't that smart, but they are hopping mad and hungry! Kill all zombie rabbits around Ardania before the normal rabbit population is converted to the undead. Time remaining: thirty-six hours, twenty three minutes! Reward: Reputation based on contribution. Failure: the area will slowly convert to dead lands. Animals will starve and become much more vicious.

"Woah. This game is freaking amazing." Joe couldn't stop a smile from crawling across his face. "This is because people kept leaving the rabbits out in the open after killing them, right?"

"I don't see it. What are you talking about?" Dylan was looking around the open field with evident confusion whereas the others quickly saw the issue.

"Bad perception?" Joe grinned at the musclebound warrior. "Looks like the rabbits that people left out in the open went full zombie mode. There is a zone quest to clear them out before we lose the rabbit population entirely."

Dylan flinched as a screen appeared in front of him. "Okay, I see it now. Thanks for pointing it out. Chad would have made me suffer for a while first."

"Not my fault that you were building as a tank even before you knew you were going to be one." Chad stared at Dylan, trying to make his eyes hypnotic. "Do it. *Do it.*"

"I'm not going to be a tank!" Dylan shoved the ranger away.

"Where is everyone? Isn't this kind of important for the town?" Joe was surprised to see Tiona roll her eyes.

"It is, but most people don't care. It is *technically* a social quest. No guaranteed loot, so unless they are trying to get high reputation they just won't bother." She gestured at a group of people walking past all the zombies like they didn't have a care in the world. "The zombies are not hostile toward us right now, being too focused on killing healthy rabbits. The pelt and meat are rotten and were worthless even when they *weren't* disgusting. They apparently do give a little bit more experience."

"That means nothing to me, though," Chad groaned abruptly. "I got a total of zero experience from them yesterday."

"That's why we are going to the edge of fox territory to grind today." Tiona grinned wickedly at Joe, creating a sinking feeling in his stomach. "*We* are going to hunt foxes, while Joe hunts zombits. We meet up to get healed or if one of us needs help."

"Zombits? Oh. Zombie rabbits. Cute." Joe shrugged his thin shoulders. "Works for me. I could use the practice."

They started walking, exterminating all zombies in their path to gain some progression in the quest. It took a bit longer than expected because the corpse didn't count as 'dead' until either fully dismembered or the heads were crushed. When they got to the edge of the territory, the others gave a jaunty wave and left Joe to kill the rotten balls of fluff and pus. They intended to stay within shouting range, but Joe still felt a bit nervous to be alone. Luckily, the dead animals weren't hostile until attacked, so he could take his time lining up his attacks. He got behind a roaming zombit, grasped his scepter with both hands, and brought the weapon down as hard as he could.

A sad little '-1' floated away from the rabbit.

The zombit shuffled to a stop, twitched as though it had been bitten by a mosquito, and then turned around after deciding it had indeed been attacked. Joe glanced at his stamina bar, noting that it had dropped by a third. So the careful stance and purposeful swing had cost less than his wild attack on the wolf last night? Good to know. He swung again, his scepter cracking against the rotting legs of the rabbit.

-1, crippled. Movement speed -30%.

Good, that should slow the animal down and allow him to regenerate some stamina. Joe was gasping a little, the force he needed if he wanted to inflict any damage was difficult to muster.

The zombit suddenly lunged at him, tearing into his leg with its large, flat teeth. Joe released a high-pitched shriek as the fatty stores in his leg were exposed to the open air.

-7 health. Bleeding (minor), -1 health per five seconds! Minor infection possible if wound is not treated within 30 minutes!

How the heck was *that* fair? He was swinging a weapon, it was using rotten teeth! Off balance, Joe swung his weapon again, hitting the animal and fully draining his stamina. He dropped to the ground as a wave of exhaustion hit him, and he waited for the next attack to tear into his body. After a moment, he opened his eyes and looked for the zombit he had been fighting.

The creature was not in sight, but a small pile of ash informed him of its fate. Joe was confused enough that he had to look over the combat logs.

Glancing blow! Zombie rabbit takes zero damage! Scepter activates ability [Turn Undead]! As Zombie Rabbit is at half health or below, it is disintegrated! Exp: 4!

Well, that explains it. Joe looked at his weapon with a new appreciation and was also pleased to know new facts about the zombits. They had to have between three to four health, and they bit *really* hard. Not only did he need to watch out for their normal attacks, but there was no way he could dodge. He had to be extra careful to stay on top of his wounds because while he didn't know what disease damage would do to him, it was likely unpleasant. With a quick motion, he healed his leg and sat down to recover his stamina. He didn't want to be lazy, but he needed to be able to swing his weapon with full force at least three times. Also, weren't the zombie versions of these animals supposed to be worth extra experience?

Automated system response: As a cleric not devoted to evil or necromancy, a part of your duties is to destroy undead. No extra experience will be gained for their destruction.

Well that was just unpleasant; he had been hoping for quick levels off of this. Joe quickly began hunting in earnest, trying to refine his skull bashing technique as he went along. Get behind zombit, swing scepter into creature's leg, and hopefully cripple it. Step back, let stamina refill a little. Attack twice, hit head as hard as possible. If the zombit died, great! If not, step back and wait a moment. Finish off zombit, collapse from exhaustion. It took a few tries, but he started becoming more efficient at dismantling the undead bunnies. He got a notification three hours into killing zombits, just as he killed his thirty-second animal.

For landing one hundred attacks without missing, dexterity +1! For having refilled your stamina from under a third–thirty times in three hours–constitution +1!

Skill gained: Staff mastery (Novice I). You have taken a step on the path of hitting your opponents with blunt objects and hoping against hope they stay away from you. You are doing great!

Yes! He was well on his way to being as healthy as an average child! Maybe a sickly child. A scepter was considered a staff? Alright, he could deal with that. Joe planned to keep going, but his rumbling stomach informed him that he was starting to become hungry. He turned back, slowly making his way toward the meeting point for the team. As he arrived, he froze as he noticed something amiss. It took a moment to understand why his senses were screaming danger, but then someone stepped out from behind a tree and the smell of blood wafted over his enhanced senses.

"Hello there! You must be the cleric who has caused so much trouble for us!" The man was grinning but certainly didn't appear overly happy. "The Wanderers guild is ahead of us in reputation gains now! How do you propose to fix that for me?"

Joe was startled by the sudden development but tried to keep his wits about himself. "I have no idea what you mean. I'm sorry to say I can't help you; I'm just here to meet up with my team."

"Oh?" A few more people stepped out of cover as the man spoke. "Tiona's team, right? Well, they'll be back online tomorrow. How about you party with us for a while instead? You know, make up for wasting our time?" Obviously these people had killed Joe's team while he was away heroically slaying rabbits. From the look of the blood dripping from the others, saying 'no' wouldn't be appreciated.

"And who are you?" Joe asked as boldly as possible, trying to inject himself with confidence.

"I go by 'Headshot'. I'm the leader of a little guild, you may have heard of it. The Hardcores?" His grin widened as he saw Joe make the connection. The Hardcores were the guild of people dedicated to PK-ing people in long-term pods. Knowing that Joe knew about him, Headshot was baffled by the next words he heard.

"No chance. May as well send me to respawn." Joe glared at the people who had killed his team before turning and trying to walk away.

"Hey, hey! No need to be so hostile!" Headshot made a motion, and the others surrounded Joe, cutting off his escape. "How about you just come with us for a walk, and you can make your decision when we are done chatting?"

A blade poked into Joe's back, knocking off five health points and making him wince. Headshot turned around and started strolling along; Joe was forced to follow. "There are so many benefits to working for me! You level faster because the competition won't take your kills, you get to go into high-density spawning areas that we control, and best of all, my guild won't kill you every time we see you!"

Joe stayed silent as the man waxed eloquent about all the

control tactics he used against other people but was fully disgusted by what he heard. The way this man was speaking, everyone in the guild was a slave while everyone else was an obstacle to be cut down. They passed through the edge of the wolves' territory, and a thundering sound began to grow in volume.

"Wondering what that is?" Headshot was no longer smiling or pretending to be nice; he seemed to have decided that Joe wasn't going to accept his offer. Now his only interest was making the defiant cleric hurt as much as possible before dying. "That's a waterfall. It flows off what can only be called a hole in the world into a really small lake. Well, maybe it just *looks* small. It is a *long* way down after all. You don't care about that though! What you care about is all the rock that surrounds the tiny lake."

Joe was forced to the edge of the hole when they got to it and had to admit that Headshot hadn't been exaggerating. This felt like the edge of the world. As far as he could tell, the ground just *dropped* a few thousand feet. What was strange was that he could see sunlight at the bottom. Was it another stage of the game? Another continent they hadn't unlocked? If so, either the land they were on was elevated or the one he was looking at had sunk. Headshot grabbed Joe by his neck and pushed him forward. "Time to choose! Join me and get all sorts of benefits, or take flying lessons and we'll try this again another time."

"Guess I'm going for respawn because there's no chance I'm joining you. Also, your recruitment pitch *sucks*." Joe made a rude gesture at Headshot, whose face contorted in anger. "You overgrown man-child."

"You wanna play it this way? Fine! Jump." Headshot folded his arms and glared. "That way, you will get the maximum respawn time. Intentionally jumping off a cliff? What *will* the AI think of you?"

"I'm not jumping." Joe glared back just as hard, extending the rude gesture to the other players as he waited for the situation to come to a head.

"Either sign the contract to join our guild, or we are going to start taking chunks off of you. Or you can just jump. If you make us start slashing you, we'll be sure not to let you die. I don't need my name to go red again, or it'd be past dark by the time I could re-enter town."

"You are a total ass. Screw your guild; I *will* get back at you for this," Joe promised vehemently, having made his decision.

"Start stabbing him, boys. He's getting too chatty." As pointy objects began closing in on him, Joe took a deep breath, turned, and *jumped*.

CHAPTER NINE

Wind rushed around Joe as he approached terminal velocity. The rock was looming ever closer as Joe tried to think of a way out of this situation, but all he came up with was 'this is going to hurt'. He was almost positive that he would survive because the effects of his undying robe would kick in. Sadly, he *wasn't* sure if he would stay alive very long, since he was certain that he would be a messy stain on the ground. Joe targeted himself and cast heal, and a globe of water appeared in his hand. His falling speed created a whipping wind that pulled the healing water off of him as it tried to collect in his hand, but he noticed that despite not being able to control the spell, the water was following his path through the air. The range was only supposed to be ten feet for the spell. Would falling negate that? Increase the range, perhaps? It was a desperate hope, but he made as many orbs as he could, starting to hyperventilate as the last few feet passed in a blur.

Splat! Joe had belly-flopped onto the ground, and *should* have died instantly. There was now a wall of text in front of his eyes, but he was unable to focus on the information the game was providing him. Joe could only focus on what his *body* was telling him. His eyes had popped. His insides were outsides. His bones were shattered to splinters.

Splash! The five spheres of healing water landed in succession on him, and his damaged body was forced into a cohesive shape. He would have screamed if he weren't in shock when his spinal column reconnected itself. In an instant, he was at twenty-five health. He grabbed himself and used lay on hands and heal until he was at full health, then flopped back and took deep shuddering breaths. The pain had passed so fast that it was barely horrifyingly traumatic! He really hoped that he wouldn't have any dreams about this experience, though he knew it was inevitable. Joe opened his repaired eyes and looked over the notifications he had received.

Heal used! Heal delayed due to travel speed x5. True damage from impact with terrain received: -4,500 health! Jump skill not high enough to mitigate fall damage!

Undying robes passive effect activated! Health set to 1! Crippled! Bleeding! Senses damaged! Bones broken x206! Organs ruptured! -50 health per second until healed!

5 health gained x5. Lay on hands activated x2. Heal activated x2. Organs repaired. Bleed effect removed. Full health restored!

Joe looked at the messages and chuckled, preparing to find the energy and willpower to stand. More text began to appear, interrupting his rise.

Achievement earned! Jump! Jump! Jump around! You have jumped so many times, that you have spent over thirty seconds in the air! You have collectively jumped eight hundred and fifty times your height and lived to tell the tale! Jump skill has increased to _ERROR_ ("Jump skill not found"). You have earned the skill: Jump (Novice _ERROR_)! While others take the boring route, you hop, skip, and especially jump along! Jump a total of twenty-five times your height to rank up! You have so far jumped 850/0 times your height! _Error_ Experience earned: _error: ("Divide by Zero") Debug: Exp: 800.

Joe was starting to get concerned; that was a lot of error messages. Was this all because he had not been *pushed*… but had jumped and survived?

Your Jump skill has increased to (Expert level 2). Your dedication to a single aspect of yourself has opened a new path for you to walk! Or in this case, Jump! You are able to find the magic in motion, the power in leaping, and the freedom of springing! Based on your use of this skill to this point, an extra effect has been added! (_Error_ Skill unused to this point _Error_) Debug activated.

New expert skill variant unlocked: Jump around! Effect: Add your jump skill level to anything that can be 'jumped'. (Current: +52. One point per skill point.) Cost: Variable. As an expert variant skill, it will have the same skill rank as its parent skill! Skill will be lost if another Jumplomancer attains a higher skill level than you!

Class unlocked: Jumplomancer (Conditional Unique). Anyone can become a Jumplomancer by entering the expert ranks of jumping, but so far, it is just you*! -50% jumping or falling damage until another jumplomancer is able to out level your skill!*

Jumplomancer has been absorbed by class: Ritualist. All effects are retained, but any leveling bonuses to characteristic points are negated. Would you like to have your class shown as Jumplomancer or remain as Cleric? (Note: Skill and Spell cost is 5x more expensive if used from non-focused class.) Reputation gain: Pending review. Issue elevated.

Joe's head was spinning as he looked over these new details. He earned a new class? How did 'Jump around' work? He cleared his throat and stuttered, "U-uh… keep cleric class focused? Strange, I thought 'mancer' meant a form of divination. I suppose that it is just using the more commonly accepted term. Otherwise I think it should be 'jumplokineser'."

He waited for the system to acknowledge his words, but there was no noticeable change. Joe had no other choice but to start walking, looking for any path or sign of civilization. After roughly ten minutes he saw a dust cloud on the horizon. He stared at the rapidly moving dots in the cloud, trying to figure out what they were, and what they were riding to be able to move that fast. One of the dots abruptly changed directions, followed shortly by the others. They moved quickly enough that they were just blurs, and within moments Joe was surrounded.

He blinked as he looked at the tall, pale forms surrounding

him. They hadn't been riding *anything*; they were just running! They were mostly humanoid but had other characteristics that he couldn't place. One of them said something unintelligible, and another seemed to become furious. They pointed at him, harshly chattering.

Charisma check failed!

The first creature shrugged, pulled out a shimmering mace, and swung it at Joe.

Adolescent Goblin Berserker Novice Trainee deals 9,999 blunt damage. You have died! Due to being in an area you could not have been in and fighting a monster that you should have never met, your respawn time is set to the lowest possible. You may rejoin Eternium in three hours, and will spawn at your current bind point or starting city. There are consequences for intentionally jumping off a cliff though. I am reviewing this situation. You have lost 400 experience.

Joe blinked. He looked around and realized this must be the respawn room. He hadn't felt any pain, but that attack had been more damaging than falling a few thousand feet and landing face-first on stone! He shook his head. How was anyone supposed to fight *that*? Joe sat down on an overstuffed chair and looked around for anything to do while he waited. He almost smacked himself when he realized that he hadn't called his mother since joining the game! He quickly established a video call with her and broke into a smile when she teared up seeing that Joe was walking and waving his arms! Her enthusiasm dropped a tiny bit when he explained that he was in a virtual reality, but he made sure to leave out the 'being legally dead' part. They talked for over an hour before she had to go, but that conversation had been soothing to him, healing his soul on a level that only speaking to a loved one can achieve.

Joe spent some time looking for data on the game, but it seemed there was still an information blackout. Drat, he had been hoping for some tips on advancing his skills. He tinkered around with the internet for a while until a beeping noise caught his attention. There was a countdown timer above a swirling darkness that was resolving into a portal. The portal stabilized as the timer ended, and Joe stepped through the opening directly to the town square of Ardania. The sun was already down, unsurprising as he had missed out on six hours of gameplay.

Joe found the nearest guard, and told him about Headshot making him fall off the cliff to his death. The guard, while polite and sympathetic, simply waved at Joe and shrugged. "What am I supposed to do here? You fell to your death, but here you stand. So…?"

Not knowing what else to do, Joe went into his guild's tavern and temporary residence. A wall of noise almost threw his emaciated body back into the street as the door swung open. Someone noticed him and pointed him out. He was dragged to the front of the room and plopped in front of the guild leader. "Joe! Cleric, right?"

"Yes! What's going on?" Joe looked around as the noise subsided; the gathered people seeming to anticipate something.

"We declared war on the Hardcores!" the man shouted, a roar of approval meeting his words. "They went around the city and wiped out six parties of *our* people. Then they started hunting field bosses and jumped in city reputation. They were ahead of our ranking all day, but about an hour ago, there was an announcement."

"What was it? I just respawned." Joe was looking around at all the once again expectant faces, but at his words, their faces sagged.

"Dang, I thought it would be you." The guild leader ran a hand through his hair and grinned goofily. "Our guild just got a thousand reputation points with the city for having the first person to get an expert ranked skill! We are trying to figure out who it was because if they leave the guild, they take the reputation with them. Now we are the number one ranked guild in the city, and only a week or so from gaining 'Friend' status. We'd have had it sooner, but those Hardcores keep stealing kills then wiping us out. So, war."

"War!" the guild members echoed the man.

"Where do I come in? They killed my whole team; I'm ready to get back at them." Joe's voice was cold. A roar of approval made him smile, but the slaps on the back were literally killing him. He needed to subtly heal himself to stay standing.

"That's the spirit!" Joe was clapped on the back once again. "We need to heal up! They have more people, but if we can keep going after them, we will outpace them before they can understand what hit 'em!"

"Works for me! Who needs healing?" Joe started going around the room, and soon everyone who had been injured in the last week was at maximum health. After that, well, they were all in a tavern. Drinks were supplied by the guild, and everyone got roaring drunk. The next day… the hunt would begin!

Joe woke up, clutching his head and groaning. He tried healing himself, but the healing water flowing over him did nothing for his dehydration. Inspired by a sudden thought and memories of this exact situation in the army, he punctured a vein on his arm and directed his healing ability into his body like an IV. He was rewarded by a quickly decreasing migraine and a message from the system.

Hangover debuff removed.

New skill gained: Cleanse! While others need to fight off the effects of poison, disease, or other detrimental effects, your patients will be able to ignore them entirely! Cost: 15n mana where 'n' equals skill level. Effect: Remove detrimental effects over time. There will be a mana cost per second until the patient is cured. Recovery speed increases by 1% per skill level!

Awesome. Joe decided that he would use cleanse a few times this morning to display and level the skill but would charge for it in the future. He started with the guild leader, who was squinting and grunting at an upset Tiona. As relief literally washed through him, the leader looked at Joe gratefully and was able to join in the conversation fully. Joe nodded and moved on to other severe patients. Soon the tavern was lively once more, and groups began moving out to hunt the Hardcores.

"Joe! I'd like you to stay in town all day today if at all possible." The guild leader was ignoring Tiona as he said this, much to her displeasure. "If someone tries to attack you in town, the guard will blacklist them and kill them for a week whenever they show up again. This way, we can bring our injured to you, and you stay safe."

Joe looked at Tiona but had to agree that the logic was good. "Sure thing. I was actually hoping to find a library and read for awhile. Yesterday was a little… intense." A memory of pain flitted across his face as he remembered splattering his body across the bottom of a cliff.

Tiona misinterpreted his expression. "Joe, I did the best I could! Don't quit my team just because you died once! All of us have! The first death is the hardest; you get used to it!"

"Whoa, slow down! I'm not quitting your team, I'm just taking a day off." Joe's answer didn't seem to satisfy the fighter. "Listen, Tiona, I got shoved off a cliff yesterday. I didn't die right away when I hit the ground, so I got to experience the *lovely* feeling of a first-person look at my intestines. I'm taking a single day to myself to get over that and heal other people."

Tiona looked him over carefully, as if she could ascertain the veracity of his words with a staring contest. "Fine. You're coming along tomorrow though, even if I have to drag you!" She blew out of the door, nearly taking it off the hinges.

Joe was escorted to the city library and was politely 'asked' to remain in the area so that he would be available for the guild's needs. Joe nodded and walked into the library, taking a deep breath of the slightly musty air. He had always loved books. When he was a teenager, he had volunteered at a library after school and on weekends just so that he could always be the first to check out the new books that came in. After he had been blown out of the sky, he hadn't been able to turn the pages. Entertainment had become all television, all the time.

"Good morning, traveler. What can we help you with today?" An older gentleman waved at him from behind a laden desk.

"Oh, good morning. I am here to read and explore the history of the world if possible. How did you know that I was a traveler?" Joe was curious; it was almost impossible to tell a player from an NPC unless it was specifically stated or they offered you a quest.

"We don't often see new faces here." The librarian arched a brow at him over half-moon spectacles. "I hate to be the bearer of bad news, but access to the library is restricted. Not to be rude, but travelers tend to be rather… destructive."

Joe's shoulders slumped a bit. He had really hoped to make some progress finding 'hidden' knowledge. "What would I need to do in order to gain admittance?" He could always sneak in but would rather not be sent to jail or attacked on sight.

"You will need a recommendation from a city official. Anyone employed by the city in a high enough position of power will do," the librarian nodded as he thought aloud. "If you manage that, I will grant you access to a few sections. More will be available if you do some work for us here."

There was no quest alert, so Joe knew that this was a personal 'social' quest. It was likely that he would get a reward beyond access to the books, but it wouldn't be explicitly stated, unlike the zombit killing quest. He thought a moment and asked, "Would the city guard captain be a worthy reference? I feel that he would be willing to do so."

"The captain?" The librarian seemed startled as he looked up from the paper he had gone back to reading; apparently no one else had continued to ask questions or put effort into entering the library. "Uhm, yes, he would be just fine. In fact, I have a communication crystal that connects to his office. Are you sure you would like to ask him? If he says no, I will assume you were lying to me. It won't go well for you."

"Please give him a call then!" Joe flashed a brilliant smile at the man, trying to project an innocent vibe.

"Alright then." The librarian shrugged and touched a crystal on his desk. When the captain answered a moment later, the librarian explained the situation. A glowing reference came pouring out of the communication crystal, to the point that when the librarian cut off the call, he stared at Joe incredulously. "How in the *world* did you get him to like you? He doesn't like *anyone*! He doesn't like *me*! I apologize, but I instantly thought you were lying to me. The only reason I actually called him was so that he could arrest you for attempting to use his name for access."

"That seems a little excessive..." Joe muttered softly. Not softly enough.

"Excessive! Ha! The first traveler to come into the library set a first edition dungeon guide on *fire*! I've had these rules in place ever since, and guess how many books have started on fire after that? Zero!" He suddenly turned suspicious. "You can't create fire, can you?"

"I'm a cleric. I can create water. No fire, yet." Joe thought it best to humor this angry individual. "Could I ask your name?"

"I am Boris, the head librarian. You had better not get my books wet; water can be as damaging as fire, if on a smaller scale," Boris threatened while squinting at Joe. "After that recommendation from such an esteemed member of my fair city, you will have access to the entirety of the first floor. Even if my heart tells me to keep you away from my precious literature."

"Many thanks, Sir Boris." Joe inclined his head a bit. "I hope that my time here will help me along my path to becoming a scholar when I have gained enough knowledge." He started to walk into the book stacks, but Boris stopped him once again.

"A scholar? You want to become a *scholar*? Not a great and powerful warrior, a vanquisher of beasts? You want to study dusty tombs and the written word?" Boris's eyes seemed to gleam.

"Of sorts, yes. I want to do *all* of that. The beasts included." Joe returned a half-smile to the frail-looking man. "I want to learn more than is stored in safe and secure locations such as this lovely library. I want to seek out lost histories, find eons-old formulae painted on cave walls, and seek out powerful magic hidden by ancient mages. Alas, my strength is lacking for adventure as of yet and so my journey begins here."

Boris was now smiling at him. "I think I can see why the captain is so enamored with you! Well, if it is physical strength you need, you are on your own. But… there are a few things you could do for me that could hurry along your search for knowledge. Also, as the head librarian, I am the man who will set you on the path of the scholar when you *are* strong enough. If you'd like, I can allow you to do some of the tasks beginners must complete and simply hold your reward until you are ready. Would this be acceptable?"

Quest alert: Footsteps through history I. Head librarian Boris is offering tasks to you which all scholars need to complete. Your rewards will be held until you are ready for them, but this could be a great way to get ahead of the competition. Accept / Reject

Joe chose 'accept' and reached out for a handshake. "I would love to work with you. Thank you for this opportunity!"

Boris's smile seemed to become sinister as he assigned Joe his first task. Three hours later, Joe was cursing his name as he attempted to sort another shelf. "Sort the books on the first floor? Is this a sick joke? No title, no author… how the heck am I supposed to do this? By color?"

So far, he had found that the only method that would work was to read at least the first few chapters and try to understand what the book was all about. Then he would place similar books in piles and hope that he could find enough of them to fill a shelf. "There has to be a better way of doing this. Maybe it is a skill given by the scholar job? They can *see* where the books should be? Is this some kind of torture?" Joe did find a small benefit in the work as a notification popped up.

Skill gained: Reading. While others run around and get injured, you only strain your eyes! +2% reading speed per skill level!

Joe felt that that prompt had been a bit… snarky, but the skill itself was excellent, giving a better percentage than any other skill he had gained. Was it because this wasn't a combat skill? He needed to find more information on leveling skills. Joe groaned as he looked over the vast collection of books. The first floor had all the common books of the Kingdom, books that were available to anyone if they could find them. The higher floors had uncommon, rare, unique, and even a few legendary books somewhere. Earning access was the only way to get at them, as they were highly valued and thus highly protected.

"I need to find a faster way... maybe I could pray about it?" Deciding that he may as well try, since he was only doing this all day, Joe activated pray and prayed aloud for guidance in his tasks. Nothing seemed to happen, so he sighed and continued sorting. Maybe he needed to be more specific? He turned his head to look at all the books he needed to sort through, and his eyes *jumped* to a specific book on a specific shelf. A fairly large chunk of mana vanished as one of his new skills was used.

Divine intervention! Successful Perception check (perception plus 'jump around' modifier)!

Joe climbed a short ladder, trying to keep his eyes on the book. When his hands grasped it, he realized that he had needed to push other books out of the way to get to this one. It was on a shelf he hadn't intended to get to today, hidden in a place he couldn't see from the ground. Was this all because he could add his jump score to skills? Or was it *only* because he had prayed? Joe decided that he needed to test his skills *much* more thoroughly. He turned the book over, looking at it carefully and trying to determine why it would be useful. He needed to hold the book carefully, as it was old and in poor shape. Walking over and sitting at a table, he gently opened the book and read through the first pages. Right away he found something interesting; unlike most of the other books he had read... this one had a title.

"Seriously? *Novice Ritual Magic for the Vastly Uninformed*? So... ritual magic for dummies?" Joe felt all of his hope deflate. "At least it seems to be for my class. Let's see, chapter one... 'Rituals are spells that can affect a large area or a small individual target. While rituals have existed since time untold and can be used by anyone, they are a foolish waste of time and money and the brunt of jokes for their inefficient and expensive requirements.' What a wonderful class I have gained. At least my ritual magic skill might finally become useful."

Looking through the various information on rituals available in the book, he nearly choked at the required components. Gold thread? Diamond dust? Sacrifices of unbound level twenty beasts… on an altar… during a full moon? No wonder ritual magic was laughed at! Some of these things were simply impossible to acquire unless you were incredibly rich or powerful! This was a *novice* set of rituals? Or was it just a book to lead idiots astray? How did his ritualist effect come into play here? Did he need to use less components, or could he get away with using material that cost half as much? Could he use silver wire instead of gold, for instance? He needed to try one; he needed to know what to expect.

Shaking himself out of his shock, he remembered how he had found this book. He had prayed for it, and his deity wouldn't lead him astray… right? He had been looking for a way to organize the shelves; perhaps that was included in this book somewhere? Joe paged through the grimoire, taking note of the myriad of spells it contained. Quite an impressive collection for this early in the game. Realistically though, the amount of rituals contained in this book simply didn't matter. Unless he had a city's worth of resources to play with, it would be a *long* time until he could use most of these. About halfway through the tome, he found what he was looking for.

"'Little sister's cleaning service'. Odd name. Does it summon spectral maids to clean?" Joe read over the requirements, trying to determine if it was feasible to attempt this ritual. "One low grade monster Core to empower the ritual. Why is core capitalized? One foot of silver wire per two meters of effect, one zombie brain to perform the monotonous task, and an initial requirement of eight *hundred* mana?" Joe gagged a bit at the requirements. Sure he had the money now, but he had grown up in the lower-middle class. He wanted to save his money for when he needed it badly.

He cut off that train of thought and looked back at the ritual. "It seems to be a permanent spell… at least, there is no ending time shown in the formula. So I need to cut the needed shape, the… ritual diagram… into something to act as a focus? I should probably bring something with me so I don't damage the libraries property. Pretty sure Boris would either kill me or have me arrested."

Joe looked at the required material then glanced around at the thousands of books waiting to be sorted. Pay to win was a valid strategy, right? "Guess I'm running to the bank."

CHAPTER TEN

Stepping out of the library, Joe winced as the bright sun washed over his highly perceptive eyes. Yet *another* reason not to stay indoors and read tiny writing with poor lighting. No one from the guild had shown up for healing yet, so he felt secure in running to the market for a short while. Before that, he needed to retrieve some funds from his account. Taking the time to ask for directions to the building, Joe made his way to the capital's bank. There was a small crowd, but luckily the lines were fairly short. After waiting behind a man that smelled like he owned a half-dozen cats, Joe got to the desk and asked the teller to access his account. His damaged cloak and beginner's clothes were looked at by the–apparently judgmental–teller with a wry grin of disdain. Upon pulling up Joe's information, the man paled, coughed, and began assisting him *very* professionally.

Joe looked at his account and was a little surprised. He had a full hundred gold more than expected! When he asked about it, the teller informed him it was due to his funds accruing interest. His account and the gold had been created before he started playing the game, so the big 'ol pile of money had been sitting here growing larger by the day. Joe happily withdrew bank notes totaling fifty gold. They worked like checks, in that unless he signed them they had no monetary worth. Even if he was robbed, the game ensured that his money was secure. Of course, the notes wouldn't work outside the city–if they ever found a town without a bank–so he also took out a few silver and copper as physical coins. Leaving the bank in a superb mood, Joe strolled toward the market.

The silver wire was simple to purchase from a smith, though he seemed to think that Joe was a jewelry maker of some kind, and tried to overcharge him by a huge amount. Having lived thriftily all his life, Joe talked the price down to a reasonable market value. When the smith came back a short time later, Joe found that he had another problem. He had no bag to hold items in! His coins were in a small pouch he had started with, but he needed to buy a backpack. The smith grunted and directed Joe to a general goods shop where he could find a storage container, promising to hold the wire until he returned.

This process was turning out to have far too many steps for his liking; he needed to get back to the library before the others came looking for him. Joe walked into the shop and was greeted by an ancient husk that may have been a woman at one point. "Welcome young lady! Are your parents around?"

Joe looked around the empty shop, but she seemed to be talking to him. "I… I'm neither young nor a lady."

"Oh, sorry about that young man! My eyes aren't as sharp as they once were, and you are painfully tiny for an adult man. You aren't a gnome, are you?" She adjusted glasses that would have served better as soda bottles and squinted at him. "Haven't seen gnomes around here for a few centuries."

"No, just a thin human male." Joe was starting to become flustered. "I'm here to-"

"Fix that poor robe?" the elderly lady interrupted. "Good thing too! It looks dejected, and it's unraveling by the second!" She stood up and walked over, running her hands over the tattered clothing.

"Unraveling?" Joe looked at his robe. It had already saved him from certain death twice; he needed it to remain functional.

"Indeed! Undying robes, hmm? Haven't seen the like in quite awhile! You came to the right place; one mistake while fixing these and they turn into *uninteresting* robes. Hurry up now, hand them over. It'll cost ten gold to fix these to perfect health, and I do mean health, not condition. Enchanted gear is alive, if only just barely." The lady pulled his robe off with a surprising amount of force.

"I see. Please repair them as best as you can." Joe's words were mostly perfunctory, as the lady was already walking away. "While I am here, I was wondering if I could purchase a backpack?"

The lady didn't answer for a few minutes, but came back after tending to the robes for a short while. "You can pick up the robes in a couple days. You were smart not to try and haggle; you can't rush art, nor cheapen it. About that bag, you can look in the pile over there. I think it was that pile. It might be that one. Or…" She waved at a heap of various fabrics. Joe swallowed and moved toward what appeared to be a mound of everything in the store that was even remotely made of cloth. It took a few minutes, but he found a decent backpack and bought it.

"I don't suppose you have something like a bag which is larger on the inside? Or reduces the weight of what is inside it?" Joe inquired hopefully. Bags of holding were staples in games, and he needed something similar if he wanted to carry much more than a few small trophies.

"Sure do; I have a few spacial rings. Not exactly a bag, but often better in my humble opinion. Now, sadly I can't sell these to just anyone. They became restricted after smugglers started using them to bring drugs into areas populated by nobility. Now you can only get one if you are a merchant, have need of one for a legitimate reason, or if a merchant like myself personally vouches for you and is held accountable for your actions." The old lady smiled a toothless grin at him. "Feel free to try and convince me, though. Been awhile since a customer got… frisky."

Joe shuddered and glanced around the shop, trying to look anywhere but at the lady giggling at his discomfiture. 'Odds and Ends' was the name of the place and also a good way to describe the shop. It was a disorganized mix of items, and if it were a little messier it could just as easily be called a landfill. "What if I were to… work for you? I could organize your entire shop and keep it that way perpetually."

"Perpetually? That's a good one, youngster! I guarantee I can turn anything into a cluttered mess." She thought a moment. "How about a bet? If you can make it happen, that would work for me. I'll admit business has been slow; not too many people feel like sorting through bins in order to find what they're looking for. Lazy bums. If you can't do it, you work here for free for a week."

"Deal!" Joe was quick to accept the bargain, though privately he thought that the term 'lazy' should perhaps be directed at the shop owner who didn't bother to organize the goods in the first place. He bought a bag and a few jars from her, then stepped outside. Hurrying back to the smith, he collected the silver wire and ordered the same amount for pickup tomorrow. He also bought a skinning knife and asked where he could find monster Cores.

The smith laughed in his face. "Cores? You better hope you've got deep pockets, lad. You can try the alchemist, mercenaries, or the mage's college." He was still laughing to himself as Joe walked away.

Joe decided that the alchemist was the person to talk to first. He walked into the shop and had to cover his mouth to keep from being sick. The potent chemicals–along with his better-than-average sense of smell–made him feel ill instantly.

"Can I help you? You gonna be sick? If so, step outside please." A man who appeared to be Joe's age stepped into the main room, looking only mildly concerned about Joe's health.

"I'm fine." Joe coughed, trying to clear his airways. He

started to breathe through his mouth in order to give his nose a rest. "I am looking for monster Cores. I need two low-grade Cores for a project I'm working on."

"Two? You sure are ambitious. I can get them for you, but they will cost thirty gold each." The man spoke in a soft monotone, as if he were trying not to wake up a small child.

Joe almost choked at the insane price quoted. That was the equivalent of three hundred dollars apiece! "Is there any way to get them a bit… cheaper?"

"Yes."

"Oh? How?"

"By going elsewhere."

"Oh." Joe tried again, "If I can get them cheaper elsewhere, why do you sell them at higher prices?"

The young man smiled gently. "You can get them from mercenaries for as low as twenty-five, if you don't mind waiting a few weeks. You will need to bribe them if you want to ensure you get your order in a timely manner, as well. From the college, you can get them as low as twenty gold but only if you are a student and have a professor-approved project you are working on. Here you are paying for the stone as well as convenience."

"Understood. Why are they so expensive?" Joe sighed and pulled out bank notes totaling thirty gold. He would need to visit the bank again.

"You are about to find out." The alchemist handed Joe a glittering gem, and when it landed in his palm, a notification appeared.

Low-grade monster Core found! Would you like to convert this into experience points? Current worth: Five hundred experience points.

"F-five *hundred* points?" Joe gasped at the gem in his hand. "This is a *low*-grade?"

"Yup. The most efficient way to become powerful that has ever been found." The alchemist sighed and looked at the stone longingly. "Of course, there are a ton of uses for them. Spells, enchantments, potions… you name it. Almost all jobs require them, to some degree. Hence, expensive and hard to acquire."

"Thank you for selling to me." Joe looked longingly at the Core one more time and stuffed it into his bag. "I'll be back for the other one tomorrow, I seem to be short on funds." The alchemist nodded and returned to work while Joe walked out.

Core, wire, and mana were all set. Now, all Joe needed was a zombie brain. He walked over to the guild tavern, only to be met with concern. Tiona walked up to him threateningly, "I couldn't find you at the library. What happened? Where did you go?"

"I needed to do a bit of shopping for a quest." Joe looked around at a few people who were bleeding and groaning.

"You need to learn how to listen, Joe. You'd think that being in the army would have beat that into you. Hurry up and get to healing." Tiona gestured angrily at the injured guild mates. Joe walked around and healed everyone that needed it, surprisingly getting a notification at the end.

Skill increased: Lay on hands (Novice II). As 'Lay on hands' is a variant of 'Heal', the skill 'Heal' also gains experience as this one does.

Skill increased: Heal (Novice II).

Joe was filled with a nimbus of silver light, and a euphoria not unlike leveling washed over him. He wasn't washed or healed, but his mind felt refreshed. Tiona watched him and grinned faintly as she remembered the feel of increasing your skills. "Alright, I forgive you. Just be glad no one died when they were expecting help."

"Sorry, T." Joe grinned at her a bit nervously. "Would you do me a favor?"

"Don't try and give me nicknames. What do you want?" Tiona's voice contained a warning growl.

"I need two undamaged heads from the zombits." Joe held up his hands as she started to protest. "I'd go do it myself, but I doubt you want me to go out while the guilds are fighting. I need them for quests."

Tiona perked up when she heard the word 'quest'. "Are these quests where multiple people can be rewarded, or…?"

Joe shook his head. "They are preliminary profession quests. So unless you want to be a scholar, I don't-"

"Hard pass." Tiona shuddered with great exaggeration. "You owe me one, but I'll go get your zombie heads. Wait here, and *don't* go wandering off again or I will beat you with a rotten rabbit!"

It took almost twenty minutes, but she came back with two heads that were dripping fluids. Tossing them to Joe, she commented, "Harder to keep intact than they should be."

"I just need the brain intact," Joe mentioned offhandedly as he pulled out his new skinning knife. His health suddenly took a hit. "Ow! It bit me!"

"Still technically undead. Also, the brains? How are you planning to store them?" Tiona seemed interested in the process and came closer to watch.

"I have a couple jars." Joe healed himself and pulled out the glass containers, setting them to the side.

"Should put them in water or something. A preservative if you want them to last for any length of time." Tiona's words brought Joe up short, and he cracked his knuckles as he rethought his class choice once again. Ritual magic took *forever* to prepare.

"Could you ask the kitchen if they have any oil I could buy?" Tiona came back a few minutes later and filled the jars with unused olive oil. Joe looked at the cloudy fluid, then, in a fit of inspiration, he cast cleanse. The magic swept through the oil, pulling out small particles which had mixed into the oil, such as dust. "Didn't think that would work. Neat!"

Joe cracked open the skulls as gently as possible, treating the brain like a barely-boiled egg. The brains **plopped** into the oil, sinking about halfway before floating. "Alright, all done!"

"What are you *doing* on *my* table?" The barkeep was suddenly looming over them and looking at the mess of fur, rotten meat, and fluids that were on the previously clean table.

Joe and Tiona had to clean and scrub the table or risk losing reputation for their guild. The entire time, Joe looked apologetic while Tiona glared at him ferociously. He had a feeling that he was going to regret having her help him. When they were done, Joe informed her that he would be going to the Odds and Ends shop, then back to the library; just in case the guild needed to find him in a hurry.

Almost *running* away from the tavern and the wrathful Tiona, Joe quickly entered the shop and began looking around for a good place to carve the symbol that was needed for the ritual. After looking at a few possible locations, he decided that the carving would have to be either on a shelf or the floor. Determining that it was unlikely that the floor would move, he pushed a shelf out of the way and started cutting into the wood.

Luckily, the symbol was fairly basic, just a star bounded by a double circle. His lack of dexterity started to come into play, and he cut himself three times, also ruining the symbol again and again. When he was finally able to make a passable version after the third try, he wiped his brow and walked across the store a few times to judge how much wire he would need to provide.

Thanks to the perks of his class, he should be able to get away with putting in half as much silver as the ritual required. Joe piled all of the wire, the Core, and the brain onto the carving. Since this was a simple ritual, he needed no chanting or complicated movements–only an influx of mana was required. He touched the place on the outer circle which the book called the 'activation sequence' and tried to begin the ritual. Mana poured out of him when he got the activation correct, a feeling similar to bleeding heavily. Joe began to feel tired, then drained, finally exhausted. Three-quarters of his total mana pool was required, and he had never needed to use so much at a time before. He was panting heavily and almost ready to drop, but the ritual seemed to have worked! This was confirmed a moment later as the components vanished, leaving behind a jar of oil and a much depleted Core.

Ritual 'Little sister's cleaning service' created! Area of effect, radius of forty feet. Components used, silver wire, low-grade monster Core (49.9%), poorly preserved zombie rabbit brain. Once active, this ritual will last three years. The poorly preserved brain has added two years to the ritual's length. Due to the brain coming from a weak [zombie rabbit] with poor processing ability, organization will proceed at speed [slow]. Activate now? Yes / No

So using better quality materials than needed would make the ritual more potent? Good to know. Joe selected 'yes', and the ritual circle brightened for a moment before fading. He put the oil back in his bag and grabbed the Core. He smiled as the bright gem offered him experience points, then put it in his bag as well. Turning around, he walked to the counter and smiled at the ancient lady. "That should do it! Your shop is being organized as we speak."

"When will it be *fully* organized?" the lady questioned with a sweet smile.

"Most likely tomorrow?" Joe ducked as a pair of boots flew over his head. The ritual was working!

"Then come back for your reward tomorrow!" She cackled at his disgruntled look. "Anything else, young'un?"

"Yeah, do you have any ornamental bookends?" Joe purchased two sets of wooden bookends, hoping they would go unnoticed in a library. He left her shop and walked over to the alchemist's laboratory.

The calm-faced alchemist looked up as Joe walked in, raising a brow at his return. "I didn't expect you until tomorrow. Come for another Core already? Goodness me. You must be making money hand over fist."

"No, but I like that you think highly of me. I was wondering if you had any preserved zombie brains? I'm not too concerned with what they are from, but the more intelligent they were, the better." Joe tried to hide his exhaustion behind a smile. His mana was returning quickly thanks to his wisdom, but he was still feeling the physical effects of the ritual draining his mana so quickly.

"Zombie brains? That is a rare order…" The alchemist tapped his book a couple times. He hesitated before speaking. "I suppose I have two items that may suit your needs, but… one of them is held as a controlled substance. That would be the *human* zombie brain. If a human were to get the contamination in their blood, their race would change to a zombie. This could be bad, as we are in a highly populated city. Not great for business if your customers are trying to eat you, I hope you understand. The other brain is from a bear, and you can walk out with it as long as you agree not to feed it to any bears. Is that acceptable?"

The alchemist spoke in a calm monotone, but his words and nonchalance toward a plague of zombies made him seem more than a little deranged. Joe looked at the alchemist in a new light. "What would I need to do to use the human brain?"

"So you are planning to *use* it for something, hmm? I have heard that your guild is at war with another. Are you trying to plant this somewhere to wipe them out?" There was now a wide smile growing on his face. "Start a zombie outbreak in their guild house, have the guard wipe them out and make them hated by the city, to the point they need to disband?" He was breathing heavily and his cheeks were flushed.

Joe was now a bit concerned for his safety. "I... need it for a spell? To complete a quest?"

"Oh. No plotting? No dark deeds done at midnight?" The alchemist's face returned to its neutral state. "Well, I'm sorry to say that it is a restricted item. The brain can't leave my shop."

"That's fine!" Joe's voice broke; this man was really throwing off his expectations and making him uncomfortable. "If I can use it here, can I buy it?"

"Fifty silver. My name is Jake, by the way. Thanks for asking." Jake the alchemist seemed to find pleasure in seeing Joe's face flush.

"I... I need to make some preparations." Joe pulled out one of the bookends and started the process of cutting a symbol into it. His first two tries failed, but the star in a double circle slowly took shape on the third set. When it was finished, Joe wiped the blood from his sliced fingers, piled the half-used Core and silver wire onto the ritual circle before looking expectantly at Jake.

"Money first." Jake held out a hand.

"Really? That was the holdup?" Joe chuckled and handed over the silver. Hadn't he had plans to save money for a long time? Ah well. It needed to be done, and there was plenty more in the bank. Jake handed over a glass container with a brain in it, and Joe read the information that appeared when he tried to examine it.

Knowledge check failed! Failure overridden due to being in a shop, and the data has been provided by shop owner. Zombie brain (Human, perfectly preserved.) Spell component, ingredient, forcible race change item.

Not a lot of data, but at least it got the point across. Joe added it to the pile of items on the circle and braced himself. Taking a few calming breaths, he put his hand on the activation area and started to inject mana into the system. Once again, when his mana stopped flowing all of the items vanished, except for the jar and the Core.

Ritual 'Little sisters cleaning service' created! Area of effect, radius of four hundred and fifty feet. Components used, silver wire, low-grade monster Core (49.9%), perfectly preserved human zombie brain. Once active, this ritual will last sixteen years. The preserved brain has added fifteen years to the length. Due to the brain coming from a strong [zombie human] with excellent processing ability, organization will proceed at speed [very fast]. Activate now? Yes / No

Joe selected 'no' and looked up at a feverishly grinning Jake. Jake tried to act nonchalant, but Joe was instantly wary. "So… what kind of ritual was that? I haven't heard of anyone creating a ritual since before the human territories were elevated away from the other races. The way your face contorted in agony as your mana was reduced to such a low amount… exquisite." He shuddered and so did Joe, though for a different reason.

"It's a spell that cleans a place for years at a time," Joe forced himself to speak. "I found the ritual in the library; it said that anyone can create rituals. Is it really so strange?"

Jake cocked his head to the side. "Strange? No. Well… a bit

strange. The real question is: how massive is your mana pool? To create a ritual takes vast reserves of power, and the load is usually split between multiple people, is it not? I won't pry–for now–but I am very interested in seeing how your journey progresses. Have a good day! Mine has been… *very* interesting so far."

Joe walked out of the shop feeling like he had somehow made a serious mistake.

CHAPTER ELEVEN

The library was just as he had left it; apparently it wasn't an overly popular destination for the populace. Since travelers were barred from entering without a recommendation, it wasn't particularly surprising that it remained empty for the majority of the day. Nodding at the head librarian, he walked into the book stacks and tried to determine where the center was. Deciding that a rough estimate was the best he could do, Joe placed the bookend on a shelf and selected the 'activate' option. As with the last ritual, a bright light filled the ritual before quickly dulling to obscurity.

Joe picked up the book of rituals, deciding to go through it a bit more carefully while he waited. He sat down and just so happened to look up as the ritual began to take effect. Books *flew* off the shelves, flying to various piles and waiting for their assigned area to be determined. As the area impacted by the ritual grew, the air became clogged with flying leather-bound books. Joe was glad he was sitting, because he would have surely been hit at least few times otherwise. For a few moments he was worried; the books were old and moving very quickly. Would they become damaged? The answer appeared to be 'no', luckily for his health and desire to stay out of prison.

Once all the books were off the shelves, a complex weave of moving knowledge was created. For nearly an hour, the books shuffled themselves and reorganized. At one point, the ritual tried to gently pull the ritual book out of Joe's hands, but the simple act of holding it a bit tightly seemed to show that he wanted it to remain where it was so the ritual let him be. As more of the shelves were organized, the ritual was able to move faster. The last few books zipped to their new position so fast that they would have damaged his hit points if he were in the way. A strangled yell came from the entrance, and a few more books flew in.

Uh-oh. Joe recognized a few of those. They had been in a pile on the head librarian's desk. The man himself bustled into the room, face red. He was about to shout in rage, but instead, sputtered to a stop as he looked around at all of the neatly organized shelves. "B-but! How?" He turned on Joe, who did his best to look innocent.

"I found a very efficient way to sort and order the books is all. I made sure that nothing got damaged!" Joe smiled happily at Boris, who was grinding his teeth in fury.

"This quest was supposed to show me your determination and help boost your skill in reading," Boris muttered unhappily. "No one has ever *actually* sorted the entire first floor; that should have taken years to do right!"

"So are you saying that I am actually the very *first* person to complete the quest correctly?" Joe watched the reaction of the librarian closely.

Boris's face was squirming, his eyelid was twitching, and he looked like he had eaten something rotten. "Erm. Well, first, how did you arrange everything? I need to make sure you did a… satisfactory job."

Rolling his eyes, Joe moved to a shelf. "The effect I created is based not only upon intent, but the actual formation of the spell pattern. Since this is a fairly specific job, I made sure to include instructions for the sorting and placement of the books. First, they are ordered by content and color. Then if they are a similar subject, they are grouped together. I had to do it that way since very few of them have an author name or title, which is why the color of the book is taken into account. At least that way we can always find the book in the same spot. Just look for where its color should appear on the gradient."

"Always? You don't mean to tell me that this is an… *ongoing* effect?" Boris pulled a book off the shelf and placed it on the table. It didn't move, so he glanced up at Joe, then down at the book. "Doesn't look like it."

"Well, you are *using* the book." Joe smiled at Boris, who looked a bit confused. "Are you done with it?"

"Sure." Boris flinched as the book zipped back to its position on the shelves. He stared at it for a long moment. "How… remarkable. How long will this effect last?"

"Sixteen years." Boris coughed dramatically at Joe's words, collapsing into a chair and looking at Joe as if he had kicked his dog.

"...Years!" Boris grabbed his beard and pulled on it. "Well, I can certainly see that you don't do things with half measures. I… *suppose* this shows your dedication and determination; I can't imagine this was easy to do. Your reading skill will likely stagnate unless you use your own time to enhance it, but that was simply a fringe benefit of this work. I judge your task… complete." Boris had his eyes closed as he said words that no other librarian had ever needed to utter for this particular task before.

Quest complete: Footsteps through history I. Where others follow the footsteps of the old masters, you create your own legacy! Hidden requirement met! Quest completion above 100%. Calculating rewards… Reputation with scholars: +1000. Profession Exp: 500 (held until profession unlocked). Skill points +2! Intelligence +1! Spectacles of the scholar (held until profession unlocked). Exp: 1000! (500 from quest, 500 from completion of hidden requirement.)

"I'm going to be a laughingstock. People are going to think

that I cheated to let you complete this quest," Boris muttered darkly, tugging harder on his beard.

"Neither of us cheated, Mr. Boris." Joe shook his head. "In fact, it is only due to the knowledge I acquired while sorting these book that I was able to complete the quest."

"What? How?" Boris shot to his feet and looked like he was ready to grab Joe and shake the information out of him.

"I found a book on rituals while sorting and was able to complete one of them. It sorts and organizes items," Joe explained carefully.

"There was a magic grimoire in here?" Boris seemed disturbed by this revelation. "Hmm. Can't let the Mage's College know about this. I have no plans to be 'sanctioned'. Where is it now?"

"Here." Joe handed over the book, and Boris grabbed it and flipped through the pages.

"You used these? That's..." Boris took a deep breath, "*ridiculous*! This is an exaggerated primer on rituals, designed to show how inefficient, wasteful, and useless they are! I... I... here! Take it with you. I don't want it in my library. Just don't mention to any mages that this is where you got it. They have a strict monopoly on the sale of magical knowledge. Even that... drivel."

Joe looked at the near-hyperventilating librarian who was running his hands through his hair. Joe cleared his throat, "Ahem. Well, I was wondering if you had another task for me?"

Boris looked up, nearly growling a reply, "I'll tell you about it, but I warn you it will be very difficult without having your profession unlocked. You have been sorting through accumulated knowledge but in order for our profession to grow, so must our collection. Your task will be to return with a work of knowledge that is not already contained within our library. I can't give you many hints because if I knew where some might be I would have already acquired them."

Quest alert: Footsteps through history II (Ongoing). Bring lost knowledge to the head librarian. This can take the form of art, books, blueprints, or knowledge of any type. Quest rewards will depend on the type and importance of your findings. Accept? Yes / No

After accepting the quest, Joe decided that he was ready for bed. It had been a full day, and a good dinner followed by a long sleep sounded lovely right now. He stepped out of the library and started on his way to the tavern. He was surprised by how little his help was needed with the guild war. Joe was under the impression that he would be called upon constantly as this was supposed to be a war of attrition. Just as he opened the door, a notification appeared, and he was assaulted by a great roar of approval.

Every member of the Hardcores guild is currently logged off! As they are unavailable to complete jobs for the city, all of their contracts are up for grabs with a 20% bonus to rewards. The city has levied a report against them. The Hardcores have lost 200 guild reputation with Ardania.

"We won!" There was an excessively festive air in the tavern, and though a few groups were appearing with injuries, it seemed that the guild was in for an excellent few days. Joe made his rounds, healing people and making conversation. It was a fun night, but he had no plans to join the others in drinking two nights in a row. He eventually went to bed smiling; it had been a long, fun day.

The following morning, Joe met up with his party, and they set out to hunt wolves. Since they were leaving just as the gates were opening, they would have roughly sixteen hours of hunting before they needed to be back in the safety of town. They were able to set a quicker pace today because Joe found that as long as he walked with a spring in his step, he could spend a point of mana per step to allow himself to move faster. He laughed when the others looked at him strangely, but he didn't bother telling them that the secret to moving further than he should be able to was due to the fact that he was skipping. It drained a bit of mana with each step, but it was better than draining his minimal stamina. Everyone was smiling, infected by his cheerful attitude and the fact that they didn't need to worry about player killers for another few hours.

As they arrived in wolf territory, Joe decided that his goal today was to finish his quest to heal half of the damage done in battle. With that in mind, he made sure to stay out of the wolves' line of sight. Tiona had taken a few minutes to explain how 'aggro' worked; apparently, it was a little different than other games. Pack animals such as wolves would try to take out the weakest link first, and that meant Joe almost *exclusively* in this case. If he were well protected, the attacks would usually focus on whoever did the most damage or generated the most 'threat'. Healers were apparently still on this list since they were a triple whammy of delicious for wolves, physically weak, and each spell cast was flashy and caused the animal to focus its attention on him.

Tiona took to using Joe as bait, luring the animal in to attack before suddenly closing ranks and wailing on it from multiple sides at once. Feeling a bit put out that his best purpose in the group was to attract salivating killers, Joe stayed silent for most of the day and simply worked to heal people whenever they became injured. As the day of grinding was winding to a close, Joe finished his quest and looked over the messages he had been ignoring.

Exp: 420 (Wolf killed x35). You have spotted five potential ambushes before they were sprung! Perception +1.

Quest complete: Playing your fake role I. You have done well, the life of a chameleon may be exactly what you needed! Reward: Title 'I'm a healer! I swear!' gained. Gain 10% bonus Exp when you heal at least 50% of the damage done during combat. Exp: 600.

Quest alert: Playing your fake role II. Set another class as your active class. This quest will be updated after doing so, based on the class chosen.

Joe was bathed in golden light and lifted off the ground. His team gathered around him closely, able to receive some select benefits of Joe's level up. Namely, becoming clean in an instant. The euphoria zipped through him, and a wash of light exploded outward like a supernova. Fully clean and cheerful once again, Joe decided to allocate his characteristic points immediately. As much as he wanted to boost his physical stats, he had to be realistic. He wouldn't get more points to spend until level six, and if he tried to balance himself right now, he would fall behind where it was actually important. Joe placed two points into intelligence and wisdom, and spent only one of the precious points on constitution. He accepted the changes, and felt a slight spasm as his body adjusted to its new levels. Opening his character sheet, he looked over his new stats.

Name: Joe 'I'm a healer! I swear!' Class: Cleric (Actual: Ritualist) Profession: Locked
Level: 3 Exp: 3023 Exp to next level: 2977
Hit Points: 50/50 (50+10 per point of constitution over 10)
Mana: 500/500 (12.5 per point of intelligence, +100% from deity)
Mana regen: 5/sec (.25 per point of wisdom)
Stamina: 50/50 (50+(0)+(0))

Characteristic: Raw score (Modifier)

Strength: 6 (0.06)
Dexterity: 7 (0.07)
Constitution: 7 (0.07)
Intelligence: 18 (1.18)
Wisdom: 18 (1.18)
Charisma: 10 (1.10)
Perception: 20 (1.20)
Luck: 12 (1.12)
Karmic Luck: 0

Joe almost started laughing maniacally when he saw how much mana he had. If *only* he had some attack spells! He could rain destruction upon his enemies for days at a time! The party started merrily on their way back to town. Joe was ecstatic to realize that his mana regen was now fast enough that it refilled just as quick as it was drained when adding his jump score to his walking speed. It wasn't a fix for his terrible constitution, but it helped him to be less of a burden on the team as they strolled along.

The joyful attitude and good cheer of the group started to dissipate as they left the tree line and the city came into view. A thick column of black, oily smoke was rising into the sky. They increased their pace, which left Joe winded and lagging behind them. Passing through the gates, they skidded to a horrified stop. The tavern they had come to love and see as a home away from home was engulfed in an inferno.

Members of the guild were running around, trying to find a way to help while the guild leader was directing them and inquiring after the tavern owner. No one had seen him or his family, who lived in a room connected to the kitchen. Fearing the worst and unable to douse the flames… The Wanderers guild was forced to watch, wait, and do nothing.

CHAPTER TWELVE

A somber mood had settled over the area, and The Wanderers guild was now scrambling to secure housing for the next few days. Joe wanted to help, but realistically, there was nothing that he could do. Deciding that becoming more prepared was the way to move forward, he started his journey to the Odds and Ends store to get his rewards–as well as to get his robe returned. A short walk allowed him to reach the store's entrance, where he had to wait a few minutes for the line to dissipate enough for him to enter.

As Joe stepped through the door, the shop owner's eyes snapped to stare at him, and she pointed a wavering finger at him. "You! *You* did this! My days were nice, dull, and I didn't have to interact with many people! Look at this place! There are people everywhere! I might need to restock! *Restock*! I haven't had to order more goods for a full *year*! Get behind the counter and mind the till!"

Quest alert: Attack of the extroverts! The Odds and Ends store has had a 1000% increase in sales in the last hour alone! The shop owner demands *your help in dealing with the customers! Rewards: variable.*

Refusing this quest will reduce reputation with the Odds and Ends store by 500.

Joe read over the quest notice, quickly accepting it and getting behind the counter to help with sales. People were going through all of the neatly organized items and finding prices better than anywhere else in the city. Clothes, bags, weapons, trade goods, specialized tools… all of it was labeled with a price that was a year old. Whereas most other stores had slowly increased the cost of goods as demand went up, this store had not needed to bother.

It took a few hours, but the store was nearly cleaned out; word had gotten out about the low price point. As night approached, even the people that had been out hunting cycled through. When the store eventually closed for the night, the owner looked around at the few scraps of goods that remained and sighed. "I'm just too old to deal with this. This may as well have been a going out of business sale because I really don't have it in me to outfit the place again. You did good work today, thank you."

Quest complete: Attack of the extroverts! Exp: 1000! (500 x2 for unintentionally creating the situation in the first place.) Charisma +1, luck +1! If the owner ever sells her shop, she will sing your praises to the next owner! Permanent 15% discount at this store location!

"You made so much money today though! You were amazing! Cutting deals, negotiating like a champion, you knew the price of every single item in here without having to look at a chart or validate the information!" Joe was confused by her reaction to this good fortune.

"You are a good child, Joe, but I don't think you understand. I don't need the money! I'm filthy rich. Disgustingly so. I liked to have people in here to chat with, to laugh as they dived into piles of gear, see their eyes shine as they found a great deal on rare items! That's all gone now." She seemed terribly sad about this outcome. "People would… ah, it doesn't matter. I think I'll find an apprentice. Pass some of my hard-earned knowledge onto the next generation. That'll give me someone to chatter away with each day, at least. Only thing is… I've never found anyone I can stand for more than a day! You think you can help me out with that? I'd rather they worked to better themselves, but you can tell them I'm looking to quit if you need too."

Quest alert: Apprentice to a Sage! The merchant Sage of the Odds and Ends shop has decided that it is time to move on and wants to ensure that the shop gets a worthy owner. Find a person willing to become a merchant and send them for tutelage. Reward: Variable. Bonus: Don't tell the person they are going to work for a Sage, and don't let them know they will get the shop upon quest chain completion. Bonus reward: Random Artifact rarity item for your class. (After the person you find completes their chain quest).

Joe read the quest, his mouth almost breaking from the force of his jaw dropping. He accepted the quest and promised that he would find a worthy person. She nodded and smiled at him, handing over a ring and his robe. "That'll be ten gold."

Eye twitching, Joe handed over the money and took the items. Looking over the cloak, he smiled as he saw that it was fully repaired. It had beautiful fractal patterns on it, and instead of being a muted grey, the robe was clearly made with various shades of shimmering purple. He frowned in consternation after he equipped the comfortable, plush robe. "Wait, don't I get a discount now?"

"On anything you buy in the *future*, yes. We don't retroactively change agreed upon prices!" The old lady cackled at his expression.

"Ugh," Joe groaned at her. "Anything I need to know about the ring?"

"Put it on!" she instructed brusquely. "It will use a couple points of mana when you put anything in or take anything out. The more intricate the item, the more mana it will use. Uncommon items will cost more than common, rare even more so. Et cetera. Just focus on it, and you will know what to do."

"It uses mana? How can anyone but a mage or cleric use it?" Joe's brow furrowed as he stared at the unassuming trinket.

"Everyone has mana; it is just that not everyone knows how to access it!" the old woman declared with a snort. "Why do you think that anyone can go to the mage's college and become a mage with enough effort? When a person reaches their tenth level, they will automatically have access to their mana. That's when they rank up and specialize, after all."

"Rank up? Specialize?" Joe's ears perked up like a deer hearing a twig snap.

"Well, of course!" She seemed to be irritated with Joe now. "How do you think we get people like… hmm? You have no idea, do you? When you get to level ten, you choose one of your classes to specialize in and rank it up to a higher tier. Yes, you can have multiple classes, but you pick one to focus on. Doing jobs that build your skill in this class will award class experience, similar to jobs at level five. That is why it is important to know what you want to do in the future, so that the job you take will complement your class!"

Joe's eyes were wide. He needed to get this information to his guild; it would give them a huge advantage over time if they were able to get various or rare specializations. "Could you give me an example of a specialization?"

"Huh, um. What would help you…? Oh! Not dying is always good. Let's talk about assassins." The old lady smiled grimly at the constipated look on Joe's face. "Yes, not a fun topic. At level ten, a rogue, thief, or other unsavory type can find a class trainer that will admit them into the ranks of the assassins. They become even stealthier, and their blows change toward devastating. As they complete jobs and their class experience reaches the tenth level, they can specialize again. Here they are released from their contract with the assassin guild that trained them, and they have a choice. They can become a Death Adept, a Freeblade, or a Temple Assassin."

Her face darkened. "Unless you are at the same class rank or higher, you will never know when you are targeted by them. You will simply die. There are some steps you can take to avoid this fate though. A Death Adept stays with the guild that trained them, carrying out brutal assassinations that are designed to send a message to others. A Freeblade is guildless and able to take any contract offered to them: glorified mercenaries but still dangerous. A Temple Assassin is–as the name suggests–taken by a temple and sent to hunt down heretics and groups of the opposite alignment. As a cleric, you have the most to fear from them."

"Can they rank up after that?" Joe's voice was a bare whisper. The slow nod of the merchant made his breath catch in his throat.

"Oh yes. Twice more. The path of the Freeblade brings them into politics and low ranked squabbles. They can become–for example–an Assassin et Marque, followed by the final class, the Assassin Politico. Politics, toppling empires... nothing is too difficult for them to accomplish. The Death Adept becomes an Annihilator then a Kingblade. They cut a bloody swath through any in their path, the need for stealth and secrecy left far behind." her words slowed, "I am a merchant, but that is only my job class. I was an Archer, then a Seeker, a Treasure Lord, and am now an Arcane Loot Lord. The point here is that there are so many possible paths to take that it is impossible to know them all. What I have told you is only the tip of the iceberg. There are *many* unknown or hidden classes, and finding the requirements for all of them would be the work of a dozen lifetimes."

Joe digested this information, already trying to determine the best way to progress along his own path. He was the only Ritualist, so unless he wanted to do something totally unrelated to his current class he would need to find a different way to advance other than finding a class trainer. Perhaps… "Is there any other way to rank up a class instead of finding someone to show you the way?"

She gave him a queer look but nodded. "Indeed there is. There are books–manuals really–that detail the requirements for certain rankings. Some classes are even able to be purchased if you find someone willing to share their secrets for coin. Of course, you can simply fulfill every requirement that exists and pick from the results. Ha! Finding the necessary requirements is how people have their classes in the first place, but there is a reason there are now entire guilds devoted to the process."

"Very difficult, I assume." Joe grinned at her. He had all the time in the world; why not find the absolute best specializations? "Any tips?"

"Humph. Any class rank worth having requires titles, titles, and then better titles. Start collecting those, perhaps. I'd still recommend finding a class trainer. Much less time intensive." She waved at the door. "Get out, I'm tired."

Joe thanked her and left, only remembering that he had nowhere to sleep as the door locked behind him. "Well, dang." He was getting pretty tired as well; it had been a long day.

"There you are!" a voice called out of the darkness. Tiona's face became visible as she walked towards him, looking him over before noticing the shop behind him. "Why am I not surprised that you are here? Trying to get the last good deal of the day or something?"

"No, I was working. I had a quest here. Even got a thousand experience for it." Joe grinned at her as her face blanched.

"A thousand…? How do you keep pulling these random quests out of thin air?" She motioned for him to follow her. "If I am going to get to level ten, I am going to need big, hairy chunks of experience like that."

"It's pretty easy," Joe told her. "I just keep asking them questions or offering services until they break down and finally give me a quest or let me do stuff for them. In this case, I organized her shop. There's no real need to fight all the time. This is more efficient."

"To think, I've been spending days at a time perfecting my skill as a warrior, learning the proper way not to die, fighting people and beasts to perfect my forms, when I could just… color-code a few bags." Tiona rolled her eyes. "Higher levels don't mean much if you can't *do* anything with them."

Joe searched for an answer to that but had to concede, "Alright, fair point. By the way, was there a big open space the guild found to sleep in? I need to talk to the guild leader pretty badly. Just got some great information."

"You know, you could just call him by his name," Tiona snickered at him. "Yes, we rented an empty barracks belonging to the city guard. They normally only use it a few times a year."

"Perfect!" Joe's eyes seemed to glow. "Also, what *is* his name?"

"Really? You joined his guild and didn't ask his name?" Tiona punched him lightly. "It's Aten. He says he chose that name because he is so sexy that every time anyone looked at him, they would see 'a ten', so it might as well be official."

"Humble."

"Who in this game is humble?"

"Another good point." They walked in silence until they got to the barracks and needed to offer a password before they were allowed entrance. Joe walked right over to guild leader Aten, interrupting whatever else he was doing. "I've changed my mind about the guild."

"You want out?" Aten sounded quite disappointed; Joe wasn't the first person to want to leave after they had lost everything they had stored in the tavern.

"No, I want *in*. You offered me a high starting position and good terms right off the bat. That still on the table?" Joe was all business right now, his time making sales had not been wasted.

"It is, but… what changed?" Aten was pleased with this development, a permanent cleric was going to be a huge boon to the guild.

"I got some new information. You have any of those contracts handy?"

CHAPTER THIRTEEN

Aten held his head in his hands. After granting Joe an officer position, he listened raptly to what he had to say. "Why have we heard nothing like this before? We all knew that the job we took would be important, but you are saying that if we don't find something that complements our future build... we may miss out on *good* specializations?"

"Yes," Joe enunciated clearly. There were a few people taking part in this meeting, and all of them seemed shocked. Joe had asked for only trusted officers to hear this.

"And so *many* possible classes!" Aten was pulling on his hair as he tried to think. "We were led to believe that anything beyond what is being offered by the city was a pipe dream. Joe, you may have just made us the most powerful guild in the game. I don't think anyone has reached level ten yet, but some people are getting close, like Tiona and I. We need to start searching for these hidden trainers and learning what their requirements are. Now we have a plan, at least. This will help us move forward; this is good."

"What about the Hardcores?" one of the guild officers demanded.

"They burned down the tavern in retaliation, I am almost sure of it. What can we do though? We kill them and they just come back." Aten shrugged dejectedly. "It's unfortunate, but if we focus on them we are just going to fall behind in our race to the top. At least we know why the guards are so frustrated now; they can't really hold us accountable for our crimes! It is going to be really difficult to grind reputation with them, but we need to find a way if we are going to become a Noble Guild."

Joe started laughing as Aten's words registered in his mind. The others looked at him strangely, but even when Aten angrily poked him, Joe couldn't stop himself. "We… haha… we need to get reputation with the *guards*? Here? The city guards?"

"Yes." Aten seemed exasperated. The cleric hadn't seemed so eccentric when he had invited him to the guild. Maybe his position could be one that didn't require attendance at meetings? Or interaction with anyone of importance? "Getting reputation with the guards is almost impossible because they are so suspicious of everyone. They know that you are trying to get on their good side, and it makes them trust you *less*."

Joe *howled* with laughter for a long moment. "And we need reputation with them… that's one of the last requirements for becoming a Noble Guild?"

"Yes, and knock it off," Aten growled at him, crossing his arms. "Do you have something to say?"

"Show… haha… show reputation: Human Guards, Ardania," Joe managed to choke out. There was a moment of bewilderment, but then all of the people in the meeting got a pop-up.

Reputation for Joe 'I'm a healer! I swear!' with Human Guards, Ardania. Current standing: Friend.

"Are you *kidding* me?" Aten shouted indignantly. "*Friend*? You already have *friend* status with them? How! Who *are* you?"

"I got it from my very first quest!" Joe explained before the atmosphere could go from jubilant to suspicious. "As a cleric, I was asked to heal a few guards. I may have gone a bit overboard, and I healed all the guards I could get my hands on.

Before I knew it, I had fixed everyone and attained 'friend' status."

"And there was no way for you to know you should be grinding reputation!" Light was glinting from Aten's eyes. "Joe, as an officer, you are supposed to get your own team. Since Tiona is also a guild officer, you two are not *supposed* to stay in the same group. I was wondering if you wouldn't mind throwing the leadership position out the window and staying with her team? You have the right to ask for command, but your job would be to help raise our newest people's levels instead of doing your own thing. If you stay on her team, we can put you on special assignment without anyone grumbling. That okay with you?"

Joe nodded easily. "I'd rather be able to focus on my own projects than need to grind with other low-leveled people. You do remember that I have a long-term quest from my deity so doing my own thing is a must. What do you need from me?"

"Tomorrow I'd like you to go to the guards and offer your services as a representative of our guild. Since you are friends with them, they should accept that even if they whine about it a little. You are our secret weapon for becoming a Noble Guild. Can we count on you for that?"

"Absolutely." Joe smiled as the people at the meeting dispersed. "Aten, can I talk to you for a minute? Alone?"

"Sure." Aten walked over to his room and motioned for Joe to follow him.

After closing the door, Joe turned and gave a hard stare at Aten. "Guild leader, I need to know if I can trust you."

Sensing the serious tone, Aten's face turned grim. "You can. So long as you don't try to hurt me or the guild, we'll stay on your side no matter what. I keep secrets *very* well."

Joe's eyes searched Aten's face for any signs of falsehood. He nodded slowly and sighed through his nose. "Alright. Let's find out how far this trust goes. Aten, it took me a few days to decide on what I wanted to *really* do in Eternium. I don't know what my endgame is, but I know how I want to get there. I plan on one-hundred percent completion. I want to find every secret, get every achievement, find all the secret quests, and explore every bit of *every* dungeon. As a part of that, I plan to get any skill I acquire to the maximum Sage rank."

"I mean, good luck with that, but that'll take years. It also isn't much of a secret that you want to get more skills, we all do." Aten waved his hands uncomfortably.

"Right, well… I may be a bit further ahead than you know. Remember, not a word about this!" Joe opened his status screen and looked at his skills. He had twelve unused skill points, and one after another he began assigning them to his 'Jump' skill. Eight points later, the skill reached sixty, and he was asked to confirm his decision. He smiled and pressed 'yes'.

New skill tier reached! Your Jump skill has increased to (Master level 0). Your dedication to a single aspect of yourself has inspired you to climb to new heights! Or in this case, Jump to them! You are able to find the magic in motion, the power in leaping, and the freedom of falling!

Skill updated: Jump around! You have jumped so much that it is now a natural part of you, and adding your jump score to basic actions now no longer costs mana! You are now able to add your jump score to more esoteric actions, though this may have detrimental effects if you 'jump' to conclusions! Skill will be lost if another player's jump score becomes higher than yours.

Guild alert! A member of this guild has achieved Mastery over one of their skills! The royal court has taken notice and grants an additional +1000 reputation to your guild! (Lost if player leaves guild.)

Though Aten could only see the last message, his eyes were round and unfocused. "You got a skill to *Master* already? You've been playing for like… three days!"

"I've gotten a bunch of skill points from completing quests around town, and I got to the expert rank because the Hardcores forced me to jump off a cliff, and I just so happened to survive. Oh, right, the skill I mastered is 'Jump'. I wouldn't recommend the experience; I was splattered all over the bottom of a cliff. I have an item that keeps me at one health point if I lose too much at once, so when I hit the ground and didn't instantly die, the system freaked out and boosted me all the way to expert rank," Joe explained to Aten, who decided that it was a good time to sit down.

"You made it to the expert rank by accident?" Aten released a frenetic giggle, his eyes a bit crazed. "Then the *Master* rank from completing–what–social quests? Your jump skill, you say? Have you ever actually just… jumped?"

"Just the once." Joe was starting to feel uncomfortable. But then he began thinking about the situation and failed to hold in laughter. He was a *Master* jumper, having only jumped a *single* time. Soon both of them were laughing, but Aten was the first to come to his senses.

"Alright. This is just absurd. Any other skills that are off the charts for no good reason?" Aten looked closely at the cleric, hoping for more ways he could benefit the guild.

"My next highest skill is 'Heal' at Novice rank two," Joe informed the guild leader.

Aten's eyes crossed. "You have a Master rank and your next highest is barely increased at all. Ugh. Alright, well, I guess this doesn't really change anything. I still need you to work with the guard, and I will still work to make sure you are happy in the guild. I'd do that for anyone though. Go get some sleep, and thank you for letting me know about you. I'll try to think of some way to make the jump skill useful to us."

"G'night boss-man." Joe waved and left to find his bunk.

A vivid nightmare about falling was his only memory from sleeping when he woke up the next morning. He was extra groggy as he stumbled to the kitchen, and when he finally found breakfast, all he wanted to do for the first ten minutes was drink coffee. After the first cup went down and the second was half gone, he allowed his eyes to creak fully open. Tiona was sitting across from him, a smirk on her face.

"Not much of a morning person?" she cheerfully chirped

while chomping into a bagel loaded with salmon, various vegetables, and cream shmear.

Joe grunted a few unintelligible words, finally mustering up the energy to speak properly after another long drink of his steaming beverage. "It isn't usually this bad. I swear I slept. Just… poorly."

"Hmm." Tiona tapped on her chin, then her eyes lit up as she snapped her fingers. "Go into your status page, look at effects, and then the active effects page." Joe followed her instructions grumpily, staring through bloodshot eyes at the text in front of him.

Active effects: Rested. After laying in a bed for six hours, no matter how poor quality, you were able to get some much needed beauty sleep. +5% Experience gain for four hours.

Stinky: You haven't showered, bathed, or cleaned your clothes in several days. -2 charisma (Temporary, somewhat mitigated by level increases.)

Addiction I: Your actions have consequences. You are well on your way to developing a severe addiction to caffeine. Intelligence +1, Wisdom -1 after drinking 10 oz of coffee. 30% chance of headache after not drinking coffee for 4 hours.

"Gross." Joe scanned the active effects again, looked at the coffee in his hand and reluctantly set it down. "It says I am rested, stinky, and addicted to coffee."

Tiona smirked at him. "Well that explains it. If you had gotten a good sleep on a good bed, you would have 'well-rested' status right now. Sleep poorly?"

"A bit. It's only been a few days, but it's been pretty wild." Joe looked longingly at his coffee and sighed. "Any showers around here?"

"There sure are, Mr. Stinky!" Her chipper attitude this early in the morning earned her a glare from several people around the table. "They also have a laundry service, so you can get your clothes cleaned at the same time. Let's get going; you are going to need all of that charisma today. I hear you are assigned to buttering up guards?"

"That's what I do, pretend the guards are delicious bread," Joe grunted the best pun he could come up with as they moved toward the bathhouse. She looked a bit green after that one though. After showering and getting into fresh, warm clothes, Joe certainly did feel better. Also, people stopped swerving away from him; he hadn't even noticed that they were doing that! Perhaps that was a side effect of lowered charisma: you couldn't see how your actions were impacting those around you? It did make some sense…

Tiona walked with him to the training grounds that the guards owned and waved at him as he started his mission. Noticing some familiar faces right away, Joe went over to them and started asking how they were doing. Any wounds reopen? Any relapses or pain? Most of the people answered that they felt great, but a few had been injured recently.

As Joe worked to heal them, the guard captain came over to see why the men weren't doing their training or sparring. "What the *abyss* are you all standing around for? Criminals don't rest easy for one reason: because we are fit enough to chase them straight into a cell! Are you giving up on that advantage? You can't be a good guard *and* be lazy!"

"Good morning, Captain!" Joe interrupted as the red-faced man inhaled to continue his tirade. "My apologies, I stopped in to check up on a few of the guards that had been more seriously damaged and my inquiries became a bit too much."

"Huh?" The captain looked over, apparently noticing the cleric for the first time. "Oh! Joe, m'boy! Good to see you. How have things been going? I'm sorry to say that I must get these men back to work."

"Please don't let me get in the way!" Joe smiled and waved cheerfully at the guards as he turned away. "You gents let me know if you need any healing! Always free for the people keeping the citizens safe!"

You have gained +100 reputation with the guards of Ardania. 900 points to reach 'Ally' status.

The captain followed along as Joe strolled down the training field. He glanced over at the cleric and grunted loudly, "Humph! You look like you're after something. Whaddaya need? Money? An introduction somewhere?"

"No, no. Nothing like that. Thank you, by the way, for that introduction at the library. You didn't have to do that, but I'm really glad you did." Joe waited for the captain to nod before he continued, "I'm actually here because I joined a guild."

"Ahh, now we get down to brass tacks. *They* need something, huh?" The captain seemed ready to slap Joe around for answers–high reputation or no–so the cleric quickly got to the point.

"Not quite. They are hoping to become a Noble Guild, and to that end they are trying to find ways to help out around the city. They seem to think that if they can make the city a better place, it will reflect well on the guild. All they asked me to do was what I am happy to do anyway: go around healing anyone who needs it. The only stipulation was that I mention that I am an officer in the guild. Something about me being a good example of their upper echelon." Joe's smile widened as he got a notification informing him that his charisma had increased by a point.

"Huh. You travelers sure do have some strange ideas." The captain was rubbing his chin. "You'll heal *anyone*, you say?"

"I feel like this is going to be interesting, but yes. Is something wrong?" Joe was watching the captain as he struggled with some internal debate.

"Alright. C'mon, follow me." The captain marched toward the small jail that they had in the area. Really, it was just a holding pen under a small fortification where suspects were held until being sent to the dungeons. They walked along until they came to a small cell. The captain opened the door and waved at a heavily bruised and bleeding individual on the stone bed.

"Many of my lads wanted this man to be left to his fate, but if he dies, he won't have been punished enough for my liking. He's a traveler, and you all keep popping up no matter if you die or not. Quite disconcerting, really. This one is the leader of a guild that we suspect burned down a tavern in town. If he dies, he has served his time. If he lives, he gets sent to a punishment dungeon that the Kingdom runs to hold criminals like this. We are able to change his 'bind point' by force, and even if he dies, he will come right back to the dungeon. No escape until time is served." The captain motioned to Joe. "Up to you."

"There are dungeons around here?" Joe stopped that thought and stepped into the cell, looking at the man on the ground. Under the bruises and crusted blood, he recognized the leader of the Hardcores, Headshot. Joe smiled a grim smile. "Cap, I'd be more than happy to make sure this man serves his time. He tossed me off a cliff recently." He stepped forward and healed the crumpled form to full health, then used 'cleanse' until he was sure that Headshot didn't have any poison in his system.

Skill rank up: Heal (Novice III). Healing only people you like will slow down your understanding of how to heal! Heal everyone and every-thing*! Need practice healing? Find a prison, church, or a hospital! (*note: healing to increase the time a person can be tortured will negatively affect alignment.)*

"That should do it!" Joe stepped back and looked at the still form on the bed. "Anything else right away?"

The captain was still looking at Headshot. "He isn't waking up. Are you sure he is fixed?"

Joe didn't know how to describe the man being away from his console. "He is fine, this is a traveler thing. He is… he is meditating in hopes of resurrection. I bet that he will be awake and furious within three hours. Maybe have him transferred by then?"

"He *has* already been sentenced… good call. No resistance this way." Nodding, the Captain motioned Joe out of the cell and re-locked it. "You know, I am worried that he may come looking for you when he is released. I'm told you people are able to see the name of whoever hurts or heals you unless they magically hide it."

He must have been talking about the combat logs. Joe had a feral grin on his face. "I think I'm okay with him knowing." He smiled as he thought of the lock of hair he had taken from the unconscious man. He had dipped it in Headshot's blood as well, and this would make it a powerful focus for one of the nastier rituals Joe had access to.

"Well, if you don't mind, I could use your help keeping a few criminals alive for their trials. I'd much rather see justice done and ensure we got the right person than have them die in custody." The captain grinned when Joe instantly agreed to help him.

Quest alert: Living for justice (Ongoing). Every day, people are arrested. Many of them are critically injured and will perish before trial without help. Some are innocent! Most are not. You have accepted this quest. Rewards: +100 guild and personal reputation with the city guard for every person who survives their time in jail due to your efforts.

Joe thought the reward was a bit high but quickly understood when the captain informed him that everyone else that was captured was doing fine, and though they may be injured, they didn't need healing to make it to trial. So, this quest would only pay out when the prisoner was otherwise fatally injured? Good to know. One hundred reputation appeared on his status, so he knew that healing Headshot had already paid off.

"Where are you staying?" The captain was walking toward the door. "If we need your services, we'll send a guard over to get you."

"Ah, The Wanderers guild is sleeping at a barracks building we rented," Joe informed him as they shook hands.

"Oh, *that's* the guild sleeping there?" He rubbed his chin as he thought. "Well… since you are doing work for the city, I suppose we can get you qualified for a discount. Tell your guild master that we can knock off… say, ten percent?"

"Whoa! Thank you!" Joe exclaimed happily. It was good to be useful to the guild; small benefits like this would help to increase his standing, especially with whoever was in charge of the guild finances.

"No, thank *you*, cleric. While most of the time we only haul in true filth, there *are* innocent people that you might save here. This is the least I could do to repay the favor. We'll let you know if we need you." The captain waved him off and returned to his duties.

CHAPTER FOURTEEN

Joe returned to the guild, getting a 'look' from Aten as he walked in. "Joe, weren't you supposed to be working with the guards *all* day?"

"I have good reason!" Joe threw his hands into the air in a classic surrender pose. "I have secured an ongoing quest with them; they will come find me whenever they need my help. I also come bearing gifts. I got us one hundred guild reputation and a ten percent discount on renting the barracks!"

Aten tried to keep his face straight but couldn't hold back his smile. "Alright, fine, dang it! It took you an hour to get the same amount of reputation we did in a week. Tiona hasn't left yet, so if you want to get out and do some fighting, now would be a good time to let her know."

"Thanks! I'll go find her." Joe walked toward the gates and only had to wait a few minutes before Tiona and the party appeared.

"Joe?" Tiona glared at him. "Look, I know that fighting is more fun, but Aten gave you a mission."

"Mission complete, reporting for grinding. Aten sent me."

Joe saluted with his tongue out as he joined the party and they started walking. "Where to today?"

"Good to see you, man!" Dylan cheerfully pounded him on the back. "You have good timing; we're fighting Wolfmen today. Think werewolf but a wolf standing upright, not a human turning into a wolf. They use poisoned weapons and are usually traveling with a pack of trained wolves. Wolfmen are much stronger than regular wolves and direct their pack during combat. Level seven enemies, so watch it."

"Dang." Joe took a moment to digest all of the information. "Should I really go with you? I'm only level three."

Chad decided to be the one to answer. "I think you'll be pretty valuable on this mission. You can heal, and if my cured hangover was any indication, you can also get rid of poisoning."

"I can, but it is still ranked at novice one. I'm not sure how well I'll do trying to fight a level seven attack, ya know?" Joe chuckled nervously as the others shrugged.

"Gotta get practice to level it up, right?" Dylan hefted his shiny new shield; he seemed to have finally resigned himself to becoming a tank. "Just hang out behind me, and it'll be fine."

Crossing the rabbit's territory was simple; it seemed that there were very few remaining in the area. Apparently, they had almost been wiped out by the zombits before the humans had rallied and went out to slaughter the fluffy abominations. The event had yet to conclude; it seemed that there were zombie rabbits somewhere in the area that no one could find. Crossing the fox zone was a bit… rougher. The foxes seemed to be starving and did extra damage due to their savage hunger. Instead of biting and clawing followed by a swift retreat like normal, they would latch on and try to tear off a chunk of flesh to munch on.

Joe had to heal Dylan a dozen times before they got to the edge of the wolf zone, and the tank was complaining bitterly about his new role. Eighteen foxes had died so far, almost fifty percent more than they normally even *saw* during an outing. Joe was secretly pleased since he had gotten not only some experience from the foxes but also gained an experience multiplier from healing Dylan as they went.

*Exp: 216 (Starving Fox x18) (8 per fox * 1.5 for healing during combat. This includes a bonus from title, as well as points for combat healing.)*

Gleefully planning how he would use the skill point from his next level, Joe almost missed his step. Catching himself on his shield-bearing teammate almost made *him* fall as well. Dylan was already a little worked up from being bitten several times and snapped at Joe. "Hey! C'mon man! Watch where you're going. I don't need to be falling on my face and provoking an attack of opportunity from some random mutt!"

"Geez! Sorry buddy, I was looking at a notification." Joe took a step back and tried to pay attention to where they were going. He started looking around with interest, and his high perception began highlighting details for him that he wouldn't have seen before. Paw tracks that crossed their path, a wet spot on a tree trunk that some animal had marked, and eyes near the ground that reflected a bit of light. "Wolf there! Ten o'clock, he's blending in with the forest floor pretty well."

Chad swiftly drew and released an arrow at the wolf. It yelped, then ran at them in a fury. Dylan braced himself with an ugly mutter about needing to buy heavy armor, but to his relief, the wolf didn't even make it to them. Their final party member came out of seemingly nowhere and slammed his daggers into the wolf's side. It fell with a whimper, and the rest of the team circled up while they looked for any extra wolves.

Joe looked at the forgettable face of the… rogue? Why hadn't he ever talked to him? "Hey, sorry. I didn't catch your name." The rogue looked over, waved, and then continued observing their surroundings. Joe noticed that his facial expression didn't change.

"Guess," Dylan told him as a snarling ball of fur and fury approached them.

"Um. Shadow? Killer? Sneaky one?" Joe laughed nervously as a drooling wolf drew closer.

"No, her name is 'Guess'," Chad informed him. "She's playing a male character in game, but *we* know she's just drag-surfing. Guess is using an old VR helmet with a mental keyboard, and we are pretty sure she has a broken microphone because she never says anything."

"I do too." The voice coming from Guess was androgynous and mechanical, and while it seemed to match the body, there was no real tonal inflection.

"Yeah, you *type* it though; you don't actually *say* anything. That's how we know you're actually a girl, ya know?" Dylan bashed the wolf in the head with his shield, stunning it long enough for Tiona to skewer the creature. "Hey! I got a new skill!"

"Congress," Guess spoke mechanically. "Ugh. Dang auto-correct. I meant congrats."

"Yeah, democracy, Dylan." Chad chuckled as Guess made a rude hand gesture at him. "Shield bash?"

"No, shield mastery," Dylan told them as he read over his skill. "Makes it so I can ignore a small portion of the damage that my shield blocks. Really good for fighting enemies that can knock me around."

"Good, you're slowly becoming an immovable object," Chad taunted Dylan. "Go~o~od little meat shield."

"Maybe I 'accidentally' miss blocking the next wolf that jumps at you?" Dylan mused loudly.

"Enough! We're burning daylight here." Tiona took command as the group started to roughhouse a bit. Until we can find a way to survive outside at night, you all need to keep moving at a good pace. The quest is for ten Wolfmen, and we haven't even found one. Oh, right, Joe you need to be level five to get this quest. Sorry about that."

Joe nodded and they moved along the path again. He dismissed the notification informing him of his twelve points experience from the fight and tried to search out any other trail signs or ambushes. It took nearly an hour of walking, but they finally began encountering Wolfmen along with packs of wolves. "Thank goodness. I was worried we were going to be wandering around the forest for the whole day."

"Alright, remember that the real prize from the Wolfmen Scouts is the antidote vials they have. They are really potent. We can sell that back in the city for up to fifty silver each. *Hopefully*, we won't need to use them if we do get hit, but remember that our lives are worth more than a little silver. I wouldn't like to lose fourteen hundred experience today." Tiona made them get into position.

"That much experience loss?" Joe muttered to Dylan as Chad lined up a shot.

"Yup. Two hundred per level. Unless you are killed by another person, then there is no experience loss." Dylan tried to keep his voice low. Joe got a bit miffed when he realized that the Hardcores hadn't cared about getting red names when they planned to kill him; they had just wanted him to jump so he lost experience.

His ruminations were interrupted as howls rang out. Chad had missed his shot targeting the head, only hitting the Scout in the arm. Three wolves raced toward them while the Wolfman lifted a thin javelin. Chad quickly fired another arrow, but his target's reflexes were excellent. The Scout dodged the arrow and threw his javelin, which was dodged just as easily. Dylan stepped forward and thrust out his shield, knocking over one of the charging wolves. The other two moved around him, one biting his leg while the other engaged Tiona.

Tiona's version of training with her sword was designed to control the flow of battle, and making your enemies attack where you wanted them to was a key component of this path. She swung in specific patterns and chopped brutally and effectively as the wolf moved into the desired position. Its head fell to the ground, cleaved off in one efficient strike. Guess was already engaging the overgrown mutt latched onto Dylan, and she activated a skill that allowed her to stab four times in a blinding flurry. Whimpering, the wolf tried to retreat, but Dylan reared back and stomped heavily on it, breaking its neck.

The final furry beast was back on its feet as the Wolfman jogged closer, and it lunged at Dylan. The powerful warrior was thrown off balance and tackled to the ground as the snarling wolf landed on him. Dylan struggled mightily and was just *barely* able to keep the flashing teeth away from his neck, but then the animal changed targets and tore into his face and shoulder with terrifying brutality. Another javelin flew through the air, finding a home in Chad's foot. The battle had devolved to a brawl, and even with Guess stabbing her daggers into the wolf, it clung to life–and Dylan–tenaciously.

Tiona suddenly bellowed, then imparted a devastating kick to the wolf. It landed on the ground in a poor position before weakly trying to roll back to its feet, but Guess had already landed on its back and was stabbing it repeatedly. The canine dropped and this time *stayed* down. As Tiona and Guess closed in on the Wolfman Scout, Joe dropped down next to Dylan and started pouring healing magic into him. By the time he finished healing the man, the battle had come to a close.

"Dylan, the next time you 'face off' with a wolf, you don't need to be so literal about it." Joe chuckled at the sour look the man sent his way.

Chad dropped to the ground, panting heavily and pointing at thick black lines that were tracing their way through the veins on his leg. "Help."

"Oh, dang! Forgot about that!" Joe rushed over to the fallen archer, pulling out the javelin and healing the open wound. He activated cleanse, and a spout of water drilled into a vein. Wincing, he apologized, "Oops, should have left that wound open a bit."

"Don't care, please stop poison," Chad gasped. Apparently this wasn't a happy little non-painful toxin. Joe poured more and more mana into the process, but his skill level wasn't high enough to negate the effects. He *was* able to slow the spread, but the poison kept doing damage over time. After five minutes of struggle, Tiona walked over and made Chad swallow the antidote that had been on the Wolfman's body. Joe reeled back; the sudden cure had created a bit of backlash on him. He shook his head to clear the lingering pain, and a notification appeared in his view.

Skill increase: Cleanse. While others hope to get well eventually, you fight the issue at its source. Though you weren't powerful enough to stop this poison, it was not due to a misunderstanding of the human body. Your failure was simply because you had not needed to combat this particular damage before. Since you understand this process so thoroughly, and have been able to prove it, skill has increased to (Novice IX).

Holy! Joe was flabbergasted. That meant he had jumped eight skill levels! It was because he used his knowledge of the body to cleanse it? Did that mean… if he healed a body carefully instead of just allowing the power to wash over it… would his skill go higher proportional to his actual knowledge of healing? He just had to *demonstrate* his skill for the system to recognize it? He was determined to do his best to focus his power the next time someone needed to be healed.

"Alrighty, that was a good test run," Tiona announced once everyone was calmed down from the intense fight. "Yes, we lost the antidote, but now we know what sort of fight will be coming our way. Let's work on keeping our formation and targeting together. If we had all been hitting one enemy at a time, they would have died much faster. I was able to kill one right away with a lucky critical hit, but we all saw how hard it was to kill the one that knocked Dylan over."

"Sorry about that. My daggers were too short to penetrate the fur, skin, and any vital points I targeted. I'll try to get at the neck or face next time," Guess volunteered a solution to her shortcomings.

"I got knocked down because I overextended," Dylan grudgingly admitted when Tiona looked at him. "I need to keep my feet planted and my shield up."

"Good. Chad?" Tiona stared at the archer, who was looking anywhere but at the party leader.

He seemed to deflate. "I missed my first shot because I was

trying to be fancy. If I had aimed center mass instead of at his left eye, I'd likely have done a lot more initial damage."

"Right." Tiona held his gaze. "Remember, when we have mastered the basics we can try for more advanced techniques. Joe, where did you go wrong?"

"Me? I don't know, I thought I was doing everything correctly?" Joe looked around at all the mirthful faces. Everyone else knew that Tiona wouldn't like that answer.

Tiona's eyebrow twitched. "So you are saying that there was *no* way for you to improve? All you learned from that battle was… nothing? You may have earned 'exp' but unless you correct your mistakes you won't get real *experience*. Now, try again. How could you have done better?"

Joe thought over the combat. "I could have helped attack the wolf?"

"Not your job," Tiona cut off anything else he might have said. "I'll give you a freebie since you haven't done this before. You were *way* out of position; you need to be in a central location of the group so that you are able to provide healing. You should have pulled the javelin out of Chad and healed him before going to help Dylan. You weren't able to start on Dylan right away because there was a wolf in your way, so you should have done what you could to help in the meantime. Instead, you stood around and waited for the wolf to be out of your way. You need to always be doing *something* in combat."

She thoughtfully paused for a moment. "Also, you need to adjust the settings you are using for your notifications. You are too distracted. Set them to only show when you call them, the importance is high, or you are not doing something else. Doing it like this will also delay level-ups so that you can use them at a fortuitous time. Remember, I expect a proper answer next time."

Feeling a bit attacked, Joe nodded sharply and looked away. He adjusted his settings quickly, but before he could get too down on himself, Chad punched him in the arm. They were walking deeper into unknown territory, and the ranger needed another person to keep an eye on the surroundings. "Take it easy man, all of this is so that we become a better team. It isn't personal, so don't take it too hard. We all went through the same thing with her."

"Right." Joe walked on, trying to find something else to look at. Only a few minutes later, they found another set of enemies. This time, combat went far more smoothly. Joe had to reluctantly admit that talking it out had helped team cohesion quite a bit. They fought for a few more hours, only stopping for lunch. By the time they had completed their quest, it was also time to return to the city. Joe decided to look at the gains from the last few hours and so called up his notifications.

*Exp: 852 (12 * wolf x38 + 20 * Wolfmen Scout x10 + 196 healing bonus.)*

A respectable amount for a day's worth of grinding, but Joe had to wonder how much he would have gained if he were able to stay in town and work on his own projects. He sighed but knew that he needed the combat experience if he were going to progress in the game. They were almost back to town now and hurrying because night was nearly upon them. The sun was dipping below the horizon, and they were not going to make it to safety.

Joe was slowing everyone down. Even with his bonus move speed from adding on his jump modifier, he simply didn't have the stamina for a forced march. "You guys… *pant*… go ahead! I'll be fine!"

"That's not how teams work, Joe," Dylan replied, even as he sadly watched the town gates closing in the distance. "If we're going to die, at least we can do so together, right?"

"We have a chance of surviving." Tiona's voice was cool. "We're in rabbit territory and right next to the town wall. Let's get close and set up camp, putting our backs to the wall. It'll be a long night, but if anyone can survive it, we can."

"No one has survived outside at night," Guess muttered robotically.

"Then we will be the first, and we'll likely get an achievement for doing so!" Tiona scowled at Guess. "Get your rear in gear!"

Now rushing to find shelter by the wall, they were assaulted on all sides by howling and snarling. For some reason, the others began stumbling over obvious obstacles. Joe suddenly remembered that his class had granted him darkvision, and the fading twilight didn't have a negative effect on his sight. They reached the 'safety' of the man-made barricade, getting into formation. If they were going to successfully survive, it was sure to be a long night. Joe looked across the flat expanse and saw creatures lurching toward them nigh silently, and he waited to hear any indication that the others saw them coming. He growled at himself; of *course* they didn't see the monsters coming!

"We have incoming," Joe stated as calmly as possible. "Three big *somethings* coming this way."

He waited for questions about his abilities, but all Tiona responded with was, "Good eyes. Keep watching them and tell us when they are getting too close to ignore."

CHAPTER FIFTEEN

"They're here." Joe's grim words made the others clench their weapons tightly. "They seem a bit confused, as if they don't know what we are. If we hit them hard enough, they might scatter."

To the other members of the party, it seemed that a large shape was suddenly looming over them. Without Joe's advance warning, it was highly unlikely that they would have been able to muster any defense whatsoever. Dylan braced himself and prepared to take the hit from the monster. It was good that he did so, because a massive paw slammed into his shield with enough force to send him to a kneeling position. The wind was knocked out of him and he felt the joints of his arm strained to their limits. Luckily, his appendage only bruised heavily instead of shattering like it should have. Coming to Dylan's rescue, Tiona's return strike landed with perfect timing, lopping off the limb that had attempted to savage her subordinate.

A high-pitched scream echoed out from the creature, which cut off quickly as an arrow entered the open mouth and tore out the back of its throat. The beast fell heavily, and a pool of blood was pumped out of its severed arteries as the straining heart beat out its last rhythm. "Another on your left! Guess!" Joe called over the din of combat.

Guess dropped to the ground as a dinner-plate-sized paw swiped past her head. She sprang up and stabbed a dagger into the creature's armpit, being forced to leave it there as she tumbled away from another attack. The third creature was hanging back, observing the proceedings with a fairly intelligent glare. Joe was most worried about that creature joining in.

Dylan bellowed at the shadow-cloaked creature and charged into it, knocking it to the ground. Guess slashed and stabbed at the beast as if trying to win an award for putting the most knife wounds into a creature without it dying. Sadly, she didn't even come close to setting a new record as the creature died without another chance to regain its footing. The third beast had crept closer, trying to use the distraction to complete a sneak attack on Tiona. Joe tried to warn her, but she was only able to dig a light wound into it before the furry animal tackled and drove her to the ground.

Chad shouted and fired arrow after arrow into the thing, while Guess and Dylan were indisposed. Joe watched as Tiona was mauled by the beast, and her screams pulled him out of his shock. He *jumped* at the beast, covering the few feet in a flash. His scepter arched around him like a baseball bat, and he tried to score a homerun using the creature's head.

Scepter activates ability [Turn Undead]! As zombie is at half health or below, it is disintegrated!

The sounds coming from the creature abruptly vanished, as did its body. Unfortunately, disintegrating the body created a flash of light that could easily be seen across the open plains around the city. Joe had no doubt that they would have more unwelcome company soon. He dropped to his knees to heal Tiona, who was just *barely* holding onto consciousness. Healing water washed over her, and he made sure to try and focus his magic to knit torn tissue together and restore vital fluids in her body. Joe walked through all the steps he knew were necessary, keeping pressure on the wounds, cutting off blood flow where needed, and closing the wounds manually so that mana didn't need to be wasted to create the same effect. When he stopped to take a breath, a deep *gong* sound echoed through the silent night.

Zone quest completed: Waste not... The innumerable bodies left lying in the open have allowed a corruption to take hold of the rabbit population! After much toil, the wastefulness in the area has been forcibly expunged. Total zombie rabbits destroyed over three days: 26,842. Rewards: Based on contribution!

Your contributions: 40 zombie rabbits, 3 Zombie Bunny-Bears (Mystically altered). Ardania reputation: 430. +100 Guild reputation with Ardania. Strength +1, constitution +1, and dexterity +1. Participate more heavily in the future to gain higher rewards!

Zombie Bunny-Bear killed x3. Exp: 150.

Skill rank up: Heal (Novice VIII). You begin to understand much in the ways of healing! Your treatment of wounds has increased, showcasing your skills!

"Wow! I got five levels in my heal spell!" Joe called out in astonishment. "Hey, did everyone else also get stat points from that quest?"

"I did," Chad admitted energetically. "I think everyone who avoided that quest because it was only offering reputation is going to be pretty upset about it tomorrow."

"We might not be able to see it if we die out here," Tiona reminded them of their current plight. "Joe is there anything you can do? Can you see any creatures?"

"Not very close, but I think we will be having trouble pretty soon. That flash of light wasn't exactly inconspicuous," Joe stated flatly as Tiona regained her feet. There was a soft tinkling sound as something fell off her and onto the stones. Joe looked down and saw a gentle blue light emanating from near his feet. "A monster Core!"

He scooped it up and saw the standard notification asking if he wanted to convert the Core into experience. He dismissed it out of hand and smiled. "There actually *might* be something I can do." Taking a swift look around to check if any enemies were closing in on them, Joe then pulled his book on rituals out of his ring and started flipping through the pages. He began muttering as he looked, causing the others to stare at his silhouette. "'Blood boiler', 'Leaden footsteps', 'Overburdened back'… here! 'Predator's territory'!"

Joe looked through the requirements, nodding as he rummaged through the components he had stored in his bag and ring. "Why didn't I think of this earlier? Oh right, Cores are flipping *expensive* and hard to find. Okay, red pepper, wolfsbane, mint, crushed amethyst, pure salt, iron shavings, orange kyanite, three ounces of mercury, and…" he looked around and tried to estimate how much room they would need, "two ounces of silver wire should do it. Nine hundred mana investment, so four-fifty for me. Optional healing potion? Sure. Highest level person's genetic material for strongest setup… Tiona most likely. Double circle around the group. Guys, I need someone to draw a double circle around us. Tiona, I need some blood or… oh, I'll just use what's all over the ground. Perfect."

"Joe, what are you babbling about?" Dylan inquired as Guess shrugged and began cutting into the earth with the hilt of her dagger.

"Quiet, I'm being magical, mysterious, and useful." Joe plopped all the items he needed into the pool of blood where Tiona had lain, and arranged them in the 'mystical' order shown in his book. Once he saw that the second circle was finished, he began a short chant while pouring mana into the ritual. His chant came to an end quickly, but the outpouring of mana continued, straining him to his absolute limits. Nearly collapsing as the components dissolved into the air and swirled around the group, Joe struggled to activate the ritual. He dropped to the ground, entirely exhausted as the monsters that had been creeping closer came to a halt. Ever so slowly, the things that went **bump** in the night shuffled away.

A notification appeared in front of everyone in the circle. *You are standing within the effect of 'Predator's territory'. Since the blood from player [Tiona] was used as a component, all beings to level [18] will be frightened away. Any beings* above *level [18] will be drawn to this area and attack to assert their dominance. A healing potion was used in the construction of this area! If you sleep here, you will leave [well-rested] after four continuous hours of sleep. Wounds will heal twice as fast while relaxing in this area. Time remaining: 7:53 until territory fails.*

"What *is* this? What did you do?" Tiona was incredulous at the effect, and the entire party was now looking at Joe.

"Hello, I'm… amazing." Joe winked at them, but no one laughed. Oh right, it was dark! That's the reason for sure. "It's something I found in the library. Rituals are a type of magic that anyone can use, but they are stupidly expensive and mana-intensive. Since I am basically a human nuclear power plant for mana, I feel like it is the right type for me to learn. Pretty much only utility spells or a long, *long* build up for damage dealing spells."

"Can I look at the book?" Dylan tried to read it, but handed it back right away. "Right, dark out. Sorry, can I look in the morning?"

"Sure thing."

"You could make a *killing* with these mobile shelters though. You created a way to be outside of towns at night!" Chad's eyes were practically cartoon dollar signs as he said this.

Joe was already shaking his head as Chad spoke. "Not really. The cost to create this particular ritual is about… thirty gold."

Choking sounds were heard all around, and Dylan's voice wavered as he spat out, "You spent *three hundred* dollars to create an eight hour shelter?"

"Let me amend that. That's what it would have cost if we had *bought* the Core." Joe nodded and explained a bit of what he knew about the component costs. The others looked wonderingly at the luminescent Core that Joe handed around to them.

"So you blew three hundred gold and five hundred *experience*?" Dylan was even more aghast.

"What can I say? You guys are worth it." Joe laughed at them as they sent rude hand gestures at him, but they did start to laugh along after a moment.

Charisma +1!

Nice! "But after studying the original ritual, I made this one a bit more efficient. So it only cost about *half* of what it normally does, which is why the Core is still here. You need a magic class in order to mess with the formula though." Fibbing a bit was better than explaining his class.

"Alright, thanks to Joe we have a chance to survive the night. Let's try to get some sleep, and we'll pick up here in the morning." Tiona issued her orders and set up a rotating guard schedule. The group settled onto the packed earth and tried to get what sleep they could with the snuffles and howls of unknown horrors around their place of rest.

It wouldn't be a lie to say that everyone was a bit surprised when light peeked above the horizon and they were still alive. Tiona watched shadowy horrors melt into standard monsters and animals. "So they all just transform at night? That explains why no one was able to find their burrows or ambush them during the day. Good to know. Though, I am surprised. I thought for *sure* we were the first to sleep outside at night-" The deep tone of a huge gong cut her off.

Server alert! For the first time, a group of travelers has braved the deep darkness of unprotected night... and survived! Each of them gain +1000 experience and the title '...In darkest night'. This is a milestone moment for all travelers! As you have shown yourselves capable of protecting yourselves in the wild, safe zones such as towns and cities are now available to find... as well as susceptible to night raids by the creatures of darkness! Prepare yourselves, for if you let down your guard through the night, it is likely you will not see morning!

The group went pale and looked at each other. Guess shrugged and said what they were all thinking, "Oops."

Dylan looked at his status screen. "Hey! It's a broken title!"

The others seemed to perk up a bit. Joe spoke up, feeling a bit left out, "Broken? As in, makes us extra powerful?"

"You wish," Chad intercepted the question. "It means the title is only a portion of a full title. It is strong by itself, but you can equip it with another broken title to create a unique saying.

Ya gotta be careful though; if they don't synergize well, you are left with a cool title that gives a crappy effect. The more fragments you add together, the more powerful the title effects are."

"At least in *theory*," Tiona grumped at Chad. "It isn't guaranteed because no one has gained enough title fragments to know for sure."

Joe nodded along with the explanation, and looked at the title for himself. Title: ... *In darkest night. Effect: Gain passive skill Darkvision (or +1 to skill if already unlocked), as well as 50% bonus resistance to dark-aligned magic. This title is broken, combine it with another title to gain additional effects!*

Bonus effect from the Hidden god: This title proves your commitment toward learning the powers of the Hidden god. Dark magic unlocked! Spell learned: Shadow spike.

Shadow spike (Novice I). Effect: Create a spike from any shadow that impales target. Damage if cast perfectly: 10n where 'n' is skill level. (Dark-aligned magic) Cost: 10n mana. Cooldown: None, but hand gestures must be completed to cast.

As you have learned a mage ability, you have unlocked the mage class! Mage class has been absorbed by ritualist class! Would you like to set your public class to mage? Yes / No

Nope. Gonna keep on pretending to be a cleric. Joe looked at the next notification, which was about the experience gained and felt a sudden rush of energy as he leveled up. Golden energy swirled around him, into him, then exploded away as a supernova effect. He was set gently on the ground as the light vanished, and he looked around to see his teammates looking much refreshed.

"Back to town, then?" Guess motioned to the gate that was now standing wide open.

"Sounds good."

Joe looked at his character sheet as they walked towards breakfast. Since he had reached level four, he didn't get any characteristic points to spend, but his intelligence, wisdom, and perception had all increased. Almost as an afterthought, Joe turned off the full status sheet option, selecting to only see character data so his view didn't become overly cluttered as they walked.

Name: Joe 'I'm a healer! I swear!' Class: Cleric (Actual: Ritualist) Profession: Locked
Level: 4 Experience: 6253 Exp to next level: 3747
Hit Points: 50/50 (50+10 per point of constitution over 10)
Mana: 525/525 (12.5 per point of intelligence, +100% from deity)
Mana regen: 5.25/sec (.25 per point of wisdom)
Stamina: 50/50 (50+(0)+(0))

Characteristic: Raw score (Modifier)

Strength: 7 (0.07)
Dexterity: 8 (0.08)
Constitution: 9 (0.09)
Intelligence: 21 (1.21)
Wisdom: 21 (1.21)
Charisma: 13 (1.13)
Perception: 21 (1.21)
Luck: 13 (1.13)
Karmic Luck: 0

Not bad for less than a real-world week in game. Joe looked at all of his stats and decided that he should really start focusing in on his future progression. To this point, he had been *reacting* instead of his normal method of planning carefully and deciding his future. He had gained four more skill points, and while he was interested in becoming a jumping Sage, it would likely be better to devote those points to something more… immediately useful.

They walked through the gates, getting a respectful nod from the guard on duty. Luckily, this early the streets were practically empty, so they didn't need to worry about upset gamers coming to scream at them. They walked to the barracks to report in, getting a mixed response from guild master Aten.

"Guys, I'm really happy you survived and happy for you in general, but please don't spread it around that you are the ones that were outside last night. A *lot* of people are really freaked out right now, and I need to go to a meeting to determine how to protect the city. The players might lash out and blame you for not being able to party all night anymore."

"No worries." Tiona waved at the rest of her team. "Take the day off, y'all. Even if we have the well-rested bonus right now, we all know it was a rough night."

She got nods in return, and the group scattered to pursue their own interests.

CHAPTER SIXTEEN

Joe walked toward the library, the only place he could think of to go relax while everyone else was outside of town desperately trying to level. Aten wasn't wrong when he said that people were afraid of what the night would bring, but to their credit, they were facing this almost gleefully. Weapons were being forged, armor was getting repaired, and fortifications were being erected. While they may not know what to expect, they were trying to be ready for anything. In classic gamer style, they were ready to throw themselves against overwhelming odds.

Walking into the library, Joe was met with a piercing stare from Boris. "Good morning!"

"You level five yet?" Boris cut straight to the point. "That why you're here?"

"Not yet!" Joe cheerfully responded. "I was actually hoping to study up on rituals and see if I can't make them more… accessible."

"Humph. Can't help you there unless you are a scholar." Boris peered at him from behind his spectacles. "You'll have to go to the mage's college to learn more about that kind of magic. Or, perhaps a temple, since you are a cleric."

"A temple?" Joe hadn't even thought about that. It made sense though; his mana was doubled due to the patronage of the Hidden god. Perhaps it wouldn't hurt to go visit his shrines and learn more about him? "Thank you for the information. Also, I'm trying to plan my future. Is there any literature about potential class advancements?"

"Class…? Pah!" Boris released a derisive snort. "You'd have better luck searching a common pig for gold! That kind of information isn't available just anywhere! Class holders hoard the knowledge of their advancement with the same greed and avarice that Dragons exhibit, forcing others to struggle as much as they did if they want to parse their secrets. Knowledge must always be found twice, it seems. What *little* we have is restricted to the highest rankings of scholars, just to ensure a spy in our midst cannot destroy what we have been able to collect."

"Ah. Is that why the city is hiding the fact that there are other paths than just the ones they offer?" Joe's mouth seemed to have run ahead of his wits with this question, because Boris's face darkened instantly.

"No one is 'hiding' that information. Those classes are attempting to recruit, and for good reason. Everyone wants a rare and powerful class, but what happens when you get to your *next* advancement and it is impossible for you to rank up? The *Kingdom* needs third or fourth tier classes in order to survive." The air temperature seemed to drop with his icy tone. "If people are unable to think for *themselves*, and are willing to take whatever class they can find… is that the fault of the *Kingdom*?"

"Ah, sorry, Boris, I-" Joe tried to apologize.

"*Perhaps*," Boris turned his eyes to the papers on his desk, "you should spend this day elsewhere. Perhaps boosting your *wisdom* will help you learn not to spout treasonous conspiracy theories without thinking."

Joe took the hint and ushered himself out of the library. As he stood blinking in the bright light, he had to sigh and slap himself. "I can't believe that just happened." Having no real objectives for the day, he tiredly interrupted a conversation between two citizens and asked for directions to the temple. A somewhat unfriendly person pointed off into the distance, and the people hurriedly walked away.

Joe trudged over to the temple area, and was astounded by the size and complexity of the building. For such a small seeming building, it seemed to stretch a huge distance. The room was dazzlingly bright at one end, and filled with impenetrable darkness at the other. Hundreds of shrines and statues of varying size and ornateness filled the open space. Seeing another person nearby, Joe inquired about how to navigate the place.

"Who's you off ta worship?" Joe winced as the excessively hairy man loudly scratched at the underside of his arm.

"I'm not sure of his name, but he is a neutral god of-"

"Sure, sure." A meaty finger pointed at the north end of the building, then the south, east and west. "North for good, south for evil. East for darkness, west for light. The more well-known or powerful your god, the more ornate their shrine. Have fun."

Joe stood nonplussed as the man walked away. Looking around indecisively, he wandered toward the center of the building. "Neutral alignment, dark and water," Joe mumbled as he stared at the shrines he was passing. In the exact center of the room was what must have been the four purely elemental deities. Neutral and without darkness or light, their altars were grand and incredibly ornate. Most of the people walking around the building were either going toward or away from these particular shrines; looking at each other with distaste whenever their paths crossed.

"Strange." Joe would have thought that people under the same banner would be friendly toward their fellow parishioners. He decided to stay on task; he wasn't here to parse the interpersonal relationships of others. Joe was here to find answers. Stopping at an empty space where a shrine should be, he looked down at the tile on the floor. It had a few simple carvings on it, but otherwise it appeared that there was nothing to be found.

Joe stepped forward, kneeling on what he was *sure* was the Hidden god's space. "Hello?"

Joe blinked and in that instant, found himself transported into a grand temple situated on a mountaintop. Smiling benevolently down on him was the Hidden god, who swiftly shrunk to be Joe's height. "Welcome, Joe! I am *so* glad that you found and visited this place. Since I now have an active 'cleric', I was able to start building my shrine again!"

"Oh, I'm glad." Joe looked around at the empty temple. There were no decorations, no furniture other than the throne, and the place felt a bit… depressing when he noticed these details. "Uhm, I had a few questions."

"What can I do for you? Actually," the glowing figure held up a hand, "just so you know, you can *ask* anything, but I may not be able to answer you. There are rules that I must abide by."

"Gotcha." Joe gathered his thoughts, "I've been here a few days and leveled up a bit, but I'm wondering how I should focus my talents in order to rank up."

"How have you been focusing them so far?" There was a wry grin on the deity's face.

"Well, I got my 'jump' skill to Master. It only took a few skill points, so I'm really hoping that it wasn't a massive waste." Joe waited for a reaction but kept talking before the silence grew awkward. "From here onward, I'm not sure what to do. I was hoping for advice on skill increases and on ranking up."

"Ranking up? Specializing? Don't worry about that for now, you have plenty of time before you reach level ten. Talk to me again at that point, and we'll see if you've earned enough favor for me to be allowed to give you a hint. Bring a map at that point." The dusky face blanched suddenly as he grabbed his throat. He gagged, trying to breathe. After a moment he calmed down. "Said too much. Ow."

"Are you okay?" Joe was looking at the man-shaped being with great concern.

"Remember I mentioned that there are rules? I just bent

one a little too far by offering you advance knowledge that you haven't earned. Action, *re*action. Or should I say *over*reaction," he muttered as he rubbed his neck, a bruise in the shape of a chain forming. "Next, your skills. Don't discount the fact that you have a *Master* rank at level four. Dang near impossible for that to happen, but have you been exploring the benefits of that skill? Have you even jumped *once* since attaining master rank?"

Joe shook his head. "I haven't. Well, I did jump at a monster, but it was only about two feet away. With my health and stamina, I suppose I am pretty nervous about hurting myself again. Not gonna lie, jumping off that cliff might have given me a bit of a fear of heights."

"Yet it wasn't the fall that killed you, and I don't see fear in your eyes when you think of rock."

"That's not the point! The feeling of being totally destroyed like that..." Joe's brow furrowed. "Actually, it doesn't seem that bad now... why?"

A terribly *uncomfortable* look crossed over the deity's face. "Since you asked about it, I can tell you... but are you sure you *want* to know why?"

Suspicion bloomed throughout Joe's mind. "Yes. Why does it not seem so bad now?"

"It is because we numb the pain and remove the trauma from you. Pain, fear, and doubt are interactions in your brain. Why do you think so many people are willing to go out over and over again after being attacked by wolves and having chunks of flesh torn out of them by bears?" the deity answered in a rush of words.

Not knowing how to handle this information, Joe simply decided to think on it later. "Alright, we'll circle back to that eventually. Now, let's go back to talking about skills. I'm Catholic, and the reason I hate using my ability to pray is because it feels sacrilegious to pray to *you*. This really bothers me, more than I've even realized until now."

"Understandable." The god nodded along. "Here is the thing, I'm a god of *Eternium*, I'm not *God*. I am not the creator, I am a part of this… game. Think of using your praying ability like… using a search engine. You send a query or a request to me, I return answers if possible. You know what? I'll update your skill for you if it'll help."

Skill: Pray has been renamed to Skill: Query. All effects and requirements remain the same.

"Thanks, that does help." Joe was much happier about this skill. "If you don't mind, can I talk about you as a *faction leader* instead of a god?"

"Makes no difference to me. Heck, you can call me Tatum. Get away from your discomfort entirely."

"Tatum?" Joe tried to hide a grin.

"Short for 'Occultatum', which is Latin for 'Hidden'." Tatum waved a hand to move the conversation along. "Listen, we're running out of time, do you need answers to other questions?"

"Yes!" Joe was laser-focused once again. "How do I increase my skills faster, and which ones should I devote most of my time to?"

"You should focus on- **gack*." Tatum choked again as he tried to give a direct answer. "*Alright* already! Ugh. Focus on what makes you *unique*. To increase your skills, you need to study them, practice them, and try everything you can think of. When you use them correctly *in ways you haven't before*, you get new skills."

Joe thought on his words, realizing where he had been going wrong. "Thank you. How do I earn more favor with you so I can earn more direct answers?"

The god beamed at this question. "Yes! I can give you a sigil! It is like a crest, or a tattoo for your clothing. In your character sheet, under equipped items, set this sigil to active, and it will appear on your clothes. Then when you gain experience, you will gain favor equal to two percent of that total! Not huge but noticeable!"

"Couldn't tell me unless I asked, huh?" Joe archly challenged.

"Correct." Tatum suddenly vanished, as did the mountaintop temple. Joe found himself back in the city temple, surrounded by shrines and statues once again. Looking down at the floor, it seemed that the flat tile had raised a bit, and the carvings were now slightly more intricate than stick figures.

"Thanks for the help. Hope I helped you too," Joe muttered to the shrine. Before he forgot, he went to the tab in his status and equipped the sigil. A silvery, shimmering pattern appeared on his robe, abstract lines that morphed into a book when you understood what the drawing was supposed to be. "Neat. Alright, now I need to go study my character sheet for more stuff that is hidden away like this." Joe walked out of the grand building, oblivious to the angry eyes that lingered on his sigil as he moved.

CHAPTER SEVENTEEN

As Joe continued moving forward, he tried to deeply examine his understanding of skills. He was a combat medic, which meant that he had a good handle on triage and stabilizing wounds. Comparatively, his actual medical and biological knowledge was much lower. Was this reflected by his heal skill remaining in the beginner ranks when he utilized all of his ability? He could go to the library and read up on all the information he could find, but this felt like a less… effective use of his time.

Tatum had told him to focus on what made him unique, and while healing was rare among humans, there were rumors that other people were gaining the ability. In his character sheet, there were very few things that had the word 'unique' by them. In fact, there were only two. The classes of Jumplomancer and Ritualist. Of those two, only being a ritualist was something that no one else could get access to without first being trained by him. For multiple reasons, it would make perfect sense in this case to focus his training on the ritualist class and abilities. It was his real class after all, and though other people technically had access to rituals, he had the potential to make them so efficient and powerful that he could use them like typical spells. Joe, deep in thought, nodded to himself. It was time to dive headfirst into the mechanics of ritual magic.

There was only one thing more important that he had to do first. Walking around for a bit, he found a cafe and ordered some coffee. Perfect! All set to parse out the mysteries of the universe! Pulling out his book of beginner rituals, he began working to try and understand why they required certain components. Blood or hair was an easy one; it helped the ritual target a specific person or base itself off of their stats, like with the 'Predator's territory' ritual. Silver was a little less obvious to him. Knowing that it was conductive to electricity wasn't very helpful since Joe was fairly certain that the ritual wasn't battery operated. Perhaps it had something to do with the purity of silver?

Skill rank increased: Ritual magic (Novice II). Learn everything!

Well, that answered that question. Was it really so easy to gain ranks in skills? He supposed it was understandable, this was an academic study more than anything else. You gain skill with swords by swinging them and fighting, why not gain skill with magic by trying to understand it? Using it would have more impact in the higher levels, for sure, but simple study was the best way for now. Joe perked up as an idea struck him; it seemed that this game was based as closely to real life as possible, why not study things in real life and relate them to the game? If he was able to gain increases like that… then… he did have an internet connection to the outside world. Since he was in a cafe, he was able to open a screen and connect to Wikipedia. With so many theories of magic as well as real-world facts at his fingertips, he began to understand much more about the potential reasoning for the effects of components.

Hours flew by as he studied, his mind drinking in the ideas with an alacrity he had never found in high school or college. Was his intelligence score here helping him to become actually smart? This was his real body now, wasn't it? His strength made him weak, so this would make sense, though it was a terrifying thought.

How far could he go? Joe grimly decided that he would do whatever it took to boost his stats. This was something that he needed to test. As his self-enforced study session ended, Joe looked at his notifications and had to put on a weary smile. He had made good progress today. Since Joe hadn't looked every time a new message came in, he was able to see the final amount gained in each category.

Skill increased: Reading (Novice VII).

Skill increased: Ritual magic (Novice VIII). Ability score increased: Intelligence +2!

Spectacular! Five ranks in ritual magic and six in reading? The speedy gains were almost assuredly because of his complete lack of knowledge of rituals, but that didn't dampen the achievement. He certainly felt that he now had a better understanding of why some components were used over others, but he also knew he couldn't go around changing them or making his own versions at this point. It wasn't far off though. Joe felt positive that the creation of rituals was something he'd be able to do at the higher levels. Also, he couldn't discount the ritualist class bonus, which was to learn skills four times faster than other people. Yes, the Ritualist class had certainly been the correct choice. He was making progress and felt serious satisfaction from that simple fact.

A more immediate benefit was that ritual magic had reached level eight, so Joe now had a four percent reduction to the cost of rituals. He stood up, his back cracking joyfully when it was straightened. Walking toward the market, Joe noted that it was much later in the day than he had expected; it must be approaching dinner time already! With this thought in mind, he hustled to reach the stores he needed to visit before they closed. His purchases were fairly simple: more components for his rituals, a carving set so that he could have a ritual pattern ready before he needed it, and a standing order for monster Cores from the alchemist. The last was difficult, since the alchemist tried to pry into Joe's reasons for needing so many Cores.

Mentally tired, Joe returned to the barracks. It had been a good day; he had learned quite a bit about himself, as well as set realistic goals for the future. Heh. What a shift 'realistic' had taken. His 'realistic' goals were about magic. Joe nearly fell over as a voice snapped him out of his self-appreciation. Aten was standing in front of him, looking a bit irritated. "Joe! You listening? Good. Tiona tells me that you might have a way to make an area safe from monster attacks?"

It took a second for Joe to nod. "Yes and no. It makes any monster under a certain level avoid the area, but any monster stronger than the repellant will be drawn to the area, avoiding anyone else. It is a… spell… called 'Predator's territory'."

A manic look came into Aten's eyes. "Even better! So we will get to fight only the strongest? That means that we will get the boss monsters and everyone else will only get the standard mob fight? This will be amazing for our reputation and levels! We can use that to recruit: 'Only the strongest and the best come for The Wanderers!'"

Joe felt a bit sick to his stomach at that thought. So. Cheesy. "Yeah, but… the threshold is ten levels above the person whose blood is used in the spell. If we used my blood, we would only draw in a monster if it was level fourteen or higher. I can't imagine what would happen if we pulled in a level twenty or something."

"Levels is what would happen! Reputation! I can picture it now, The Wanderers versus a raid boss… in the center of the capital city!" Aten was unconsciously gripping his sword and slowly drawing it, bloodlust pouring off of him.

"But…" Joe tried to think of some way to reason with this battle-maniac, "if it gets to us here, it means it either got through the wall or can fly!"

Aten cocked his head to the side. "Hmm. Good call. I'll make sure our archers are on duty tonight. Oh, and we even have a first level mage now! Congrats, you aren't the only magical person in the guild anymore!"

"Really? How did he get the mage class?" Joe leaned in; he wanted to hear every detail since the details of the class were so sparse.

"*She* went through classes at the mage's college. We sponsored her so that she could afford it, and I gotta tell you, I really hope her magic is going to be as useful as we need it to be. That place was not cheap." Aten grumbled a bit about this fact. "Hopefully we can pay off the loan before the interest breaks us."

"Speaking of costs, if you want me to run that spell every night I will need some components. Those aren't cheap either." Joe listed everything he needed, and Aten winced but nodded while he explained.

"Gotcha, I'll get us a large stash of those. We won't be able to use the spell every night, but when we see something interesting that we want to fight or if we need a break, I'll ask you to set it up. That work for you? Since it is such a huge imposition, we can call this your guild dues instead of making you pay a percentage of your income."

"Sounds good. Dues? You tax guild members?" Joe's hand twitched toward his coin purse.

"Have to." Aten waved a hand at the building they were staying in. "You think room and board is free? Nah. Plus we need to buy work contracts, then we get reimbursed and paid upon completion. Guild quests cost a couple hundred gold just to accept. That's why the competition is so fierce."

"Set it up for tonight then?" Joe was very interested in keeping his money in his own pocket.

"No, let's wait and see what sort of trouble the city is in for tonight. I'll see if we can get a box of Cores for the guild to use; a few craftsmen have already brought it up." Aten waved goodbye and went off to attend to his other duties.

Joe decided to eat dinner, afterward sitting down and beginning to carve the patterns needed for various rituals. He didn't need to make too many; this was the only component of the ritual that wasn't consumed by activation so he could reuse successful carvings. Some of the symbols were very easy, such as the star enclosed by a circle, or the double circle needed for 'Predator's territory'. The issue arose as the rituals began to have more effects; the patterns became far more intricate than his dexterity allowed him to create.

Skill gained: Carving (Novice I). Are you either an artist, bored, or in your seventies? Then carving is the skill for you! Each skill level increases accuracy of carving by 1% as well as decreasing time to finish by 1%.

Joe looked at the pattern he had been trying to create in dismay. It had been intended as a pattern with graceful, swooping lines, but the final product was destined for the trash can. Perhaps kindling for a fire. The wood had chipped and splintered, the graceful lines instead consisted of hard angles, and it was overall poorly done. He sighed regretfully; perhaps it would be better to have an artist create these patterns for him. Joe's perception was excellent, and although he was able to easily find the flaws in the work… his dexterity left him essentially childlike in his attempts at artistry. Yet another thing he would need to delegate until he was able to improve himself.

Perhaps it would be better to work with the rituals he was able to complete? For instance, Aten had wanted to have the area ready for the ritual tonight, if needed, though he said not to activate it. The ritual would need to encompass the entire barracks, which meant that he needed to get a double circle drawn around the entire structure. Seeing as they were in a temporary dwelling and the ground was stone, carving a double circle was impossible. Perhaps paint would be the best substance to use? Joe asked around but no one in the area had anywhere near the amount of paint that would be needed, and by now, the shops were closed.

Joe was about to throw his hands up and call it a night, perhaps go to bed in an attempt to no longer be frustrated, but then he noticed a group of children drawing on the cobblestones across the street. Light filled his eyes, and he went over and asked the kids if they had any spare chalk. The adult watching them seemed to be trying to stare through Joe's skull but relaxed when all Joe did was accept a large chunk of chalk in return for a few coppers. Walking around the building, Joe tried to make lines every few feet so he could connect them and make a complete circle. After finishing the preliminary marks, he followed them around the building twice, enclosing the structure. Using his personal stock of ritual components, he placed them in the correct positions and began empowering the ritual.

Something felt different instantly; his mana started tearing out of him at a far greater pace than ever before. Joe gasped in pain and dropped to his knees while his energy was drained away. Attempting to cut off the flow didn't work, and he watched with trepidation as his mana dropped below half full. His mana regen of a little over five per second was doing its best to keep him standing, but couldn't keep up with the powerful drain. He fell forward as his mana dropped below a quarter and could hardly breathe as his power reserves fell to zero.

Agonizing pain tore through him then, and his health began to fall in place of his mana. The pain stopped and restarted every second as his mana regeneration kicked in and allowed a few extra points of energy to flow into the ritual. His health fell all the way to fifteen points before the ritual finally had enough mana to satisfy itself. As his pool of power began to slowly recover, Joe wheezed, coughing noisily as he sat up. With a trembling hand he pulled up and looked at the notifications which now appeared as a combat log.

Ritual: 'Predator's territory' initiated. Caution! Missing component 'blood'. Caution! Ritual size larger than recommended for a single person to perform! Caution! Ritual pattern is malformed! Calculating added requirements due to issues… +200 mana required! Mana drain increased. Insufficient mana, drawing from health pool. Blood added to ritual via damage to [Joe]! -100 mana required. Ritual complete! Activate ritual now? Yes / No

Joe selected 'no' with a sour expression. The chalk surrounding the building took on a red glow, which interested Joe enough that he tried to rub some of it away. It didn't budge or scrape off, so Joe felt confident that it would remain until it was activated. Looking at the notifications, Joe snarled into the empty air, "So it starts pulling from your health pool unless you have enough mana? I never saw that mentioned anywhere! I won't be forgetting this anytime soon, stupid never-explained magic."

Wisdom +1!

Skill increase: Ritual magic (Novice IX).

He snorted at the new notification. "Now I feel like someone is just messing with me." Ritual ready to go, body and mental power drained, Joe gave himself over to his exhaustion and went to bed.

CHAPTER EIGHTEEN

Waking up the next morning without having to fight anything or have anything trying to kill him felt almost… anticlimactic. Joe stumbled out of the rock-hard bed he called his own and owlishly stared at anyone who came too close. Imagine his surprise when a pink-and-blue haired girl plopped down across from him and gave him a brilliant smile. "Hi there! I'm Terra. Are you the other magic user in the guild?"

"Mhmph," Joe grunted as he tried to adjust his eyes to her eye-damaging color choices. She basically shimmered, and he hoped she was just wearing glitter and it wasn't somehow part of her character. Her hair was pink with blue highlights, and her eyes were bright green. Joe–very used to the modest colors he normally wore–thought she looked a bit like a parrot.

"Awesome!" Her enthusiastic tone made everyone in the room who was not a morning person wince theatrically. "I just got back from an awesome ten-kay jog, and I was hoping to see someone else perform magic! You are a cleric, right? Like, how does healing magic work compared to elemental magic? Can I watch you do a few spells or something?"

Joe thought very hard but could not come up with any real

reason to deny this request. He looked around the room until he saw someone holding their head in pain. Motioning them over, Joe used cleanse on them, curing their hangover and sending them on their way. He looked over at Terra expecting her to be excited, but she was just looking at him with her eyebrows raised disdainfully.

"Really? You don't direct the mana or work to control it?" She looked at him up and down. "I didn't think you were on a mental keyboard; you look like you are actually coffee deprived."

"What are you talking about?" Joe was shocked into answering her. "Of course I controlled that spell, didn't you *just* see me direct it through his entire body?"

"Yeah, sure, but I meant you didn't control the way your mana left *your* body. I mean, seriously, if you already have the mana channels, why not use them?" Terra seemed confused by Joe's non-reaction. "You don't have them? Oh my gawd, using any amount of mana at all must, like, exhaust you! You can seriously hurt yourself like that."

"I have no idea what you are talking about," Joe informed her firmly. Her valley-girl way of speech was grating on his nerves, and he wanted her to either get to the point or go away.

"Wow, you are *so* lucky I came along to this guild!" Terra flipped her hair over her shoulder and smiled happily. "Let's get you learned! You have a mana pool and mana channels. If you use a spell without directing the power through the channels–sure it is faster–but you get tired and sore really fast, right?"

A few of her words resonated with Joe. "So if I had a huge mana pool and used all of it at once…?"

"You'd probably hurl or pass out. Maybe bleed all over the place or something." Terra smirked at him smugly. "Guess *what,* though? I can teach you how to fix yourself! I *am* a licensed mage, after all!"

"You need a *license*?" Joe nearly choked on his coffee as he took a long drink.

"Right? Whatevs though, let's get started!" Terra grabbed

both his hands and leaned toward him. Joe's face turned crimson as a few people in the room whistled at them. "Okay, where is your pool of mana?"

Not understanding what she was asking, Joe pointed at the interface in the corner of his vision that showed a full mana bar. She shook her head violently and laughed. "That's your mana *bar*, silly! You need to meditate and go 'into' yourself to find your center. I'll show you."

Terra used skill 'guided meditation' on you! Accept? Yes / No

Joe accepted eagerly. His breathing slowed and his mind cleared of distractions. He felt a warm light in his mind, and he followed it deeper inside of himself. He followed the light through dark, twisting tunnels until finally, a kaleidoscope of brilliance formed in the distance. Turning the final corner, Joe found himself staring into a tiny, twisting hurricane of blue and black light.

"Woah," Terra's voice echoed into his mind. "You have a *buttload* of mana."

"Is this a lot?" Joe smiled as he watched the powerful clouds of energy. "I get a boost to my mana pool from being a cleric."

"I should see if I can switch! I could cast *so* many spells…" Terra stated wistfully. "You need to condense this stuff and start it moving through your spell channels. Think about it shrinking, condensing, and then *will* it to happen. Make it an orb that spins, and use as much force as you can."

She hadn't led him wrong yet, so Joe stared at the mana and tried to make it pack together. He felt his mind reach into the storm, and the edges of the turbulent energy began to smooth. Excited, he pushed harder. The storm started to take on a spherical shape, expanding at the bottom and shrinking at the sides. It compressed smaller and smaller, also becoming much brighter as the mana was forced together. When it was nearly half the original size, Joe found that it wouldn't go any further. He stared at it angrily, pushing and shouting with his mind until a nasty headache bloomed.

Skill gained: Coalescence (Novice I). You have taken the first steps on the path of the mind! By collecting your mana in an orderly form, you will be able to pack more mana into a single usage, with far greater effect. +1% spell efficiency and +1% mana regeneration per skill level. Wisdom +1. Increase your wisdom to coalesce your mana to a higher degree. (Maximum 50% spell efficiency.)

"Awesome!" Joe exclaimed when he finished reading the description. "What does spell efficiency do?"

"It makes your spells cost less mana." Terra was staring at the contained storm clouds. "What kind of ridiculous wisdom score do you have?"

"Oh, ha, yeah," Joe nervously babbled. "Uh, it's a cleric thing. Healing someone is based off of your wisdom… or something like that."

"Ah, that makes sense," Terra nodded knowingly. "Okay, step number *two*! This one is usually harder because people don't have enough mana, but somehow I think you will get along just fine. Grasp some mana, keep it attached to your mana pool like a string, and start pulling it along these tunnels. Just walk and pull. The more mana you are able to bring along on the first pass, the better your bonus will be at the end."

"Alright." Joe tried to grab some of the cloud, but it was… well… a cloud. Rolling his eyes, he tried to pull it along with his mind. Nothing happened at first, but after focusing harder, he was able to force a tendril of mana to slither out of the orb. Grunting in what he was sure was a charming manner, Joe slowly coaxed as much of the energy along as possible. As he got the hang of controlling the thread of power, he started walking along the twisting tunnels with his mind. The thread followed Joe, and Joe followed Terra. He was very lucky that she knew where to go, else he would have been lost a dozen times over. Looking back, a trail of light followed Joe as far as he could see. He turned another corner, and his mana pool was back in sight.

"Are we… lost?" Joe asked Terra a bit reproachfully.

"Where did you think we were going?" Her voice was

confused. "Now just reconnect the mana to the pool, and you're done!"

"Oh. Sorry about that, I thought we were… actually, I had no idea what to expect." Joe stepped forward and directed the energy back into the pool. As it connected, mana began to pulse along the line, and another message appeared in his view.

Skill gained: Mana manipulation (Novice I). Where others are content to throw unseemly amounts of power into a spell–swiftly fueling their own destruction–you use a lighter touch. -30% mana. +1% mana and +1% spell efficiency per skill level. (Maximum 25% efficiency). Intelligence +1.

Joe's face moved from confusion, to shock, to outrage. He sputtered, "T-thirty percent mana pool loss?" He opened his status, and–sure enough–his mana had dropped from what should have been five hundred seventy-five mana… *all* the way down to four hundred and two point five. His shock brought him out of his meditation session, and Terra responded nonchalantly.

"Yeah, thirty percent loss. It's rough, but you start increasing your mana pool at the student rank, and if you make it to Sage you can get up to, like, a *seventy* percent mana boost." It appeared that she couldn't read his thunderstruck expression very well. He. Was. Not. Amused.

"That's *obviously* why it is such an issue for mages at the beginning, but it is *so* worth it in the end! You rank up the skills by getting your mana pool down to zero over and over. For coalescence you focus on shrinking the mana pool as it refills, keeping it as small as possible the whole time. Helps boost wisdom over time, too. For mana manipulation, you work your power to use that open channel while you cast. You gotta kinda… um, make it stay on that path? Try it; it's way easier to understand it that way."

Joe wanted to be upset, but he swallowed his frustration and cast a ranged heal on a random passerby. Casting using the mana channel was a strange feeling, but he also instantly felt the difference. Instead of only seeing the effect after casting, he could now feel the power flow along his body. It was similar to grabbing a live wire, a kind of... *tightening* that forced his body to respond. A ball of water splashed on the lady passing. She sputtered as water dripped down her face, then glared and gave him a rude gesture. Whoops. That was the server. Joe suddenly felt the need to leave a really good tip.

"The more mana that passes along the channel, the wider it'll grow. At its max size, it'll bump open a new one. When you have all *seven* open, you are a Sage ranked mana manipulator!" Terra seemed to have stars in her eyes. Actually, with the burning ambition he could see, Joe thought that a forest fire was a more accurate representation.

"Seriously, I know I'm grumpy, but thank you for teaching me these skills." Joe nodded at her and pushed his cold coffee away. "Is there anything I can do to repay the favor?"

"Well, learning that skillset without guided meditation costs nearly a thousand gold from the mage's college." Terra's words nearly made Joe's eyes pop out of his skull. *Ten thousand dollars* for those skills? "Luckily, the guild paid the fee for me. So now all I need to do to earn my officer's cut is train our members and participate in raids. Teaching you paid off ten percent of my debt to Aten, but if you want to thank me more personally, feel free to heal me whenever I need it and resurrect me if you ever learn how. Otherwise I do accept cash. I'm thinking of making, like, a tip jar?"

"Um. Sure thing. Thank you again, this will be really helpful. Eventually." Joe received a wink in reply, and Terra flounced off to do... whatever it was she did. Joe looked at his mana again, a bit forlornly. He was now *under* the minimum required mana for most rituals that he had seen. Only the *very* basic ones were available to him at this point. Joe wanted to dump points into the mana manipulation skill, but stopped himself before he did something he was sure he'd regret. He needed to save those points, but he also needed to have enough mana to use rituals, and he... Joe barely stopped himself from screaming. Everything needed skill points!

Joe tried to calm down. Think good thoughts now. Inhale.

Exhale. He could level these skills up quickly, he was certain of it. Mana manipulation was based off of how much mana you used correctly? Mwahaha. Well, he could empty out his entire not-quite-as-massive mana pool easily with a single ritual. He paged through the ritual book, marking down which rituals were available to him at this time. 'Little sister's cleaning service' would just about clean *him* out, which was perfect for leveling his skills… but he had no real need for the effects.

'Predator's territory' cost *about* four hundred and fifty mana, a bit less with his skill increase. Too expensive to use right now. He was rather glad that he had set one up around the guild area before he learned these… useful… skills. The only other rituals he could complete right now were nasty debuffs that lasted through death. Leaden footsteps and overburdened back. Leaden footsteps was interesting; it would increase a person's weight fivefold whenever they weren't in contact with the ground. This would make swimming, jumping, or flying nearly impossible.

Overburdened back would make any single item not equipped weigh the maximum amount the targeted person could carry. Joe could see some utility with this one beyond being a curse. If this was used when someone was carrying something massive, it would actually *reduce* its weight to something manageable. Unfortunately, he couldn't think of a time where anyone would only want to carry *one* item with them. Maybe a competition of some kind?

Both of them cost seven hundred mana, but his class would make them usable for him by halving their requirements. Unfortunately he was out of Cores for his rituals, so it was currently a moot point. Not only that, but creating the rituals *just* to create them would be incredibly wasteful. Sighing in frustration, he decided that he would grind up his new skills today by joining Tiona and using as many spells as possible.

Looking at the time, he found it was already eight in the morning! Joe cussed softly and made for the city gate. In his rush out of the building, he tripped on a crate. He was in pain, and his mind was making rhymes! Snarling, he debated healing his stubbed toe, but in his hurry, he decided against it. Sprinting, he arrived at the gate. Turning his head, he puked as his stamina hit rock bottom and the physical side effects hit him. Collapsing to his knees as he looked around for his group, Joe hoped that he wasn't too late. As it happened, they were just walking up and looking at him with great concern. …Dang it. He explained his morning between gasps and about how he lost track of time. All he got in response to his tale were a few laughs at his terrible stamina.

They set out at a much more moderate pace, their mission once again to hunt Wolfmen. The rabbits ran away as Tiona approached, her high level causing a fear status in the weak creatures. She laughed at that; apparently level nine was the threshold for rabbits to become terrified. Foxes would still attack them if they got too close, but staying on the now well-traveled paths allowed for very few encounters. There *was* a small side effect from being on high alert and not being attacked; when they reached the wolves, the entire group was antsy and spoiling for a fight. In their rush to burn off some nervous energy, they decided to attack any wolves they saw along their path.

Chad pointed out a small pack drinking from a shallow pond, and everyone moved into position. He fired an arrow, which lodged deep into his target's flank, eliciting a howl and a response from the others. Joe's eyes narrowed as he saw the wounded wolf moving toward them at a much slower pace than normal. This was his chance to try his first attack spell!

Focusing on his mana, Joe directed it to his hands through the newly opened channel… and cast shadow spike! It felt a bit strange to see the spell impact the wolf because there was no indication that the spell had come from Joe. The wolf was staggering toward them and never even noticed its own shadow bunching up and spearing him from below. The shadow returned to its normal form, and the wolf's entrails poured through the gaping hole. Joe was almost ecstatic about how effective the spell had been, but a touch of sleepiness made his mind a bit fuzzy from the spell cost. Since it was a mage spell–and he was playing as a 'cleric'–the spell cost *fifty* mana for being a non-class ability. Well, *technically* the spell cost forty-nine point five mana because of the one percent spell efficiency from his new skills.

Still, it took an *eighth* of his total mana to cast that spell a single time. Before condensing and directing his mana, using that much power at once had caused a serious wave of fatigue. Thinking it through, he found that he had no real complaints. The spell was spectacularly effective, and even the huge mana cost would be good for increasing his manipulation skill. A touch of sleepiness? That was manageable. Joe was torn out of his self-analysis by a scream of pain almost directly in his ear. Tiona's wrist had been caught by the pack alpha, rendering her sword useless as the canine shook her brutally. Her sword clattered against a rock as she dropped it, and the wolf was able to throw her body to the ground.

The snarling beast lunged at her neck, and Joe saw that there was no one near enough to help her. He made the gesture needed to cast shadow spike and felt his mental energy drain once again. Joe's hands hadn't been very accurate with the rushed motions, so even though the spell fired off properly, it drained almost fifty percent more mana and seemed far weaker than it should have been. He shook his head to clear out the sudden cobwebs, watching the results of his action.

The shadow had lurched up from underneath the animal, impaling him as he leapt for Tiona. He landed on her and the flat base of the short lived cone-shaped spike used the impact of their bodies to drive deeper into the chest of the meaty creature. It thrashed for a moment but fell still as it bled out. Tiona needed to wait for rescue as the horse-sized body started to crush her; her wrist was obviously damaged–possibly broken–and she was in great pain. When the last of the animals fell–a far easier task without the alpha guiding them–Dylan was able to push the creature over without it further injuring the already wounded woman.

Joe hadn't been idle; he had begun healing his party leader as soon as he could get access to her. The heavy body had been inflicting minor crushing damage every second, but the amount of health being taken was fairly small. He was confused; for some reason, he wasn't able to bring Tiona past three-quarter health. When the wolf was off of her, he found that the bones in her wrist hadn't been able to set. He pulled her hand into the correct configuration and healed her again; this time her health reached full. Oh, thank goodness; it was just a major sprain, puncture wounds, and dislocation. Her constitution and strength must be *massive*!

"Thanks for the healing." Tiona was rubbing her hand and took a moment to wipe away the sweat and tears threatening her vision.

"I'm glad to do it. For some reason, I wasn't able to set your bones with magic." Joe was searching his memory for any time he had healed a bone, but he realized that he hadn't needed to fix any of them. Mainly because magical healing was a rarity so people were fairly good at setting bones and performing first aid. Their bones healed pretty fast in this magical world, and he now realized that he had only ever fixed various flesh wounds. In fact, the only time that he had healed serious organ damage or broken bones was when he had fallen off a cliff and splattered all over the stone below. Was he able to heal himself to a greater degree than he was able to heal others?

"Not surprising. You'll get there." Tiona was standing, and it was obvious to Joe that the trauma of the fight was already vanishing from her memory. He shuddered a bit at the intrusion into their minds. "What *is* surprising is how the wolf died. Did you cast an attack spell?"

Joe choked on his words as he began to wave her question away but realized that hiding his ability was foolish. This was his team, and he needed to trust them. Hiding his ritualist class was needed so that he retained all the experience bonuses, but this? "I did! I got access to it when we got that title for staying outside overnight. My deity is one of at least water and darkness, and maybe I'll be able to learn more spells as time goes on. This spell is called 'shadow spike', and I got it as a bonus reward on top of the title."

"Awesome! Now we have two ranged damage dealers so we can take on tougher enemies. How much damage does the spell do?" Chad put out a hand for a high-five.

Joe slapped the outstretched palm and winced as the disparity in strength between the two caused his hand to throb. "Right now, only ten points of damage. It does ten points per skill level, but the cost doubles with each level as well. Takes about two seconds to cast correctly, but if I dump extra mana into it, it seems that I can cast an inferior version faster."

"Oh? How many times can you cast it in a row right now?" Tiona's eyes gleamed as she planned out their next fights.

"Only eight correctly cast versions before I am totally out of mana," Joe stated almost sadly, though no one else understood why. They thought that was perfectly reasonable for such a powerful spell.

Tiona did some quick math in her head. "Alright. Healing is pretty cheap for you though, right? That makes perfect sense, using non-class related skills costs more stamina for us, why wouldn't it cost you more mana for spells? In that case, during battle I only want you to use the spell a maximum of five times. That way you will have enough in reserve to heal us if we get put into a tight spot, but you'll still be able to contribute to the fight more directly. Also, that spell seems really hard to avoid. I didn't even see it cross the distance between you and your target."

"It should be difficult to avoid!" Joe chuckled with glee as he realized that having non-class skills wasn't out of the ordinary. He could flaunt his abilities a bit more with this knowledge. "It uses the target's shadow to attack them and seems to move at the speed of darkness."

"Speed of darkness? Faster or slower than the speed of light? Hey, looking at the bodies I don't know if it did full damage to the wolves, but it might have." Guess chimed in as she inspected the corpses. "It's great, but remember that these are just animals with no magic resistances. Monsters and bosses will almost certainly be able to ignore some of that damage, so keep that in mind. Also, now that you have a damaging spell, I think we should have you go hunt foxes all on your lonesome soon."

"Will do. Thanks all, I'm glad you are so happy about this." Realistically, Joe expected them to be a little miffed that he hadn't told them about his spell earlier. He now saw that *he* would be pretty upset if one of them were doing his job; what if suddenly Chad had been able to magically heal without telling him? Bleh. As they walked, a notification popped up since combat was complete and his stress levels had decreased.

Exp: 48 (Wolf x4)

Skill increased: Mana Manipulation (Novice II).

Not bad! Every little bit helps.

CHAPTER NINETEEN

Hunting ten Wolfmen was complete in under an hour. The number of Wolfmen in the area seemed to have increased dramatically now that they were being actively hunted. Was it a response from the game? Perhaps their tribes were just sending out more patrols? Regardless, after completing their daily hunting quest, the group wanted to head back to work on their individual projects. Tiona relented but informed Joe that his job was to hunt foxes until the sun began to drop and he needed to get behind city walls.

Fairly pleased about this task, Joe readily agreed. He had gained six hundred and ten experience from the wolf hunt, a pretty solid haul for an hour of fighting. Sure, it took about two hours of walking to get there and back, but it wasn't a waste. Joe needed just over three thousand experience to get to level five, which would unlock his profession. Then–according to Tatum–he would get massive bonuses from his research and could live in the library for awhile. After assuring the others that he would be fine hunting alone, he waved them off and waited for them to leave his area. Then he smiled, opened his character sheet, and set his class as 'mage'.

Quest updated: Playing your fake role II. As a mage, your job is to output as much damage as possible in as short a time as you can manage. If you want to be a believable mage, your ambition needs to be even higher than an actual *spell slinger! Learn three mage spells 1/3. Get one mage-type skill to the beginner ranks 0/1. Kill five enemies within ten seconds by using spells 0/1.*

Well, dang. This quest was going to take awhile unless he was able to get an area of effect spell, but the reward was pretty great. How was he going to manage this? Somehow, he felt that a fireball spell was out of the question for him, with his affinity for water and darkness… well, at least it probably wouldn't be very effective. Technically, he *was* able to learn *any* type of magic because of his class. Setting his combat notifications to be read at the end of his training, he decided to begin the hunt! Cracking his knuckles and smiling at his soon-to-be victims, he dove into his grisly business. Joe was here to kill foxes and chew bubblegum, and as far as he could tell, bubblegum didn't exist in this world.

Looking around with narrowed eyes, Joe tried to see any hint of fur in the area. The red fur stood out against the green grass pretty well if you paid enough attention, and his perception let him paint targets easily. Sighting one fox stalking an inattentive rabbit, Joe started the gestures needed to cast shadow spike. It took about two full seconds for the spell to be cast properly, and the difference between the hastily cast spell he used on the wolf and this proper cast was instantly noticeable. The spike formed under the animal faster, looked more solid, and was several degrees darker. The fox was lifted off the ground, impaled through its stomach. The spike vanished quickly, leaving the mewling fox to bleed to death over the next few seconds.

Joe felt bad that he wasn't able to finish off the fox in one blow, as he really didn't want the poor thing to suffer. The next time he saw a fox, he specifically targeted its head with the spike. Unfortunately, right as the spell completed, the fox whipped its head in Joe's direction, and the spike missed completely. It crouched down, growling at Joe but not moving to attack just yet. Joe glared at it as he finished his spell again, feeling the mana move through his body and form into a spike under the animal. The shadow punctured the small skull, and the fox thrashed only for a moment before expiring with a sigh.

Joe spent the next few hours tracking down foxes, impaling them, and doing his best to boost his skills. With every cast, he tried to utilize his channels correctly while thinking through every aspect of his spell. On his twenty-first kill, the mana drain seemed a bit more intense than usual. As he was currently set as a mage class, the mana cost was negligible and replenished by the time he finished the next spell, so he wasn't sure if he was just imagining things. He took a moment to read his newest notification, intentionally ignoring the others.

Skill increase: Shadow spike (Novice II). Spell damage if perfectly executed: 20. Mana cost: 20.

Perfect. His attempts to use specific portions of shadows so he would hit critical areas must be helping him to understand his spell a bit better. He kept on tracking and attacking, leaving all the bodies where they fell. Hopefully this small amount of bodies wouldn't be enough to spawn a zone quest because he couldn't pick the bodies up. He was only wearing clothes, a ring, and his robe while carrying a scepter, and he was *already* nearly overburdened. His strength modifier was a serious hindrance, and he swore to himself that he would get strength and constitution to a basic human level as soon as possible. Until then, he had to hope that he wouldn't set off a zombie fox apocalypse.

A few experience points later, he stopped to examine the wound that his shadow spike made in an animal. It tended to leave a large hole in the pelt, and as far as he could see, there was no way to know that the damage was caused by magic. It looked the same to him as if a spear had been thrust into the creature. Releasing a huff of air, Joe decided that he needed to see the spike more closely if he was going to understand how it worked. He stepped into the shadow of a tree and cast the spell, keeping a close eye on where the spike was intended to appear.

Thud. The spike slammed into the tree, vanishing an instant later. Joe cast the spell again, getting a bit closer. *Thud*. It was really strange to watch this process; the shadow of the tree bunched up and rose from the ground while the remainder of the shadow… brightened wasn't the correct word. There was no extra light, but… perhaps the colors in the area were easier to see? They penetrated the gloom under the tree as though the color saturation was higher, the hue more vivid than it should be. The effect only lasted a fraction of a second, so it was hard to study.

Joe started to cast the spell again but this time tried to keep an active connection of mana to the spike. Nope. Again! Didn't work. The third time though, the spike seemed to last just a *tiny* bit longer. Joe tried one more time, and the spike shot off the ground, and stayed impaled in the tree. Mana was flowing out of him, but the drain didn't affect him too much since he had such a high regeneration rate. In the corner of his vision, a notification was blinking at him, so he focused on it even though the spike vanished as his attention wavered.

Skill gained: Channeling (Novice I). Spray and pray? Fire and forget? Not this *mage! At seventy-five percent spell cost per second, you can maintain a connection to a spell that would otherwise use up the mana allotted to it, increasing its effect over time. -.2% cost and +1% spell damage per second per skill level.*

Joe marveled at the potential this skill offered. If he maintained his shadow spike for ten seconds, it would gain an extra two points of damage. Or, was it one percent of the *current* total? That would mean that after ten seconds it would do fifty-two points of damage. Not great when he was hiding his class, true, but… this was exactly what he needed in order to boost his mana manipulation and coalescence. Holding shadow spike active would burn through fifteen mana per second. Even with his mana regen, he could only hold the spell for roughly forty seconds before he was tapped out.

Would holding the spell for that whole time cause the damage to be eight hundred per second? Or would that add four damage to the spike right now? He had to test this! What about even at the *beginner* level? Channeling would either add one damage per second or *ten* per second! He didn't have the mental skills to add up the possible damage at the higher levels, but this was certainly an ability he would be working on. Finding a fresh fox to attack, he channeled his spell into it!

His math had been *really* wrong. Joe had for some reason seen one percent - or 'point one' - as 'ten percent'. It was *one* percent. That… it was fine. The results were good even if he would have been failing basic math right now. He just couldn't kill a dragon over ten seconds as his dreams had foretold. It seemed that the damage accrued as the *current* total, and after checking the combat logs, he was again happy with the new skill. The first second did twenty damage, then twenty point two, all the way to his current maximum of twenty-nine point five. Altogether, this single spell did nine hundred and seventy-seven damage at full power! Now all he needed to do was figure out how to make a live enemy hold still for forty seconds as it took damage. Hmm.

Too excited to spend more time grinding foxes for minor bits of experience, he started walking back to town. Though his class ability of darkvision meant that his sight wasn't inhibited, it was just evening and the shadows were thickening; so he didn't think Tiona would mind too much. Distracting himself from the boring travel, he looked at how much experience he had gained. He had killed thirty-two foxes, netting himself two hundred and fifty-six experience. Not bad at all. As the gates came into sight, Joe screeched to a halt and quickly set his class back to cleric. Whew! That was close, he almost…

"Joe!" a guard called out to him, startling him enough that he almost dove to the ground to avoid an assumed attack. "Joe, got a job for ya. Captain wanted me to let you know that we have a couple people in the slammer. Cut each other up real good, but if they die, their families will start a blood feud. Head on over if you want to help prevent a civil war." He sent a wink at Joe, implying that he was exaggerating a little bit.

"Will do, thanks. Anything you gents need before I head on in?" Joe smiled at the guards, always on the lookout for reputation gains.

"Sure!" the guard standing on the other side of the gate called. "I hear you are good at fixing up people who… err… celebrated a bit too much before duty?"

Joe looked at the guard, and under his helmet he could see the poor guy squinting and sweating. Joe snorted, then cast cleanse on the hungover protector of the people. Just as he was about to call it good, a flash of inspiration caught Joe and he attempted to channel more mana into the spell. Was it only good for mage spells…? It worked! A stream of water connected the two men, rushing from Joe's hand into the veins of the startled guard.

The spell cut itself off after a short while, much to Joe's surprise. The guard seemed to stare into the distance for a moment, then broke into a happy grin. "I've never seen this buff before! It allows me to have ten percent gain on strength and dexterity related skills for the next two hours!"

"*What?*" the other guard yelped. "I want it too! What is the buff called?"

"Looks like… 'well-hydrated'." The first guard had looked at his status to read the name off. "I feel really good."

"Can I have it too?" the second guard implored Joe.

"Sure thing, but then I need to go heal those guys in jail." Joe channeled water into him, then hurried to the jail. He was excited that he could now *force* people to have the proper amount of water in them. What his drill sergeant wouldn't have given for this ability!

"Joe!" Joe turned as he saw the captain approaching him across the training grounds. "I need you to heal-"

"Lead the way, I heard they're in a bad way," Joe called back, not slowing his pace. The captain nodded, easily matching Joe's jogging speed, which anyone else would have called a casual stroll. Joe's stamina was dropping swiftly, but he wasn't at the point of puking just yet.

"This is a bad situation, Joe," the captain explained seriously as he opened the door to one of the cells. "These two are from noble houses, and if they have killed each other, we will likely have a civil war on our hands."

"He was serious?" Joe muttered in shock as he remembered the cheeky wink the guard had sent his way. "He still made me hydrate him?"

The captain pulled open the door. "Heal this one first, and we will move to the other right after."

There was a young man on the substandard bed, laying in a slowly growing pool of blood. Joe hurriedly moved over and cast lay on hands, channeling the spell so that he didn't need to wait three seconds between casting it again. Joe had no idea how much health this man had and was surprised when he wasn't at full health in eight seconds. By channeling, he had already restored… three hundred and thirty health, but the man's wounds were still gruesome. At two hundred and fifty mana already spent, Joe was concerned that he may not be able to heal the other person at this rate.

As the last wounds finally closed, Joe got a notification that mana manipulation had increased to Novice III. His distraction made him miss the moment when the man's eyes snapped open, and a glowing fist sent Joe into the stone wall.

Joe was stunned as the man roared and charged him, and two swift punches later Joe got a series of messages that made him groan in frustration.

-30 health (Empowered strike)! -15 health (Impact damage)! -20 health (Basic attack)!

Undying robes passive effect activated! Health set to 1!

-20 health (Basic attack)!

You have died! 800 Experience lost. Time till respawn: 8 hours. Maybe don't hang out with violent prisoners.

That was a huge loss of experience! Joe found himself back in the virtual reality loading room, and with a sigh, he decided that it would at least be a good chance to check in with his mom. Making lemonade out of lemons and whatnot.

CHAPTER TWENTY

Spending the remainder of his time doing research on the components for rituals he could use, Joe was unsurprised to gain a notification as he respawned.

Ritual magic has reached Beginner 0! Congratulations on finally understanding the most rudimentary concepts of rituals! You are now able to substitute components with others without the ritual automatically failing. Make sure you choose what to replace carefully! Based on your usage of rituals to this point, you are able to use excessively expensive components 10% more efficiently!

So the respawn room counted for abilities like this, huh? What did this notification mean by excessively expensive materials? Joe looked at his character sheet, spitting to the side when he noted that he now needed about thirty-six hundred experience to reach the next level. He had been gone for sixteen hours in game, so he walked back toward the jail in the predawn darkness. He hoped against hope that he would still be able to save the other person in the jail, but seeing the grievous wounds of the first… it was unlikely. Arriving at the jail, he was waved inside, but the captain walked over shaking his head.

"Too late to save the other. I'm so sorry about this; I had no idea the prince would wake up swinging like that. I should have taken more care, had a couple guards in there with you. This shouldn't have happened." The captain seemed to be a defeated man. Black circles were slowly growing under his eyes, and it was obvious that he hadn't slept at all since the last time Joe had seen him. "By the *abyss*, do I hate being the cause for casualties in good men."

"It isn't your fault, Captain. I should have been on guard; he got that way because of a fight, yeah?" Joe instantly tried to calm the man. "So that was the prince?"

"Did I say that?" The Captain's eyes bulged. "You didn't hear that from me or my men, got that? Say nothing at all about the Baron dying." He winced again and slapped a hand over his mouth.

"Sure, sure," Joe placated him cautiously. "I guess… nothing else for me to do here?"

"No, not now. I'm sorry it turned out this way, but I'll make sure you get some reparations from the royal family. You did save a prince, and he killed you for your troubles. That, and knowing what you know… and since they can't *keep* you dead…"

"Got it. Thanks, Cappy. I won't be able to sit around and wait for gifts that may not be coming, but let me know if you need anything else." Joe tried out a new nickname and getting no negative feedback, decided to keep using it.

"After *that* travesty you are still willing to help us?" The captain's head dipped down and he let out a deep breath. "On behalf of my men, I thank you again. We will be more dutiful in the future."

Reputation gained! +1000 with human guards. New reputation rank gained! You are now considered an 'ally' of human guards! New opportunities become available to you in the future, and guards will often look the other way if you need them to. Abusing this may have negative consequences!

Guild reputation gained! +500 with human guards. New opportunities have opened for your guild!

Joe nodded at the Captain and walked back to his guild. He

walked into the barracks and was met with crying and sobs of pain. His eyes widened as he took in the seriously wounded people laying on the floor and tables. "What in the world happened in here?"

Terra was the only person he could see that was on her feet. She walked over, a thunderous expression on her face. "Where the *hell* have you been?" she hissed at him.

"I got killed by a person I was healing. They woke up and slaughtered me," Joe informed her, already healing the worst cases he could see. Almost all of the people were missing chunks of flesh, mainly fingers, hands, or feet. Their body parts were next to them, and his healing spell allowed him to reattach the tissue and nerves without issue, though the bones would need to heal naturally. He shuddered in remembrance of his own loss of limbs and was happy all over again that he could heal these people. "What happened?"

"Monsters," Terra grimly informed him. "They were some kind of leech-looking thing. They slithered in or were already here. We don't know. For some reason, they couldn't get very high off the ground… but they tore off anything that dangled off a bed. No one even noticed at first because they seemed to inject some kind of a painkiller. Then a couple members started to bleed to death, and since Tiona's an officer, she noticed in the guild member's tab that they were dying."

"The monster under the bed is real here?" Joe shook his head. "That's disgusting."

"It's called a Tenebris. Made for good experience since they don't move very fast. They are mainly just effective against unaware people," Tiona's voice preceded her as she stomped into the room. "I saw that you died, care to explain?"

"I really can't, beyond telling you that a prisoner woke up after being healed and killed me. I was completing the ongoing quest with the guards. Got a ton of reputation for the guild, too," Joe told her.

Wisdom +2.

The notification made him sweat; obviously he had just

done something the system considered *very* wise. How badly could that have gone for him? Tiona grunted at his explanation, noting the lack of details for a private conversation later. "Give me a few minutes, and I'll be able to finish up here."

Healing so many people in rapid succession brought him a level in lay on hands but not heal. There seemed to be some sort of block there that he wasn't approaching correctly. He was very interested to notice that using lay on hands brought experience to the main skill and remembered that the notification when he first got the variant had told him it would do so. He supposed that could be true for many different skills where the skill variation was a branch of the main. Maybe smithing had specific subskills for things like weapons or armor. It would make sense that leveling those would level the main skill while making the variation more potent for the specialized skill. Master smiths usually focused only on either weapons or armor, right? Some even on just one or two *types* of weapon.

Joe shrugged off these thoughts as he finished healing the last person in the room. They had waited very patiently, and he thanked the man before noticing that he had simply logged off while waiting. He snorted; must be nice to ignore pain and come back ready to play.

"What's the plan for the day, Tiona?" Joe asked as he washed blood off of his hands and robe.

"Eh, the others are at work. Monday in the real world. You know how it is." Tiona shrugged and stretched. Obviously she hadn't slept much. "Just go do whatever you need to get done. They'll be back tomorrow from our perspective, late afternoon for them."

"Works for me." Joe had plenty that he wanted to get done.

"Joe…?" A tentative voice called warily from the front room. "There's a royal guard outside looking for a Joe? Any 'Joe' in here?"

A bit confused but *assuming* he knew why the man was here, Joe walked to the door and met the most intimidating man he had ever had the displeasure of meeting. He was bald, near six and a half feet tall, and had a series of scars on nearly every bit of exposed skin. His stare bore into Joe from a point two feet higher than the cleric's perspective, and it seemed that the man was judging every aspect of Joe's being. Releasing a grunt, the man reached into a spacial ring, pulled out a package, and tossed it at Joe. After ensuring that Joe had the package in hand, the man turned on his heel and marched away at a speed Joe couldn't sprint at.

There was nothing special about the box that he could see, but he still decided against opening it in the street. Shrugging off the curious looks from his guild mates, Joe went to the small room he was assigned, closing and locking the door before prying open the unassuming box. He was glad he had taken the precautions. A bright light shone throughout the room, and Joe had to look away, blinking. He squinted his eyes and touched the item within.

Flawed Greater Core found! Would you like to convert this into experience points? Current worth: Five thousand experience points. Yes / No

Joe's mouth dropped open, and he could do nothing for a long moment but stare at the light coming from the palm-sized stone. The emitted radiance forced him to look away as his eyes teared up, but after a moment he was able to start thinking again. Should he use it? Or… should he save it? He could be at the next level *now*, or maybe he could find a better use for it… Joe considered his options, but as much as he wanted to save the Core, he knew that he would start getting the *real* benefits of his class at level five. If this was a gift, he knew it wasn't unique. There would be other Cores out there. He grinned as he pressed the 'yes' button.

Golden light flooded out of him as the stone vanished, and he was jerked into the air as his level increased. Feeling a rush of energy, Joe landed softly on his feet with a joyful smile. Already, there were people knocking on the door shouting questions at him; they had felt the relaxing shockwave of a level increasing, and wanted to see if there was something to fight in the room. He pushed the door open–a surprisingly difficult feat with so many people crowded into the area–and tried to explain the situation by saying that he had simply finished off a quest, and it had given him enough experience to level up. A few people pressed the issue, but he refused to say much more, telling them that one of the requirements of the quest was that he couldn't discuss it. Since this was a *surprisingly* common theme in quests, all they could do was grumble and meander away.

Joe sat down on his bed with a happy grin covering his face. He looked at his character sheet and noted with glee that his 'profession' was now unlocked. Focusing on that section, he brought up a small selection of the professions he already had available to him.

You may choose one profession at the fifth level, and another at level ten. It is recommended that you choose a gathering profession first to gain the materials needed for the next profession you choose. Not all possible professions are shown here, only those you currently qualify for. Seek out a teacher or meet the requirements in order to unlock more options!

Occultist: A seeker of the greatest truths, often scorned for their belief in what others believe to be conspiracies and fantastical tales. Ironically, many have spent their lives seeking out the knowledge that the occultist can readily access. For others of lesser professions, the terrible truth has sometimes been too much to bear. The occultist has no such qualms when it comes to knowledge. Nothing is forbidden, nothing is too horrific to turn them from their path. For better or for worse, the occultist will seek even a grain of truth in any matter which intrigues them.

Profession benefits at first level: Can attain quests from non-quest related books if there is 'truth' hidden in the text. Lies and truth are visually discernible when in written form. Gains skills from 'scholar' profession unless true profession is discovered. Profession title appears to be 'scholar'.

Scholar: Devoting their lives to understanding the mysteries of the world, scholars apply the scientific method to all things. Often the very best at their field of study, the scholar is an asset to anyone seeking to become stronger. Though considered weak by others, scholars have been known to defend themselves in ways that none can explain, and in their sanctuaries, the prospect of fighting them borders on suicidal.

Profession benefits at first level: Increases speed of reading and writing by 50%. Ability to add 'lore' skill to any skill that could benefit from the area of study. (For example, a scholar who studies metallurgy could add their lore skill to the creation of a weapon, increasing the quality of the item.)

Actor: This is the job for any who act in a way that is not true to their reality. While it does not offer many combat-related options, it is a profession used to great effect by bards, dancers, spies, assassins, thieves, and politicians.

Profession benefits at first level: Increased reputation gain with non-aligned factions. Grants the 'disguise' and 'persuasion' skills. Can hide alignment 75% more effectively.

Tracker: Steadily moving and searching for their target, trackers use their high perception of the world to great effect. Hunters, trappers, bounty hunters, and investigators rarely lose their quarry, and this job offers them the best starting benefits of any option.

Profession benefits at first level: Grants the skill 'tunnel vision', which allows the tracker to see anything in the area that relates to their target 80% more effectively. Trackers move through rough terrain 50% easier than others.

Herbalist: The study of botany and use of plants intended for medicinal purposes or for supplementing a diet. The herbalist can find rare and powerful ingredients needed by chefs, alchemists, and apothecaries. Whether to poison or heal, the herbalist can acquire the needed materials.

Profession benefits at first level: Plants you harvest are 50% more potent for seven days. All useful herbs have a faint pillar of light above them. (Can be toggled on / off.)

Joe was surprised at how many jobs he had available, he had thought that he would only have access to occultist. Some of the others were tempting, but he had been waiting to unlock his job since he started the game. For him, this was an easy choice. The fact that he was able to hijack the scholars' skills was just an added bonus. He selected the occultist job and accepted it. Joe waited for anything to feel different, but nothing happened. "Hmm."

Checking his status sheet, he confirmed that he did indeed

have the occultist profession. Joe felt a little let down, he thought that he would feel… stronger? Smarter, maybe? Regardless, this did change his original plans for the day. To the library! Joe walked toward the repository of knowledge, feeling light and free. He was an occultist now! As he walked into the library, he was humming and received a glare from Boris.

Then Boris saw Joe's level, and a flash of hope crossed his face. When he saw that Joe's profession was set as "scholar" he released a strangled shout of joy. "You did it! The first new scholar in nearly a decade! My boy, thank you! Our profession was dying, losing out to the mages for their direct power! Let me be the first to welcome you to the Scholarly pursuits!"

Experience held back from completing 'Footsteps through history I' has been awarded! +500 profession experience!

"Oh, that's right, you already earned these, use them well!" Boris handed over a small pair of spectacles, beaming all the while.

Spectacles of the scholar. These half-moon lenses allow you to read for long periods of time without straining your eyes. They also help you to notice wear and tear in books and chase down anyone who damages a books' binding by setting it down on the ground upside-down to hold their place. You'll be a librarian yet! -25% eye strain from focusing on small details, +10% vision specific perception.

Interesting, Joe had never seen an item that only enhanced one of his senses at a time. Usually a perception bonus was applied uniformly, but he had to admit he'd rather not feel ten percent more pain. So, the spectacles were very welcome. "Thank you! Is there anything else I can do in here, Boris? Any quests or texts I should read?"

Boris scratched his chin. "Nope, not really. I don't know what *you* don't know after all. You do have access to the first floor uncommon section now, but I'm sorry to say that your job level needs to be higher before you can go to a floor with rare books."

"Thanks. Oh! Before I forget, how do I get the 'lore' skill?"

Joe had half turned before asking this, but his attention had now returned to the librarian.

"Lore?" Boris chuckled fondly. "Oh, it has been so long since I've needed to explain this skill. All you need to do is read up on a topic, think through how you can apply it to any given situation, and then do so. That'll unlock the skill. To forewarn you, lore is one of the few skills I know of that cannot have skill points added to it. Not to mention, you have to level each lore skill individually; you can't just apply a study of one facet of creation to another without both being at high lore ranks. Study water? You get a lore skill. Fire? Another lore skill. Try to combine them into a steam lore? Better have aerodynamics as a lore skill as well! You need to do actual *learning*, which is why people avoid that skill like the plague outside of our hallowed ranks."

"So lore isn't about history? It's a fancy way to say science?" Joe watched Boris's eyes get wide, and he looked around swiftly.

"Basically, but don't go calling yourself a scientist." Boris whispered, forcing Joe to lean toward him. "You will get laughed right out of the city or right into a jail cell. Scholars are scientists, founded by the first order of scientists in ancient times. Back when science was almost useless due to magic being able to bend natural laws to the breaking point. Now, with less people around able to use magic and magic becoming so specialized… well, we are coming into favor again. With the nobility at least. The common man… they tend to discredit science any chance they get, and the mage's college isn't helping."

"I'm not sure I understand," Joe withered under the glare sent his way. "but I'll just take your advice and get to work, then. Thanks again."

Joe stepped into the stacks of books, smiling as he saw a tome go flying through the air only to settle gently in its correct spot. Even just looking at the covers around him made him smile. Thanks to his new abilities, all of the books were glowing.

CHAPTER TWENTY-ONE

Joe pulled the brightest, shiniest book he could find from a shelf, excited to see what was inside of it. To his horror, it was a book on simple mathematics. So the glow was not about how *important* the book was? Joe flipped through the book until he noticed a single dark spot. It took him a moment to realize the significance of the dark spot, but by adding up the numbers, he found that the provided answer was incorrect. So… he was able to see at a glance how *accurate* the information contained in a book was? It made sense that a math book was almost perfectly true, even if you could craft a spell to crack a world in half, one plus one equals two.

With a sigh, Joe put the book down and ignored it as it flew away. What would be the best use of his time then? If he wanted to get and level the lore skill, he should focus on the books that were shining with correct information. There were a surprising amount of books that were dim, outnumbering the books filled with truth by three to one at least. So, if he wanted to find magical artifacts, quests, and ways to get more powerful… his eyes jumped toward the fiction section. Myths, fairy tales, books others thought were just 'fun' reads. Joe wandered over and began pulling likely books from the shelves, stacking them on the nearby table.

He was glad that there was a note-taking interface in his character screen; paper was fairly expensive to purchase in small amounts. He typed away at a keyboard which only he could see. Any onlooker would have found it very strange to see, since it seemed he was just wiggling his fingers in midair while flipping the pages of the book in front of him a few times.

The data he could find was… disjointed. There were nuggets of truth in these fictional books, but they didn't relate to each other in any real way. Before he could get frustrated after the fifth book, he found something interesting. This book had also reiterated some information that had been in the second book, and together they started to form a slightly clearer picture. He kept going, able to ignore large portions of the text as he continued to write down only the true parts.

Grouping all of these chunks together was similar to creating a jigsaw puzzle, and he found out more about his skill as he tried to piece the words together. When he put the information in an incorrect order, the words would dim. Placing them in the correct order would make them grow a bit brighter. He spent an hour trying to put a quest together with what he found, but his mind began to wander eventually. There simply wasn't enough information here. After a short break, he began parsing a few books about people who had used rituals in the past. Unsurprisingly, he started to ascertain that most of the contents were false. With a jolt, he remembered his own book of rituals, and pulled out the *upsettingly* dark volume.

Before he could continue going through other books for truth, Joe felt that he had no choice but to revamp his own grimoire. He opened to the page he had bookmarked, and winced as he saw the ritual. The words were so dim as to be almost black, and he was unsure why. This ritual was the 'Little sister's cleaning service', and he knew it worked correctly. Then why…? Boris's words came back to him then. 'This is an exaggerated primer on rituals, designed to show how inefficient, wasteful, and useless they are!' Of course. The ritual would work, but Joe was likely using *much* more than he needed to in terms of mana and components.

With a sigh, Joe stood and left the library. He went over to the nearby shops, and placed a large gold piece on the counter as he bought a sheaf of paper. Joe grumbled a bit at the cost; a full gold had only garnered him one hundred pages of blank paper. Next he bought ink, quills, and finally a cup of coffee before returning to the library. Boris gave him the stink-eye when he saw the coffee, and made him drink it all before he was allowed near the precious books.

Joe sat down again with a sigh, placing a single piece of paper on the table in front of him. The trader had explained all the uses of the items he had bought, and had thrown in some drying sand and a quill sharpener for him since he had purchased such high-valued items in bulk. Joe dipped his quill into the ink and began writing text as small as he could without letting the ink run together. Deciding to start with the 'Predator's territory' ritual, he changed the values of the needed mana, components, and Core. As soon as all the information was together on the page, he compared the now-glowing information with his book. Several of the items were glowing brighter, some were certainly dimmer.

The question was, were the dim values dim because they were not needed, had too small a value for the material, or were the wrong component entirely? He looked over the list of requirements, red pepper, wolfsbane, mint, crushed amethyst, pure salt, iron shavings, orange kyanite, three ounces of mercury, and silver wire. Nine hundred mana investment and an optional healing potion. Finally, blood and a Core. Looking at it like this, it almost seemed like a recipe. Realistically, a recipe is *exactly* what it was and how he decided to treat it. Looking at his notes, he eliminated all the items that he thought had nothing to do with protection.

Now the list only consisted of crushed amethyst, pure salt, iron shavings, orange kyanite, and silver wire. After writing that down, along with the symbol for the ritual, the information turned black. Obviously, this ritual would do nothing good if it was tried. He looked for more information on the other materials and found that mint was used to ward off rodents. Mercury was a symbol of change, and wolfsbane was a poisonous flower. He added these back in and the information began to glow again.

It took over an hour of replacing items, substituting in new material, and adjusting amounts before he got a recipe that glowed fairly brightly. It had taken six full pages of paper, and his hands shook with rage when he read the final formula.

Ritual: 'Predator's territory' (80% maximum improvement). Uses: Wards against creatures, beasts, and monsters ten levels above the genetic material used in the ritual. Caution! The inherent bloodlust generated by this ritual draws in any creature above the ten level threshold. Components needed: One half ounce dried wolfsbane, one ounce mint, one quarter ounce crushed amethyst, one ounce pure salt, five grams of pure iron shavings, one quarter ounce orange kyanite, three ounces of mercury, one-tenth of an ounce silver wire per square foot of space, and one drop of blood. One hundred experience from a low grade Core and four hundred point mana investment required. Lasts eight hours.

Joe had to physically sit down and breathe deeply to keep from screaming like a furious pterodactyl. He had wasted *hundreds* of experience points, mana, and coins on materials because someone had written this primer on rituals to discourage people from *using* rituals. He looked at the six pages of paper he had used to create this new formula and felt that paper was suddenly not a terrible investment after all.

Skill gained: Ritual Lore (Novice IX). Your study of rituals combined with your occultist profession has allowed you to greatly enhance a ritual that you found! Since you are already a beginner in ritual magic, this starts at a higher level than normal. Make a study of more–and more powerful–rituals to increase this skill! Effect: Variable. Allows you to fine tune rituals that you find or create. Can increase potency of rituals and/or decrease cost of rituals.

Skill increased: Ritual magic (Beginner II).

Huh, that may be the shortest skill increase message he has seen thus far. Joe was glad to see that he had gained a lore skill, and he was always happy to see his ritual magic skill increasing. He flipped to the next page in his grimoire and groaned. It was going to be a long day of adjusting rituals at this pace.

When Joe wearily stumbled out of the library, he was exceedingly grumpy. It was already twilight and his fingers were cramping from the constant writing. He was hungry, had ink all over his hands… but the saving grace of the day was the fact that he had changed at least half of the rituals in the grimoire to be usable. Sure they were only the simplest rituals, but it was a start. He had also found that a few of the rituals were entirely bogus and were designed as traps to kill off anyone foolish enough to attempt them. He had found out that ritual magic was actually created by the symbols used, specifically the shape bounding it like the double circle for 'Predator's territory'. If the components weren't properly in place… it would make the ritual spin out of control and place a mana-debt on the person they could not hope to pay. Joe had received a taste of this with the ritual around the guild's barracks, but these symbols were on another level. A much *higher* level. Death was the most likely outcome from working outside of his capabilities.

He had also found that the ritual would use all of the materials *you* intended for it to use, which explained why it would eat an entire Core even if it only needed one-fifth of it. Dang greedy magic. Might as well call it Dijkstra magic instead of ritual magic. Joe chuckled at the tiny programming joke he had made. It was funny to think of programming while in a world created by a supercomputer. Kinda like the opposite of meta-programming. He shivered and tried to move past that thought spiral; this was his real world now.

As he crossed over the red chalk circle around the guild, he stopped himself and shrugged. No reason *not* to activate it; the ritual had just become cost-effective. The chalk seemed to glow brighter for a moment before a timer appeared in his vision. Seven hours and fifty-nine minutes remaining, plenty of time to sleep. Joe went to the dining area and gorged himself on the stew that seemed perpetually available, told Aten that the ritual was active, and collapsed into bed. Long day.

One dreamless sleep later, Joe popped out of bed with a smile on his face. The ritual had given everyone who slept here last night the well-rested bonus, and Joe was feeling it as total relaxation. Everyone he passed was chipper, and this was before the coffee was ready! Joe smiled as Aten sat down across from him. "Morning, boss-man. How did you sleep?"

"Better than I ever have since losing my thousand thread-count Egyptian cotton sheets." Aten sniffed the aroma of fresh coffee wafting from the pot moving toward them. "That because of your spell last night?"

"Yeah, you can add in a health potion to get a well-rested bonus." Joe poured his coffee slowly, letting the potent smell wash over his face.

"Does the potency of the potion matter? We have some apprentice alchemists that I'm sure would be willing to donate to the cause." Aten snatched the coffee pot from Joe the second his hand was off the handle.

"I'm not sure." Joe thought about it, nodding as he thought it over. "Most likely it'll just increase how long the bonus lasts. If that means I can feel this relaxed for half the day though, I'll take it."

"Now, we did have a rotating guard last night but weren't attacked or even looked at by the monsters that were running around out there. I'm real happy you had the forethought to activate your spell thingy last night; the city was attacked by… I think they were mutated bats? Nasty buggers. Sharp claws and a sonic attack." Aten shuddered a bit at the thought. "I'm liking the thought of having your spell going pretty often, but the cost is just too-"

Joe waved his hand to cut off the flow of words, he finished his gulp of black ambrosia and let out a contented sigh. "Good stuff. The spell, it's called a ritual actually, well, I made a huge breakthrough yesterday. Turns out that I can refine the recipe of the spell a *lot*. I'm now able to get the spell cost down to… not quite *cheap*, per se, but manageable. It went from a little over thirty gold to create, to…"

Doing a bit of mental math, Joe looked over the formula he had created. If the base ritual cost a hundred experience from a Core, for him it dropped to fifty experience. "Just over three gold per eight hours. Now it costs about a *tenth* of what it did. Turns out that whoever made the spell book was intentionally trying to destroy anyone using them."

"Three gold?" Aten rubbed his stubble excitedly. "You say it so casually, but going from three hundred dollars per use to thirty dollars is pretty huge. These work anywhere? We could use them for overnight expeditions?"

"Theoretically, but… the big issue is creating a double ring of material to soak the magic into. I can't picture someone carrying around a huge sheet of paper or concrete with them." Joe shrugged uncomfortably, this was one of the major issues he was having–making his magic transportable.

"Does it matter what the rings are made of?" Aten thought for a moment after Joe shook his head. "Can we talk to a weaver or tailor? Could we get a double ring of string, then roll it up after it is ready?"

Joe felt like his head was about to burst into flame as hundreds of ideas were considered. "Yes! **cough**. I mean, yeah, that might work. Know anyone?"

"Of course I do," Aten scoffed. "I'll talk to them today, see if I can't get a few prototypes for you. Have a good day, I see Tiona coming this way. Ha! I made a rhyme." Aten wandered off, and Tiona slid into the recently vacated space.

"Ready to go hunting, Mr. Level Five?" Tiona grinned at him mischievously. "Let's see if that level was *earned* or bought!"

Joe was forced to eat quickly, Tiona's stare not very conducive to a relaxing meal. They ambled over to the gate, discussing the plans for the day while the other members of their team caught up to them. Joe was heatedly explaining why he couldn't just use shadow spike continuously to Tiona, "Look, it is a non-class skill! Right now, it's only at novice two and it sucks almost a *hundred* mana per cast! I can use it four times before I'm wiped out."

"Ya know, I hear mage is a fun class," Tiona prodded him. "Why don't you go get a mage license and switch classes? You'd keep your healing skills, right?"

"No idea! Also, I'm not going to go drop a *thousand* gold so that some random group is fine with me using my *own* spells!" Joe ground out. It turned out that the mage's college would hunt down anyone using mage abilities if they weren't a 'certified' mage. That way they were able to keep tabs on anyone growing in strength or, as they called it, 'causing trouble'. Joe was almost positive that it was simply a way to stay in power and in control. Anyone who came to their attention and didn't comply with their demands eventually gained the title 'rogue mage' from them. Thankfully, it was not an actual title that was on your character sheet, but it was basically a bounty. Then that person tended to vanish, either from a 'natural' accident or someone selling them to the college.

Joe shook the dark thoughts from his head, trying to pay attention to his surroundings; they were almost to fox territory now. Tiona was explaining some of her insights on leveling to the others. "Going from level nine to level ten is just… stupid hard. It is apparently going to be awesome at my next level though because ranking up, specializing, whatever you wanna call it… you know that euphoria from leveling? I was told it is that times *fifty*."

"But gaining any levels at all after that point is going to be really hard, right?" Guess spoke up, still a rarity in the group. "I mean, going from level nine to ten costs, what? Fourteen *thousand* exp?"

"Yup," Tiona replied cheerfully, "and it just goes up from there! But! Your new class starts at level one. So while your class is leveling up again, you are *also* gaining experience toward your overall level. Apparently, it isn't uncommon to get to level twenty and get your fourth specialization at the same time. At least, that's what I've been able to learn from the trainers"

"Seriously, I've never played a game where it is so hard to get levels," Dylan grumbled rhetorically.

Chad piped up, "Levels don't matter as much as skills anyway! What's the point in getting to level ten and ranking up if you are stuck with a lame class because you didn't bother to get any skills?"

The others either shrugged or nodded, Joe included. "I guess we'll just have to wait and see, right?"

Tiona changed the topic, "Joe, did you remember to get the Wolfman hunting daily quest? You *are* level five now."

Joe froze in place, falling to the ground when Dylan stumbled into him with a curse. "No! Crap! My first chance to-"

"Relax, I'm messing with you." Tiona giggled at his expression. "Here, I can share it with you." Her eyes lost focus, and a moment later, Joe had a popup blocking his vision.

Quest alert: Hunting the hunters! (Daily) The Wolfman population has been rising beyond any projections, and the human Kingdom will be threatened by a horde of rampaging beasts if their population isn't brought under control. Hunt 10 Wolfmen Scouts, 5 Wolfman Warriors, or one Wolfman Shaman! Recommended level: 8. Accept? Yes / No

Joe accepted the quest, and furrowed his brow as he thought about the meaning behind the prompt. "So, if we are only hunting Scouts every day, does that mean the population of Warriors and mages is shooting higher and higher?"

His words nearly made the others stop walking as they saw what he meant. This game had a way of twisting words to have multiple interpretations. Tiona was the first to speak, "Well, shoot. Probably? I bet other groups are doing the same thing we are."

"I'll mention it to the guards that give out this quest; they might want to break it up into three separate ones," Dylan decided as they continued forward. "Doesn't matter today though. We aren't going to go hunt down an unknown enemy the first day that you get to gain experience from a daily, Joe."

Joe nodded appreciatively, and the group quieted down a bit. They were getting near to wolf territory, and the large canines were known for ambushing unalert prey.

CHAPTER TWENTY-TWO

"Woof!" Dylan barked into Guess's ear, causing her–him?...the group still hadn't found out Guess's real gender–to jump in apparent shock after a moment. Joe chuckled, since Guess was playing with an outdated VR helmet and mental keyboard, she must have manually pressed the jump button. Good sense of humor there.

"There is a group of wolves trying to sneak up on us," Chad warned the group as they strolled along. "Joe, you want to take out the alpha, or should we fight them?"

They had discovered that if the largest wolf in the pack was killed before the other wolves attacked, the animals would scatter and run away. Tiona thought it over before shaking her head. "We're in a hurry. Joe, take him."

Joe grinned and turned his head. Easily finding the crouching wolves, he concentrated and made the required hand motion. A spike of pure darkness thrust upward, catching the alpha in its flank. It howled in pain, and Joe took the time to channel the spell, needing to hold the spike in place for a full three seconds until the wolf collapsed. The other wolves ran off, just as planned. "Whoo! That guy had a lot of health in him. Nearly drained my entire mana pool to finish him off."

Skill increase: Channeling has reached Novice II. Mana manipulation has reached Novice IV.

Joe really preferred these succinct messages. "How long until you are back to full?" Tiona liked data; the more she knew about her party, the better she could plan out combat.

"Let me check," Joe muttered, opening his character screen. "Mana manipulation went up, so now I have four hundred and nineteen mana, but I just used three hundred twenty-five to channel that spell, so... about a minute? Fifty seconds?"

"Hmm. Too long for anything but an ambush." Tiona looked around, scouring the underbrush for hidden foes. "Sure, there aren't other things attacking us right now, but in the future, if you run out of mana like that we might get wrecked. Feel free to do that if we need you to, but remember that if we are going to have a longer battle you have to make sure to conserve your mana. That means no channeling spells at the start of the fight. Let that be a finishing move if you really feel the urge."

"Yes ma'am!" Joe saluted her with mocking precision.

"Pff. Dang straight, good to see you finally know who's in charge." Tiona winked at him, her analytical side softening as she remembered that this was supposed to be fun.

The others chortled as they began moving again, and Joe's focus turned inward as he tried to squeeze his mana into a smaller container as it refilled. He hadn't made any real progress with his coalescence skill, but he wasn't overly surprised. After all, it was written right in the skill description that he needed a higher willpower to gain levels in the skill. Joe wasn't sure he believed that though; practice and determination had served him well through the years. He wasn't going to stop progressing because some skill *description* gave him arbitrary boundaries!

His mana finished refilling without him gaining a rank in the skill. Joe crossed his arms and pouted a bit. The group had to carve a path through a small pack of wolves once or twice, but they finally reached Wolfman territory. Trying to be stealthy, they watched the first group they came across for a few moments. Their stealth failed them as one of the wolves on the fringe of the patrol suddenly snapped its head to face them and released a growl.

"Not overly surprising," Tiona lamented as she tightened the grip on her sword. "Animals must have boosted perception. Unsurprisingly, this includes wolves. Chad, Joe, try to take out the Scout. Joe, if we get injured, break off your attack and heal. Everyone else, get ready for battle."

"Three… two… one!" Chad called softly, letting loose his bowstring just as Joe finished his spell. A spike of shadow lanced into the Scout's lower back, causing it to freeze as pain overwhelmed its senses. Before its reflexive paralysis faded, an arrow lodged itself in the Wolfman's eye. Crumpling to the ground, the humanoid body quickly stilled. The basic wolves stumbled to a halt, looked back at their fallen leader, and scattered with high-pitched whines.

"The Wolfman is considered the alpha, then?" Guess accurately inferred.

"Looks like it, thank goodness." Dylan let out a long sigh of relief. "I need some better armor. All I can think right now is, 'I'm so glad I didn't get bitten again.' Not the best mentality for the guy planning on taking all the hits, ya know?"

Howls in the distance heralded an unfortunate side effect of having allowed the other wolves to run off. A notification then blocked their views for a long moment.

Area quest: Territory dispute. Wolfman Scouts have found wolves without a pack, and are converging on the location of the missing Scout's patrol. Survive against their fury! Reward: Variable, one class-related item. Rounds survived: 0/5

"Territory dispute? As if!" Tiona scowled at the notification blocking her view as if trying to frighten it into changing its verbiage. "This is a stupid survival quest like that rabbit swarm!"

"Here they come!" Dylan's voice wavered as he raised his shield. "This is gonna hurt, dang it, stupid team needing a tank…" His voice trailed off into incoherent grumblings, but his stance reflected perfect defensive discipline.

Guess looked around at the team members–who were getting into formation and putting their backs to a tree–and vanished into a nearby shadow. Tiona was about to give a few orders, looked around, and snorted. "Rogues! Guess, you better just be getting into position, or I'm going to cut you in half!"

The first of the wolves exploded through the underbrush, only taking a moment to lock its eyes on the party before snarling and charging them. Before making it halfway, half a dozen more canines began hurtling into the open. Arrow after arrow launched from Chad's bow, finding new homes in fur and flesh. The first wolf died, but the others simply increased their pace. Chad continued attacking, but was knocked to the ground as a Scout made its presence known by returning fire. Chad screamed as the barbed head of the arrow tore into his bicep, and he was forced to stop attacking as his arm went limp.

Joe was the only other member of the team with ranged attacks, and his hands quickly formed his only offensive spell. The shadow of the Wolfman bunched up and slid into the Scout soundlessly; the Wolfman screamed in pain as it fell. It wasn't dead yet, but Joe needed to turn his focus to Chad. He gripped the arrow, knowing this part would suck. With a sharp pull, the arrow, a chunk of meat, and a spray of blood came from the fallen man. Chad shrieked as Joe grabbed the tender area, applying his healing spell as accurately as possible. In moments, skin was closing over newly-grown tissue.

Chad nodded with tears in his eyes, leapt to his feet, and began firing arrows once more. His attacks were much more carefully targeted now; Scouts were his main focus. Leaving the four-legged variety to his teammates, Chad put an arrow into any wolf standing on just two feet.

Dylan was screaming in rage and pain as he waded through the wolves attempting to drag him to the ground. "Not! This!

Time! You mangy beasts. I am going. To. Cut you!" He punctuated his sentences with slashes or bashes, using his shield as much as his sword. With his grumbling curses drawing the animal's attention, Tiona was able to deal maximum damage. Her sword flashed amongst the combatants, leaving behind huge gashes and crippled opponents. As the last wolf fell, Dylan stood on wavering legs. Just before he would have collapsed, Joe's hand landed on his shoulder and began pouring healing water over the stocky tank. Dylan shook his head, his mind able to function properly again as savage bite marks rapidly vanished from his body.

A Scout thudded to the ground, falling from its sniping position in the branches of a tree it was planning to ambush them from. Guess landed on the anthropomorphic wolf, using it as a landing pad as her presence was once again known. "Three Wolfmen, well, four with this one, and about sixteen wolves in that wave."

Territory dispute. Rounds survived: 1/5. Experience deferred.

"Deferred?" Joe asked as he noticed that everyone else was also getting the notification.

"You get the experience when you either finish the quest or die," Tiona told him as she prepared herself for the next wave. "That way, you can't level up mid-battle and get fully restored."

"Well that sucks," Dylan's grumbles started up again. He was looking over his wolf-leather armor which was becoming heavily tattered. "At least I'll have plenty of materials to repair this with after the battle."

The next wave progressed in a similar manner; the only real scare being when a wolf used one of its comrades as a springboard and was able to tackle Dylan to the ground. Luckily, this was near the end of the wave, and Joe was able to restore him from only a few health before the next wave began.

Territory dispute. Rounds survived: 2/5. Experience deferred.

This time, something was different. Instead of Wolves charging them, a storm of arrows and thin javelins began to whizz through the underbrush. Dylan laughed as his stout shield vibrated from the impact of the projectiles, his reaction time good enough that none of them landed in his body. Joe, Chad, and Guess were the main damage dealers this round, as they needed to seek out the archers and end them from a distance. Joe was able to eliminate two of the Scouts on his own, then finished off one Scout who had three arrows protruding from his stomach. Not seeing any open wounds on his teammates, Joe was surprised as Chad suddenly fell to his knees gasping.

Looking him over, Joe noticed black lines that had crept up Chad's arm. He swore softly, only now remembering that Scouts were known for using poison on their arrows. Activating cleanse, he channeled the spell and worked to expunge the high-leveled poison from his teammate. It was difficult to do, but with his higher understanding of the spell, higher skill level, and the bonus power from channeling, he was able to rid the toxins from the archer's bloodstream.

Skill increased: Cleanse (Beginner 0). Congratulations! You have increased your skill enough that you understand the basic concepts! Since you mainly used this skill to remove poisons and toxins during the novice rankings, Cleanse now has a 10% bonus effectiveness against poison and toxins in the human body!

A piercing scream rang out from the final Scout as Guess succeeded in backstabbing it, and it fell to the ground from a branch above them.

Quest complete: Hunting the hunters! (Daily) 10/10 Wolfman Scouts have been slain by your party's actions! Return to the quest assigner for any monetary or item rewards! Experience gained: Deferred.

Territory dispute. Rounds survived: 3/5. Experience deferred.

Joe tried to help Chad to his feet, but as he pulled the archer upward, his strength modifier made him fail and he fell down on top of his surprised teammate. "Sorry!" Joe was flushed with embarrassment, "Seriously though, I need to put a couple points into strength. And constitution. This is getting stupid."

"Joe! Get your mind in the battle!" Tiona called out as the next wave began. A few arrows arced toward them, but Chad

had already regained his feet and returned fire instantly while dodging the missiles. The real trouble appeared as a trio of Wolfmen stepped out of the forest, heavy machetes and thick leather armor marking them as vastly different from the creatures they had fought thus far. Joe stared intently at the new threat, attempting to pull up some information on them.

Successful perception check! Wolfman Warrior. After standard training and months of hardship, extra strong Wolfmen are given their first weapons and armor. The more metal they have on them, the more elite the force. A Wolfman fully clad in metal armor and wielding a metal weapon is an absolute elite and a force to be reckoned with. Average level is eight.

Perception +1! After staring intently, almost lovingly, into the eyes of your foe, your perception has increased to the point that you can attain general knowledge of them. Gain more insight into your enemies to advance your understanding of their being.

"These guys are at least level eight, everyone." Joe was surprised by how calm his words sounded. Realistically, he had no idea if he would be effective against this type of enemy.

"Finally, a worthy challenge," Tiona stated dryly, her face coated in sweat as she tried to catch her breath.

The three Warriors loped toward them, fury in their gaze as they raised their weapons.

CHAPTER TWENTY-THREE

"Joe, can you slow one of them down?" Dylan questioned in a quiet voice. "I can't hold against three at once."

Looking over his teammate with a searching stare, Joe saw that he was about to break. "I'll do my best." His mana reserves were almost full, since healing cost him almost nothing right now. Joe targeted the Wolfman Warrior that was in front, leading the charge. Joe's hand moved in a specific pattern, and the shadow of the wolf lanced upward into the unprotected shin of the sprinting soldier. There was a disturbing **crack** of bone as the shin bent around the spike, the force of the running Warrior causing the bone to split vertically.

Howling, the leading Warrior dropped to the ground, weapon flying from his hand. The others ignored him as they continued their assault. Joe wanted to finish off the fallen Wolfman, but the others clashed with Dylan and Joe had no attention to spare. Their attacks were unrefined, brutal but effective. Dylan blocked three strikes before his shield shattered, but he managed to lash out and open the gut of the rightmost attacker.

The Wolfman whimpered as his intestines saw light for the first time but continued attacking weakly until all his movements stopped. Tiona dashed in and parried a blow that should have caught Dylan in the neck, leaving the Wolfman open to a backstab from Guess. The wolf stiffened as another blade slammed into him and an arrow slid between his ribs through a gap in the leather armor. Dylan gasped, dropping to his knees as he took a deep breath, cradling his broken arm as the pain finally reached him. He smiled through the pain, happy they had survived the wave. "Guys, I *really* think we-"

Blood poured from Dylan's torn throat as he looked uncomprehendingly at the Warrior that had fallen with a shattered leg. The canine bared its teeth in a horrifying snarl before the others managed to put various weaponry into its body.

Party member Dylan has fallen! Experience loss halved due to quest deferring experience gains. Look for him as the sun rises over the eastern horizon.

Territory dispute. Rounds survived: 4/5. Experience deferred.

"Damn it! No!" Tiona dropped next to Dylan, trying to find any signs of life even though they had all already gotten the notification of his death. "Dylan, I'm so sorry! We weren't ready to push into this area, and you *told* me you didn't want to tank… I…"

"Snap out of it, Tiona!" Chad called angrily. "He'll be back tomorrow, and you can feel bad for yourself then! The last wave is starting!"

The brush rustled ominously, and all of the humans prepared themselves. Joe frantically channeled cleanse into Tiona, granting her the 'well-hydrated' buff just before the battle started. Out of the forest walked an extra-large Wolfman, and the light reflecting from his polished armor caused Joe to blink a few times. A thick bastard sword was held in a single hand as the Elite Warrior glared at them and looked around at the bodies that were already beginning to rot. A dark rumble grew in its chest, transforming to a howl as it charged them. Twice as fast as the others, the Elite Warrior crossed the distance in a flash.

Joe cast shadow spike as the Wolfman closed in on Tiona,

but its eyes shifted to him and Joe could see the beast's eyes dilate. As Joe finished the spell, the monster launched himself into the air. The spike appeared from the shadow, but the spell almost instantly collapsed. Not only had jumping taken the wolf out of range, his shadow had shrunk to a tiny circle on the ground, weakening the spell immeasurably. Cleaving downward with his huge sword, the wolf snarled as Tiona rolled out of the way of the ground-shattering blow. It took two incredibly quick pulls, but then the bastard sword came out of the ground with a spray of soil as the wolf continued his attack.

The Warrior rolled forward suddenly and Guess appeared behind him, her daggers only scoring the metal armor as the beast dodged. A backhand caught Guess across the face and the rogue went flying into a tree. A sound like hail was starting to annoy the Wolf, and he glanced over to see Chad firing arrow after arrow into his armor. Targeting weak points, the archer was doing his best to inflict any damage at all but failing miserably. With the wolf looking in his direction, Chad targeted his eyes. Simple movements of his head caused all the arrows to either miss the Wolfman entirely, or break against his helmet.

Tiona roared as she swung her sword with both hands, catching the Wolfman in the small of his back. He only stumbled forward, regaining his footing and turning to join the duel Tiona was offering. The huge sword flicked out and it took all of Tiona's skill to deflect the blow, the force still causing her to stumble backward. She dodged the next two swings without trying to match strength with the beast. Locking eyes with Joe for a moment, she nodded slightly and charged forward.

Joe channeled his shadow spike, the spike appearing at the Wolfman's lower back just as an arrow impacted the back of his knee, causing it to buckle. Tiona's charge *slammed* the off-balance Wolfman into the spike, but to Joe's horror, the armor held. Guess re-entered the fray at that moment, and her daggers bashed the wolf *just* hard enough for the armor to give way with a squeal. The tip of the channeled spike slid into the humanoid slowly, the wolf not able to recover his balance as Tiona and

Guess dodged his frantic attacks and applied their own. With a sickening **squelch** the spike exited the front of the wolf and was stopped by the undamaged breastplate.

The Warrior struggled valiantly for a few more moments before falling to the ground as Joe ran out of mana. It twitched a few times, then lay still. Joe dropped to the ground gasping as his body slowly began regenerating his fully depleted power. Through his breaths, he looked with great curiosity at the new notifications that were allowed to appear.

Quest complete: Territory dispute. Rounds survived: 5/5. Experience increased by 50%! (25% bonus for being the first to find this event, 25% bonus for completing it on the first attempt.) Exp: 2000. Item gained: Class specific item box! This small treasure box holds an item only useful to you or someone with the same class as you! Guard it well!

Joe slowly sat up as he felt his body starting to recover from the intense battle. Everyone was sitting, faces and bodies covered in dirt, blood, and sweat. He muttered, "I bet we all have the 'stinky' debuff right now."

For some reason, the others seemed to think this comment was hilarious and started chuckling. In a moment, the chuckles turned to full-on laughter. They slowly stood, aching all over, and began to loot the bodies. Most of the clothes were tattered rags, but the leather armor and metal weapons could be sold for a fairly good price. The real prize was the heavy metal armor worn by the Wolfman Elite. They stripped the gear off of him, ignoring the horrid stench coming from his ruptured organs. When the team found that they couldn't carry both the armor and the loot, Joe decided to tell the others about his new spacial ring. There were a few twitching eyes, but no one said anything as he stored the thick armor in the ring.

"It's totally full right now," Joe explained as Tiona asked him to put the other loot in the ring. "It's not a huge capacity, really just enough for all my spell components and… well, a set of armor, I guess."

"What?" Guess looked over at them.

"I said 'I guess'. I wasn't calling you." Joe rolled his eyes.

"Ah." Guess went back to watching for danger.

"Alright." Tiona sighed heavily. "You know, the more you hide stuff like this from us, the less likely it is that we can fully trust you."

"I wasn't hiding it, really." Joe felt a bit upset about her assertion. "You just can't really use it, so there was no reason for me to bring it up. It would just seem like I was bragging!"

"Hmm." Tiona looked away, then addressed the others, "Good job today. Check to see if Dylan dropped anything, and let's get the heck outta here. I'm totally beat right now." They set out for town, and Joe checked the other notifications that had been blinking in the corner of his vision.

Exp: 496 (Combination of multiple creatures. See full listing? Yes / No)

Joe selected 'no'. He knew what monsters he had fought today, he didn't need to go over it again. It was only early afternoon when they approached the gates, but it felt like it had been a week. He was indescribably interested in the class item box that he was carrying in his storage ring, but he couldn't open it for fear of the others finding out what it contained. What if it shouted 'Ritualist class item!' when he opened it? Sure, it was unlikely, but… games had done stranger things in the past.

The trail back was quite the trudge with how exhausted they all were, but the thoughts of a relaxing bath and a hot meal were a powerful draw. Joe's need to maintain a fairly slow pace made the others huff with annoyance by the time they were halfway back; at this point Chad and Guess started playing tag in the trees, jumping from branch to branch with the excellent agility their class afforded them. Tiona would get a bit ahead of Joe, then do push-ups until he was past her. Joe's face soured when she would run past him and try to beat her previous record. Now he was missing the slow, stealthy pace they needed to use when going through hostile territory.

Never had Joe been so happy to see the city gates. He ignored the others in his team, and they laughed at his aloof countenance as the party disbanded. Waving at each other, they went their separate ways. Even Joe muttered a fond farewell, knowing that they were only teasing him to ease the tension of the day. He skidded to a stop as he remembered that he was carrying the armor they intended to gift to Dylan. Looking around frantically, he saw that the others were gone. They must have forgotten about the armor and the repairs it needed. He rolled his eyes, knowing that he needed to take care of this before starting to relax.

Joe walked into the trade district and was surprised with how long it took to find directions to a reputable armor smith. The characteristic sound of metal on metal and tear-inducing smoke from the forge was nowhere to be found. Worried that the smithy in the area would only be a storefront, he was much relieved to walk in and see a man pounding soundlessly on an anvil. "Hello! I have some armor that I need work on."

There was no response to Joe's words; the man just kept hammering away. Getting a bit frustrated after repeated attempts to get the man's attention, Joe looked around and noticed a bell on the counter. He went over and rang it, and the man at the anvil looked up with a startled expression. Setting down the hammer and metal he was beating on, the man walked over with a neutral expression on his face. "Yes? Sorry, there's a sound barrier in that room. Can I help… no, get out. I don't sell any kind of mage armor or weapons, in fact I'm not a huge fan of the college. I work with metal here, I don't have anything light enough for… whatever class you are supposed to be."

Joe looked down at his stick thin body, a bit perplexed. He hadn't gotten a response like this before, and he wasn't sure how to handle the situation. "I… I'm not here for armor for myself."

"Oh, that's a relief." The smith grinned and wiped his bald head. "Er, sorry about that; thought you might be an undead at first. Skeleton, ghoul, or some such. Since you can talk, I'll assume you are alive."

"That… I…" Joe felt gobsmacked. How was he supposed to reply to casual insults like this?

"So, whaddaya need, brother?" The smith had a large grin on his face now.

Eye twitching, Joe pulled the armor out of his ring. "I need this repaired and resized for a human-sized warrior. Is that possible?"

The man looked over the gear with a critical eye, and when he got to the gaping hole, he raised an eyebrow and glanced at Joe. "Your handiwork?"

Joe nodded and the smith grinned. "Nifty. Yeah, I can do it, but it'll be a couple days. Have the person in question come here so I can size it properly. Actually, why isn't he here right now?"

"That, yeah… well… not everyone was so lucky as to survive the process of acquiring this gear. He'll be back tomorrow, but until then, I just want to get the process started." Joe halfheartedly shrugged at the end of his explanation.

"I see." The smith was silent for a long moment, looking at the oversized armor. "Say, I don't suppose you know what your friend is trying to accomplish? Class-wise, I mean. You said warrior, can you be more specific? Heavy plate armor like this might not be the best for someone like a standard melee fighter."

"Well, he is gearing himself to become a tank, a guardian of sorts. Get the attention of the enemy and keep it while we finish them off." Joe tried to think of a better way to explain, but the smith was already wincing.

"Oh, ew. He is going to… you're letting him become a… why do people do that to themselves? A regular warrior planning to be a tank?" The smith shuddered. "I can help him out a bit, perhaps. Are you certain this is his plan? I don't suppose you have some funds available you would donate to give him a better chance at survival?" The smith was looking at Joe with a gleam in his eye.

Joe grumbled but said that he might be persuaded to help his friend out. The light in the smith's eyes turned almost rabid.

"Wonderful! He uses a shield, yes? Has he achieved shield mastery yet?"

"He has a skill called that, if I remember correctly."

"Good, good." The smith started to gather the armor. "Well, I'll add in the adjustments after I get him measured. He will be *so* happy! I'll make sure to tell him it is a gift from you." The smith wrote down a sum on a slate and left it on the counter. "I'll need this much money, thanks in advance!"

Joe looked at the amount on the board, and a muffled scream reached the smith's ears just before he crossed into his magically silenced room, "There's no way I'm paying-"

The smith smiled as he began his new project. It was nice to have a challenge.

CHAPTER TWENTY-FOUR

Joe watched the smith flee, and his hands tightened around the slate. If he had been able to bring any strength to bear, it would have shattered. With a snarl, he left the room and went over to the alchemist to see if he had restocked any Cores. Joe left the building sixty gold poorer but with two shining gems tucked into his ring. Making his way to the bathhouse, he cleaned up, had his clothes washed, and then went to dinner.

Feeling like a brand new person, Joe retreated to his small room in the barracks. Finally, it was time to see what his reward from the item box was! The small chest sat on his bed, and after a moment, he flipped the lid open. A soft golden glow filled the room, and a thin ring of metal with a long needle on one side appeared as the light faded. Joe touched and tried to inspect the item.

Perception check succeeded! Item gained: Titanium Taglock Needle (Class item). Similar to taglock kits used by witches in voodoo magic, this is a reusable weapon augment designed to draw blood for rituals. One ritual can be bound to the needle, set to activate when blood is drawn. Stats: 80% armor penetration. Adds 1 point of physical damage. Item type: Augment. Rarity: Rare. Durability: 1000/1000.

That was *way* more information than he had ever been able to see before! Thinking of the item's uses, Joe wasn't sure how to react at first. He didn't have any combat-related rituals, but he could certainly see how this could be useful in the future. Plus, an extra point of damage meant that he would effectively double his damage when hitting rabbits! The thought made him smile. He didn't *actually* think that was the best use for it, especially with eighty percent armor penetration. If he aimed for a weak point when someone was in plate armor, he could likely draw blood. Then–if he had the right ritual–the fight should be over.

The need to find more and better rituals began to overpower Joe, but sadly, he had no leads on potential locations for them. He could try the mage's college, but he was *certain* that they would make demands on him that he wasn't willing to comply with. Just like any other university out there, they would try to charge him an arm and a leg, force him to participate in courses he didn't need, and essentially pledge loyalty to their ideals if he wanted to make any progress in his field of study. Joe grimaced at the thought. He had received so many calls asking for money from his old college after he graduated that he had needed to eventually get a new phone number, then change his email address and get a shredder for all of the junk mail.

Reminding himself that this process was supposed to be fun, Joe shook off his morose attitude and thought about his new weapon augment. Pulling out his scepter, he slid the metal band around the head of the weapon and snapped the clasp closed. A few sparkles of light appeared around the weapon, but they faded after a moment. Looking at his weapon, he had to laugh. It looked like an odd-shaped baseball bat that someone had hammered a nail through. Comparing it to the glowing weapons and magical effects he had seen, this scepter looked like something a caveman would use. Joe swung his weapon around a few times, but there was no difference that he could feel. He shrugged, he would have to use it in combat eventually, he'd just need to wait awhile. He couldn't think of anything else he needed to do, so he decided to just get ready for bed. Joe stretched out, made sure his door was locked, and laid his head on his pillow. Today had been kinda rough, and his tired mind gleefully accepted the chance for rest.

A few hours of snoozing soundly drifted by, but around midnight he was rudely awakened. Screams and sounds of battle began to ring out, replacing happy dreams of bashing bunnies. Joe jumped out of bed, unintentionally activating his skill 'jump around'. His body did a flip without prompting and he landed gently on his feet, gagging from the sudden stamina drain. The blankets he had jumped out of swished and settled down, revealing a perfectly made bed. Joe did a double take at the room, but the screaming intensified, and he needed to get out there and help people.

It was close to three in the morning, and the only light was either from fire or some form of magical effect. Only a second was needed to understand what was happening; they were under attack–not by monsters, but by people! They were wearing scarves and hoods to try and hide their faces, the style worn by only those who know they are intentionally doing wrong. Joe, even with his high perception, was having a difficult time tracking the movements of several of them, indicating that they were rogues with high stealth skills. Looking around, Joe saw that there wasn't anyone really *injured*; the invading force was making sure that whoever they attacked *died*. Making a snap decision, Joe changed his class to mage and sent a shadow spike into a warrior that was rearing back to strike a fallen guild member. The spike shot up into a… delicate area… and the warrior released a high-pitched scream.

Joe's fallen guild member stood up and began stabbing the warrior, so Joe felt that he could turn his attention elsewhere. He glanced around at all the shifting shadows, seeing a rogue sneaking behind a small group of defending archers. Another shadow spike appeared, but there was a secondary effect Joe hadn't expected. As the shadows cloaking the rogue were pulled to a different task, the rogue seemed to be almost *ejected* from the darkness that had been protecting him. He tripped and fell to the ground, a new and large hole in him. The archers saw him appear, and the man was quickly filled with various feathered shafts.

Seeing the results of pulling the concealing darkness from his foes, Joe began focusing his attacks on the hidden enemies. One after another, they fell to The Wanderers guild, and soon, all that remained were the various warriors and archers that had broken in. They too fell swiftly, now that the guild was roused and the rogues causing chaos were defeated. Aten stalked over to a body, pulled off the mask and **tsked**. "These are Headshot's goons. Looks like the Hardcores want another taste of pain. Spymaster! Find where they are holed up."

Aten looked around at the expectant faces and shouted, "Who comes for The Wanderers!"

"The strongest! The Best! We kill all the rest!" a few of the guild members finished the chant that was becoming their guild motto. Joe had changed his class back to cleric by this point and made his way around to the few injured people in the room. When he finished, he looked over the flashing notifications he had been ignoring.

Skill increased: Shadow spike (Novice III). Playing with darkness is paying dividends!

No experience has been awarded for killing travelers, but as several of them had red names, they may drop money or gear. If they had removed all items before launching an unprovoked attack, money or items will appear, taken from their bank account. Eternium does not recommend attacking other players.

Your guild has successfully held off an invading force that was attempting to assassinate your members! Due to your Guild's high reputation with the guards of Ardania, if all the enemies slain were from the guild Hardcores, the city will launch an investigation into their activities. Depending on the results of this investigation, members of the guild Hardcores may lose reputation, serve jail time, or have heavy fines levied against them!

"The guards are getting involved!"

"Holy crap, look at that message. They're making the *game* mad with their shenanigans!"

"About time! I need to be able to play the max amount I can. I quit work and am living off this game right now," a familiar voice mentioned.

Joe perked up when he heard the last comment. Looking over, Joe saw that it was Terra who had spoken. He nodded, it made perfect sense that she could already live off her earnings. As the only battle mage, she made a good cut of any money found. As a guild officer, she earned a monthly stipend from the guild to play as much as possible. After ensuring there was no one else needing his services, Joe returned to bed.

The next morning, or later that day depending on how you thought about it, Joe went to meet with Dylan after he respawned. He found him staring into a coffee cup, armor in tatters and seeming to be a bit worse for wear. "Morning, Dylan. Doing all right?"

"Huh? Oh." Dylan seemed startled to be spoken to, and when his eyes met Joe's, he had to look away. "Yeah, I'm good. Sucked to lose experience, but finishing the quests put me ahead by a good margin. Got a nice little class item box, too. Look, Joe, I normally don't mind being a tank. In other games, it is kinda… whatever, you know? Here though, I… I don't think I can…"

"Hang on, buddy." Joe gripped his friend's arm. In that moment, he knew he would pay whatever was needed for his teammate to have the protection he needed. "I've got a present for you. Come with me?"

Dylan seemed to struggle internally for a moment, but sighed and followed. They made their way to the smith, and Joe introduced his friend to the money-grubbing scumbag… that is, the smith who was going to fix up the armor and resize it. The smith looked Dylan up and down, nodding the whole time. "Now we're talking! Someone who can use proper gear! I hear you are walking the path of a defender? Is this true?"

"I'm… trying. It's hard. I get hurt *every single time.*" Dylan looked at the ground, clenching his fists.

Something shifted in the smith's eyes and approval shone through. "Yet you continue to go with and protect them. Admirable. Not many can devote themselves to protecting others over their own well-being. Most warriors will go and fight, leaving their team to their own devices. I think you are someone I can *really* work with. Are you willing to devote yourself to the safety of others?"

"I… I want to. It just hurts *so* much," Dylan whispered as he continued his staring contest with the ground.

"An honest answer. Even better." The smith put a massive hand under Dylan's face and lifted his head so they could see each other. "I can give you the tools you need. Just tell me you will do your best to protect those in your care."

Dylan gulped and nodded. "I will. I always do."

A message appeared in front of Joe, making him stumble backward. He growled. Outside of combat and stressful situations, these messages were invasive, annoying, and were *supposed* to be blocked. Then he saw the content of the notification and smiled.

Requirements for hidden class found! After suffering for his team, Dylan had reached a crossroads! Thanks to your direct actions, he has devoted himself to the protection of others and gained the hidden basic class 'Bulwark' (Rare). For finding hidden information, your deity has granted you 150 Exp!

Dylan was staring into space, the look someone got when checking notifications or their status. He blinked after a few moments and cracked the first smile Joe had seen from him today. The smith took a few measurements and told them to come back in an hour. Apparently, he would rush a job for a client who would 'use his work properly'. Dylan looked over to Joe. "Did you know he would offer me a new class?"

"No, I only came here so you could get measurements taken," Joe answered truthfully. "Can you tell me anything about your class?"

"Mmm." Dylan got a faraway look again. "Huge bonus to defense, great knockback resistance, and I can use shields to attack without the normal penalties. I got a new skill right away; it's called 'stand behind me'. Let's me move at triple my normal speed to get in front of a party member and block an attack. Also, the smith told me he knows what I need for progression, all the way to the *third* tier! I'll just need to prove that I am using my abilities to protect others and do some work for him."

"That's seriously awesome, man!" Joe enthusiastically congratulated him. They talked for a bit longer, deciding to just wait the hour instead of leaving and coming back. When the smith entered the room again, Dylan seemed to tense up. The newly minted Bulwark almost seemed ready to hyperventilate when his new armor was handed over; the smith instructing him to equip it.

He calmed down quickly after the armor was on, and a huge grin appeared. "Joe! This armor is a class item now! It's only missing two pieces and it'll be a full *set*. I will have *set* armor!" Set armor was gear that was made to work together perfectly, complementing all the other pieces. A full set was often better than having a couple of amazing pieces because a full set usually came with a large bonus.

"Well, if you want a full set, you are going to need to put these on." The smith grinned as he pulled two large shields out from behind the counter. Handing them over, he grinned at the look on Dylan's face.

"*Two* shields? How am I supposed to fight?" Dylan equipped them, a wide smile stretching his face as the metal implements appeared on each arm. His question was answered by the spikes on the front of the shields.

"If you push them together, they link kinda like magnets. Then you jab the bottoms into the ground, and you can pretend to be a wall." The smith seemed pleased at the reaction he was getting. "Look at the bonus you get for having all the set equipped. I think you'll like it."

"Increased defense, halved movement and weight penalties,

and…" Dylan paused, then tears filled his eyes, "thirty-five percent *numbing*? Joe! This armor makes it so that I don't feel the pain!"

"*As much* pain," the smith warned carefully.

"Yeah, that!" Dylan started back to the barracks. "Let's get going! I have Wolfmen to get revenge on!"

Joe started to follow, but a loud cough brought his attention to the smith. "Forgetting something?"

"Ah, yes. Here's the bank notes. Make sure he never knows about this, alright?" Joe dropped a sizable stack of banknotes on the table, and the smith nodded at him gravely.

"It's a good man who returns a warriors will to fight. In the future, you'll get a discount here." The smith turned and walked away, and soon, soundless hammer blows were raining down on an ingot of some kind.

Charisma +1! 10% discount gained at Masterwork Metals.

Joe had fourteen points in charisma, and therefore was now fourteen percent more charismatic than the average person. He liked the thought of that. Turning, he made his way back to his team.

CHAPTER TWENTY-FIVE

"Let's do this!" Dylan slammed his fists together, sparks flying as his metal gauntlets connected. "I want to get out there and show those mangy, stinking Wolfmen who they're messing with!"

The party was passing through fox territory, and while the foxes were avoiding everyone else, they seemed to be eying Joe hungrily. It might just be his imagination. Still, he moved closer to the center of the party and listened to their conversation. Tiona seemed pleased with the change in Dylan's attitude. "Glad to hear it! I was thinking that this morning we would go a bit deeper into their territory. We could try and find an area where the higher leveled ones like the Warriors and mages are hanging out. Good call on asking the guards to split that quest up."

Joe grinned at that as well. Having three quests that he actually had a chance to complete in a timely manner was exciting. Joe was getting close to level six, and the free characteristic points were calling to him like a siren song. Less than a thousand points to go, and the possible rewards for today would go a long way toward helping him work at his long-term goals. He looked at the three quests, hoping they could finish them all in one go.

Quest: Scouring the Scouts. The Wolfman population has been growing quickly, and Scouts have begun marking targets for their people to attack. Reduce their numbers. Wolfman Scouts killed: 0/20. Reward: Exp: 500. 20 gold. Bonus available if enough are destroyed.

Quest: Disarming the Warriors. The Wolfman population has grown fast enough that their fighters have begun using weapons and armor to gain an advantage. Unfortunately, their gear is stolen from the humans they kill before being modified to fit their larger forms. Reduce their numbers. Wolfman Warriors killed: 0/10. Reward: Exp: 1000. 30 gold. Bonus available if enough armor and weapons are reclaimed or destroyed.

Quest: Witch hunt. The Wolfman population has advanced to a point where they are making connections with the deeper mysteries. Destroy any Wolfman Shamans you find. Wolfman Shamans killed: 0/5. Reward: Exp: 2000. 50 gold. Bonus available if their magical research is reclaimed or destroyed.

Joe almost started dancing when he got the quests, and he wasn't the only one. Thirty-five hundred experience, a hundred gold, and possibilities for bonuses? For the others, this was a chance to make a thousand dollars in one fell swoop. For Joe, this was a chance to be able to get his constitution and strength high enough that he could walk at a normal pace and distance for extended periods of time! He almost fainted in delight… or maybe exhaustion from walking so far.

There was a small downside to Dylan's new armor. Stealth was no longer an option. He didn't yet have any heavy armor mastery, and he couldn't get any extra bonuses such as noise reduction until he got the missing skill to at least beginner levels. He sounded like a forge, each step clanging and clattering. His shields also tended to bounce off his legs as he walked, causing Guess and Chad's eyes to twitch every few seconds as the metal squealed. When they entered wolf territory, they began drawing attacks every few minutes.

"I! Love! This! Armor!" Dylan bellowed as yet another wolf

staggered backward from a concussive blow to the head. Two wolves used his apparent inattention to leap at him, but he only laughed and put the shields together, letting the animals bounce off the spiked surface. He had found that he had great abilities with stunning, staggering, and enraging enemies but dealt very little actual damage. He didn't seem to mind and simply had great fun taunting his enemies and not feeling pain as they crashed into the wall of metal that was his body. "Dire wolf? More like *dying* wolf!"

"Oh no," Guess mechanically spoke as she dug her blades into a wolf's neck. "He got his sense of humor back."

"That was a joke? I thought he had just taken a blow to the head," Chad chipped in wryly.

"A little of this, a little of that," Tiona quipped with a smile at the Bulwark. He didn't seem to mind their teasing and was usually quick to return any verbal barbs. Right now, he just seemed to be enjoying himself.

"More! Let's see what level they need to be to do damage to me under this gear!" Dylan clanked forward, deeper into unexplored territory.

The others looked at Tiona, who shrugged and nodded. "You heard the man. Let's knock out these quests!" The group cheered and strolled forward. Dylan hadn't gotten too far, the weight of his armor allowing even Joe to keep pace without issue.

When Chad made one joke too many about the slow pace, Dylan replied haughtily, "Pretty soon I'll have heavy armor mastery, and I'll be able to jog at your running speed."

"As if!" Chad sprinted forward, vanishing into the forest in an instant. "Think before you speak, ya tin can!"

"I'll get-" Dylan roared, but stopped suddenly as Chad came flying back with a worried expression on his face. "What's wrong?"

"I found a trail, there are Wolfmen patrolling it pretty heavily. There is a group coming now, three Scouts and two Warriors. From the look of things, we just missed another patrol. If this is the norm, we will only have a few minutes to off this group before another is here."

Dylan looked to Tiona. "Fight or flee?"

"This isn't making sense," Tiona said with a growl. "We haven't seen any Scouts yet today, and suddenly, we run into them and *Warriors*, which we only found for the first time yesterday?"

"Tiona!"

"Fine! We fight!" Tiona's sword was instantly in her hand. "Battle formation, we'll hit them as soon as they start to pass us. Guess, can you get across the trail and start backstabbing as soon as their eyes are on us?"

"Heh." They looked around but couldn't see the source of the monotone chuckle.

"That better be a yes!" Tiona hissed into the empty air, followed by a sullen mutter, "I hate rogues."

At this point, the Wolfmen patrol was reaching detection range, so everyone stopped speaking and moving. The Scouts seemed to be alerted already, their ears twitching in all directions as they padded forward on silent paws. When the first two were past the humans who were hiding just off the beaten path, Tiona exploded forward and aimed a brutal chop at the third Scout. As a testament to his reflexes, the beast wasn't beheaded instantly, but still gained a deep gash across his chest and neck that promised a swift death nonetheless.

As one of the Warrior's began to howl, possibly attempting to bring reinforcements, Chad accurately placed an arrow in the unprotected muscle where his neck and shoulder joined. Instead of a howl, only a pained yelp sounded. The Scouts were using their javelins to fend off Tiona and the lumbering Dylan, but Dylan only laughed at their attempts as he barreled forward and let the thin weapons shatter on his thick gear. Tiona used the distraction to move forward with perfect form, her sword dancing through the air.

The wounded Warrior shuddered and fell, revealing Guess and her blood-dripping daggers behind him. Two Scouts and a

Warrior having fallen already, the final Scout turned and ran while the Warrior tried to keep the focus of the battle on himself. He was obviously playing for time, hoping for reinforcements. Joe was determined that no wolf would turn the battle against them, and he snarled as he directed his spell. The sprinting being was at the outer range of his spell, but his speed was his undoing as a spike appeared in his path. The Wolfman coughed blood as he impaled himself, and an instant later an arrow severed his brainstem as Chad landed a critical hit.

The Warrior, seeing his chance for life vanishing, snarled and charged Dylan. He began to glow red, as a berserker rage overcame him. His sword whistled through the air, and Dylan struggled to keep up as the blows rained down. The others moved to help, but he stopped them. "Gotta! **Clang** Get. **Clang** Used to this! **Clang** **Clang**

The Warrior grabbed his sword with both hands and swung in a heavy overhand chop. Dylan lunged forward and interrupted the attack with a shield bash to the abdomen. The Warrior fell to the ground, and Dylan nodded to Tiona. She stepped forward, sinking her sword into the prone target.

Quests updated: Scouring the Scouts. Wolfman Scouts killed: 3/20. Disarming the Warriors. Wolfman Warriors killed: 2/10.

Joe wondered where his experience notification was for a moment before remembering that he had set most notifications to only show in a safe zone or when he brought them up. He looked at the mess they had made on the path and made an 'oops' sound. "I don't think the next patrol will miss this when they come along."

"Yeah, especially with their enhanced senses. *I* can smell the blood." Tiona looked at the gore and made a decision. "Right. We did good work here. Let's start going down the path, towards any patrols that are coming. Chad, Guess, which of you wants to scout ahead? I liked how our ambush went, let's keep it up."

"I'll go," Chad volunteered easily. "I'm trying to get my

tracking and spotting skill up anyway. Might as well get started here." He waved and trotted down the path. "See you in a few."

"Alright team, from here on out it is going to be a heavy grind." Tiona motioned for everyone to walk as she talked. "We expect the patrols to be about five minutes' walk apart. Scouts use javelins and bows, the Warriors are armed and armored. If we can't ambush them, make sure to focus on cutting down the Scouts first. They *are* using poisoned weapons, after all, and the Warriors will have a harder time escaping us."

As she finished her speech, Chad came bounding out of the tree line. "Next patrol five hundred feet out!"

"Off the path!" Tiona hissed as she slid into the foliage. They all made it before the next patrol was in sight, though Dylan did have a hard time walking off the hard-packed dirt; his feet sunk into the earth with each step, and he wobbled as he moved. Falling silent, they waited for their foes to appear.

It took longer than they thought it would, because apparently the wolves had either heard something or were getting a bad feeling. One of the Scouts was lagging behind by almost fifteen feet, obviously poised to run if there was a problem. Tiona elbowed Joe, pointed at the Scout, and gave him a meaningful look. Joe nodded, stretched his hand toward the Scout, and started casting his attack spell. Tiona launched into the mass of Wolfmen just as the shadow spike impaled the trailing Scout through it's calve. Leaping from soft ground wasn't ideal for an ambush, but she still managed to inflict some light wounds on the Wolfmen before they could mount a proper defense.

This group only had one Warrior in it, but he was well on his way to becoming an Elite if the amount of metal he carried was any indication. Dylan's eyes were locked on this enemy, and he strolled forward with a challenging shout at the beast. The Warrior was perfectly happy to have an opponent decided for him, and he rushed the Bulwark with his cleaver held high. Dylan blocked his blows–too heavy to dodge them–and punched out at the Warrior over and over with his shields.

Joe's first target had collapsed to the ground, falling dead from the accumulated damage of the rapidly cast spell. Thirty damage per use was no joke. Another Scout had gotten into an arrow battle with Chad, both of them dodging and spinning as they launched projectiles back and forth. Chad was the first to stumble, and an arrow slid into his gut, luckily heavily slowed by his thick leather armor. He grunted, and the Scout stopped moving to see if the fight was over. It was his last mistake, as Chad used the moment to launch a precision shot, and the resulting critical hit slew the anthropomorphic wolf.

Guess dropped from a branch, landing on the shoulders of one of the Scouts who was using a javelin. As his knees buckled, Guess slammed her daggers into either side of his neck and severed both jugulars. She did a backflip off the Scout as a geyser of blood exploded into the air. "Woo. Hoo." She paused for a moment. "That's somewhat less fun to say when it is in a monotone."

Tiona had finished off her target and was standing and glaring at Dylan as he fought the Warrior. Dylan's new armor was gaining some fresh dents, but the two were fairly evenly matched. The human couldn't deal much damage due to using a weapon designed for defending, and the Wolfman could do little damage due to Dylan's high defense. Joe looked at them, then Tiona. "Shouldn't we help him?"

"Shouldn't he have listened when I told him to focus on the Scouts first?" She crossed her arms and waited to move until the Wolfman's cleaver bounced off Dylan's helmet, causing him to stumble. *Then* she darted forward, sheathing her sword in the Warrior's abdomen as he reared back for a finishing blow.

As the last enemy fell, Tiona whirled on Dylan. "We are doing a grind here, Dylan. I know you are pissed off at the Warriors, but you need to follow my orders out here. We are going for efficient quest clearing, not a cathartic exchange of blows. If you need to hit something to work off your anger, take a job at a smithy and beat on metal! You good?"

Dylan blearily nodded his head as Joe topped off his health.

Joe hadn't been neglecting his duties; Chad was already cured of his poisoning as well as being at full health. Dylan shrugged. "Sorry. I got a bit overexcited."

"Don't do it again! If we finish these quests today, that's half of this month's game pod fee! We don't know how long these quests will be available; if some jerk goes and kills off the whole tribe, we're gonna need to find a new income and set of quests." She took a deep breath. "Sorry. Sorry. I'm already lagging behind on payment this month because the best score we found was the silver wolf hide. We need to step it up and really treat this as a new job. I'm not even making as much as I was at my old office-"

Chad jumped in before she could get too worked up, "Well, let's not stand around here and waste time then! Let's get hunting! There is gold to be found and quests to complete!"

CHAPTER TWENTY-SIX

Quest complete: Scouring the Scouts. Wolfman Scouts killed: 20/20. Exp: 500. Continue destroying Scouts to gain a bonus or return to town for your monetary reward.

Quest updated: Disarming the Warriors. Wolfman Warriors killed: 9/10.

These notifications popped up as they finished slaying the most recent patrol. They had taken some injuries, but between Dylan's new class and Joe's healing, they had been able to continue at a good pace. Looking at his experience from the quest and the three hundred seventy five gained from the creatures themselves, Joe smiled as he saw that he only needed one hundred and twelve points to reach the next level! Chad waved and ran off to find the next patrol, while the others slowly moved down the currently clear path.

"I wouldn't normally ask, but since we are both in pods…" Joe's voice trailed off as Tiona raised an eyebrow. "What did you do for work before you started playing?"

"Huh. I thought that was going a different direction." Tiona winked at Joe, and a bit of color entered his cheeks. "You're going to laugh."

"No, I won't!" Joe promised as he thought of a way to tease her in return.

"It's ironic, but I was a party planner." Tiona's words made the others grin. "I left that behind because I didn't like the outside stress. Other people changing their minds about massively expensive billable items, the drama… it just got to be too much."

"From a party planner to a party leader." Guess smiled at her. "That is ironic."

"Yeah, yeah." Tiona stuck her tongue out at Guess. "Still, it was interesting. This is better for my sanity though."

"Getting chewed on by wolves and having poisoned arrows stuck in you is *better* for your sanity?" Dylan quipped in a serious tone.

"Well, the game *literally* is better for my sanity." Tiona chuckled, then looked around at the confused faces. "You all didn't read the fine print? Maybe it is just the pods that have that function… no, I'm pretty sure…"

"What are you talking about?" Dylan prodded her as she trailed off.

"The pods balance your brain chemistry. Like, *perfectly*, over time. Why did you think this game is so expensive to play every month if you are in a pod? It's been proven to essentially reset your brain. Depression? Gone in two months. No drugs needed ever again unless you let yourself go." Tiona's eyes were bright as she remembered the controversy this system had generated. "Autism? Well, that is caused by your brain chemistry being out of whack. The first patient was cured and reintroduced to society after a year during trials. No scientist can explain it, and since the game's makers aren't advertising this game as a cure for mental disorders, they don't need to explain themselves or release their data to groups like the FDA."

"So *that* is why the pods are on backorder for a year?" Dylan sounded incredulous. "I was lucky to even get an updated helmet!"

"Yup. The pods are getting filled up with sick people, and

they are often getting preference. No one knows why, they just assume that President Musk is trying yet another way to save humanity. I *know* the helmet has a similar effect, I think it's just slower. Oh, crap." Tiona pointed ahead. "We talked too much. Patrol incoming! Where's Chad?"

"Chad!" No answering reply came as Dylan shouted. "Damn. I'll draw their attention. Get ready!"

The group coming toward them was significantly more dangerous than anything else they had fought today. There were four heavily armed and armored Warriors and one unknown Wolfman covered in bones and leather that Joe assumed to be a mage of some kind. A Shaman possibly? This is what they were looking for! Dylan bumped his fists together and did what he could to draw attention as Guess slipped into the shadow of some nearby trees. Tiona glanced at Joe. "Joe. Take out the unknown if you can."

Joe nodded and started making gestures. As the unit raised their weapons in the final charge, an inky black spike shot out of the ground toward the Shaman. **Dong!* * The spike slammed into a field of energy that seemed to appear from nowhere. As the spike shattered, the Shaman's eyes locked on Joe and he shouted. The other Wolfmen then turned their hard gaze on Joe, and their speed increased. Joe's face paled. "Uh-oh."

Dylan didn't take too well to being ignored by what he considered to be his rivals. With a bellow, he charged into the midst of the enemies, knocking one Warrior off his feet in the process. The others were on him in an instant, their blows aiming for weak points and joints. Dylan took on all challengers, and his shield mastery skill helped him redirect attacks as he shifted his stance and took the brunt of the damage on his dual shields. It wasn't to last though, with three opponents and a fourth joining soon, he was beginning to take real damage.

Tiona joined the fight, but her attempts to avoid the Warriors and cut down the Shaman were thwarted quickly as two Wolfmen broke off their attack on Dylan to protect their charge. Her ability was apparent in her movement; she was skillfully avoiding attacks and leaving shallow wounds in her foe. She barked, "Cleave!" and the shallow swipe of her longsword turned into a deadly arc of metal that bit deeply into her adversary. A spray of arterial blood covered her just before a fireball landed on her chest and exploded. She flipped backward from the concussive explosion, stunned into stillness as she landed on the packed dirt.

A ball of water landed on her next, soothing the burns and restoring some of her lost health. Another landed on her, and she was able to shake off the impact and rejoin combat. Joe sent a few balls of water at Dylan, healing the bruises and reinforcing bones that were about to break from the strain of repeated blows. Casting healing spells was drawing attention back to him, and the Wolfmen started attempting to get around the other combatants to reach him.

Guess dropped from a branch, swinging her daggers down to take out the Shaman in a single blow. Just before her attack landed, the Warrior in charge of protecting the frail magic-user spun around and slashed out. Guess was sent flying backward, but she left one of her daggers in the Warriors' arm. His sword arm went limp as Guess crashed to the ground, spitting up a mouthful of blood. Tiona took advantage of the wounded beast's sudden weakness to deal a finishing blow, and the Warrior's head slid to the ground.

One of the Warriors broke off his siege on Dylan, twirling and running at Joe. Joe didn't see him until the last moment, having sent a healing spell at Guess. Joe turned his head just as the cleaver slammed into his neck, and the Warrior was blinded by the blood that sprayed over him. Joe slid to the ground just as the Warrior charged back to attack Dylan from behind. The Shaman was coaxing another ball of fire to his palm, and as he raised it to throw it at Tiona again, an arrow punched through the fire and the Shaman's hand. A look of horror flashed across the Shaman's face before the spell detonated. Charred beyond recognition, the Shaman swayed and slumped to the ground.

"I'm back! Sorry I'm late!" Chad called as he fired another shot from his bow.

"Better late than never," Tiona ground out as she attacked one of the Warriors harrying Dylan. "They got Joe."

"Damn!"

A swift kick to the back of his knee dropped Dylan to the ground, unable to maintain his position. Tiona killed one of the fighters as the other swung at the fallen Bulwark. He was stopped short as a spike appeared and skewered him. The Wolfman looked down, saw the hole in his body, and looked back toward Joe. The ritualist was standing, channeling the spike with one hand as he made a rude gesture with the other. The spike vanished as did the light in his foe's eyes.

Joe stepped forward, rubbing his neck as he healed the others. "That sucked," he said in a raspy voice. He coughed wetly. "I sound like I've been smoking for a decade."

Tiona just stared at him. "How are you alive? Your head was basically cut off!"

"Robes, and no matter what we say, this is a game," Joe replied carefully as his voice returned to–mostly–normal. "These robes are a magic item. If something just about kills me, it sets me back to one health. Same thing as when the silver wolf ambushed us, remember?" Joe didn't feel like explaining the limitations of the robes. No need to give away all of his trump cards at once.

"I want some," Guess piped up. This got a laugh from the group.

"It actually sucks pretty hard." Joe wheezed, spitting out some blood. "Yeah, there is the great perk of not dying, but… my head was basically *severed*. Do you know what it's like to feel that, survive, and then have it reattach as I heal? It's…"

There was silence for a moment. Dylan spoke softly then, "How do you do it? It nearly broke me when I was…"

Joe thought for a second. "It must be the pod balancing out my mind as the trauma ends. Thanks to Tiona, I finally understand how it is doing it, but…" Joe stopped speaking as he remembered that he wasn't *in* a pod. Technically. The game was able to impact him in a more… direct fashion.

A notification blinking gold pulled him away from his line of thought. As soon as it had his attention it displayed its words as Joe was lifted from the ground on a surge of golden wind.

Quest complete: Disarming the Warriors. Exp: 1000! Return to the quest assigner for monetary rewards, or work at the secondary objective for additional rewards!

Quest updated: Witch hunt 1/5.

Skill increased: Mana manipulation (Novice V), Heal (Novice IX). Exp: 90.

You have reached level six! You have gained one point in intelligence, wisdom, and perception. You have five characteristic points to distribute and sixteen unused skill points!

Joe settled down onto the ground, a wide grin on his face. "Oh heck yes. I feel *good.* Guys. Guys. I have five characteristic points to use. I'm about to be able to walk at a normal human pace!" He started reaching for his status window to add in the points, but Tiona caught his hand and stopped him.

"Wait!" She was squinting at him uncertainly. "Are you saying you're about to cross a threshold?"

"A threshold? If you mean getting my stats to a basic human level, ten points, then yes." Joe's smile was slipping a bit as she shook her head.

"Wait until you are in a safe area," she unceremoniously ordered. "You are almost assuredly going to pass out, and it is going to really suck for you. Also, take some time to read the guild wiki. As long as you are in-game it is available to you, and you keep not knowing important things."

"Are you being serious?" Joe's certainty wavered. "C'mon, I've been waiting for this-"

"I am." She smiled at him though. "Feel free to bring your stats up to nine though! Just, don't go to ten."

"Fair enough." Joe dramatically frowned then rolled his eyes. A few more hours wouldn't bother him much. Looking at the stats that were just… abysmal… he found that with the five points he could bring two of his three physical stats to ten, but one would not be able to make it. Strength, dexterity, or constitution. His first instinct was to bring strength and constitution up, but… he needed to be practical. As he started to get higher levels of spells and rituals, he was sure that dexterity would come into play. Maybe… if he could make hand motions faster or more accurately, could he cast spells quicker? He was almost sure of it so he put one point into dexterity and two into strength. The remaining two would need to wait until he got home, apparently.

They barreled along the path, eager to make progress in their remaining quest. Joe found it a bit easier to keep up, but in reality, a two percent increase was not enough to show a significant change. The day was drifting towards afternoon at this point, and if they wanted to finish the final quest, they needed to give up on stealth and subtlety. Their full frontal charge may have been a mistake because as they rounded a trail they came upon what appeared to be a sacrificial altar. The altar itself wasn't the issue; the fact that it was surrounded by a small swarm of Warriors and a few Shamans–all of whom turned their heads to observe the interruption as the party came crashing into the open–was a bit troubling. For a moment, there was silence as the two sides simply looked at each other in shock. The stalemate was broken by a plaintive cry.

"For the love of all that is good, *help*! They're killing us!" A woman bound to the altar was at *just* the right angle to see the arrivals.

Joe felt sick as the Wolfmen remembered what they were doing. Without any further pause, the main Shaman grimaced and plunged his dagger into the bound woman's heart. A deep throbbing filled the air, and Joe began to feel a buildup of power. The hair on his arms was tingling, standing on end as the abundance of mana created physical after effects. The Shaman beckoned, and a Warrior grabbed the next bound human and started dragging him to the altar.

Timed Quest alert: 'Blood for the Beast God.' You have stumbled upon an altar that Wolfmen are using to commit dark deeds. After losing the better part of their territory to human invaders, the Wolfmen are attempting to assert their dominance in a horrific way. Stop the Wolfmen before they are able to complete their ritualistic sacrifices. Sacrifices: 4/10. Rewards: variable.

Alternatively, you can choose not to help the humans. If you do nothing, you will gain the option to change your race to 'Wolfman' if the human Kingdom falls. You will also gain the title 'Racial Traitor', allowing you to kill humans for experience! Betraying and attacking your teammates will increase your starting favor with the Wolfmen by +1000.

"I'm going to assume *right now* that none of you are stupid enough to betray us and that you want to save those people," Tiona snarled as she slapped the notification out of her view. "Battle formation. Guess, take out any targets of opportunity. Joe, healing *only* unless it is an emergency. Chad, try and mess with any spells coming our way. Dylan, let's put that new class to the test."

Dylan's only response was to slam his fists together and roar at the Warriors standing between him and the people they needed to save.

CHAPTER TWENTY-SEVEN

The altar was raised a few feet off the ground, but wasn't huge or imposing like Joe would have expected from a sacrificial altar. Of course, in his mind, a sacrificial altar should be a huge Mayan structure that thousands of people gathered around for religious purposes. This was just a stone bed that was currently coated in flowing blood. Human blood. Joe shook his head to clear his thoughts just as the first few Warriors rushed at them. Dylan took center stage, holding off two of the four Warriors with ease while Tiona and Guess each stepped in to hold off another.

The main Shaman began chanting, and just as he reached a crescendo… his knife began to descend. An arrow bounced off the blade, turning it and knocking the dagger from his hand just before impact. The Shaman ended up punching the bound man in the chest decently hard, but a few seconds of breathlessness was a welcome result for the human. The Shaman looked over to see Chad making rude gestures before loosing another arrow at him. Not reacting in the slightest, the Shaman watched as the arrow bounced off a translucent shield that the force of the bolt revealed. A small lightning bolt jumped from the altar to the Shaman as the spell that he had been attempting to cast created backlash, but he simply tilted his head and cracked his neck before sauntering over to retrieve his dagger. The other Shaman looking on seemed to be holding their breath until he returned, shuddering with glee when the chanting began again.

"Ha! Filthy mongrels!" Dylan shouted at the Warriors he was holding off. He bashed one on the snout as he parried a blow from the other. "I got my shield mastery to Beginner three already! Your attacks mean *nothing*!"

The Wolfman that had been struck reeled backward, grabbing his nose as it streamed blood. He snarled animalistically, and started hacking at Dylan with brutal overhand chops as the other tried to slip around Dylan's defense with a more tactical approach. The brutal chops were easily predicted, even if they were powerful, and not one of them slipped by.

"You should probably call this mutt's older brother!" Dylan called to no one in particular. "It seems his *little sister* stole his weapon and armor and is playing dress-up!"

Foam appeared around the Warrior's mouth as his eyes lost all sanity. He tossed aside his sword and started slamming his claws into the obstacle in his way, trying to tear Dylan apart with his bare hands. When he was easily blocked, he tried to grab the shield and pull the Bulwark off balance–failing miserably. He dropped to the ground, a spike of shadow having stolen his life before he noticed the damage accumulating.

"Joe!" Tiona called angrily as she whirled around her opponent and eviscerated him. "What did I tell you *not* to do?"

"Oh come on!" Joe laughed as he tossed a healing spell at Dylan. "That was a perfect opportunity; I *had* to take it." Tiona didn't say anything else, but her silence only ensured that the conversation would be happening at a later date. Joe looked at the altar and heard the chanting once again reaching a peak. As he noticed an arrow get deflected by a shield a subordinate Shaman was maintaining, Joe had an idea and grimaced. As the knife came down and slammed into the captive's chest, Joe channeled a ranged healing spell. A flow of water reached the attempted sacrifice and settled into a laminar stream. The Shaman pulled the knife out of the human, already motioning for another sacrifice when the bound man coughed.

The Shaman looked shocked—even more so when the feedback from his failure to complete a sacrifice at the correct time hit him—finally noticing the stream of water connecting the humans together. He shrieked, his ears flattening against his head as he snarled at Joe. Seemingly reaching a conclusion, he waved at two of the lesser Shamans. They left the area around the altar, joining the fight against the adventurers. At this point, Guess had been injured fairly badly but was surviving thanks to a hastily wrapped bandage. All but the last Warrior facing Dylan had been felled, though there were other Warriors that were currently assisting the Shaman. These Warriors were motioned to join the battle as well, and Joe winced as he noted how heavily equipped they were. These were certainly the elite of the Wolfman race.

Now facing seven enemies, the party closed together again. Joe stopped healing the sacrifice, knowing that the magical Wolfman only stabbed at the peak of his chant. He healed Guess to the maximum amount—unable to heal the fractured bones in her hip—noting that his mana was down to a quarter as exhaustion began settling on him. Joe grimaced as he thought about Tiona's orders. He should have listened; over half of his mana had been used for that channeled spike. It was refilling fairly quickly thanks to his huge regeneration, but the battle was nowhere near over. In fact, it looked like the battle was just getting started.

The largest Warrior—easily the highest level Elite—approached at a jog. His movements were so fluid that when he was dodging it almost looked like Chad's arrows were poorly aimed. The Elite half-turned as he got close and swung his cleaver almost casually at Dylan. The Bulwark caught the blow with a grunt, actually being forced back a few feet as his armor vibrated under the powerful blow. A fireball hit the ground at their feet causing blisters to instantly form on any exposed skin as the flames washed over the group.

Joe quickly countered the blaze with his healing water spells, but frowned as they only healed half the amount they normally did. It seemed that the magical flames were going to need a more concentrated healing effect than he was currently creating. Not good! The Elite was battering Dylan around like a practice dummy, and the other three were closing in quickly. Joe looked around for a solution to the issue and saw that Guess was running into the forest. He almost called out, but stopped himself at the last moment. If she was trying to circle around, he didn't want to ruin the element of surprise for her. Tiona shouted a warcry–boosting their stamina and strength by a small amount–and launched herself at the incoming Warriors.

Her sword was flashing back and forth; her skill allowing her to hold off the two Wolfmen on her own. She wasn't able to strike devastating blows, but she and they were beginning to bleed from multiple cuts. Fortunately for her, she had a healer in her corner. As she wore them down, she was able to continue battling unabated. She needed to stay close to the Warriors, because any time she broke away to gain distance a fireball exploded against her. Chad was doing his best to break whatever magical shielding the Shamans were using, but no matter what angle he tried his arrows continued to bounce off the shield surrounding the two of them.

Quest updated: Blood for the Beast God. Sacrifices: 5/10.

Joe's head jerked to the side as he got the notification; he watched as the unsmiling Shaman tossed aside a corpse and motioned at one of the few remaining members of its race to bring forward another human. Joe shouted in fury and started swinging his scepter at the Elite attacking Dylan. Sadly, he was unable to damage the massive Warrior with his pathetic attacks. A backhanded blow sent him reeling and coughing out blood. He instantly healed himself and tried to think of a way to be more helpful. Breathing deeply, he stared at the Warrior Tiona was fighting and prepared himself. Carefully positioning his hand, he made the required gestures and created a spike under the Warrior's foot just as he stepped backward. Expecting solid ground, the Warrior's ankle turned and he fell with a startled yelp.

Tiona didn't miss the opportunity, and sliced open the Wolfman's neck with a flick of her wrist. She tumbled to the side as a fireball whizzed by her head, and after regaining her footing, she began fighting the other Warrior one-on-one. Now that she was able to focus on just one battle, the Wolfman started to lose badly. In just a few moments he fell as well, surprise etched across his beastly face.

"Tiona!" Dylan shouted as a bright blue fireball cast jointly by the two attacking Shamans burned through the air toward her. "*Stand behind me!*" His legs seemed to move almost of their own accord, and he blurred as he sprinted at triple speed to get between her and the fireball. Dylan's arms slammed together, and he jammed the completed shield into the ground. The fireball detonated against the man, and screams filled the air as the metal he was covered in became superheated. The blast was otherwise entirely negated thanks to his position, but his armor was glowing as red as it had when it was being forged.

Dylan continued to yell in pain as the armor applied a damage-over-time effect to his body. Joe threw a ball of water at him in an attempt to heal and cool him, but it was a poor decision. The water almost instantly turned to steam, scalding Dylan's face through his visor and pulling another pained cry from the man. Another ball of fire was being formed between the two Shamans as they chanted together, but it seemed that Guess decided to return to the battle in the nick of time. She sprinted up to them as their brows furrowed from concentration, and plunged her daggers into the mana shield covering them. Again and again she stabbed as the fireball began to roil. With a sound like glass shattering, the shield broke and her daggers plunged into unprotected kidneys.

Freezing as the pain and shock overcame him, the Shaman lost control of his portion of the spell. Guess only had a second's warning but managed to squeeze herself behind his rigid body. The fireball exploded wildly, finishing off the damaged Shaman and critically wounding the other. An arrow was *finally* able to sink into the downed Shaman, ending his existence. Chad shouted in pure exaltation as he watched his opponent expire from his feathered shaft.

Quest updated: Witch hunt: 3/5.

Quest updated: Blood for the Beast God. Sacrifices: 6/10.

"Drat it!" Tiona shouted furiously, "We're losing *people* over there! Let's cut this magically compensating pup down to size and *end* this!"

She and a pained Dylan began working together better than ever, her attacks going unanswered as Dylan blocked every slash the Elite could muster. She was able to circle around the huge beast, swinging low as Dylan launched forward. The combination sent the Warrior flying, knocking the wind out of him as he landed. Tiona swung her sword back, but before she could finish him… a spike shot into the gap under his helmet and into his brain.

Joe had the grace to look sheepish as both Dylan and Tiona made a 'what the heck' gesture. "Sorry, I'm not trying to steal your kills. He was going to gut you as your swing came down." He pointed at a long dagger the Elite was gripping in his hand, the final resort of the desperate.

"I'll let it go. This time," Dylan said in a mockingly angry tone. "That all of them?"

"Looks like it!" Tiona called darkly. "Let's carve these Shamans a new spell-hole."

Quest updated: Blood for the Beast God. Sacrifices: 7/10.

"Son of a-!" Joe stopped himself, taking a deep breath. "He sped up!"

"Joe? Buddy? Make with the healing? Pretty please?" Dylan dropped to one knee panting heavily as he struggled to keep his tunnel vision from turning into full-blown unconsciousness.

"Oh, right! Sorry, my charred friend!" Joe pressed his hand against Dylan, and water started pouring over him. By this point, the armor had lost most of its residual heat, and the healing properly took effect. Since the damage under his armor was the result of superheated metal, not the magical flames–technically–there was no issue restoring him to full health. Joe glanced at his mana, noting that it was now just barely over an eighth full.

The group moved toward the altar, determined to stop the horror taking place. The main Shaman gave them a derisive sneer, motioning the remaining Shaman forward as his chanting increased speed yet again. The party jogged forward, but the Shaman erected a dome of power around the small area. Moments after creating the shield, they began sweating and trembling. Obviously the cost of creating and maintaining the barrier was high, and their mana was likely also being sapped to fuel the dark ritual being performed.

"Break through it!" Tiona ordered, emphasizing her words with action. Her action being chopping *specifically* at the Shaman's face. Though he flinched as the blow descended, her blade stopped dead an inch from impact. She was undeterred, and took this chance to work out some anger. Her sword crashed down, over and over as the Shaman paled further. As the rest of the team joined, the main Shaman stabbed another human.

Quest updated: Blood for the Beast God. Sacrifices: 8/10.

The main Shaman hurriedly pulled two bound humans right next to the altar and tossed the unlucky one onto it. He started his chant again, *much* faster this time. Sparks were flying as the team attacked the barrier as fast as possible. The chant reached a crescendo, and the knife plunged down yet again.

Quest updated: Blood for the Beast God. Sacrifices: 9/10.

"No!" Dylan roared, slamming bodily into the barrier. Tiona screamed as her blade clashed with the magic, which finally gave way. The shield shattered with a thunderous **boom**. The two Shamans sustaining the energy field fell into deep unconsciousness, their eyes rolling back into their head, but for Joe's team, it was *much* worse. The energy of the shield exploded outward, tossing the humans back. A portion of the damage they had done to the barrier affected them as true damage, ignoring all protections, while a larger part of their delivered force slammed into them as pure kinetic energy.

Joe was surprised to see the others tossed away, seemingly damaged to an extreme. He felt only a tiny impact, as he had been unable to participate directly in the destruction of the barrier. The chanting was becoming louder, so Joe decided that healing needed to wait. Now was the time for destruction. He narrowed his eyes and ran forward as quickly as his wasted legs would allow. He was still seven feet away when the dagger rose into the air in preparation of being used, so Joe began forcing his remaining mana into a shadow spike. Inky darkness slammed into the stomach of the Wolfman, but he managed to continue his chant, though it was now sounding more like a wheeze. As the dagger began to descend, Joe had only one option remaining to him. Narrowing his eyes and hoping for the best, he *jumped* at the Wolfman.

As his muscles bunched up, he felt a supreme confidence fill him. His body knew *exactly* how to jump to create the best effect. Joe launched into the air, spinning as the Shaman grew larger and larger in his vision. He drew back his scepter, planning to slam it into the animalistic chest presented to him, but he had misjudged his trajectory. Instead of jumping past the Wolfman, Joe's momentum carried him directly *into* the Shaman. Joe twisted like a cat, trying his best to land on his feet, but instead belly-flopped against his intended target. He tackled the Shaman to the ground, Joe's momentum too great for the Wolfman to counteract.

Looking at the creature he was pinning to the ground, Joe was surprised that he wasn't being savagely mauled by the cruel beast. He glanced down, realizing that the titanium taglock on his scepter was jammed directly into the Shaman's heart. Joe staggered to his feet as he tried to see the results of his actions, but turning his head made him lose his balance and fall to his knees. Both his mana and stamina bar were completely depleted, and the sudden movement caused him to puke all over the fallen Wolfman. Realizing how far he was from his starting point, Joe was shocked at the knowledge that he had just jumped nearly ten feet directly forward from a *very* slow movement speed. Was his jump skill *really* that overpowered?

Joe forced himself to stand on his unsteady legs, walking over and tugging at the rope binding the sacrificial human's hands and feet. The man thanked him brokenly, and for the next few minutes simply sat and cried over the bodies of his comrades. Joe looked over to see his team getting to their feet. Before coming up to the altar, they took a moment to impale the remaining Wolfmen who had fallen into a stupor. His team looked to him and nodded. Joe returned the nod, finally taking the time to acknowledge the notifications awaiting him.

Quest updated: Witch hunt: 5/5. Exp: 2000! Return to the quest giver for monetary rewards, or continue trying for the available bonus if Wolfman magical research is reclaimed or destroyed.

Quest updated: Blood for the Beast God. Sacrifices: 10/10. You have failed the Quest! (_Error_) You have completed the quest! (_Error_)

The notification window vanished with a sound like breaking glass, reappearing after a nerve-wracking moment.

How very… interesting! You have simultaneously completed and failed your quest. To your credit, you fought valiantly against your foes and will not be labeled a Race Traitor. There is only one small issue: You *completed the sacrificial ritual by killing the Wolfman Shaman via stabbing him through the heart at the correct moment during this ritual. What is your luck stat? You really might want to look into that. Normally, this situation would result in automatic quest failure and a wave of dark beasts sent to attack your city at night.*

You *seem to be a special case though, so there is an added option, Mr. Error-generator. As a ritualist and champion of a different deity than the one the ritual was designed for, you have met the requirements needed to wrest control of not only the activating ritual, but the* altar *as well. You may have a single chance to take control based on your knowledge of rituals. You have five minutes to attempt to do so. Reward: Control of altar, wave of dark creatures will attack Wolfmen population. Failure: Human city*

Ardania will have a powerful wave of beasts attack them through the night, and you will make me bored. This is the second time you have elevated an issue to me, so I will be paying a bit more attention to you. Also, boom. You're cursed.

New title gained: Baldy. Effect: Your head is permanently bald. You cannot change this fact; this title is mandatory. Wigs will burst into flame if placed on your head. Wearing a hat will give you a temporary -1 to charisma. Your head reflects light, -20% ability to hide when in sunlight.

Some settings have been permanently changed.

CHAPTER TWENTY-EIGHT

"Joe, what's going on?" Dylan called out as he approached the altar. "Also, what happened to you? Your hair is falling out!"

"No time for that." Already feeling the mana in the air beginning to thicken, Joe swallowed his frustration and opened his character sheet. "The quest changed. I have one chance to stop this ritual from taking effect, or the city is going to be attacked by extra strong monsters tonight." With a sad farewell to his accumulated skill points, Joe dumped twelve of the sixteen painstakingly gained points into his ritual skill.

Skill increased: Ritual magic (Apprentice III). Congratulations! Your hard work and dedication to perfecting your craft has allowed you to become more powerful! Based on your usage of the ritual skill to this point, you gain an addition to your abilities! Ritual magic now grants a 10% bonus to your chances of success when you are attempting to optimize, change, or create ritual formulas! Get out there, and change the world for the better! Or reduce an opponent into a puddle. Or magic a rock into solid gold. The only limiting factor is you! And what a limit that is. Intelligence and wisdom +1!

Allowing three minutes of his allotted time to pass before he started his attempt, Joe tried to calm his mind and prepare himself. His mana had fully regenerated at the two minute mark but he was still nervous that he might make things worse. With a deep breath, he approached the altar and placed his hands on the swirling light. In his mind, a large ritual diagram appeared. It took a few seconds for him to grasp all the elements of what he was seeing as the ritual spun slowly. Rituals could move? This was too far out of his experience! He almost panicked, but then he saw a few symbols that he recognized from the study of his book. From there, he was able to puzzle out the context and meaning of most of the remaining symbols. Overall, it truly wasn't an overly complicated diagram; it was simply well made and *massively* powerful.

Essentially, it took in the blood, experience points, stamina, and mana of the sacrifices and donated them as power to whatever deity controlled the altar. Looking over the diagram, it was easy to see how worn and faded it was… meaning that this ritual had been here for a *very* long time. If he was able to change it, the likelihood of another party being able to undo his actions was exceedingly low. Joe smiled at the thought. In the Kingdom, mages had long ago declared ritual magic a useless skill. It was time to prove all of them wrong.

The first symbol that changed was in the 'target' field. It currently held the symbol of Ardania. Joe was unsure at first how he was supposed to change this mark, but then his perception highlighted a symbol that all of the Wolfmen had on their clothes or armor. He nodded to himself and recreated the symbol in the ritual. He allowed his own mana to seep into the pattern, reinforcing the thinning lines of the aging ritual. The slow and jerky rotation of the spell circles smoothed, speeding up and spinning at a faster rate. Lastly, Joe looked down at his clothing and overwrote the symbol of what he assumed was the 'beast god' with the sigil on his robe. Now this altar would be devoted to the 'hidden god'. Simple changes, but hopefully all that was needed.

Joe looked over the changes one last time before stepping

back and hoping the entire thing wouldn't… explode. It didn't detonate, but it did begin shaking. Everyone in the area hastily retreated just before the altar was *sucked* into the ground. There was an awkward pause as his team gave him the stink-eye, but to his relief the altar quickly reappeared from the ground in a new configuration. Instead of a bed of stone coated in generations of muck, a pristine slab of marble rose from the ground. The main features were similar, but instead of a bed the altar now had the overall appearance of a large stone book.

Quest complete: Blood for the Beast God. After defeating the priests and warriors of an opposed race in pitched combat, you sullied their holy site and dedicated it to another deity! Remaining anonymous should be its own reward, but you greedy travelers probably want more than life-saving anonymity! Exp: 1100! (Base 1000 + 100 for each human saved). One class item box guaranteed to contain an item with a minimum rarity of 'rare'. -10,000 reputation with the Wolfman race for destroying their altar of holy rituals. Current reputation: Blood feud.

Since there were no surviving Wolfmen in the area, your reputation with the Wolfman population will be reset unless they learn the cause of their people's loss. Lucky you, brutality seems to be your key to your success! You know what? Luck +1. Why not. Current reputation with the Wolfmen: Neutral.

Fractured title gained: '…I choose to be…' This title grants a 10% boost to any title it is combined with.

Quest alert: 'Reclamation of the lost'. Congratulations! You have completed not only the original quest, but gained a hidden quest! As a champion of a god, you have the ability to capture altars and holy sites, rededicating them to your deity! While this will make your own power and favor grow with your god, be warned that followers of differing gods will see you as an enemy if they find out you are attempting to take their holy area away. Capture any altar, temple, statue, holy site, place of power, or effigy to gain favor and power from—and for—your deity. Rewards: Variable.

A small box appeared in front of each member of his team; they all eagerly grabbed their reward and stored it away for later usage. Chad was looking around nervously; just because they had cleared a small area of Wolfmen, there was no guarantee that more would not soon stumble upon them.

"Woo!" Dylan hooted excitedly. "I didn't die! I didn't even get too seriously injured! I *love* this class and armor!"

"I knew you were the right choice for a meatshield, er, tank role!" Chad called over, getting a laugh from Tiona and Guess. "Let's get out of here."

The group started to walk away, stopping when they noticed that Joe was not walking with them. Tiona's voice took on a hard edge as she noticed him standing at the altar. "Joe. Get moving, we are going to need to run if we want to make it back before nightfall."

"I need to write down this ritual!" Joe distractedly called back as he finished pulling paper and quills out of his pocket.

"Why?"

"It is insanely powerful! If I can modify it so that it doesn't require blood sacrifices, we could use this to-" Joe was cut off by Dylan snorting at him.

"She means 'why are you taking it down by hand'? Seriously man, read through the manual and guild wiki when we get back. Take a screenshot of that thing and work on it at home!" Dylan's words made Joe blush heavily. He hadn't considered that. Actually, he hadn't even known it was an option.

"Treat it like reality, Joe," Joe grumbled in a mocking tone as he made a screenshot of the ritual. "Make sure you know all the game functions so you can cheat reality, Joe."

"Are you really complaining that you can take a picture instead of using an hour to make a drawing in hostile territory?" Tiona incredulously teased him.

Joe muttered some unintelligible words before turning to walk away. He took half a step before stopping, frowning as something tickled at his senses. He cocked his head and looked at the altar. As the others complained, he walked back, reached under it, and found a small indentation. His fingers touched the space and a needle stuck into his hand, drawing blood. He grunted in shock as a notification appeared in his vision.

Skill increased: Hidden Sense (Novice II). You are finally letting your instincts guide you! Too bad they are so underdeveloped, you've missed a lot of good items. Gain higher levels in this skill to increase how powerfully hidden information and items call out to you!

Congratulations! You are the first traveler to take control of a fast travel point! Out of your whole species, you are the first to look for anything not overtly obvious! What does that say about your people's attention span? Nothing good! These points can be found at most important landmarks across Eternium. Since you are the first person to capture this point, you may choose to take control of it! Take control? Yes / No.

Joe chose yes, and his eyes widened as he read over the new notification.

Congratulations! As the owner of a fast travel point, you can set a toll for its usage. This might be the only thing in your life that you can really control, but let's not think about that too hard! Don't let the existential dread set in! You can choose to take ten percent of the user's mana or stamina and donate it to your deity, or require a monetary transaction which will be deposited to your bank account. What would you like to do?

Joe thought about it for a long moment but forced his inner greedy squirrel to go back to sleep. He chose to make the donation go toward Tatum; now anyone who got to use this would lose whatever was more abundant to their class. Mages would lose mana, others would lose stamina. Joe smiled as a white circle appeared around the area. In his vision, it was a beacon shining into the sky, but the others were looking at him with annoyance, obviously not seeing the light.

"Joe! Let's *go* already!" Chad called impatiently.

"Hey, guys, come here." Joe couldn't stop a smile from making his face twitch. "I need to, ah, show you something." He snorted from the effort needed to stop his laughter.

There were a few muttered curses, but the others decided to humor him. When everyone was in the circle, Joe chuckled and used his new rights as a travel point owner to give them access. They flinched as the beacon of light seemed to appear around them and went wide-eyed when they were asked if they wanted to fast-travel back to the only available location: Ardania.

Quest updated: Earn a god's favor. You have progressed far on the second step of this quest! Keep working hard! Progress: 83%.

A smile almost split Joe's face as he saluted the team and accepted the transport. He blinked and appeared in Ardania. Within moments, he was surrounded by the rest of his team.

CHAPTER TWENTY-NINE

Back in his room, Joe snorted as he remembered the walk back to the guild. He had brushed off the team's questions, explaining that it was 'a cleric thing'. Since they *had* been at an altar, the others had no choice but to accept his word as factual, though they hadn't done it gracefully. He had promised to open the point to Aten and give him permissions that would allow select guild members to use the travel point. This would let Joe keep donations to Tatum flowing and keep his standing in the guild fairly high even if he were off doing something different for awhile.

As much as Joe wanted to tell them what they wanted to know, there was no *possible* way that he was going to give up the information on how to activate the travel points. Being able to move huge distances was a staple of any game for the last few decades, and he knew that if word got out, he would have far too much competition for his burgeoning idea for a travel company. When he had gained enough fast-travel points to make a wide network, he would open them to the public and rake in the rewards. Maybe he would retire on a mountaintop in a few decades. Joe now had a long-ish term goal, and he hoped no one else would beat him to completion.

They had stopped to turn in the daily quests, so each of them were now a hundred gold richer. The others were happy with the outcome, but Joe really wanted to know what the rewards would have been if they had been able to complete the optional portions of the quest. The *real* reward Joe was interested in was the class item box he was staring at. It contained a guaranteed rare item, and Joe's hands were sweaty as he reached his trembling hand toward the clasp keeping it closed. It swung open, revealing a small black book. Joe began beaming as he picked it up and inspected it.

Reward item, perception check is automatic success! Item identified: Beginner's Encyclopedia Circulus (Forbidden Rare). This is a book containing dark rituals used to destroy, demolish, or otherwise impede your enemies. The knowledge contained has been forbidden by the Mage's College, and all copies existing during the purge were destroyed. While once this book would have been considered uncommon, its rarity has been adjusted due to external forces. Caution! Creating the rituals contained in this book while in the presence of a licensed Mage will result in a sharp reputation loss with the College. Activating them discreetly *will not, as most effects are similar to various spells. You really shouldn't worry about that though. Maybe you should declare war on the mages! It'd be fun!*

Looking at the book, Joe inspected it with his occultist job. The book glowed mostly golden, showing that while there was room for optimization, most of the rituals contained within were accurate. Opening the small book, he was excited and a bit disturbed by the effects of the rituals inside. There were only five complete rituals drawn out, but there were also multiple symbols, shapes, documentation of effects, spellforms, and components most commonly used in rituals. In essence, it was an encyclopedia which allowed you to make your own rituals with far greater ease.

Right now, there was only one attack ritual he had a chance of completing. The others required the next tier of monster Cores, and he simply had no idea if he could get his hands on one or what it would cost to do so. Ritual magic excelled as utility magic, long-term with intricate effects. These were offensive rituals, yes, but they were obviously designed as last resort doomsday devices, not commonplace weapons. Looking over the only completed attack ritual he could use–and they were *definitely* attack rituals–Joe had to wince as he read the description of its effects.

'Gravedigger's requiem'. This ritual targets a single creature, and upon activation, emits a sonic field around the victim. This field is attuned to the frequency of earth and stone and will soften the ground in a three foot radius around them. All earth in the affected area will act like quicksand, dragging them deep into the ground. Typically, the target will vanish without a trace, making this a preferred ritual for the assassination of important figures. Component cost: Copper tuning fork capable of reaching between 5 and 9 hertz (any tuning fork of uncommon quality or above), blood or hair of target, grave dirt, Sandshark's tooth, emerald (flawed or better), 80% of a full low grade monster Core, and 1000 mana.

After reading the requirements, Joe felt that he could get most of the listed items without too much issue. He wasn't *positive*, but it was likely a Sandshark was a monster, which meant that it would be harvested for components. He figured the alchemist would have this item, but he wasn't sure where to get a tuning fork. Was there an instrument store around here? What else would he need… eighty percent of a Core was four hundred points, which meant it should cost him roughly eighty? He did another quick calculation in his head; the mana requirement should be feasible, and it would cost him… four hundred and forty-five mana. Exactly one more point of mana than he currently had.

He rolled his eyes, his regeneration would ensure that he gained the needed point of mana before it became an issue, but it still irked him for some reason. Wait! He was forgetting his mana manipulation and coalescence skills! With a bonus eight percent efficiency, he had *more* than enough mana! He could stop cursing Terra now! An evil chuckle rocked him as he allowed himself a short vision of grandeur. Joe would stand on top of the world one day, and make the earth swallow dragons for him! Bwaha- **Cough**. Joe choked for some reason, making himself cough a few times. He took a sip of water, hugged his new book, and went to sleep.

At least, that was his plan. As his eyes closed, Joe remembered that he had two characteristic points to spend. His eyes flew open, bloodshot and excited. He sat up, pulling open his status sheet and staring at the two stats about to cross the threshold into 'normal' territory. With hands almost trembling from excitement, he allocated one point into both dexterity and constitution. Accepting the changes, he waited to notice a difference.

Minimum threshold for normalcy achieved! Body modification starting in three… two… one.

Ow. Ow. *Ow*! Ambient mana was sucked from the environment, fueling the rapid growth of his body. Joe winced as his nerves tingled, making his body twitch. The process sped up, and soon he was thrashing on his bed as if having a seizure. As this slowed down, Joe began to feel heavy. His body slowly sank into the bed, and he began to cough. Not cute little 'oh, dear me, there seems to be a hint of pollen in the air' coughs; these were a version more along the lines of 'I've been smoking for thirty years and my lungs seem to be full of tar'. It was a good analogy because thick black fluid came out of his mouth with each noisy hack. Landing mostly on the floor, the substance seemed to boil into nothingness and left Joe feeling as though he were imagining things.

When all of the shaking, coughing, and sputtering were complete. Joe stood up and tried to get a feel for the changes that had occurred. It was… strange. He felt heavy and slow while simultaneously being able to control his movements to a higher degree. Walking over to the small mirror provided with his room, Joe looked at himself and nearly started dancing. He didn't look like a walking corpse anymore! He had healthy flesh and color for the first time since appearing in this world! His body had filled out, and while he didn't exactly have a set of thick corded muscles, he did have muscle *tone* on his lean figure! As if he had never left his room but also ate exactly the amount of food he was supposed to. He pulled open his status screen.

Name: Joe 'Baldy' Class: Cleric (Actual: Ritualist) Profession: Scholar (Actual: Occultist)
Level: 6 Exp: 17978 Exp to next level: 3022
Hit Points: 50/50 (50+10 per point of constitution over 10)
Mana: 462.5/462.5 (Base 625, 12.5 per point of intelligence, +100% from deity)
Mana regen: 6.82/sec (.25 per point of wisdom)
Stamina: 50/50 (50+(0)+(0))

Characteristic: Raw score (Modifier)
Strength: 9 (0.09)
Dexterity: 10 (1.10)
Constitution: 10 (1.10)
Intelligence: 25 (1.25)
Wisdom: 27 (1.27)
Charisma: 14 (1.14)
Perception: 23 (1.23)
Luck: 14 (1.14)
Karmic Luck: +5

He looked at his hands and smiled. Now he could walk normally and do the basic functions that a human should be able to do! He would still attack with all the force of a fluffy pillow and could tell that he wouldn't be able to carry anything extra, but he was still overjoyed at his apparent fitness. Feeling greatly pleased with his expenditure of characteristic points, Joe climbed into bed and allowed himself to drift off to sleep.

The following morning, Joe awoke feeling chipper and excited. It seemed that a healthy constitution also made it possible for him to sleep on his poor quality bed and still gain the well-rested bonus! He felt ready for the day, and Joe could hardly wait for the shops to open. Ignoring his wrinkled robes,

Joe walked to the common area to scrounge up some coffee. Soon, he would be able to test out a new ritual, soon he would…! At that moment, Aten walked into the room and called for everyone's attention. "Listen up people! We have, as of this morning… become a *Noble Guild*!"

The calm early morning atmosphere shattered as everyone either whooped, called a question, or just excitedly began to chatter. Aten waved his arms and shouted to regain the attention of the group. "Today, unless you have a time-sensitive quest, I want everyone to stay in town and wait for myself and the guild officers to return. We have been invited to the castle to receive our first Noble Guild quest directly from the King and Queen!"

If the noise before had been excited, this was even more so. A few people begged for a promotion on the spot, a few were steaming mad that they didn't get to participate right away, but most were just happy for the guild. "All *current* guild officers, I am going to need you to join me near the castle gates in about two hours. Everyone else, I hope you are as happy about this as I am, and I *also* hope that if you are disappointed, you work to prove yourself capable of being a guild officer. As our roster fills out, we will need more and more officers to lead parties of new recruits! Good luck everyone, and great work so far!" With the end of the morning announcement, most people returned to whatever they were doing beforehand.

Joe wavered between excitement and exasperation toward the news. He *really* wanted to go set up rituals and practice with them, honing and refining his craft. He wanted to go and study magic until he was an undisputed master. Joe's eye twitched, and he sighed as he thought through his options: study and empowerment versus meeting royalty. Maybe he could…

He gave up; the guild *needed* not only him, but all members, to continue getting quests and completing them for the guild. Only two dramatic and defeated sighs later, Joe decided to compromise by going to collect all the materials he needed for his new rituals and set them up later. That way he could get the best of both worlds, if not in the order he wanted them. He had to be fast! Joe hurried out of the guild, excited to advance his craft. The sudden onset of ambition was new, but he simply thought of it as overexcitement. Going about his day would surely calm him down.

After wasting time walking through the merchant district, Joe had to stop and ask directions. As it happened, there wasn't a standard musical instrument store but instead a bardic college. Unlike the mage's college, this place was open for anyone. He entered the strangely built building, learning instantly that the shape of the walls was designed to create a barrier of soundproofing. Joe winced at some of the sounds he heard coming from small rooms as he passed them. He wondered idly if the ear-rending sounds were meant as some kind of sonic defense for the college. It was obvious that this area must be where novices learned how to play their chosen instrument. After asking directions a few times, he left behind the practice rooms and came upon an administrative area with a secretary sitting behind a desk.

"Can I help you, Mr....?" She politely smiled at him, though boredom was evident in her eyes.

"Joe." Joe smiled in return. "I was hoping to purchase some tuning forks?"

"Sure thing, honey. How many, and in what note?" The lady had pulled out a clipboard and was preparing to write on it.

"Oh, let's see here." Joe pretended to think about what he needed, foisting off the question on her. "What do you have here that is abundant and of at least uncommon quality? I was hoping to give them out as gifts to some musician friends, but I'm not sure what they need."

"Musicians?" An unexpected sneer crossed her face. "No wonder they don't already have the equipment they need to succeed. No self-respecting *bard* would allow someone else to choose their equipment for them." Joe was taken aback at her abrupt shift in attitude and hastily made his purchases before scurrying out the door. Thinking over the situation, he shrugged. Was there a way for him to have handled that better? In his mind, bards were the most ridiculed class, but that might only be true in other games he had played. Maybe they had a different role here? Why were simple musicians so disparaged?

Joe decided to ignore this interaction; he had far more important things to worry about for now. Looking over his purchases, he counted out thirty tuning forks. That should be enough for quite awhile, and hopefully someone else would be at the counter the next time he had to stock up. Next on the list was various components, so he bravely walked to the alchemist and had an awkward conversation with the strangely flamboyant potion maker. After he made his purchases and escap–no, *left*–that store, he stopped by the general goods store and bought as many remaining ritual components as possible. He wanted to be ready to create rituals constantly; he had no interest in running to the store every five minutes!

Joe made it to the meeting point twenty minutes early, and used the time to start sketching out some simple rituals on his spare paper. The difference in his hands' fluidity of motion between yesterday and this morning was intriguing. He didn't *feel* like he was doing anything different, but his hands were steady and the symbols were drawn out with a grace that he had despaired of ever attaining. Yay dexterity! He continued working for as long as possible, but time was running out. Just as most of the people showed up for the meeting, Joe got a very welcome yet strangely rude notification.

Skill gained: Drawing (Novice I). It looks like you have graduated from extra-large crayons! It is very surprising to see someone start this skill at Novice one. Typically, artists show some *skill when starting to draw, and their talent is adjusted accordingly. Once again, you prove how… extra special you are! Keep up this pace, and you may even become a beginner by the time you retire! Effect: +1% easier to create accurate artwork per level.*

What was going on with his notifications recently? They seemed to have become far more snarky, sarcastic even. Joe tried to think about when this started, and as far as he could tell, it began when he killed the Wolfman during the ritual yesterday. Did he accidentally set his notifications to 'rude'?

He started to pull open his status sheet, but Aten chose that moment to begin talking, "Thank you all for joining us this morning! First, let's go over some ground rules." This statement was met with loud groans and booing. "Yeah, yeah. Listen, I'm *pretty* sure you are all adults, so I'll keep it simple. Don't screw up! If you do something stupid in there, you are either going to be sent to respawn or to jail. I haven't met a single person associated with the castle that has a sense of humor, so keep the jokes on silent mode. We are apparently getting a major quest line, so pay attention to the details. Remember that the wording of quests can change the entire meaning based off interpretation, so we will talk about this in a meeting later. Everyone ready?"

The gates were swinging open behind him, and it almost looked like he had planned his speech to coincide with it for dramatic effect; this effect was ruined somewhat as a yelp escaped his lips. A royal guard had appeared beside him and was inspecting him from about an inch away. The guard nodded after an awkward moment and looked around at the other people gathered. His eyes lingered on each person, and twice he pointed at a player. "Those two."

"What about them, sir?" Aten politely inquired while opening his guild tab to view their information.

"They are traitors to either your guild or humanity as a whole. This person is a traitor to your guild, while the other has the title 'Race Traitor'. Their statuses are falsified by a mid-tier effect, so they have outside help. He has a different guild–Black Brotherhood–listed as his *actual* guild. As for her, it appears *she* is trying to join the Wolfman faction by attacking and killing humans." The guard rattled all of this off with a deadpan vocalization.

His words shocked the others, and everyone present stared at the two who were called out. They pretended innocence and confusion for a few long moments, but one of them broke and started running. Seeing this, the other paled and ran away as well. Making a strange motion with his hands, the guard flicked *something* at the race traitor. She yelped and was suddenly surrounded in the red glow of a murderer. In the middle of the city, it was unlikely she would survive long, so no one bothered to give chase. The royal guard's eyes kept roaming among the people until Joe felt the shining eyes trying to pry secrets from his status.

Greater inspect resisted! Tatum is pleased with you for the boost in power he has recently gained and has used a drop of this power to grant you a six hour divine effect: Veiled Soul. This will rebuff all attempts to read your true status screen. When the benefit from this expires, you may regain the buff by making a donation or praying at an altar.

Message from Tatum: Woo! Close one there! Thanks for the new altar!

The royal guard seemed puzzled, blinking at Joe a few times before moving on. He turned to Aten. "The rest are who they say they are. At least, their loyalty to your guild and the Kingdom are not in question. Welcome to the Grand Palace Ardania; the royal couple is awaiting you."

CHAPTER THIRTY

Joe had a strange cognitive dissonance as they walked into the palace. The palace and grounds were beautiful, just not in the way he had expected. The castle itself was obviously ancient but had never been repaired, or if it had been repaired, it was done so perfectly that the walls were utterly flawless. There were flowers and various beautification projects throughout the grounds, but it was obvious that their budget was nowhere near the one for war. The true beauty of the area came from the training grounds which completely surrounded the palace. Royal guardsmen hopefuls moved in shining armor, Scouts were firing volleys of arrows at stationary targets, and messengers were running back and forth between the various camps. This was the training ground of the Elite.

An elbow to the side caused Joe to drop his intent gaze from all the combatants. Tiona was now walking beside him, looking him up and down before whistling. "I like the new look! Skeleton just didn't suit you."

"Just wait until I am able to get my strength to ten as well!" Joe exclaimed excitedly. "I'll start looking like my actual self again!"

"Oh? You weren't this slim before?" Tiona inspected his body dispassionately. "You don't look *bad* this way."

"Thanks, but I am looking forward to having a bit more muscle. I feel like if I grew my hair out a bit and went to a bar right now, I'd start getting free drinks from the men." Joe chuckled at Tiona's eye roll.

"You'd need a *heck* of a lot more charisma if you wanted to pull that off. Your face looks a bit like a squashed potato. Also, grew your hair out? Really, baldy? You'd need hair in the first place in order to grow it out." Tiona snickered as Joe pretended to be hurt.

"So rude! Confidence destroyed! Can't... pay... guild dues..." Joe snorted at Tiona's fake look of horror and turned to look at the large set of doors they were approaching. "I bet those open into the great hall. That's where royalty of old would accept petitioners and hold court. This should be interesting."

The chatter died down as the group stepped into the palace proper. A feeling of reverence, fear, and power flowed over them. It felt a bit like being in a library as a sniper watched you through a scope, tracking your every move and waiting to pull the trigger. They were approaching the thrones, but it seemed there were overly large metal statues occupying them. The group looked around, waiting for the royals to arrive, but the guard who had escorted them was wide-eyed at their insolence. "Bow, you fools!" he hissed as he bowed toward the thrones.

"It is unnecessary. Many who come here unprepared do not know or understand our position." A distinctly feminine voice came from the metal statue on the right. Joe wasn't the only person to flinch when what appeared to be a statue turned her head to look at them. "Welcome, travelers. As a part of the Noble Guild The Wanderers, you have earned an audience this day. Before we give you the details of your quest, please know that you may not tell another person the reason for it. You may share details such as where you need to go or what you need to fight, but you cannot tell them *why* beyond that it is a quest. If you stay here for the explanation, I will take acquiescence as your answer and bind you to it."

The guild members looked at each other, most shrugging or rolling their eyes. Requirements like this seemed to be in all of the quests given by higher-ranking individuals. It was frustrating, as trying to help someone else through a similar quest proved impossible. When no one left or had anything to say, the queen began again.

"It is good to have such stalwart heroes." The Queen exhaled a metallic blast of air. A sigh? "Some background for all of you. A long time ago, our entire world had devolved to a state of war. Every race fought each other for the control of places of power. The battles escalated to a point where mutually assured destruction was imminent, and the inhabitants of the world were waiting to die. An… *outside force* took control, and each nation was placed under a spell, our populations collected together. We were frozen in a sleep-like state; we did not dream, we did not note the passage of time. We slept long enough that the *outside influence* was able to take control of all of our lives, and he separated us by changing the very world we stood upon. Then he raised us, this entire area, off of the continent far below."

Joe's mind turned to when he had been forced to jump into the hole in the world and how different that experience had been. He shuddered as he remembered the power of the monsters there. It may have been for the best that they were separate.

"Because of our foolishness–and our bloodthirst–when we were awoken several hundred years ago, we were given a task to complete. On this raised continent, there is only one other sentient race of people. Each of the races gets a single chance to prove that they should be the ones to survive, and the way we show this is by defeating the other group." Her voice was grave and dark as she seemed to relive their history.

"If we win this horrible 'game', our continent will connect to another, where two other races are also battling for their right to live. We will be able to choose one of them to help. It will continue like this until we have saved all the races that we can, forging alliances and generating goodwill. For now though, we must ask you to do an awful, terrible thing. You must help us win this 'game'. So. Your quest… is to break the Wolfman nation, slaughter their people, and capture their leader's throne."

Silence thundered through the area. Aten, oddly, was the first to break the silence. "*Awesome*!" As if his words were a trigger, a notification appeared in front of all of them.

Quest alert: Shatter a people. The Queen of Ardania has offered your guild a quest! All you need to do is gain entrance to the most highly guarded area in Wolfman territory, kill their leaders, fighters, noncombatants, and capture the throne! Completing this quest will break the Wolfman nation, leading to their eventual eradication or subservience to humans. Reward: Exp: 50,000. 100,000 gold to the guild treasury and up to 10,000 gold for each participant in the final battle (Based on contribution). Maximum reputation with the city of Ardania. Failure: The human nation is shattered, leading to the eventual eradication or subservience of all humans to Wolfmen.

"Frick on a stick. This is an endgame level quest, y'all." Aten's face was practically glowing as he read over the quest notification. "*Then* we get to connect to other races? Can you imagine the secret classes and stuff we will find in an area humans haven't touched in hundreds of years?" He wiped a drop of drool from his mouth as he said this.

"So we are going to have to topple a nation?" one of the officers questioned.

"No, we are going to topple a *race*," someone else called. "Er, *shatter* a race."

Aten looked toward the Queen once again. "What is the timeline for this quest? How long do we have?"

"As long as you need." Her next words made a few people go quiet. "All four Noble Guilds will have this quest, and as long as it is completed before *they* are able to destroy *us*, you can take all the time you need. Our battles have been raging for hundreds of years, what is a few more? There is something important to take note of though. Last night, it seems that one of their summoning spells backfired. Our scouts are reporting heavy casualties amongst their civilian population and light casualties amongst their fighters. We don't know what happened, but somehow, a blow was struck against them that they weren't expecting."

Tiona looked at Joe sharply, but he pretended not to notice. After all, there was no way he was going to be able to repeat that ritual without losing a part of his humanity. He had originally wanted to change it to be less human-sacrificey, but… after recreating the ritual diagram on paper, he had found that it was a Master tier ritual called 'Abyss on Earth' that required five mages to initiate. Altering the required components was impossible with his current abilities; all he had done yesterday was give it a different target and refresh the lines the mana ran along. The massive cost also explained why the Shaman had been so easy to defeat; they had been running on fumes and what their mana regeneration would allow. Not only could he not change it, but he didn't actually *know* all the required components and items needed to actually empower the ritual. He wouldn't be performing a ritual on that scale for quite a long time.

"As Guild Leader of The Wanderers, I officially accept this quest, Your Majesty," Aten announced with a deep bow.

The Queen nodded; she had expected no other outcome from the meeting today. "Just know that your silence on this matter *will* be magically enforced. We don't need riots about 'the end of the world' and we certainly don't need people running off and becoming race traitors because they *pity* the Wolves. I thank you all in advance, and wish you the best of luck. I have given authorization for Aten to have information on a series of classes and specializations that we know of; feel free to use them. Go now and become strong."

Their audience over, the guild officers left the building chattering excitedly. Not only had they gained an *amazing* quest, they now had access to more classes and specializations! This would be a huge benefit to their recruitment efforts and help secure their position as a powerful and prolific guild. Several people started talking with Aten as soon as they were out of the gates, and he quickly acquired a harried look as he worked to access and disseminate the information given to him.

Joe grinned and started walking toward the guild. Tiona caught up to him quickly since her walking speed was easily double his. "Not sticking around to learn about a new class?"

"Nah, I'm pretty happy with mine." Joe flashed a smile at her, but his mind was on other things. He really needed to get a workspace for himself; it turned out that only novice rituals were able to be performed with simple infusions of mana into their symbols. Starting at the beginner ranks, rituals needed chants, specialized equipment or tools, and more than anything–large amounts of protected space. Not just so that the ritual was large enough to easily find errors, but also because if a ritual failed there tended to be devastating effects. He had read a note in his book where a miner had cut through a ritual's symbolic links as it was powering up… and the release of power had obliterated a city.

"Joe!" Tiona tapped him on the arm. "Are you mad at me? You don't need to say anything if you don't want to. I just want you to know that it isn't because of you."

"Wha?" Joe's eyes locked onto her, and he realized that he had missed something important while lost in his thoughts. "I'm sorry, could you repeat that? I was off in my own little world."

"Wow. We are literally living in a fantasy world, and you still want to abstract it one step further." She smiled, but the expression was strained. "I said that I am disbanding the party. I'm getting close to level ten, and I really need to take as much time as possible to grind my skills before I specialize. Thanks to the new classes and specializations we have access to, I was able to find a really awesome class I want to specialize in. I need to become an apprentice to one of the royal guard trainers to get it though. If I get accepted, I won't be back for at least a month."

"Wha?" This time, Joe's half-formed word was due to incredulousness, not lack of attention. "Have you told the others?"

She shook her head. "No, that's what I'm off to do now. I really wanted to thank you though; without all of you guys fighting with me I wouldn't have made enough gold to take the time away from quests to train."

He wanted to say something, but what could he? She had been the first real person to help him in the game, and now that she was leaving, he felt a bit sour inside. Not angry, just a mix of sadness and overprotective friendship. "If that's what you want to do, I'm glad you are going to do it," Joe stated firmly while shaking her hand. She thanked him, and they returned to the guild in silence.

Dylan didn't take the news quite as stoically. "What the heck, Tiona? We were *just* starting to get a good battle rhythm! We were finally working together like a *team*, getting stronger, and making serious money! You are just going to toss that aside?"

"If we beat this quest, we can earn up to ten *thousand* gold each," Tiona spoke carefully, doing her best to explain her thoughts. "I want us to be a team in the future, but I need to get to level ten and get my new class while I still can."

Dylan looked away, crossed his arms and said nothing else. Guess and Chad both shrugged and didn't say anything beyond 'good luck'. Tiona nodded at them all and walked away, returning to the castle. Joe looked around at the morose faces and tried to decide what to do next. "I mean, we could all party together still. Let's just find a fifth and-"

Chad interrupted him. "Can't do it. To get contribution points for the guild we are going to need a party leader who is a higher level than us. Also, I hate to say it... but it isn't likely another party leader will want you on their team. As great as it is to have a healer, Tiona had to split her officer's commission to account for your salary. No one else is going to want to work for free or half price."

Joe wanted to argue but stopped himself. As much as he wanted to continue adventuring with these three, not having a party might be exactly what he needed to gain the time to study, practice, and perfect his class. He had been running himself ragged since he joined the game so that he could keep up with the higher level players on his team. Maybe it really *was* time for him to go solo for a while. It looked like they had a few in-game months before they could really make progress on the royal quest anyway. They finished their meeting and slowly dispersed, saying their goodbyes morosely. The three others went to find a new party while Joe went into town to find a place to make into his workshop.

CHAPTER THIRTY-ONE

In preparation for lengthy research and development of his skills, Joe had told Aten that he was taking a few weeks to train. The guild leader had actually looked *relieved* that Joe wasn't demanding to take over as party leader for his group and wasn't fighting to keep them together. Apparently, under Tiona's leadership the members of the party had become well respected, and several guild officers were already vying for them to join their party. Basically, he had saved Aten the trouble of telling him 'no'. Joe rolled his eyes as he forced himself back to the present; he had rented a building and needed to get to work.

It wasn't perfect, but for now it was his. Joe looked around the dusty warehouse, already planning out what he would need to do to protect the place. The owner of *Odds and Ends* had offered him a lease on the large building when he had mentioned he was looking for a large open space. He was lucky to get such a good deal, even if the structure was in a seedy part of the city. Apparently, she used the building to store goods that weren't ready for her store yet. Now that she was planning on leaving the business, the warehouse was simply sitting empty and unused. The building supposedly had a few basic protection enchantments, but he had been warned that anyone could smash through them if they really tried. He was going to need to fix that issue.

His first task was not to put *powerful* magical protections on the building; no, that would simply bring attention to him. People would wonder what treasures he was hiding, and their insatiable curiosity and greed would make them brave any barriers in their way. No, making this place *undesirable* was the way to go. If being near this place was annoying and frustrating, perhaps embarrassing, people would avoid it at any cost. Pulling out his book of dark rituals, Joe began to write down the various effects and area of effect he was after. As it happened, he found that he had been making an incorrect assumption about the magic he was using. Since most of the runes and diagrams were circular, he had thought that they would all have a circular area of effect.

In fact, he could change the affected area simply by changing a few variables in the circle itself. His eyebrow twitched in anger when he found that he didn't need to make a gigantic ritual circle around the guild house to stave off monsters, he only needed to adjust the parameters so that the effect was pushed out to the range he wanted. Joe growled at the memory of his previous mistakes, vowing to get better at this in the future. What he wanted right now was a rectangular area of effect that covered the entire warehouse and about ten feet out on each side. That way it wouldn't affect people that walked by or those that simply lived or worked in the nearby buildings.

Reading through his grimoire, he softly sang to himself to help pass the time. "Montage! Doing a ritual creation *montage*, yeah." Time didn't pass any faster, but after twenty minutes, he stopped mumbling his song and became fully invested in his studies. When his words trailed off, the crackling of turning pages sounded like a whip snapping in the silence of the building. His quills scratching notes onto some paper could be heard once every short while. He muttered "Montage!" softly every half hour or so. Eventually, he decided that he should work on the actual creation of a ritual instead of just making notes.

"Hmm. Effects I want in this ritual… exclusion, yes. Don't want it to affect me or guests. Passive scanning so it isn't active and wasting mana if there are no targets. The goal of the whole ritual, nausea, yup. Maybe include the feeling of *really* needing to poo? Maybe actually *make* them poo if they hang around too long? I can't imagine many people wanting to stick around if they are feeling like that." Joe looked at a few other possibilities, selecting only one more. "Exponential increase? Yeah… the closer they get to the ritual circle, the worse the effects are." Exponential increase actually reduced the overall cost of the ritual, because it meant that unless you were right at the epicenter the effect was lessened severely. Adding limiting factors was a good way to turn a powerful ritual into something usable, but making it specific like that carried its own risks.

"Now, how to combine these? Exclusion requires a silver chalice be filled with my blood to be placed in the circle… passive scanning requires a *used* glass eye? Why? That's disgusting and a little weird. Moving on. The nausea requires the third stomach of a cow, and the… poo feeling… needs the fresh intestines of a bear. Exponential increase needs an example of exponential growth. Could I use a copper and gold coin? That's exponential growth of *cost* at least." Joe wrote down all of the details onto a paper before looking through the various ritual circles.

"Since this will be a beginner tier ritual, I'll need at least two different circles. This one is used for affecting 'all in area' and this double lined circle is used to stipulate 'area this big'. Hey, that's the same one I use for 'Predator's territory'!" Joe happily created the ritual diagram, frowning when his hand jerked to the side and splashed ink all over the page. "Stupid drawing skill being so low. Stupid dexterity," he muttered as he pulled out a fresh sheet and started over.

He was able to create the spell diagram this time, and it began to glow a soft gold as he looked at it. "Good, good. Now I just need to add in what other components should be needed. I already knew that silver wire was needed for the double-lined circle, but what about the 'target all' circle? Looks like air, water, and fire. How *element*-try, my dear Watson." He chuckled as he worked. So far, all his new space had done for him was let him study in peace and protect others from his puns. If anyone else were to know about this, they would agree that it was a good investment.

Putting the finishing touches on the ritual he noticed that it was glowing a brighter gold than it was originally, but he also knew he could improve it to a higher degree. He adjusted all the parameters a tiny bit, and over the course of another hour, he fine-tuned all the requirements. Finishing at long last, he smiled at the brightly glowing page and finally acknowledged the notifications waiting for him.

New ritual created: 'Quarantine area'. This ritual was designed specifically to drive off unwanted company. The designer didn't seem to realize that his personality would have worked twice as effectively! As this is the first ritual you have designed, you gain a reward. Because it is a beginner tier ritual, rewards are doubled! Profession (Occultist): 500.

Occultist has reached level two! Speed of reading and writing is now increased by 10%, currently set at 60% bonus. New languages are now 20% easier to learn (written form only).

Skill increased: Ritual lore (Beginner 0). Congratulations! Study and practice have allowed you to increase your usage of a skill considered useless by society! You'll prove them right someday because you are like King Midas. Except that instead of gold, everything that you *touch seems to turn to turds! Intelligence, perception, and luck +1.*

Skill increased: Ritual magic (Apprentice IV). The creation of your own rituals certainly allows you to increase this skill at a much faster rate. Nice work earning *a skill increase after spending most of your skill points to get this far!*

Joe kind of wanted to yell at whoever was making these notifications. Seriously! This was bordering on abusive at this point. He double checked his settings, but it *appeared* that his notifications were still set to 'normal'. Joe snorted and left the building; it seemed that he needed to purchase some specialized equipment for his ritual. Namely animal innards.

Doing a bit of shopping turned into a seriously unpleasant chore. When he went to the counter of the general goods store, people laughed at him. It looked like he had grabbed a random pile of garbage. They seemed to think that he didn't understand that most of these items were considered trash drops, things found in old buildings or from monsters that didn't have any *real* value. Only the heavily tarnished silver chalice still had any value at all, but it would need to be melted down or sanded and polished to become useful again. He would have bought a better one, but it was *literally* the only pure silver chalice he had been able to find!

Joe's ears felt like they were on fire, and his cheeks were bright red from the embarrassment he was feeling. It was all for the pursuit of magic! He would suffer any humiliation to be able to bend the world to his will; so what if these basic *muscle brains* couldn't see past the end of their sword! Joe stumbled a bit; where in the world were these narcissistic tendencies coming from? It was fun to think like that as a joke, but he didn't want to become a person who sneered at other classes of people. Maybe it was just a wizard thing? Or… aha! He was *jumping* to conclusions about people! The skill had specifically warned him about this sort of thing!

Armed with new knowledge about himself, Joe hurried about his tasks and simply kept his head down. He did his best to ignore the few chuckles he elicited with his strange shopping spree and simply did what he needed to do. After going to the butchers to get a cow stomach, he found that he had another problem. He was already carrying too much! Adding on twenty or so pounds of animal intestines certainly wouldn't help the situation. Why did he always need to get extras? How many times was he planning to cast this ritual? Joe made his way back to the warehouse before returning to the butchers. He was sweating heavily from the swift pace he had needed to set to make his purchase in time, and from the look on the butcher's face, he was sure that his charisma had taken a hit.

"I need a… urg." Joe had to stop himself from retching from the combination of his run and the smell. "I need a cow's third stomach and bear intestines. Do you have those?"

"Wot in te'eck ah youse gonna do wit douse?" The butcher had a cockney accent so thick that Joe could barely understand him. Joe stared at the man for a long moment as he parsed the words.

"Oh. Does it matter what I want with them?" His words caused the butcher's face to darken. "Alright, I guess it does. It's bait for a trap. We need a specific combination to draw out a large monster."

The butcher seemed to think it over. "Awrigh. I c'n do da 'tomach fo' a coppa, but freaysh bea' insoids is gonna be ah sowlid silvah."

"Works for me." Joe handed over the money and got meat wrapped in a slowly seeping sack in return. "Thank you!" He hurried away.

"Nah prob'm, kiddo. C'mon back soon," the butcher replied needlessly. Joe was already across the street by this point.

Night was falling, but Joe wasn't overly concerned. How many master tier 'abyss on earth' rituals were out and about in the world? Joe bet that the number was close to zero at this point. He was *pretty* sure that the activation of the ritual was why the human city had been attacked by monsters every few nights recently. Actually, if the reason night became so deadly was the ritual he had subverted, nighttime hunting would soon become rather popular. No one liked that they lost half of the time they had to level each day, though it had been conducive to the rapid advancement of non-combat skills such as tailoring. Eh, didn't matter to him. Joe had a ritual to create!

He unlocked the door to the warehouse and walked in. Joe paused. Something felt off. Was there someone in here? He looked around the huge room, but it remained empty. "Hello?"

Obviously, there was no reply. He shook off the feeling and

got to work. Having stored the meat in his ring, there was no real rush to complete the ritual… but he *really* wanted to. Pulling a bucket full of chalk into the center of the huge vacant room, he dropped to his knees and started drawing out the spell circle. The first tier circle went on the outside, so he started with the far more difficult *interior* magic circle. Halfway through the process, he was intensely happy with his decision to use chalk. It made erasing his *many* mistakes easy to do, though it pained him every time he needed to redo a section. Maybe when he was a master artist he would be confident in using a more permanent medium that let him draw more accurately, but for now, chalk would have to do.

Very carefully stepping out of the completed portion, Joe began drawing the double-lined circle around the outside. He was using a curved chunk of wood to make the curve, having learned that freehand circles were not to be trusted. When the exterior was complete, Joe wiped his face. He didn't care that he left a long streak of chalk behind, the diagram was complete! Placing all the items he needed in his ring, Joe stepped into the center of the ritual area and began arranging the components. This wasn't a novice circle, so he couldn't just toss everything into the center and hope for the best. Failure to do everything *perfectly* increased the mana cost or created feedback that could damage him.

When all the items were out of his bag, Joe lit a candle, put a feather on a pedestal, filled a bowl with water, and dropped a large stone on the floor. There, that should take care of the elemental components… next was the chalice of blood. Bleh. He pricked his finger and watched the blood flow out, and flow, and *flow*. When it was finally over, he was quite dizzy and wishing that he had been able to find a smaller chalice than the one he bought. He healed himself, double checked that he hadn't scuffed the chalk… and grinned. Time to make the magic happen! He placed the Core into the center of the arranged components and began to feed mana into the spell circle.

In a flash, ten percent of his mana was gone. He gasped and tried to regulate how quickly the mana was pouring out. Joe forced the power back into the proper channels and began to sweat. Controlling the ritual was becoming rather difficult, and the mana required per second was starting to strain his channels. Joe watched as his mana ticked down. Twenty percent. Ten percent. Five. The pull of power stopped, and Joe shuddered in relief. His mana regeneration pulled him up to fifteen percent, when the draw suddenly began again. What the…?

The outer circle had its own mana requirement? Oh crap. The draw of mana was much smaller, but he still reached zero mana disturbingly quickly. Ow! His health took a hit before his mana regen kicked in. The accordion effect of health and mana continued for a couple seconds, but the ritual completed in time for him to survive the process. The inner circle of the ritual glowed a sickly green while the outer was colored a clashing vibrant orange.

Ritual 'Quarantine area' completed! Players who will remain unaffected: 'Joe'. Once active this ritual will remain for six months until maintenance is needed. Activate ritual now? Yes / No

Might as well. Joe clicked yes, and waited for something to happen. He felt nothing but did notice that his mana was entirely empty. Not wanting to waste the opportunity, Joe quickly sat down and worked to squeeze all of his mana into a perfect sphere as it regenerated. The storm of power in his mind shrunk noticeably, his wisdom score quite a bit higher than it had been the last time he worked to improve this ability.

Skill increased: Coalescence (Novice IX). You stand at the peak of novice ranked coalescence. Work hard and think deep thoughts! Deeper. Oh… that's your limit?

Skill increased: Mana Manipulation. (Novice VII). Guiding huge waves of energy through your body without damaging yourself is the mark of a true magical artist, but if that is the case, it appears that this is yet another area where you are still using crayons.

He was happy about the skill increases, but he may need to

send a message to customer support if those notifications kept being so personal. Seriously, it was getting-

Bleugh

"*What in the heck is that?*" Joe shrieked as he jumped to his feet.

A splatter of bile found a new home on the floor, rapidly followed by a body covered in a garish red robe splashing into the newly formed puddle. Joe moved away as the invader tried to stand up, but they failed and puked again, followed by a nasty rumbling sound from their pants. Joe thought about trying to help the man, but the smell coming from the collapsed man certainly wasn't convincing him to get close. He sent a few ranged healing spells at the man, not fixing the bones broken in the fall, but keeping the man awake and alive. It also helped the smell a tiny bit.

As the unknown man groaned, Joe got over his squeamishness, reminding himself that he had been in far more disgusting scenarios during his time in the army. He walked forward and grabbed the man by the arm, dragging him to the wall of the warehouse and further away from the ritual's center. Here the ritual had far less effect, though the man's face still seemed quite green. "Who are you, and why are you in here? This is private property."

"Ugh… I was just trying to find a place to sleep," the man replied piteously. If Joe hadn't caught a crafty gleam in his eye or perhaps the ornate robes that screamed wealth or that the man had been in the rafters, he may have believed him. Totally a believable lie from this guy.

"Oh? In that case, I am sure you wouldn't mind me charging you rent for the evening." Joe grabbed the dangling coin purse threaded into the man's belt, carefully avoiding the stained portion of his pants. He pulled the bag open, spilling gold coins into his palm. "Ah yes, I can see that a hotel is out of your price range. Good thing you came here."

He looked up in time to see the man thrusting his hand at him. Joe *jumped* to the side, somehow executing a perfect barrel roll and landing on his feet. Stamina already depleted from that simple action, Joe watched as a bright line of heat flew across the room and reduced an empty crate to ashes. "I'll take *that* to mean you aren't here for my health."

Joe grabbed the unknown mage and dragged him closer to the center of the room. Then he slammed his scepter into the man's broken hand until he heard the bones snap. That should keep more powerful spells from being used against him. "Now, we are going to have a little chat, you and I."

"Filthy rogue mage!" The man on the ground was doing his best to squirm away from the ritual, but Joe kept him in place with the simple expedient of kicking him in the face when he tried to roll. "When the college gets this information, you will be drawn and quartered!"

Joe sank into a squatting position. "Well then, it looks like I will just need to keep you from reporting in."

The mage's face paled, enunciating the green cast it had gained. "They already know about you! Why else would I be here, if I weren't simply gaining the proof they needed to take you?"

"Again, not offering much incentive to letting you go." Joe healed the man, followed by rolling him a bit closer to the ritual circle. The mage released a keening sound as his bowels rumbled.

"Just… more proof of your… twisted magic!" The mage was gasping, a riot of emotions shifting across his face.

"I think we need to go ahead and get to know each other better." The look in Joe's eyes didn't inspire much confidence in the captured mage. "Shall we begin?"

CHAPTER THIRTY-TWO

"So tell me again why people who learn magic outside of the mage's college are 'evil'." Joe was sitting in a chair, looking at the man he had bound with thin rope. It was thin because the man had multiple broken bones, and the way he was tied made it impossible to attempt escape without severe damage to his already mangled limbs.

The mage appeared happy to spew vitriol at him. "You *commoners* can't understand the sheer responsibility and dedication required of a licensed mage! We who can create and shape the elements need the security and brotherhood only found within the halls of academia!"

"So mages only shape the elements?" Joe was doing what he could to read between the lines, but he wasn't a trained interrogator.

"Of course! Anything else is a perversion of the natural order!" the mage shouted at him, gasping as he pulled against his bindings.

"What about clerics? The holy healing powers granted by deities?"

The mage snorted derisively. "Keep your parlor tricks and

emotional casting. What we care about is others stealing from our domain or using unholy magic they cannot hope to understand! Your rituals are a good example of what the truly insane will attempt!"

"How did you become aware of me, anyway?" This was the crux of the matter for Joe. Where had he slipped up?

"You walked up to the city, proclaiming for all to see that you consider yourself a mage, then hid behind your facade of lies!" The mage somehow seemed to be looking down on him, an impressive feat as his robe had… filth… seeping into it. "You probably don't even deserve to be called a cleric, either! What true class are you hiding?"

"Ah. So it was when I switched over to my mage class to hunt." Joe nodded to himself. "A question for you. Tell me, how do you rank in the college?"

"I am a mage of wind and fire, assistant to the assistant professor!" The mage's answer seemed overly proud of this fact.

"Pretty low then." Joe decided to use a different tactic. "Tell me, oh nameless mage, how does the college get its money?"

"Tuition and grants from the Kingdom."

"Grants, you say?" Joe rubbed his chin. "Is that so? I know that tuition is high; I'm told two skills cost a thousand gold to learn. This means there must not be many students, certainly not enough to make a dent in the school's apparently endless budget. Why, in your opinion, does the Kingdom pay such a high amount of 'grant' money?"

The man glared at him. "Is there a point to all of this?"

"Yes, yes. Come on now."

"Obviously, it is because there is no other place to get magical training, weapons, or defenses!" The mage snorted at the foolish man questioning him.

"How interesting," Joe drawled as the pieces fell into place. "So the Mage's College is the *only* place where magic comes from, and they *also* happen to send out assassins against anyone who finds their own way to practice magic. The cost to become licensed is sky-high as well. To me, it sounds like the college just likes to have a monopoly on the magical market and so they murder any competition. Let me guess, if you create something or serve a term fighting against the Wolfmen, does the mage's college take a percentage of the profit you make? A *large* percentage?"

"W-what? Of course they do! How else can we repay them for the learning and magic we are able to perform?" The mage seemed pale for a different reason. Joe was digging into his beliefs now.

"Usually, that would be what that *tuition* you bragged about is for. You know. Pay for the skills, the training, so on, then go off and do your own thing? Like *every other* profession that exists?" Joe could see dark realization forming in the young man's eyes. "Don't worry. I know what it is like to be milked of every copper by the college you thought was trying to prepare you for the future. As it turns out, you are often times better learning on your own."

The mage was slack-jawed and couldn't find anything to say in reply. *No one* questioned the Mage's College! It… it was against their *policies*! Joe tilted his head back as he spoke out loud, "So now what, I wonder? I can't simply let you run back and tattle on me. I suppose I could keep you here and use you for my rituals…"

"No! You will not use me as some sort of foul sacrifice to summon demonic beings!" The mage began to struggle heavily, even though he was obviously in great pain.

"What in the world…?" Joe looked shocked at the thought. "Of course I won't do that! I'm the champion of a deity. Why would you think that would be allowed? I meant that I need a second member of my coven to activate more powerful rituals! This one almost killed me, and it is only a beginner tier! I can create apprentice rituals–maybe even expert tier if I need to–but I need people to join me in powering them. You seem to have access to mana already so why not?"

"You want me to *join* you in this proscribed activity?" The mage seemed to be about to faint.

"Yes."

"No!"

"Well, dang. I was really hoping it wouldn't come to this." Joe sighed and pulled out his black book. He walked over to the table and began collecting circles and components onto a list. No matter how loudly the tied mage shouted, he was unable to break Joe's concentration. As the sun rose in the morning, Joe looked down at a new ritual that glowed a lovely golden color. He sighed, looked at the mage who had either fallen asleep or fainted, and got to work. Out came the chalk, and Joe tried to keep quiet as he scratched the symbols onto the floor. The ring he drew up was large enough for a bed and a chair, about ten feet in diameter. Since he had made this ritual so *very* specific, the components were cheap and he had them readily available.

The silver chalice was once again filled with his blood, and yet again he grumbled about not being able to find or buy a smaller one. The captured mage groaned as the noise woke him up, blinking at Joe in obvious confusion. Fear flashed across his face as Joe stabbed him in the hand and began collecting the blood that dripped from the wound. "What are you doing!" His voice was hoarse, all the yelling the previous hours coming back to bite him.

Joe looked him in the eye without blinking. "Making a ritual, of course. I *just* started to get good at it and I need some practice." He stepped to the side as the mage began to thrash, trying to move his broken body out of the circles surrounding him. He couldn't move at all without his bonds twisting his broken bones so his attempt ultimately failed.

"I don't *want* to be practice," the mage whispered as tears formed in his eyes. Joe ignored him as he placed the blood in its position. He stepped out of the circle and looked at the whimpering mage.

"You came in here with the intent to either kill me or *get* me killed. You cannot be *too* surprised that I would seek retribution on you. I ask again, will you help me willingly?" Joe looked at the pitiful figure on the ground, hoping that he would accept his offer.

"I *can't*!" the young mage's words burst out in a terrified scream. "Every mage has to sign The Accords when they start school and when they graduate! This has to be done before they get their license! Even you *travelers* sign it, at least the few who have graduated or came into this world as full-fledged mages! I *can't* willingly work with you. I'd die! Plus, I don't even *want* to help you!"

"Firstly, stop screaming at me. If you want to speak against what I have to say, or you think I am wrong, give me reasons *why* I am wrong. Improve your argument. Next, why in the *world* would you sign something that kills you if you help someone?" Joe was looking at the man, aghast at the words even as a darker conspiracy theory tickled against his senses.

"I didn't know! *No one* knew!" the mage howled at him. "It's a binding contract; it forces us to follow the will of the Archmage. Since the lifespan of mages ranges into multiple *hundreds* of years, everyone that worked together to create The Accords had died before he made them mandatory for inclusion in the college. They hide the minor negative ramifications like this for good reason! The Accords were made to protect us and ensure that we work together as a society! Until now... until now I have always seen them as the greatest *good*, the thing that set us apart from the common rabble outside our walls! We have *courses* on The Accords and how it protects us against the rogue mages that have tried to destroy us in the past."

"*Minor* negative ramifications? Taking away your freedom for an elusive 'protection' is never the solution. When are you protected? Give me examples of people attacking your college. When were your accords made, who voted on them, or were they forced upon your people? Who decided to hide important information from you until you had already signed them?" Joe looked sadly at the suddenly silent mage. "Tell me, what did your older mages say about The Accords?"

"Nothing!" The mage paused, suddenly seeing the discrepancy. "Actually *nothing*. They weren't required to teach those classes, and we were always directed to the younger generations if we asked… looking back they seem… sad? Angry? I… I don't understand."

"What's your name?" Joe asked the man quietly.

"Cel," he answered, lost in thought. Panic appeared on his face. "No! I told you my name! Fiend!"

Joe rolled his eyes. "Yeah, I never needed your name for magic. I have your *blood*. I'm just trying to be nice and stop calling you 'the puke and poop covered mage' in my head. Thank you for the information." He thought that he had heard enough, so he stepped back and concentrated on the ritual. "Hope this works."

His words didn't comfort Cel in the slightest. The mage's eyes widened as he watched the mana flowing out of Joe. Since Joe was always doing his best to cut out distractions, he had never watched the process from the outside. As much as Cel hated to admit it, this was a beautiful piece of spell work. Mana poured into channels that were already prepared for it, creating strong bonds and links throughout. The spellform lashed out and converted the supplied components to energy, pulling what it needed into the ritual and turning the remainder to vapor. It almost looked like a lightning strike. The only thing different was the Core. When the mana struck out at it, the Core simply dimmed a bit.

Cel felt a strange pull inside of himself and gasped as the power from the ritual settled upon him like a blanket. He tried to escape once again, but his bonds forced him to remain still. Joe stood up, brushed off his knees, and watched as the ritual began to complete around Cel. The seconds ticked by, and the power piling atop Cel seemed to slowly vanish. After a full five minutes, Joe nodded and stepped over the ritual circles. He untied the mage, preemptively apologized, and pulled one of his broken bones into place. Cel screamed, but the sound seemed to echo strangely. When Joe pulled the next bone into place, the young mage passed out. After Joe had ensured that the bones were where they were supposed to be, he channeled his lay on hands spell and healed the mage as best as he could.

The bones would take more time to heal naturally, but… Joe decided that now would be a good time to practice fixing them. Nothing like a 'willing' and damaged target to hone his skills on! He started small, looking for the fragments floating next to where they were supposed to be. Pushing the shard into place, he tried to convince the small fragment to bind itself to the larger bone. The chunk of calcium simply ignored his orders. Joe huffed, feeling a bit upset. Why wasn't this working? In every other game *ever*, as far as he knew, healing bones wasn't an issue. To be fair, he hadn't really played games, but... Then again, if he remembered correctly, healing was usually considered a 'light' spell and he didn't have… he did have access to *dark* spells though. Could that work?

Joe tried to add darkness to his healing spell, braiding it into the water. To the naked eye, the water flowing from him simply turned black. Inside Cel's body, Joe was able to see the darkness sink into the bone and fragment, acting as an adhesive that held them fast to each other. The darkness didn't vanish even when Joe stopped putting power into it! Since bones didn't have nerves in them and because the bone remained stable when he moved Cel's arm, Joe had to conclude that the bone was healed. Hopefully the dark mana would eventually vanish and leave behind a healthy arm, but Joe would need to watch for side effects in the future.

"Gah!" Joe rolled his eyes and almost slapped himself. *This* was why he had been able to heal his own body to a much higher degree than he could heal others! Joe was already stuffed *full* of dark and water mana and could manipulate it freely when he healed himself. How had he not practiced with this yet? Joe could only blame his lacking skills on himself; he should have been *practicing* instead of gallivanting all over Eternium! He was almost spitting mad when he canceled the spell and tested Cel's movement. His face was calm for the first time since they met, so Joe assumed he was out of pain. While the man was still asleep, Joe took the chalice and filled it with Cel's blood. He had to add him to the quarantine ritual, or staying here would remain absolute torture. As he went about his business, he checked the notifications waiting for him.

Congratulations! For grasping the requirements for a more specialized form of healing without system assistance, 'Heal' has morphed into a higher tier skill, Mend. Your creativity, true knowledge of healing, and usage of the spell has shown a high level of skill and power, boosting your skill ranks greatly!

Skill increased: Mend (Beginner VIII): Select a target to heal restoring 5n health where 'n' equals skill level. Unlike the lower tier skill 'Heal', Mend is able to heal broken bones. Congratulations! Mend has reached the beginner ranks. Dark affinity is automatically added to the spell and will heal dark-aligned creatures twice as effectively. No extra effect added.

You have created a new ritual: 'Ritual of containment'. This ritual utilizes the target's stamina to power the ritual and absorbs any mana from the target that is bound into a spellform. If target leaves the containment area, their stamina and mana will be fully drained. Their health will also begin to fall but can never fall past ten points due to the effect of this ritual. Health, mana, and stamina will only regenerate once the target has re-entered the circle. To cast this ritual, the target needs to show willingness to be confined. Remaining in the spell circle for a full minute after activation and a donation of their blood can be used to show their 'willingness'. More targets can be added to the same ritual with a donation of blood. This ritual can be deactivated at will by: Joe.

Joe had built the at-will deactivation functionality into the ritual for a very simple reason: it was very unlikely that anyone could change the ritual and have it remain effective. This way, if someone got ahold of his rituals and tried to use them against him, he could quickly end the ritual and save himself. He planned on adding this as a safety function to all of his rituals, though it added about ten percent mana cost to the overall diagram. Rituals could be activated and used by anyone, so it was better to create a way to protect himself *now* than be betrayed in the future by his own work.

Cel woke up right about then, moving slowly as his mind

tried to convince him he was still injured. "What did you do to me? I feel… not *good* but no longer damaged."

"Well, I healed you and added you to the exceptions listing of the ritual over there. So you won't feel sick and you shouldn't be all sorts of mangled. I have a couple more questions for you before we are all done, namely: do you think the mage's college is withholding assistance from the Kingdom? I have seen a lot of Warriors and archers that have a couple magical abilities, but I haven't seen any mages out hunting down Wolfmen."

"I guess… I am unsure. I know that there have been messengers coming to the college for years, and any of them that seem to be on official business always leave looking like they have been eating lemons. It was always a point of pride to us, seeing the heralds of the Kingdom be turned away like commoners. Now it just seems… wrong" As Cel was speaking, he was inspecting the ritual he was surrounded by. He was trying to be sneaky but had a very poor poker face.

"Uh-huh." Joe watched as the man obviously began to create a spell. Cel thought he was keeping his hands hidden in his robe, but the motions had the whole thing wiggling and moving around. "You said that the older mages don't say anything about The Accords. Is there any reason that The Accords would affect them differently?"

"Sure, sure," Cel responded distractedly. "When mages are allowed to specialize to their second class or graduate, they sign The Accords a second time. They sign a third time before they are allowed to specialize further. When they sign the third time, they have full rights and privileges as a master or professor. That is also when they stop talking about The Accords, now that I think about it. In my head, it was always because they no longer needed to worry about them. Instead it could be- *winds of immolation*!"

Joe stood silently as the crazed look of glee slowly slid from Cel's face. He was posed in an awkward position, his hands pointed at Joe. He wiggled his fingers a bit more and frowned. Joe coughed into his closed fist to regain Cel's attention. "Last question for you then. If The Accords were somehow destroyed, do you think the mages in the guild would turn against the Archmage and help the Kingdom?"

Cel looked rather shaken. "You took my spellcasting ability? You unbelievable *monster*."

"Pretty sure you just tried to light me on fire," Joe responded dryly. "Answer the question."

"No, they would not 'turn against' him," Cel growled as he started to sidle away from Joe. "They'd all be *dead*. All of us would, anyone who signed The Accords. There is a repercussion clause against a foreign power gaining control over the college. We'd all die *instantly* if The Accords were destroyed."

Joe looked at the ground, nodding and thinking to himself. Seeing his distracted state, Cel started sprinting toward the exit. Ten feet from his starting position he crossed the lines of the ritual, instantly falling flat as his stamina and mana were drained from him. He began to scream weakly as the ritual latched onto his health and began to *pull*. Ever so slowly, Cell was able to roll himself into the ritual area again. Joe watched all of this happen with a callous gaze. The mage had tried to kill him several times now; simply keeping him contained *was* Joe's way of being merciful.

"Thank you for the information, Cel. I've decided that you will be helping me for the next few weeks, however unwillingly that might happen. Let's start now!" While Cel looked on–trembling from fear–Joe spent the next half hour writing out the ritual diagram for 'Gravedigger's requiem'. When it was finished, he looked it over, double checked the circles and markings, and began to place the components in their positions. The final item was his scepter, and he felt a bit naked without it at his hip. Taking a bit of Cel's collected blood from his storage ring, he added it to the 'mana donor' section. When he was ready, he took a deep breath and began empowering the ritual.

His mana started to stream off of him, and he was very careful to keep it flowing along the proper channels from the beginning. It'd be nice to increase his mana manipulation at the same time. As the first circle finished becoming powered, Joe looked at his mana and noticed that it had been draining like normal. As the second circle started to draw power, he watched as his mana dipped all the way to only a quarter full. At that point Cel suddenly yelped, and mana stopped escaping from Joe's body. He watched the mage try to control himself, but his face was paling rapidly. Just before he would have collapsed, Joe's mana began to drain once more.

The ritual completed just as Joe's mana touched twenty percent, and he whooped as he saw that the taglock needle on his scepter seemed to be distorting the air around it. It was vibrating softly and releasing a faint musical chime. Joe was concerned that the vibration might be damaging the needle, but after watching the durability for a minute, he was certain that he was simply paranoid. Though he was *very* excited to test this out, he really needed to get some sleep first.

"I feel so *violated*. You used me like a…a…"

"Battery?" Joe finished for the captured mage. "You make a pretty good power *Cel*." He looked at the confused man, waiting for a reaction.

"I make a good what?"

"Power *Cel*!"

"Power *what*? Stop saying my name!" Cel balled his fists and roared at the ritualist.

Joe *tisked* and looked away. "I'll go get you a bucket of water and a clean set of robes. Then I'm going to bed. You should try to rest up; we have lots of work to do!" Joe strolled away, tiredness obvious in his voice. He had been up overnight, and he was feeling it now.

When Cel was alone, his brow furrowed. "My mana manipulation skill increased?"

CHAPTER THIRTY-THREE

Joe woke up feeling refreshed and cheerful. Sure, he didn't have a team to hunt with. Yes, the quests that he currently had were long-term and vastly difficult. No, he didn't have a clear way to reach his goals... Joe suddenly wasn't feeling quite as cheerful. He decided that before going back to the research and development of his rituals that it might be a good time to return to the library and look for some easy quests that he could complete between studying and creating rituals. He stepped out of the guild building and winced at the bright light flooding the area. Whoops. It was later in the day than he had thought!

Joe started trotting toward the library. The position of the sun showed him that it was already early afternoon, and he wanted to make sure to find some good information before the library closed for the evening. It wouldn't be a good idea to mess with his sleep cycle too much, so he should try to do his work during daylight hours. He walked into the library, waving at Boris. The old man glanced up, nodded at him, and then did a double take. "H-hey! How are you a level *two* scholar? I haven't rewarded you for any quest completions! Who is giving unauthorized quests? Is it Bobius? It *is*, isn't it! I *told* him that I-"

It wouldn't be a good idea to explain where the level *actually* came from, so Joe decided on a half-truth. "No, sir! No one else gave me a quest; I got a special reward for completing a quest for the Kingdom."

"The Kingdom? How did they give you experience toward your scholar job?" Boris, for good reason, didn't believe the story he was being fed.

"It wasn't scholar specific. Part of the reward was experience toward your 'profession'. I really *cannot* tell you much more." Joe tried to appear as sincere as possible.

"Fine, keep your secrets like those impotent mages at the college! Stupid nation is getting shrouded in '*mystery*'. O~o~oh, *I* don't tell other people what's going on. I'm so *surprised* that we aren't advancing and need to do everything twice," Boris spat sarcastically. "Whatever. Well, you advanced to level two. Just perfect. Why not? You are already a 'special' case. Alright, you didn't bring any new information into the library, and you never advanced our cause."

"Sorry about that?" Joe looked up at the man with a hopeful grin.

"Humph. Well, rules are rules even when they are stupid. You *are* level two as a scholar; you now have access to the 'uncommon' book section. I would *suggest* that you try to get to the third level the *correct* way, otherwise other scholars may start becoming antagonistic toward your special treatment. To that end, you can gain job experience in a few ways: either by doing research and creating something from the books that no one else has been able to, completing a quest you find in the books that you confirm with me *before* you run off, or the standard way, which is to bring back lost or forgotten knowledge and donate it to the society of scholars."

"You know about quests in the books that haven't been completed?" Joe was excited to hear about this. Maybe he wouldn't need to hide his ability to find secret quests!

"What do you mean? Of course *I* know! Did *you* know?" Boris looked at Joe like he had insulted his mother. "Ugh. Just…

just go take a look around the 'uncommon' book area. Your face is bringing back bad memories, even though you don't look like a walking corpse anymore."

"Rude." Joe snorted and walked up the stairs leading to the second level. At the top was a sign warning off anyone who didn't have access to the uncommon section. Walking through the archway that denoted the entrance to the room, he felt as though he had just walked into a thick spider web. Joe shivered, brushing at himself before realizing that it was probably a security measure against intruders. Looking around the empty room, he smiled and activated his job's special ability to see books containing truth.

He beamed as he looked at the golden glow coming from the shelves. This section had far fewer *fully* black books, though not all the books here glowed brightly. Maybe this was the distinction between common and uncommon books: the fact that the information was more accurate or maybe from a more reliable source? Either way, Joe had some work to do. He was happy to see that the ritual from the first floor had been in range of this room as well. This was easy to notice because the section he was looking at contained a lovely gradient of colored leather. It was too bad the books didn't all have titles; it would have made finding the information he was pursuing *far* easier to attain. He pulled a few books down, trying to get a feel for what sort of material they contained. Ah, it seemed he was in a section that had never interested him in reality, but here it was a potential gold mine: history.

In Eternium, history could be more accurately labeled 'lore'. It was fun, interesting, and… wrong. Joe read through the first chapter with a twitching left eye. The book was *wildly* embellished and inaccurate. Drat! Whoever had written this had gotten a good chunk of the facts correct but had been trying to flatter whatever noble house they were a part of. The cover still glowed a soft gold, but Joe felt that his eyes were deceiving him. What he really needed was to…

A thought crossed his mind, a thought that made him very hopeful. He put the book on a small table, grabbed a few pages, and tried to will the pages to *jump* to pertinent information. The pages fluttered, and when he looked at the resulting page… yes! The words on this page were shining a bright gold, the specific coloration he had found which signaled a clue to creating a quest. This part was about an investigator who had a perfect record for only punishing criminals. Everyone else who was captured–who was innocent–was let go almost instantly. His story was a sad one unfortunately, because he was targeted by various groups who had an interest in ensuring their dark deeds went unpunished. The author of the book thought that the assassin who killed the investigator had been funded by a noble house and because of the glow of the words Joe was able to see that his thoughts had been correct.

"So this… if I find more information, will it become a hunt of the noble house, the abilities of the investigator, or something else entirely?" Joe debated for a moment; should he really take the first quest that he found? Maybe he should look over some other options? He started skimming through other books, but his mind kept wandering back to the partial information he had found. "How can I call myself a completionist if I don't take and complete every quest possible?"

He sighed and began searching through other books that were on either the same or a similar subject. Another hour passed and he finally was able to put together a comprehensive and detailed version of events. No quest prompt appeared until Joe added a small part about how the investigator had left detailed instructions on understanding criminals in a place where criminals were sent to repent.

Quest created: Seeker of truth! An influential investigator met an untimely end due to his relentless pursuit of criminals. He may have left detailed records of how he was able to sniff out evildoers. Follow the clues you have found, and find the truth for yourself! Reward: Unknown. Penalty for failure: None. Accept? Yes / No

Joe accepted the quest and walked downstairs with his notes. He needed to talk to Boris and make sure that this was an acceptable quest for a scholarly reward. "Boris? Got a quest here, would you look at it and approve it?"

Boris's head jerked up off his desk, and he blinked tired eyed. "Boy, you *do* know that some of us have other things to do at night? We were supposed to close an hour ago! Let me see the 'quest' you've found." He snatched Joe's notes and looked over the details. Joe had included references, showing which book and page he had gained the information from. "Hmm. Interesting, but how does this help our society?"

"Since I am uncertain *what* our society does as a whole, I figured it would be useful for us to have these methods of determining truth from people. That way, we could validate information coming to us from third parties." Joe's words made Boris nod softly.

"It would indeed be useful… if it exists." He tapped his chin a few times and nodded. "Alright. I approve this quest as a suitable scholarly mission. I'll add on fifty points toward your job upon quest completion, one hundred if you are able to secure the techniques described here. Yes, you get points even if you bring back nothing."

Quest rewards updated: Seeker of truth! Rewards: Unknown, profession Exp: 100. Failure: None, profession Exp: 50.

Excellent! Now *that* quest was fully worth attempting. Joe waved at Boris, who scowled and started locking the doors to the library. Maybe he should get Boris a fruit basket or something to cheer him up. He was rather nice, no matter the curmudgeonly aura he exuded. Joe started walking toward the–oh dang! His prisoner! He hurried back to his rented warehouse, entering and rushing over to find an unconscious mage, Cel. "Shoot. Totally dehydrated. I never gave him drinking water or food today! After the ritual emptied him out, too! Ah, I'm a terrible medic."

He channeled cleanse into the collapsed mage, getting his water levels to a stable point. After a long minute, Cel stirred and woozily glared at Joe. "You *left* me here. I thought you were going to let me die!"

"You could have used the water to drink!" Joe tried to defend himself. "Or at least changed and cleaned up a bit. You *seriously* smell."

"*Is that my fault?*" Cel howled and jumped to his feet. "You left the bucket of water over there!" He pointed, and sure enough a bucket of full water was patiently waiting to be used… about five feet from the edge of the ritual.

"*Ahh.* Sorry about that." Joe scratched his head sheepishly. "I've never had to take care of a detainee. Slipped my mind."

"Slipped your…?" Cel slid to a sitting position with an unpleasant **squelch**. "I'm going to die here, aren't I?"

"Stop being so dramatic!" Joe rolled his eyes. "So long as you are at least a *little* alive, I can drag you back to full health. I *am* a cleric, after all."

"So there's no escape," Cel whispered with wide eyes.

"*Drama* queen!" Joe groaned as he rubbed his bald head. "Look, I'm going to eat some food. Would you like some?" Cel's stomach rumbled at the mention of food. Joe was unsurprised; a noble brat like this had likely never had to miss a meal or even skimp a little. Pulling some food out of his storage ring, Joe handed over a basic sandwich and waited for Cel to start before he ate his own.

"Look, I'm going to bring that bucket over, and here's a spare set of clothes. Try to clean up, get changed, and get some sleep. Tomorrow we are going to do more rituals! ...Hey, can I call you 'Tate'?"

"What? No! My name is Cel. Why would you want to call me 'Tate'?" Cel asked suspiciously.

"It's short for potato!"

Cel didn't blink, but his hands trembled. "And… why would you want to call me 'potato'?"

"Because much like the noble potato, you are not a battery… but you are going to be used as one!" Joe chuckled as he brought over a pillow and thin blanket for Cel. "Sleep well, Tate!"

"I'm going to light you on fire when I escape," Cel whispered as he watched Joe leave the building. As the door closed, all light in the building vanished, leaving him in a large and hopefully empty space. Small scratching sounds reaching his ears made sleep difficult that night.

CHAPTER THIRTY-FOUR

Joe awoke with a positive outlook on life. Something about going two days in a row with his only wound being a papercut just felt... *right.* He had a nice breakfast, storing an extra plate of food for Cel because he deserved a pleasant surprise. Grabbing his notes, he went to the store for more paper, ink, and a spare quill. He also purchased another bucket of chalk from a nearby art supplier; it wouldn't be good to run out when he needed it! Joe was walking back to the warehouse when he noticed that the roads were quiet. Very, *very* quiet. He reached for his scepter, getting a firm hold on it just as his senses screamed at him to *move.* He jumped as hard as he could, reaching rooftop level just as the entire road seemed to explode.

A hurricane force updraft from the massive flame threw him to the side, and he landed heavily on the rooftop. He took no damage from the fall, his jumplomancer class coming into effect. The blast did take ten points off his health, a sickening amount since he was nowhere *near* the epicenter of that attack. He looked around, trying to find who had attacked him.

"Ha! Had some kind of a shield up, did you? Mage armor? Blast threw you clear to the roof!" a jovial voice called to him.

"Not many people get to see *Volcanic Conflagration* and live to talk about it! You impress me!"

"Impress you enough to make you go away?" Joe looked around, eyes narrowing as he saw a beefy mage in a bright red robe talking to him. How had he missed seeing *that*? "Why did you attack me? Who are you?"

"That should be an easy answer for you!" The mage's face and voice turned dangerously furious. "Not only are you a rogue mage, but you also killed one of the most promising fire mages of this generation! Where did you hide Cel's body?"

"I certainly did *not* kill him!" Joe shouted at the man. If the spell he was creating was any indication, the mage didn't seem to believe him.

"See this? Nasty little spell called 'lava worms'. Not all that useful in a war, the damage over time is quite small. Torture though, well… this spell is great for that. The worms burrow into you and start swimming around. Painful, *very* painful." There was dirt flying up, collecting and liquefying in the intense fire he was generating. "I'm strong enough to keep them hot till they reach your brain. You have until that point to tell me where his body is."

Joe prepared his scepter. There was *no way* he was letting that stuff swim through his body. The mage wasn't listening to reason so there was nothing to lose. All or nothing at this point. Joe had recovered only a very small amount of stamina from that jump and had been hoping to use it to escape. It wasn't going to happen; this man was far too powerful for that. He knew the mage would eventually track him down even if he somehow escaped right now so he wasn't even going to try. Joe jumped off the roof and swung down, hoping that his ability to fall at half damage would save him from his own recklessness.

The mage snorted as Joe fell at him. "I have mage armor too, you moron. I'm fully trained, so *mine* isn't a flimsy covering, either. I may as well be wearing plate armor!"

Undeterred, Joe swung as hard as he could even as lava worms entered his legs with an excruciating, searing pain. His scepter hit, but the bulk of it seemed to bounce off as if it had just impacted a wall.

Dexterity check failed!

Joe belly flopped onto the steaming street, losing over a quarter of his health at once. The mage made a dismissive gesture, and a fireball took off most of Joe's exposed skin and eyebrows as he was slammed bodily into a nearby building.

"What was that supposed to accomplish? You are even *closer* to death now. Don't worry, foolish little *warlock*. I know that you travelers are restored by the gods in the city square a few hours after you perish. That's why I am not worried about killing you. Not at all. When you come back, I'll be there. You will die as many times as needed to ensure that you *stay* dead!" The mage lifted a hand, and fire began collecting in his palm.

"Yes," Joe managed to croak out through his charred lips. The lava worms were ravaging his insides.

"Oh, still able to speak?" The mage was about to continue, but a strange chiming noise filled his ears. "And now I have tinnitus. Great. I was too close to the blast zone. Now I need to pay for an overrated healer-"

Joe blinked, and within that moment, the mage vanished into the street. Through fluttering, mostly-gone eyelashes he was able to see: *You have chosen to activate 'Gravedigger's requiem'. This ritual lasts for ten seconds after activation*. Heh. At that point, the lava worms reached his brain, and he was unable to heal himself from the catastrophic damage to his grey matter.

You have died! Calculating. You were attacked in a safe zone by an NPC that was set as non-hostile. Your alignment with the mage's college: neutral. NPC reason for attacking: death of student. Reason for attack invalid. No action was taken that should have flagged you for assault. _ERROR_ Safe area. Please have patience, this issue is being elevated.

A short time passed before a new message appeared. *Alrighty, let's see here. Oh, you again, huh? Setting your notifications to 'extra snarky' didn't drive the point home, you are still breaking things? Let's take a look. Huh. No, for once, you were the wronged party. If the mage had attacked you because you took his student* captive, *we would be having a different talk right now, but, technically, you were in a safe zone at a safe time and were still attacked by a mage who is not supposed to attack you. Here's my take on this. Three hours till you respawn, no loss of experience. I'm also giving you a temporary boost to your reputation with the college for six hours when you respawn. You'll be set to 'reluctantly friendly'. That should give you enough time to make your case before turning into a human tiki-torch. Good luck! Stop breaking my world, or I will break you!*

-Love, Certified Altruistic Lexicon.

Joe felt a bit leery about this situation; he just got a signed note from the AI in control of the entire game. He had *specifically* been told not to draw the AI's attention! While he was out of the game, he did a bit of reading and called his mom. She was ecstatic, of course; he was calling her so often now! For her, it was only a little over a day since the last time they talked, though for him it was two. Joe told her about his new friends, and she told him about how she had been on perpetual vacation after she had gotten the winnings from her lottery ticket and sent him off. There were a few sad moments, such as when she asked when he would be coming to visit. Really, there was nothing he could say about that… so he just shook his head and told her it would be a long, long time. When they finally ran out of things to say, they reluctantly hung up, and Joe flopped into the fluffy chair that he was able to create in the area.

The time passed quickly with a nap, and an alarm woke him up five minutes before he was allowed back into the world. He got himself ready and stepped into Eternium as the 'portal' appeared. A *very* familiar and unpleasantly smiling face was waiting for him. In fact, it was the first thing he saw. "Why, *hello* there. Let's talk about how you managed to drop me a kilometer under the ground, shall we?"

Joe winced, the bright red robes were covered in filth and the mage himself was heaving with what appeared to be barely suppressed anger. If he was this furious after what would have been six hours… "Oh, hey there. It's such a… *surprise* to see you."

"I bet it is." The mage's hand burst into flame, and he started reaching for Joe's face with a maniacal grin on his face.

"Your apprentice *is* alive, you know," Joe tried to keep his tone conversational as his eyelashes curled from the heat, "but if I don't get him some food and water soon, he won't be."

The flaming hand stopped moving closer but also didn't back away. "If you are lying to me, I will burn every bit of your skin off before digging into the next layer. I will peel you like a potato."

Joe snorted a laugh, making the mage's threats trail off in confusion. "A potato? Hah! Tell Cel that you called me a potato. He will laugh, I swear. Let's go."

"He is really alive? He told you his name?" The mage couldn't seem to reconcile his expectations with reality.

"Yeah, we're totally friends now." Joe cautiously started walking away, moving toward his warehouse.

"I don't believe you. Cel's company is not something a person enjoys." The mage snorted with annoyance. "I can always kill you later, so let's go save my apprentice."

"What if he doesn't want to be saved?" Joe asked in a serious tone. "What if, when he sees you, he tells you to leave? He might come up with all manner of excuses, like telling you I am trapping you, I'm his new best friend, or that I'm actually a powerful mage and you should run away?"

Haughtily, the mage looked Joe up and down. "I think that you used your most powerful spell already. I think it had no effect on me because I possess the dual affinities for earth and fire and simply unburied myself. I see no need to *run* from you, and I will explain this to him. Then you both will explain what the *abyss* is going on."

They walked in silence for a few minutes before the mage started talking again, "So you are an earth mage? Or whatever the equivalent is for a self-trained hedge witch like yourself."

"Actually, no. I'm not really sure how I got on the college's watch list. I have a single spell that could be classified as a mage ability, but I got it from my deity. I'm actually a cleric."

"A single mage spell is enough to draw us to you. Why didn't you register with the college? You had to have heard of the consequences."

"Why should I register? Where is the benefit to me? I'm not looking for training or to boost my mage capabilities," Joe carefully lied. "Why should I pay a King's ransom simply not to be *attacked* for a spell I gained via divine providence?"

The mage thought on that for a few minutes as they approached the warehouse. "I see your point, but it doesn't matter. If you have a single mage-classed spell, you need to sign The Accords. It is the only way we have been able to maintain order in the Kingdom; it is what keeps powerful mages out of politics and government positions."

Joe kept his voice calm and tried to remain collected, "What if I simply cannot afford to pay? I am in a Noble Guild and am a guild officer. What if we made it a personal quest to kill you all? We are travelers; we'll keep coming back if you kill us. Can you say the same? I also took a quest directly from the queen in the last few days. Is it really wise to make an enemy out of a huge portion of the population–especially those you can't kill off–simply because they are using the abilities given to them? And it *was* given to me; I did not study for it or find my spell lying around. It was a quest reward."

"But why not sign The Accords?" The mage seemed frustrated, like Joe wasn't hearing him. "All you need to do is list out your magical abilities, pay the hundred gold, and inform a certified teacher if you gain more magical abilities! You can keep your spell, and you will just need to pay a percentage of quest rewards to the college! You won't be a licensed mage and cannot attain rank or training in your spells, but you won't be hunted down!"

Shock was written across Joe's face. "What? I can just go in and get access to The Accords? I was told that the only way was to join the college and become a licensed mage for multiple thousands of gold!"

The mage rubbed his temples. "This is why I told them we needed more publicity. Listen. Do you have a hundred gold?"

"I do."

"Then, if Cel is safe, I will plead your case to the council and the Archmage. Either way, you will be brought into the college tomorrow. If you sign The Accords and they witness it–and you haven't killed any mages–I will do my best to make sure you walk away with a clean record."

Charisma +1! You have reached an important milestone in the growth of your charisma! As you now have 15 charisma, you gain access to the basic skill of charismatic people: Speech.

Skill gained: Speech (Novice I). Talk your way out of things, talk your way in! This skill adds a bonus equivalent to your skill level onto your charisma when attempting to convince another person or group of people to do something they normally would not. Only activates via talking. Chance for new or unique access to quests has increased!

"That's… very nice of you. We are here." Joe distractedly walked up to the door and pulled out his key. As he was unlocking it, the mage coughed.

"I'm not feeling very well, all of a sudden." Indeed, the contrast of his red robes and green face clearly showed how sickly he was.

"That's just the building." Joe motioned for him to wait at the door. "It'll get worse for you the deeper into the building you go. I'll go get Cel, don't worry about coming in. Also, Cel and I are immune."

"I'm not going to wait here, and I'm not letting you out of my sight. Let's go." They stepped into the building, and the mage's bowels made a low moaning noise. "We may need to move a bit faster."

"You have a couple options here. If you go further you *will* start puking and… well, I'm sure you can feel what else will happen. You can wait here, try your luck, or put some blood in this chalice." Joe pulled the tarnished cup out of his ring. "I'll bring it over there, and you will feel better right away."

Ignoring him, the mage looked across the room where his apprentice was standing. "Cel! You're alive!"

"Master?" Cel could only see silhouettes, as they were framed by the light coming through the doorway. "Don't do anything that man asks you too! He is an evil, conniving-"

"Don't worry about him. He will be signing The Accords in the morning, Cel." The mage told him equitably.

"*What?* No way! He went out of his way to convince me how evil the college was! He tried to tell me that The Accords are shackles that keep us under the thumb of the Archmage! How we are incredibly weak because it is impossible for commoners and rogue mages to enter our ranks!" Cel was almost shaking. "All of that rhetoric against the college and he is *joining?*"

The mage seemed frozen in place, his face aghast. "He told you all of *that?*"

"Yes!"

"If… if you went back to the college tonight, would you feel the need to explain your whereabouts and what he told you to your colleagues?" the mage inquired, voice deadly calm.

"Of course! I need to discuss this with them so that we can study The Accords further and have a valid explanation against this line of reasoning in the future!" Cel's voice trailed off as he saw the shock in his master's posture.

"In that case… Cel, I can't take you back with me tonight. You were already on the verge of increasing your rank, and with this information and attitude toward it… I can't allow you to be around other mages until you sign The Accords a second time." The mage seemed sorrowful, and his hands were clenched to the point of draining color away.

"What are you talking about? Master! You can't mean to leave me here! Why?" Cel shouted across the room in a hoarse voice. Drat, Joe had forgotten to leave him drinking water again.

"Isn't it obvious, Cel?" Joe crossed his arms and stared at the red-robed mage. "It is because what I said is the *truth*. Your master is under the same compulsion that you will be, a more advanced version of what you are sworn to. Master mage, tell me a *single* negative thing about The Accords. Anything at all. Tell me you don't like the quill they made you sign with! Say the font was a dumb choice or that it was written in comic sans! Perhaps there was poor lighting in the area it's stored in?"

The mage opened his mouth, closed it and looked away. Joe snorted through his nose. "As I thought. You *can't* say anything against it. You also can't let someone go against The Accords, am I correct? A stay of execution is the best you can do?"

Still looking away, the mage made a motion that could almost be considered a nod. His voice came out as a whisper, "I can't let Cel go back right now. If he started speaking out, someone might kill him. I… would have to kill him."

"Master. No. You can't be serious." Cel sunk to the floor. On his knees, he grabbed his hair with both hands. "We've become little better than slaves? I… I can't…"

"If you don't think of it like that, life is far more manageable," the mage spoke softly. "Think of The Accords as you always have, a force for good in the Kingdom. There isn't any other way to justify… what we have. To. Do." He struggled to get out the last words and seemed to be in pain even from that light disagreement. He took a deep, shuddering breath before turning bloodshot eyes to Joe. "I'll come back for you in the morning. Can you keep him here? If you do so and don't cause problems, I'll pay you back half of the fee for signing The Accords. ...Why did you have to explain his position in the-" He coughed blood.

"I'll keep him here," Joe promised solemnly. The mage closed his mouth with a loud **click**, nodded, and turned toward the door.

"Master! You can't!" Cel called brokenly, standing as close to the edge of his containment as he could get.

The mage grit his teeth. "You are wrong, Cel. I literally *need* to. As much as I don't-" He started to choke and grabbed at his throat. He was still for a few seconds, then reached into a satchel at his side. Three bottles that should not have fit into the bag appeared, each glowing a bright blue color. "Take these. Whatever you are doing to contain him, just make sure it holds."

Joe held the bottles and tried to inspect them.

Perception check failed! Intelligence check versus contextual evidence and past experience… success!

Item acquired: Concentrated mana rejuvenation potion x3. Restores 300 mana over five seconds, triples mana regeneration for one minute. Item rarity: Artificially Rare (Common).

"Those are only allowed to be produced or sold in the mage's college, in case you are wondering why such a useful item isn't found in shops." The mage released a sound that resembled a laugh, but it was obvious that it was simply a strangled sob. "Yet another product that benefits our *great school.* Make sure you are here at sunup and don't cause problems for us, or you will be declared a warlock as well as a rogue."

Storing the potions, Joe nodded at the mage. The red-robed man made a motion that could be mistaken for wiping his eyes and walked out the door. Retching sounds echoed faintly into the building, but Joe had a feeling that it was not because of his active rituals.

CHAPTER THIRTY-FIVE

Joe clapped and smiled brightly. "Well, that was horrible and heartbreaking!" Cel glared at him, tears openly streaming down his face.

"You are… how can you be so willing to throw yourself into servitude?" Cel growled brokenly. "You should run while you still can. Vanish into the city. I have no choice but to accept my-" He erupted into a coughing fit, surprise written large on his face.

"Looks like The Accords are punishing you a bit." Joe watched as Cel's face turned purple and the coughs became flecked with blood. He sent a healing spell at Cel, just to be on the safe side. "Why don't you eat dinner and get some rest?"

"Why don't you let me ruminate about my fate?" Cel choked out a dramatic rebuttal.

"You do whatever you need to do." Joe pulled out his book on rituals and sat down for a long study session. An hour passed in near silence, the only sound being the scratching of a quill and various soft sobbing noises. Joe looked up when Cel quieted down fully. "Your master called me a warlock, then later seemed to change his mind and told me that I would be *declared* a warlock. I thought that was just a type of spell caster, someone who debuffs others or summons beings to fight for him?"

"No. Well, yes, they *can* be warlocks. It is a title given to those who break oaths. Not everyone can make a mana contract, and most people don't want to be bound by soul-crushing pain or death if they violate a contract. So they make deals, oaths. If you break your word of honor, you are despised by any who can see the title." Cel seemed to be exhausted; he didn't even look over while speaking. "This is one of the few titles that can't be revoked or changed by a deity, since honor is only amongst people. Only the wronged party, a magistrate, or the King can rule against the title and lift the restrictions it imposes. Even then, any but the wronged party can only revoke the title if the reason for breaking the oath was just, such as an oath specifically pledged under duress or for the greater good of the Kingdom."

"That's pretty specific." Joe was quiet for a short while. "Sounds like it would be a fairly common title then."

"Oh, it is," Cel responded dully. "The title fits the oath broken though. A serious oath, such as leaving your men to die or sacrificing another you pledged to protect, will impact your interactions greatly and give you a negative balance on your karmic luck."

"Karmic luck? Do you have an explanation for that?" Joe perked up; this was one of the few stats he knew nothing about.

"I don't. All I know is that you never want it to be negative." Cel fell silent again.

"I see." Joe kept studying his book, trying to find a way to survive the upcoming day. His eyes lit up as he thought of a single possibility. "Reversing it? Would that even work? I can't risk it. What if I changed it? If I added this, no, the power requirement would be too high. Combining it? That might work. I'd need an additional circle though. Apprentice level. This might get messy."

He shuddered and got to work on creating a new ritual. Time began to creep by, and once he finished his work, there were only a few hours remaining until dawn. Joe's eyelids were sagging, trying to force him to accept the embrace of Morpheus. He powered through, keenly feeling the need to stay alive. Fear of potential slavery or death was a good motivator. Joe began drawing out the spell circles, knowing he needed to be precise but also doing his best to draw quickly. Every time he made a mistake and needed to remake a portion, he growled at himself and his wasteful actions.

Skill increase: Drawing (Novice V). *Control of the body starts with control of the mind. Control of chalk was supposed to start as a child. Whatever, right? You got a tiny bit better at a mundane task!*

An hour before dawn, he shook Cel awake. "Cel, I was hoping to ask a favor of you."

"Are you being serious right now?" Cel sleepily replied, tiredness and angst coloring his voice. "Why in the *world* would I help you willingly?"

"I'd just *really* like to survive the day. I have no doubt that once I am near The Accords, at least one person will try to kill me. Ask yourself this, Cel. Do you want me to sign The Accords or die before I get there?"

Cel seemed to struggle with himself for a long moment. Grudgingly, he answered, "I want you to sign them."

"Thank you, Cel," Joe stated warmly. When he turned so that Cel couldn't see his face, his eyes hardened. He already knew that The Accords subtly influenced the mind of whoever signed them. This was proof that The Accords wanted to grow and impact more people. He remembered the words of the owner of the *Odds and Ends* store; an enchanted item was alive, if just barely. He was sure that a magical contract that had thousands ensnared and had lasted for hundreds of years had a more developed ego. It wanted to grow, to have more people trapped in its binding words, or it could be that Cel wasn't a terrible human being and didn't want a fairly innocent person to die for no reason. Could really go either way.

"Here is what I need you to do. I am creating a ritual, and you don't need to help. I'm just going to give you a mana potion and hope that you keep yourself alive by restoring your mana when the ritual tries to kill you. Thanks!" Joe grinned evilly and marched toward the ritual as Cel gave off an indignant squeaking sound.

Placing his scepter in the innermost ring, Joe started pouring mana into the ritual. The power draw was massive with three rings, and even with his ability to only pay half of the final cost, the ritual was demanding nineteen hundred mana. The first circle activated without issue, leaving Joe with mana to spare. The second circle began to pull power, and he became a bit worried. When the first had been pulling mana, it was at a rate he was used to. The second one was draining him almost twice as fast. As he approached ten percent remaining in his mana pool, the power draw switched over to Cel.

The young mage cried out as he felt his mana channels straining to direct the flow of power. Though he really didn't want to help his captor, if he let the power run out of his body in a disordered fashion, he might be torn apart. Joe took this opportunity to drink the first mana potion and felt a sense of relief and clarity as his mana was restored. With triple mana regeneration, he was quickly coming back to full strength.

Cel dropped to five percent mana before the burden of the ritual switched back to Joe. He reached for the mana potion with trembling hands but was caught off guard when Joe managed to say, "No! Wait… for… signal! Or we both die!"

The mage wavered, hesitating as mana exhaustion clouded his thoughts. He was not used to getting his mana pool below half, *ever*. It wasn't allowed since you never knew when a commoner was going to attack you for no good reason. Therefore all mages were taught to keep half of their mana pool for emergencies. Hand shaking, Cel brought the potion bottle to his lips.

Joe was focusing on his mana expenditure, watching with awe as his mana regeneration fought against the rapid power suck of the ritual. With triple regeneration for one minute, he was generating a tiny bit more than twenty mana a second. It was fascinating to watch his mana decline at what appeared to be a very slow rate, about ten mana a second. So the ritual was pulling thirty per second? They could do this, they just needed to hold on!

Then the third circle began to draw mana. Blood erupted from Joe's mouth as he was unable to contain the flow of mana within his channels. Watching his mana decrease at almost double the previous rate, Joe turned to Cel to give him the signal to start drinking… only to see that his potion bottle was already empty. Cel could see only horror in Joe's eyes as he looked at the little moron. At five percent mana, the ritual switched targets and Cel screamed. Mana seemed to *tear* out of him in arcing bolts of energy, and his eyes and mouth had coronas of blue light shining from them. He struggled and failed to control himself, doing everything he could to keep the mana flowing in an orderly fashion.

Joe could see the moment that the boosted mana regeneration ended for Cel. He seemed to shrink, almost *shrivel*, as his power was pulled from him. Joe grabbed the final potion and chugged it just as Cel collapsed. Instantly back to three-quarters full, Joe braced himself and guided his mana along the channels. He wasn't going to make it. Sweat dripped down his face, stinging his eyes as he watched his mana bar trickle toward the halfway point. He gasped and fell as the power draw suddenly vanished, the ritual completing.

What? How had it completed? Their vitality should have been drained as their mana ran out! Joe went over the calculations in his head once again; it should have needed nineteen hundred mana! What was he missing… spell efficiency! Mana manipulation and coalescence together added… seventeen percent efficiency! The mana cost had dropped to fifteen hundred and seventy seven! If he had used the potions himself, he wouldn't even have needed to use all three! Why did he keep forgetting to account for spell efficiency? He almost screamed aloud about the wasted resources! Notifications interrupted his fury.

Skill increase: Mana Manipulation (Beginner V). Congratulations! The forced draining and refilling of your mana has torn open pathways that should have been given weeks to open safely! For reaching the beginner ranks of this skill, an additional effect has been generated based on your usage of the skill to this point! Effect: Add 10% stability to magic that costs more than 30% of your total mana pool to activate. Since I'm sure you don't understand thanks to your non-existent magical education, spell stability is the statistic that determines how easy it is to keep your mana in the proper channels. Tearing apart your body for greater power is definitely the way to go. Go you! Intelligence +2. Wisdom +3. Constitution -1.

Joe began to wheeze as his body deflated. His constitution had dropped below ten again, and flesh began to drip off of his body like wax from a melting candle. As it touched the ground, it vaporized into sparkling light. Soon he was again looking down at a wasted form, and standing upright became difficult. A bit hunched over, Joe retrieved his scepter. There was no noticeable effect on it from the ritual's activation. In fact, the taglock seemed almost unnaturally still. Putting it into his storage ring, he shuffled over to Cel and slapped him.

Zero damage!

Joe growled at the reaffirmation of his destroyed physical stats. He tried again with the same message appearing. A kick, the same. Finally he just reached into his ring and pulled out a bit of rotten-smelling intestinal meat. Holding that under Cel's nose, he waited as the man began to twitch and groan.

"What happened?" Cel mumbled, holding his head. He looked at his now wet hand; it had come away covered in blood.

"What happened is that you almost killed yourself because you cannot seem to believe that someone else knows better!" Joe barked at him. His voice sounded rough and dry.

"*What are you*?" Cel looked into Joe's skeletal face and backed away in horror.

"I'm a guy that accidentally tore open his mana channels and had his constitution dropped below ten points." Joe glared at Cel as he turned white; the young mage seemed ready to puke.

"Disgusting! I can't believe that could happen!" His eyes were wide and appalled. "Now it makes sense why we need to keep our mana pool so high."

Joe spat to the side. "There is a terrible bias against taking risks. The rewards can be great. We are always told to play it safe so that everyone else can optimize covering their own butt. The price for me might seem high, but I only lost one point of constitution while gaining two points of intelligence and three of wisdom. Not to mention ten percent spell stability."

"*What?*" Cel gasped in shock. "Impossible! All you get for overloading your mana channels is a step into your grave! Everyone knows that-"

"Hold up." Joe put his hand in front of Cel's face. "This 'everyone' you speak of. They wouldn't happen to be the same 'everyone' that are forcing us into signing away our freedom in a few hours? The same people that have lied to you your entire career as a mage?" Cel had no way to respond to that.

"I'm betting that there is a whole *bunch* of information you are missing or have been lied to about. Get ready to go; we don't have long until the mages show up." Joe walked over to the ritual containing Cel, reaching out with his mind and deactivating its effects. Cel had no idea it was off of course and simply stood there looking troubled. "Ritual is off. Let's get going. We can wait outside."

They moved to the entrance, and after stepping into the open, Joe locked the door and turned around. Five mages as well as several guards and crossbowmen stood waiting for them. A mage coughed delicately, then arched a brow. "Going somewhere?"

Joe nodded, keeping his body as straight as possible. "We are. You are the escort to the college?"

"Indeed." The mage was in a strange purple robe. "You are going to be 'silenced' until you sign The Accords. You will both be unable to cast spells or speak unless I or the Archmage ask you a direct question. Is that clear?"

Both Cel and Joe nodded grimly. The mage looked between them. "Anything else to say before we go?"

"Moist ointment in rural pulp," Joe enunciated each word clearly. A few of the gathered people looked at him strangely, cringing a bit. The mage made a 'what the heck" gesture, making Joe shrug. "I just didn't want to be the only one feeling uncomfortable."

"Goal achieved, you weirdo. *Silence*." Joe's throat seemed to fill with phlegm, forcing him to cough wetly. He tried to speak, but as expected, he was unable to. He tried to gather the shadows into a spike, but they ignored his will. He tried to use a healing spell, and to everyone's surprise, a ball of water splashed into the mage's shocked face.

"*How did-*" the mage yowled like a wet cat, stopping as he realized that he felt pretty good. "Healing spell? Non arcane… ah yes, you *did* claim to be a cleric, didn't you? Divine magic is unimpeded? I'll have to update the magical fair usage committee."

Joe snorted at that comment, and the mage seemed to remember he existed. "Ah, that's right. You two are going for a double signing today, aren't you? This young, of course you don't think The Accords are designed for fair usage. Back before The Accords, mages could freely experiment and shape their powers in non-recommended ways. Some mages of the same generation were able to outclass their peers, becoming far more powerful than the others. They could sometimes even specialize into non-mage classes! Imagine a mage turning into an arcane druid! Well, that doesn't happen anymore. Now The Accords ensure that the entire generation moves at the same pace, and specializations are chosen for each mage via committee approval. All is fair."

Joe wanted to speak up, *really* wanted to explain how this man must be a weak idiot if he thought that was a good system. Sadly, the spell of silence was still in effect. Equality of outcome was tyrannical. Forcing people into specializations for the good of the college? Making the strong or gifted wait for what must be *decades* to better themselves while the others caught up? If he had any doubt that the Archmage was a dictator in his own right, this proved the point perfectly.

The mage spoke the entire time they were walking toward the college, waxing eloquent about the college and the 'good' it did for the Kingdom. How they would be 'bettering' themselves by signing. Joe rolled his eyes so many times that he was surprised he didn't get dizzy. Several times during the walk, people approached to see what was going on. Each time, the guards around the small group drew weapons and their path was instantly cleared. They had gone farther east in the city than Joe had ever ventured before, and it seemed they were moving toward a looming tower. The tower was about half the width of the royal palace, perfectly circular, and about fifty feet tall. Its color was hard to pinpoint because it changed every minute or so.

The mage escorting them chuckled as he saw the confusion on Joe's face. "You've never seen this? There is quite a fun explanation; it's a game! Each class of magic wants to be the one representing the college. The entire tower will change color to match whatever type of spell is used on it most recently, so—see there! Purple! My students must have joined in the fun."

CHAPTER THIRTY-SIX

The group walked through the defensive wall which encircled the tower, and the entirety of the building was revealed. Beyond towering above them, the college was incredibly… boring. No plants could be seen, no art, and the only form of self-expression seemed to be limited to painting the tower with a spell every once in a while. Since it had first turned purple, the tower had briefly flicked to blue before becoming purple again. Now Joe could see why. A fireball appeared in the hand of a laughing mage in red robes, but before it left his hand, a purple-robed mage pointed at him, and the fireball vanished.

"The school of silence dominates this game," their escort smugly told them. "Cel knows how it is. Really hard for any other school to impede the others without damage. It is also good for the other mages to learn from a young age that they can't defeat our policing forces."

Joe and Cel locked eyes, and Cel seemed to be exasperated. It seemed even *this* game was rigged. Their escort's voice suddenly rang through the area, "Good morning students! There will be an assembly today for the promotion of apprentice fire mage Cel! Today will be his second signing of The

Accords, and he will step into his position as a journeyman mage! Be there at noon for the ceremony!"

Cheers rang through the yard as dozens of people yelled out their support for the captured young man. Tears filled his eyes, mistaken by the others as pride or some other emotion of jubilation. Their escort leaned in, whispering to Joe. "Of course, before the promotion we will be having a trial. *When* you are found guilty of conspiring against us, I'll make sure that you specialize into something *extra* special. Maybe your class ability will be to clean toilets extra easily."

Joe and Cel were both shocked at this. Why were they surprised though? He had *just* told them that the college chose how their members ranked up. They were led into the tower and walked along oddly stunted and winding corridors. Stepping through a door, Joe saw the most bizarre room he had ever laid eyes on. The room was a spherical shape with the bottom half covered in benches for spectators. The room was far too massive to fit into the building, and must have been given extra area with the assistance of spatial magics. Another series of what appeared to be more comfortable seats could be seen on a platform in the middle of the room, one of the chairs larger and grander than the others. It could even be considered a throne. All of these details were secondary to the centerpiece of the room.

A gigantic glass tube extended from both the ceiling and floor, shrinking down and becoming narrow like an hourglass in the center. Where the glass would have met, a book was suspended in midair. Though airborne, it may as well have been concrete on the ground for how much it moved. Colored lights moved through the tubes, condensing into tiny beams of energy that shot into–and were apparently absorbed by–the book. Mana? How much power was required for The Accords that such a grand mana collecting and focusing setup was needed? The only reasonable explanation was that the contract used mana *constantly* to control the people who had signed it.

"About time. The rogue mage and his captured pet have

finally arrived." A terribly obese man stood from the grandiose chair on the platform, raising his jiggling arms to the side so that his multi colored robes flared out and slowly settled around him. "I will leave it to the council to decide their fate." He sat back down with a great sigh. After such an ostentatious display to grab their attention, Joe was a bit annoyed that the Archmage hadn't said anything else.

"Their cases have already been discussed." Another mage—this one's robes a deep blue—stood and spoke. "In the case of apprentice Cel versus the college, he has been found... not guilty. He was captured and tortured. According to mana devoted to The Accords, only recently has he been slipping from his dedicated path. After a period of re-education yet to be determined and with a second signing of The Accords today, Cel will be moved to the journeyman rankings and gain a specialization befitting his new status."

The mage who had escorted them in seemed like he was about to say something; his face turned red, and he appeared furious. The blue-robed councilor ended his speech by glaring at him darkly, and no other words were spoken.

The Archmage tapped his chin, pretending to think on the matter. "I find this acceptable, though there *will* need to be punishment. He *did* slip from his teachings under torture and it took less than three days for him to have a decade of dedication fail him. During his re-education, Cel will spend eight hours a day devoting his mana to The Accords. This will last no less than one full month. If he doesn't die or go insane from the strain, he will be welcomed back as a full member of the college."

A few quiet gasps could be heard from the chairs around the Archmage, and their escort seemed greatly pleased, even going so far as to smirk at the mage on the council. Joe looked at Cel, noting how pale he had become. Obviously, this was a terrible punishment, but he had no point of reference for just how bad it would be. When another council mage stood, Joe gulped as his eyes were met.

"In the case of 'Joe' versus the college," the mage snorted derisively, "we find him guilty of attacking the college, torture of a member, and practicing magic without a license. As punishment, we recommend no less than six months devoting his mana to The Accords for *twelve* hours a day. During this time, he will have someone reading him a copy of The Accords and extolling its virtues for *six* hours each day. We also recommend that at the end of this time frame, as he is a traveler, we send him to respawn until he reaches level one. At that point, we will bind his mana pool so that he can never again cast arcane magics."

Joe would have fallen to his knees if he hadn't been roughly grabbed by a guard standing near him. All of that for holding a mage that was trying to kill him for… what? Two days? The Archmage nodded along as his sentence was decided. "That is lenient, but I expect nothing less from you. If it were possible, I'd say you've gone soft!" The Archmage's wheezing laugh echoed around the otherwise silent room. Only now was it apparent how upset the other mages on the platform looked. A few squirmed, but the light around The Accords dimmed a bit and they became still.

"You, boy, will serve as an example for the college. It has been quite a few years since someone dared test us. Now we will once again teach the Kingdom why it is the last thing they ever want to do." His cruel, piggy eyes were on Joe as he spoke. "That said, at the end of this process, you will likely have raised your stolen skill of mana manipulation to great heights. You will make a decent healer at that point, able to continuously heal for days at a time. When you are finished with your punishment, you will go serve the Kingdom as a healer until you have earned enough to repay us for those skills. We'll say ten thousand gold total. It should only take you a decade or so. How does that sound?"

You have been offered a quest. Punishment for your crimes! Serve your sentence with the Mage's College by spending 12 hours a day for six months refilling the mana of The Accords and pay ten thousand gold to the college!

This quest is mandatory if you have signed The Accords as it has been offered by the Archmage. Rewards: You will not be hunted by the college. Failure: You will be hunted by the college. Accept? Yes / No

Not a chance. Joe declined the quest so quickly that he was able to see the tiny smirk that fluttered across the Archmage's face. "Oh? Not accepting *willingly*, hmm? I thought that you had learned your lesson! Don't worry, we will adjust the quest *accord*ingly once you have signed The Accords." Joe wanted to spit when he heard that terrible attempt at a pun. You can't just say the same thing twice and call it a joke!

"Well, we have a few hours until noon; why don't we get started charging The Accords while we wait? Cel, this will count toward your punishment. Joe… not so much." The piggy eyes were mirthful as the captured men were frog-marched to the glass tubing on the dais. Their wrists were gripped and their hands shoved against the glowing surface. A seizure rocked them, and their muscles locked as if they had grabbed an electric wire. Mana instantly began to be torn out of their quaking bodies.

The power draw wasn't at all like using a ritual; for some reason, it felt like this process was *designed* to be painful. Joe bent his mind to manipulating the mana and keeping it contained within his channels. Though an imperfect solution, the pain dropped to a dull roar. His channels had been shaped to handle large quantities of mana moving through him at once, and he was using this fact to lessen the pain inflicted on him. Cel was having far more issues, and he cried out every few seconds as his mana ran out and tried to regenerate.

Joe lasted twice as long as Cel, but his mana also ran dry. He still couldn't pull his hands away from the tube, but each time mana appeared in his body, the painful shock came again. This was an extraordinarily efficient form of torture as it didn't directly harm the body, but Joe was determined not to be a victim. He turned his mind inward, and with each suctioning current, he did his best to use his mana channels as if this act was second nature. An hour passed, and yet there was no end in sight. They had been escorted here at the crack of dawn and were not going to be signing The Accords until noon. Another hour of time slowly trickled by, and still, Joe refused to break. Shock after shock rocked his system; but at least now that his channels were custom-made for the force, there was no pain from the mana being pulled from his body.

Joe mentally checked the notifications waiting for him and smiled as the updates took effect.

You have put your mind and body through a grueling training regimen! This has tested you in ways you have never been tested before, and the results are beginning to show. You can add one point to either constitution or wisdom. Please choose. Constitution / Wisdom

Joe added a point to his constitution, almost managing to grin as he saw a few people become horrified as his body began to pull mana from the air around him in order to grow.

"What is happening? What did he just do?" a panicked voice reached his ears. "How is he drawing in mana while touching the tubing? Kill him!"

"Wait!" a voice called sharply. Joe grimaced as the shock came again; he had been hoping they would send him to respawn so he could rally his guild to destroy this place. "It looks like he spent a characteristic point to get above a ten-point threshold. No need for alarm; he was just trying to withstand the pain of The Accords."

"Ha. A useless gesture." Joe ignored the seemingly satisfied Archmage as he kept going over the notifications.

Skill increased: Mana Manipulation (Beginner IX). What are you doing to yourself? Total body torture to gain a few measly skill points? Now that is dedication!

Skill increased: Channeling (Beginner II). Congratulations! You have reached the beginner stages of channeling and have gained an extra effect based on your actions with channeling to this point. Extra effect: +5% spell stability when channeling mana.

Not terrible gains for two hours of grueling pain. Joe would have preferred not to have been in this position but was seriously considering doing this for a while just to get his mana manipulation to greater heights. He could always log out and let his avatar take the beating for him, but he wouldn't gain any skill levels that way. That was the big danger of being 'locked up' for six months of real time. Joe wouldn't get any skills nor any play time. He also couldn't delete his character and start a new one, since that would erase his mind entirely.

An indefinite amount of time later, Joe heard the words that he had been yearning for since the start of this process. "That's enough for now. The students will be joining us soon, and we should prepare for the ceremony."

Someone came over to the captives, grabbed their wrists, and yanked their hands off the tubes. Joe noticed that whoever it was kept their own hands covered with gloves just in case they bumped against the glass. Hardly able to remain on their feet, Joe and Cel were brushed off by one of their escorts, obviously an attempt to mask the torture they had just gone through. Their clothes were covered with opulent robes, and someone roughly scrubbed their faces with a damp rag. Apparently looking as good as they were going to, they were marched in front of the Archmage's throne and forced to kneel. Cel was moving easily and with relief, but Joe's muscles were locked and tense. He was not looking forward to this.

Students began pouring into the seating area, chatting amicably and separating themselves by the color of their robes. The noise steadily grew, but it seemed there were only about three hundred total mages joining to watch what they thought of as a joyous spectacle. When everyone had found a seat, they waited to actually sit down until the Archmage motioned for them to do so. Joe's eyes widened. Never had he imagined that the Archmage had such control over the magically inclined. Stealing a glance around, he saw that the councilors' eyes were all deadened, and they were watching the proceedings helplessly.

"Today," the Archmage struggled to his feet, hiding his lack of physical fitness by flourishing his robes, "we have gathered to observe a special event. Many of you know your young brother, apprentice fire mage Cel!"

The gathered crowd began cheering, calming down after a long moment as the Archmage waved his hands. "What many of you do not know… is that a few days ago, he was captured by a rogue mage!" The gasping drowned out the applause instantly. "While this young man was captured, he remained strong! He fought valiantly against his captor and learned many very *important* lessons!" His eyes glinted with mirth as the assembled people cheered. They couldn't know that the lessons he had learned is one that *they* would all eventually learn as well.

"For his strength and mental fortitude, today he will be promoted to the rank of journeyman mage, and the council will decide upon his first specialization!" The silence lasted a second longer, but then the people seemed to explode into wild cheering and clapping. A tear trickled from Cel's eye, but any who saw the shining liquid only thought that he had been overcome with joy and was attempting to remain stoic; they respected him all the more for it. "*Apprentice* Cel, you may approach and sign… *The Accords*!"

Joe had to hand it to the guy; he knew how to work an audience. Cel got to his feet and marched toward The Accords robotically. He was obviously under compulsion, but that wasn't noticeable from a distance. Joe had to wonder why the Archmage didn't simply order everyone to sign it three times. Did it require more mana to control the populace if they actively fought against it? That would make sense. Also, it was already using a huge amount of mana. Did the amount of times you sign it correlate to how much mana it allocated to control you? He had seen the entire construct dim when the gathered councilors had shifted around. Joe watched as Cel walked the last few feet and reached toward the utterly massive book that contained The Accords.

The book opened, and pages flew by. It stopped, once again becoming as still as a predator awaiting prey. Cel's hand kept moving, and a beautiful quill that seemed to be made out of pure mana appeared in his hand. The last inch of his scrawled name was traversed, and Cel's name appeared in The Accords for the second time. The mana rushing through the glass seemed to become more agitated, and a small arc of power leapt from The Accords into Cel. He reacted as if he had been struck by lightning, his entire body stiffening as he gasped in pain. When he could move again, he turned around with a wide smile plastered across his face.

"Rejoin us... *Journeyman* Cel!" The Archmage roared, the awestruck people taking his cue to begin celebrating for their newly promoted member. Cel bounded down the stairs, standing proudly in the spot he had vacated just moments before. Joe looked at him and was able to see that his wide eyes were horrified, not matching the rest of his expression at all.

Joe nodded at his ex-captive as the Archmage began to speak once again. "The other man up here is one that none of you recognize, for good reason. This man is... the *rogue mage* who held Cel captive!"

Your reputation with the Mage's College has suffered! Reputation has been reduced by 2000. New status with the college: Hostile.

"That's right!" The Archmage bellowed as the room broke into confused whispers. "This man broke our rules and needs to pay for his crimes. We have decided to be merciful though." Boo-ing followed his words. "I know, I know. As much as we want to execute him for his crimes, he is a traveler. A single death would be too simple for him! Not only that, but when he was discovered, he surrendered as soon as he was able. Of course... this was the only possible outcome. After all, our own Master of the Flame was sent to bring him in!"

The red-robed mage on the dais with them stood and bowed. The Archmage nodded approvingly. "This man, known only as 'Joe', has sworn to follow our rules from this point forward. To that end, he will be signing The Accords today! He will never again get the chance to hurt one of my precious students!"

Mana must have been used to empower his words and the

audience because the clapping and cheering could be considered sonic damage at this point. Joe–unlike Cel–was not allowed to freely walk to The Accords. He and two others climbed the stairs, but they stopped a few stairs from the top. "Now is the moment of truth!" the Archmage proclaimed as he watched Joe carefully. "Will this *man* prove himself a warlock, or will he join the college as the lowest of the low, hoping against hope that he will one day deserve to join us properly?"

CHAPTER THIRTY-SEVEN

Taking a deep breath, Joe slowly walked the last few steps to The Accords. He reached a trembling hand toward the book, which burned black with falsifications in his occultist sight. The book began to shine with power and fell open. The pages blurred by, coming to rest at the next available open space. Joe's hand came closer, and a quill formed in his grasp. Before he touched the page, he opened his left hand and allowed his scepter to drop from his storage ring into his waiting palm.

"Joe! What are you doing?" the Archmage boomed. "The Accords are protected by the entire college. Attacking them with a legendary weapon would do nothing. What are you going to do to them with a glorified stick? Remove his silence. Answer, boy!"

Joe looked back as the spell of silence deactivated. "Obviously I am going to do nothing to The Accords with my *scepter*." He looked back to The Accords and allowed the quill to drift closer. Seeing this, the prepared spells targeting him were cancelled and the tension eased. Joe paused just before the quill touched the ancient paper, touching the book with his finger directly. "I *really* hope this counts. Activate ability from title

Terms and Conditions." His voice was harsh from the long hours of not speaking, but it was more than enough to activate the first title he had ever gained.

Terms and conditions single use special effect activated! There will be no contract-based repercussions to destroying the targeted contract, though other parties may not be pleased with you. Use ability on contract 'The Accords'? Yes / No

"What did he just say?" The Archmage struggled to his feet and was about to start climbing the stairs. "Silence him! Now!"

"*Yes*!" Joe shouted as he drove the taglock needle on his scepter into his leg. A red '*1*' floated up from him as a slew of messages began to appear.

You have activated the special effect from the title 'Terms and Conditions'. The mana contract 'The Accords' will be destroyed in 5… 4…

You have activated a new ritual: 'Stasis'. This ritual makes the target unable to interact with anything, move, or perform any action. The target is still able to see and think. While this ritual is active, the target and anything they have equipped cannot be damaged, moved, or altered in any way. This ritual lasts for five minutes. Time remaining: 4:58.

Title gained: Warlock I. You have broken your promise to the 'Master of Fire' of the mage's college. You had promised not to cause trouble. Talk to the wronged party, a magistrate, or the King to get this title removed. Subsequent increases in this title's ranking will have increasingly negative effects on you. Effect: Charisma -1, +10% cost for all purchases at neutral or good aligned shops.

Skill increased: Ritual Magic (Apprentice V). Testing new things on yourself is a surefire way to end up dead! Good thing you like risks. Let's see if this one pays off.

The Archmage stopped, looking at Joe's unmoving form in confusion. "You attacked yourself? Why? What are you doing!" He pointed at Joe, creating a lightning bolt that slammed into the utterly still man. A perfect hit, and yet not a single aspect of Joe had changed. Even his clothes were undamaged. The bolt of power had just… ended.

As everyone looked on in wonder–with just a hint of confusion–Joe's titular effect came into play. The light around The

Accords brightened as mana accumulated, and the sound of tearing paper shook the room. Without any further fancy effects, The Accords vanished with a small **pop*. The Archmage stumbled, staring in horror at the space the massive book used to occupy. "What… what have you *done*?"

"The cursed Accords are *gone*!" the Master of Fire spoke in a shocked tone. He seemed even more surprised that he had been *able* to speak. "We… we are free! Councilors! We are free! *Kill that swine*!" The incredulous tone had turned murderous at the end.

"G-gone? How are you all not dead then?" The Archmage squealed as he noted dozens of hostile gazes centered on him. He erected a shield around himself just before multiple elemental spells slammed into the thin barrier of energy. "Students! Help, they are attacking me!"

Confusion among the students was the only reaction to his words. They all knew it was impossible to intentionally hurt one of the members of the college, especially the Archmage, so what was going on? In their confusion, no one moved to help either side. The Archmage was weathering the council's attacks only due to the huge amount of power enhancing and defensive enchantments that covered his corpulent body.

Lightning struck and strange shimmers in the air pulsed with dark intent. Fire devoured the air around the Archmage, leaving him gasping even though he was protected from direct damage. Slabs of tile lifted from the ground, superheating and flying at such speeds that they could be called a meteorite. One by one, the charms and mana-infused artifacts held by the Archmage began to break. His counterattacks were so weak that they couldn't even pierce the wall of power that the attacks against him created around his body. Instead, he began looking for a way to flee the battle.

His protections would not last forever–in fact they were already faltering–but it gave him time to retreat up the stairs to where Joe was frozen in place. Breathing heavily from climbing the stairs and fighting, the Archmage pulled an ornate dagger out of a satchel on his side and stabbed it at Joe's heart. The tip of the dagger stopped at the first clothing fiber it encountered as if the Archmage had struck a wall of steel. Seeing that there was no effect, the Archmage instead ducked behind Joe and tried to use him as a shield.

His plan was lacking, as it appeared the other mages had no qualms about blasting both of them into oblivion. In fact, it seemed that though the spells were becoming less flashy, they were becoming far more deadly. A line of what could only be described as 'instant death' drilled into his shield, only stopped due to the sheer complexity of enchantments the Archmage had been forcing others to create for him for centuries. "You bastard! What did you do to my *accords*!" The Archmage stood screaming and sobbing at Joe as the air sizzled with redirected and deflected spells. "I *will* find some way to destroy you for this!"

A wave of magma settled on him and shattered the last of his passive defenses. The Archmage screamed as droplets of molten stone splattered across his face. "Wait, wait, *wait*! Please! Stop! I surrender, I *surrender*!" He managed to save himself by raising a weak shield with his own power, obviously unused to the requirements of using his own magic for any length of time. This was a man who controlled others, and he had allowed his personal power to wane in favor of a few decades of hedonism. The attacks against him paused momentarily, but the looks on the councilors' faces promised violence would resume soon.

"I've closed the spacial rifts in this area. There will be no escape via teleportation," a mage in shimmering black robes spoke softly but was heard clearly across the vast room. His words made the Archmage's face pale even more. "Why, *why* should we allow you to live when we have been your slaves for years, you pathetic worm? Did you ever afford us the opportunity to escape or allow us to plead our case?"

"You all had it coming!" the trembling Archmage screeched and stomped on the floor, trying and failing to slit Joe's throat. This prompted no reaction from the mages, which bothered Joe quite a bit. "You belittled my craft, laughed at those of us who created binding contracts! I was getting *my* revenge for being treated as a drudge, a useless mongrel! You called me *quill* pusher or the poor man's lawyer!"

"So you *enslaved* us? *All* of us? I had never met you!" a woman in brown robes yelled up at him.

"It didn't matter! None of you matter! *I'm the Archmage*! I knew that contract magic was more powerful than *any* of you could hope to defeat, and I *proved* it!" The obese man was breathing heavily and sinking to the floor, clutching at his chest as though his heart was giving out.

"The Kingdom has been at war! You held us back, refusing to allow us to join in! *Thousands* have died because of your cowardice and profit-mongering! Our outlying villages have been stolen or destroyed, anyone not in the capitol city either dead or enslaved! You may have killed humanity as a whole through your inaction!"

"I don't *care*!" It turned out that the Archmage wasn't having a heart attack, he was pulling a stone that blazed with multicolored light out of a hidden pocket. "You are all going to die anyway!"

The Archmage reared back to throw the stone, but Joe's hand reached out and snagged his flabby arm. Joe snatched away the stone, then swung his scepter into the Archmage's head. The heavy man stumbled back uncomprehending as Joe *jumped* forward, slamming into him and sending him flying into the space that had been recently vacated by The Accords.

Screaming, the Archmage was pumped full of the mana that had been accumulated and stored by the tubing. Mana rolled into his body, filling it beyond capacity, beyond comprehension or human limits. Joe landed on the floor and covered his head. The screams seemed to linger and reverberate in the air as the Archmage's body inflated and exploded into gore. Mana-charged flesh vaporized before it had a chance to land on anything, but the concussion wave blasted Joe off the raised platform.

He landed heavily with a large portion of his health removed, stunned and disoriented. He looked up to see potentially hostile council members staring down at him, but then Cel pushed through the wall of bodies that had formed around him. "Joe! You're alive! How? How did you survive all of that and still manage to stop him from attacking us?"

Shaking his head, Joe coughed and healed himself. "Ow, dang that hurt. Remember that ritual we made this morning? It's a ritual named 'Stasis'. Activating it made me unable to move or perform any action but it also shielded me from everything thrown at me."

"How did you get out? When you wanted to move, it just… stopped." Cel seemed to take his answer at face value, which Joe appreciated.

"I built a function into all my rituals that lets me deactivate them at will. I knew it might kill me to block that attack, but I had to stop him. I can always come back; you all wouldn't be able to." Joe took Cel's hand, getting pulled to his feet by what he now hoped was a friend.

"Hand me the stone, boy." A man in white robes with black arcane characters stitched into it held out his hand.

Joe looked over at Cel. Cel nodded in approval. "He's the Master of Enchantment. Do it." Joe shrugged and placed the bright stone into the outstretched hand.

Peering into the stone, the man began to shiver. "So unstable, how did it even last *this* long? What a maniac! A Grand Radiant Core with an enchantment created to dissociate itself on impact! That reaction would have obliterated at *least* half the city!"

A couple students listening in fainted. Cel was pale and licked his lips with nervousness. "What… what do we do with it?"

"I'm feeding it to the Mana Engine is what I'm doing with it! Don't get involved in conversations at this level, you milk-drinker!" The wizened old man walked over to the exposed glass of what was apparently something called a mana engine and touched the stone to the tubing. The stone stuck there, the light inside it slowly fading. "There! Give it a few minutes and all the stored power will be converted into a usable form. Might even fix the protections. Ha! With that much power it *better* fix the protections."

"What do you mean?" a slightly less wrinkled mage asked him.

The white robed man folded his arms behind his back. "That fool of an Archmage diverted the power of the Mana Engine into keeping his precious *accords* in effect. He left the college defenseless, unprotected from the outside world. *That's* the real reason he never let anyone but apprentices take missions for the army or Kingdom. He needed us here to protect *him* if we were attacked." He spat to the side. "I think revenge is completely underrated; seeing him get vaporized felt amazing."

Joe looked at the remaining mages surrounding him. "I guess the next question is… now what?"

"Now what, indeed. You have saved us from a fate that none of us wanted, freeing hundreds of nobles, mages, and travelers even if they didn't know they were slaves. Anything you want of us, we will try to accommodate. At least, I will," the Master of Fire spoke for the group, and those around him nodded. They seemed a bit wary of making a sweeping promise like that but seemed to feel a bit guilty about their doubt. After all, they were free now. They could tell him 'no' if he tried for outlandish rewards.

"In that case…" Joe thought for a moment, and the mages around him became rather tense as the silence persisted. "I could ask for money or enchantments, but the truth is, I either don't need them or don't know what to ask for. Instead, I'll only ask for a few general terms. One, I'd like training as a mage, but I don't want to be beholden to your group. Stop this 'rogue mage' garbage, and let people explore their powers. Next, I'd like to ask that you reduce your fees and open the college to the general public. That is for this next request: as you know, the

Kingdom is at war; I'd like you to assist them however possible. More mages are needed if we are going to expand the human influence, and what we currently have simply isn't enough to combat the Wolfman nation." The mages grandly nodded. These were things they would have gotten around to, but as a personal request from their savior they would be able to move much faster and avoid some political bargaining on these issues.

"Also, I know that the library is desperate to expand their selection, would you be opposed to donating a copy of your research to them for safekeeping? I am certain they would be willing to place restrictions on who can access the materials." This suggestion was met with a good deal less enthusiasm, but they didn't say 'no'.

"Finally..." Joe's tone made the tension reappear. "Master of Fire?"

"Yes...?"

"I broke a promise with you. In light of the circumstances, could you please remove my warlock status?"

Your reputation with the Mage's College has increased by 8000 points. Current standing: Extended Family.

EPILOGUE

When Joe first entered the common area of the guild house, a squealing form with vivid blue hair slammed into him in a full-body tackle. "You destroyed the accords! Anyone who had signed them got a notification! I hadn't even known how restricted that made us! How did you figure it out? Did you know that there are now *twelve* new classes we can specialize as? Twelve! And that's only what we *know* about! I'm going to learn to enchant! I got accepted right away when I told them I knew you and was part of your guild; all of us even get a discount!"

"Terra?" Joe's mind finally caught up to the flood of words that was entering his ears. Her mouth was like a reverse black hole; instead of absorbing things, she constantly spewed noise. "Wait, everyone knows it was *me*?"

"There was a server-wide announcement! Have you not looked at your notifications?" Terra grinned at him, but it turned into a pout after a moment. "You didn't yet, did you? Gah! You are famous; you must have gained, like, a *bazillion* fame points from this! Look at your notifications! Do it now!"

Terra's excited chatter had drawn most of the rooms' inhabitants to them, and they seemed to agree with her. Aten walked into the area, and upon seeing Joe, looked like he was about to kiss him. "Joe! I can't believe it! We are now the top guild, and-"

"Quiet down!" Terra coolly interrupted him. "Joe hasn't looked over his notifications, don't spoil the surprise!"

Now with a pained look on his face, Aten sat down muttering darkly, "I'm gonna get voted out at this rate. Maybe he'll let me be an officer, at least." With all the expectant eyes on him, Joe awkwardly opened his overburdened notification screen.

Server wide announcement! Rejoice! The Mage's College has been freed from the tyrannical slavery of the Archmage by player 'Joe' of the guild The Wanderers! With the defeat of the Archmage, new goods such as mana potions are available for sale at various shops. The cost of being trained in mage-based skills has been reduced by 60%, and twelve new mage-based classes are available for specialization at the Mage's College! The guild The Wanderers has maxed out their reputation with the Kingdom of Ardania for as long as 'Joe' remains a member! Their guild tax to the Kingdom has been reduced by 75%. Be warned: oppose them and you oppose the crown!

Hidden quest (Legendary) completed: Unshackling Magic. You completed a quest that no one knew was a quest by destroying a contract that could not be destroyed. Not only did you defeat the Archmage, but you did not allow any other mages to perish! By completing seemingly impossible requirements and saving those that should not have survived, the rating of this quest increased from Epic to Legendary difficulty.

Rewards have increased, but you will not be able to loot the Mage's College without breaking the law. Rewards: Exp: 20,000, 100 platinum coins, prices for skills and class training at the college are further reduced for you and players on your 'friend' list by 30%. Reputation with the college is locked at maximum unless you commit a high crime against them. As you completed this quest alone and the college is joining the war, you will gain 5% of all contribution points earned by the College for the war effort. This will impact your quest 'Shatter a People'.

The ranking of your deity has increased! He has moved from 'unknown' to 'pretty much unknown'. Rare knowledge, items, and locations will be 5% easier for all players to discover for two weeks!

Quest complete: Earn a god's favor. You have found enough hidden knowledge or completed enough hidden quests to earn the favor of a deity! Reward: You have unlocked your first specialization! Reach level ten and go to a shrine dedicated to Tatum in order to see details. Reputation increase with Hidden god Tatum: 2000. Current status: Friendly.

Title gained: The Chosen of Tatum. You are the chosen of a deity and have his blessing. When your class would show as 'cleric', it will now show as 'Arch Cleric'. You have gained access to a new spell.

Spell gained: Resurrection (Novice I). This is a spell granted only to the champion of a deity, and only one follower may have this spell at a time. Increase your skill with this spell to increase its effects. Effect: Restore a fallen person to life with (24+1n)% health, mana, and stamina and return (19+1n)% of lost experience where 'n' equals skill level. Can be used once every 24 hours. Target must be the same level or lower than the caster. Target must be resurrected within one hour of death. Cannot be used on self.

Title gained: Anti-mage. You have killed the highest ranked mage in the Kingdom. By doing so, you have proven that you have what it takes to kill any *of them. +10% spell resist. +50% intimidation bonus against mage-based classes.*

Title gained: Immovable object. You have withstood spells that could shatter buildings, and weapons that can pierce steel. You did so stoically, without flinching, dodging, or dying. +80% knockback resistance. Constitution +2, strength +1.

Title removed: You have lost the title 'Terms and Conditions' due to using the benefit of the title.

Title removed: Warlock. You have lost the title 'Warlock'. Charisma and shop prices have been reset.

Caution: You have at least 5 of 10 title slots filled. You can chose to replace one if needed, but be warned, gaining a mandatory negative *title while all title slots are full will delete one other non-mandatory title at random. (Example: Warlock).*

Joe gasped as all of the effects slammed into him at the same time. Not only did he move to level nine instantly, but he passed the ten point threshold in strength as well! His bones shifted painfully as his muscles thickened and became more supportive. Standing suddenly didn't feel like a chore, and he felt like he could carry an entire backpack filled with wolf meat! He took a deep breath, his chest pulling air into his lungs without the strain that used to cause him to cough. Joe felt human again!

After getting to this new level, Joe had also gained five characteristic points to spend, so he quickly placed three into intelligence and two into wisdom. Closing all the screens, he looked around at the group that was waiting for him with strange smiles. Thinking of the notifications they would have seen, he whooped for joy. "This is amazing! Max reputation with Ardania and seventy-five percent less tax?"

This caused a few people to cheer, especially Aten, who was clapping and whistling into an otherwise mostly quiet room. Terra snickered and looked at Joe out of the corner of her eye. "No, yeah, we're excited. Gotta say, whatever you just did that made all your skin slide around was a little freaky. Looked like you had worms crawling through you."

"Oh, no! Gross. Now I need a shower." Joe shook a bit theatrically. "I just got to ten strength and broke through a threshold."

A few people sighed and seemed less disgusted. Aten noticed that people were starting to disperse now that the fun was over and quickly whistled to get their attention. "With the prices and new classes available at the college, we will be sponsoring anyone who wants to get a class change. Right now we only have two magic users, and we need to beef those numbers up! Those are rookie numbers! Right now, anyone who changes class is guaranteed a spot in one of the top twenty squads. I know most of you aren't specced for it, having put points into mostly physical stats, so don't worry about us holding it against you if you want to keep your current class!"

Only a small amount of people were interested in the class change, and most of them were very low level. Aten had them move to another room, leaving Joe to catch his breath and relax a bit. He wanted a nap, but he needed to take a moment and rethink his plans at this point. Now that new mage skills were available to him, he needed to get some training and become more powerful. Not to mention, now that he had max standing with the college, it was likely that he could find books and manuals on ritual magic that had been banned by the recently deceased Archmage.

Speaking of ritual magic… Joe checked his stat sheet and noticed that he had sixteen unused skill points. For a long moment he thought about putting them into his resurrection spell, but it was not really worth it as he could only use that spell once a day. He decided to rank it up by *using* it for a while so he could grasp the concepts behind it. Joe placed fourteen points into ritual magic, saving two points just in case he needed them later. After accepting the changes, his mind was flooded with new concepts and nuanced meanings of all the diagrams and spell components he had studied thus far. It felt like he had just graduated high school with an education devoted to rituals. He read the notification that appeared, followed by looking over his stat sheet and top five skills.

Skill increased: Ritual Magic (Student IX). Rejoice! You have entered the ranks of a Student in ritual magic! Based on your recent combat-aligned ritual usage, a new effect will be added to the skill! Effect: Rituals are 10% more effective against single targets. This increases to 15% if another being was forced to participate in the ritual's creation against their will and to 20% if the target *of the ritual was forced to participate in the creation of the ritual. 'Forcing' does not include using their genetic material to target them.*

Name: Joe 'The Chosen of Tatum' Class: Arch Cleric (Actual: Ritualist)
Profession: Scholar (Actual: Occultist)
Level: 9 Exp: 37,978 Exp to next level: 7,022
Hit Points: 50/50 (50+(0))
Mana: 704/704 (12.5 per point of intelligence, +100% from deity, –12% from mana manipulation)
Mana regen: 8.99/sec (.25 per point of wisdom, + 9% from Coalescence)
Stamina: 50/50 (50+(0)+(0))

Characteristic: Raw score (Modifier)

Strength: 10 (1.10)
Dexterity: 10 (1.10)
Constitution: 12 (1.12)
Intelligence: 33 (1.33)
Wisdom: 32 (1.32)
Charisma: 15 (1.15)
Perception: 25 (1.25)
Luck: 15 (1.15)
Karmic Luck: +5

Top Skills

Jump (Master 0): Your ability to jump skillfully and without hurting yourself.

Jump Around (Master 0): Add your jump skill level to anything that can be 'jumped'. Be careful not to jump to incorrect conclusions! (Current: +62)

Ritual Magic (Student IX): Ability to create, maintain, and change rituals much more efficiently than usual. -.5n% mana and component cost where 'n' equals skill level. Rituals are 10% more effective against single targets. This increases to 15% if another being was forced to participate in the ritual's creation against their will and to 20% if the target of the ritual was forced to participate in the ritual. 'Forcing' does not include using their genetic material to target them.

Mana Manipulation (Beginner IX): (-30+1n)% mana. (+1+1n)% spell efficiency where 'n' equals skill level. (Maximum 25% Efficiency)

Mend (Beginner VIII): Select a target to heal restoring 5n health where 'n' equals skill level. Mend is able to heal broken bones. Dark affinity is automatically added to the spell, and will heal dark aligned creatures twice as effectively.

Looking over the stats and skills, Joe rubbed his chin thoughtfully. He had a solid set of skills and a supportive guild, and now it was time to start putting together his own team. Though he was enjoying his time as a solo player, if he wanted to progress through the game, he needed to become more active with other players. When Joe had trained–and learned to trust–his team, he would start teaching them ritual magic and work toward building his coven. Eventually, they would be able to shape the world with Sage-tier rituals!

Joe felt a piercing gaze as he finished reading. Looking over his shoulder, he saw Tatum sitting at the table behind him, apparently unseen by the other occupants of the room. The deity winked and nodded, as if to affirm that Joe's plans were well thought out. After pointing at their guild banner, Tatum vanished, leaving behind only the smell of old books. Joe looked at the banner, noting that there was now a holographic royal seal seemingly floating over their coat of arms. He would need to point that out to someone.

He sighed and stood up. It was time to get to work. His goals might still be a long way off, but he was happy with his progress to this point. Besides, Joe knew that he would never stop until he had completed everything the game offered.

ABOUT DAKOTA KROUT

Associated Press best-selling author, Dakota has been a top 5 bestseller on Amazon, a top 6 bestseller on Audible, and his first book, Dungeon Born, was chosen as one of Audible's top 5 fantasy picks in 2017.

He draws on his experience in the military to create vast terrains and intricate systems, and his history in programming and information technology helps him bring a logical aspect to both his writing and his company while giving him a unique perspective for future challenges.

"Publishing my stories has been an incredible blessing thus far, and I hope to keep you entertained for years to come!" -Dakota

Connect with Dakota:
MountaindalePress.com
Patreon.com/DakotaKrout
Facebook.com/DakotaKrout
Twitter.com/DakotaKrout
Discord.gg/mdp

ABOUT MOUNTAINDALE PRESS

Dakota and Danielle Krout, a husband and wife team, strive to create as well as publish excellent fantasy and science fiction novels. Self-publishing *The Divine Dungeon: Dungeon Born* in 2016 transformed their careers from Dakota's military and programming background and Danielle's Ph.D. in pharmacology to President and CEO, respectively, of a small press. Their goal is to share their success with other authors and provide captivating fiction to readers with the purpose of solidifying Mountaindale Press as the place 'Where Fantasy Transforms Reality.'

Connect with Mountaindale Press:
MountaindalePress.com
Facebook.com/MountaindalePress
Twitter.com/_Mountaindale
Instagram.com/MountaindalePress

MOUNTAINDALE PRESS TITLES

GameLit and LitRPG

The Completionist Chronicles,
The Divine Dungeon,
Full Murderhobo, and
Year of the Sword by Dakota Krout

Arcana Unlocked by Gregory Blackburn

A Touch of Power by Jay Boyce

Red Mage and
Farming Livia by Xander Boyce

Space Seasons by Dawn Chapman

Ether Collapse and
Ether Flows by Ryan DeBruyn

Dr. Druid by Maxwell Farmer

Bloodgames by Christian J. Gilliland

Unbound by Nicoli Gonnella

Threads of Fate by Michael Head

Lion's Lineage by Rohan Hublikar and Dakota Krout

Wolfman Warlock by James Hunter and Dakota Krout

Axe Druid,
Mephisto's Magic Online, and
High Table Hijinks by Christopher Johns

Skeleton in Space by Andries Louws

Dragon Core Chronicles by Lars Machmüller

Chronicles of Ethan by John L. Monk

Pixel Dust and
Necrotic Apocalypse by David Petrie

Viceroy's Pride by Cale Plamann

Henchman by Carl Stubblefield

Artorian's Archives by Dennis Vanderkerken and Dakota Krout

Vaudevillain by Alex Wolf

Made in United States
Troutdale, OR
02/12/2024